The Holiday Bake-off

The Holiday Bake-off

A DELIGHTFULLY CHARMING
CHRISTMAS ROMANCE

LINDSAY DETWILER

HARPETH ROAD
PRESS
Nashville

HARPETH ROAD PRESS

Published by Harpeth Road Press (USA)
P.O. Box 158184
Nashville, TN 37215

Paperback: 978-1-963483-03-1
eBook: 978-1-963483-02-4

The Holiday Bake-Off: A Delightfully Charming Christmas Romance

First Harpeth Road Press Edition: October 2024

Cover Design by Sarah Hansen
Cover Images © Shutterstock, Adobe, Depositphotos

To my husband, Chad

ONE

I'd just claimed my long-awaited espresso from the counter of our favorite coffee shop when I got the phone call that changed everything.

I strolled to the tiny bistro table to join my best friend, Serena, who had already made conversation with the elderly couple seeking refuge from the blustery November day at the table next to ours. I tapped Answer despite not recognizing the number, expecting to hang up immediately on the telemarketer.

Instead, my fun-loving grandma croaked, "Now please, Lucy, don't worry..."

I instantly began to worry.

Something was wrong. Without fail, my grandma started our daily phone conversations by asking if I'd met a cute boy yet to write about in my next romance novel—even when Jed and I were still together. She didn't hide her disdain for him, undeterred that I was floating on cloud nine and talking about forever. The day after Jed broke my heart, shredding my faith that love would ever be mine, she insisted the right cookie was out there for me to find—she was a baker and had a bad habit of using food analogies.

She offered no witty cookie references or cupcake connections that freezing cold November day. Instead, my heart sank as I plopped my espresso on the table, the chill in my bones not just related to the frigid temperatures Serena and I had sought to escape. Grandma's voice was raspy and distressed. She didn't offer any funny jokes or nosy questions about my dating life. The ray of sunshine that always radiated from her voice and made me smile on the darkest of days was missing.

Serena wrapped up her conversation with the adorable woman sitting near us and stood, moving closer to try to hear what had me in a panic.

"Grandma, you telling me not to worry undeniably worries me. What's going on?"

"I-I'm in the hospital, dear. It's nothing, really. A-a little hiccup with my heart is all. I just wanted to let you know in case you called the house phone and I didn't answer. It's all going to be okay, they tell me." She coughed, her voice clearly weakened from talking. Her words ebbed and flowed slowly, her tone devoid of emotion. She struggled to get the words out.

"Put your doctor on immediately," I ordered as Serena grabbed my elbow and ushered me to sit down.

"Lucy, there's no need to worry. Honestly. I'm practically good as new already. And Herb will take care of Edmund. He promised after he brought me in this morning. I just didn't want you worrying is all." Her breathing seemed labored. Was she slurring some of her words?

"Grandma, stay put. I'm on my way." My heart was pounding, and I wished I didn't live so far away. Before she could argue or again try to assure me it was nothing, I hung up, grabbed my espresso, and told Serena I needed to go.

My heart fluttered with fear as Serena and I maneuvered the insanely busy sidewalks. Thanksgiving had been the day before, and the tourists were already bustling about, ready to kick off the holiday magic with the shopping frenzy Black Friday brought. Usually, I loved the cacophony of noises, the lights, the tree at Rockefeller Center, that meatball sub from my favorite food truck down the block, and the energy of sheer chaos. Today, though, it only enhanced my anxiety. I needed to get out of the city and get to my grandma.

My hands shook as we walked, Serena asking questions I didn't know the answers to. In truth, my mind was still on the phone call, waiting to hear even more horrific news. I was no stranger to bad phone calls, after all. The last life-changing call had come four years earlier. I was twenty-two and had just moved to the city with Serena to live out my post-college dreams. That call ripped me in half and threatened to shred my hopes before they even began. Serena, sheer willpower, and nothing short of a miracle helped me survive.

But if something happened to my grandma now, my only remaining family, I didn't know how I'd survive at all.

I shoved aside the negative thoughts as Serena reassured me everything would be okay. We rushed back to our tiny apartment, my refuge for the past few years and especially the past month. My belongings were still in disarray since I'd only just moved back in after the mess my life had become. I hadn't bothered unpacking because I would be leaving soon anyway, whisking myself to a new adventure I desperately needed. Serena helped me choose a few outfits from one of my suitcases. I caught sight of the fabulous hat

I'd splurged on last week—a new style, a new city, a new me, if the inspirational podcasts were to be believed. But the new me, the adventure—it would all have to wait.

"Do you want me to come with you?" Serena asked generously. She would come to Star Creek with me in a heartbeat if I needed her to. It wouldn't be the first time she'd dropped everything to help me through a tough time.

"You have that important client you're working with. I don't want you to miss your big break at the firm because of me. I'll be okay." I tried to paint on a grin to reassure her because I really didn't want her to blow her chances.

"You know you come first," Serena replied. And the thing was, I knew it was true. Since high school, she'd been the kind of friend who really was there for me in the good and bad times, the kind I could depend on. Still, she was working her way up at the law firm, getting ready for a big case. I couldn't get in the way of her dreams. I had to do this on my own. Grandma needed me, and I would be there for her. I was strong enough to handle it.

"It's okay. I've got this." I was convincing myself as much as Serena.

"Just promise you'll text when you get there. And promise if you need me, you'll call. I'm only a few hours away."

I nodded, hugging her.

"I'll take care of everything while you're gone." She smiled, gesturing to Gary, my succulent, the only living creature I had to my name.

"I won't be gone long this time," I assured her.

"I hope not," she said. "I don't want to have my movie marathons alone again on the weekends. It's been good having you back, even though it's because of not-so-great reasons. Selfishly, I want to keep you here."

"You're a great friend," I whispered, feeling bad that for the past year, I had been mostly absent from Serena's life, caught up in a whirlwind romance and moving in with Jed. I'd sacrificed a lot of beautiful things in my life for him. I understood that, now that he was gone. Still, I didn't have the brainpower to worry or analyze that now.

"Oh, I know. You owe me so many espressos when you get back. But tell your grandma I said hello and not to cause too much trouble for those doctors."

I smiled. "Bless them if they try to pass off one of those hospital desserts as edible. They're going to hear all about what's wrong with every sweet they serve."

I did one final luggage check, remembered my laptop, and shoved it in the bag. Serena, who noticed everything, smirked as she gave me a thumbs up.

"Maybe getting a change of scenery will help things." She nodded toward the laptop.

"I hope so," I replied. That would be one good thing to come from this. Another would be that, even though it was under bad circumstances, I would get to see my grandma again.

She'd visited at the beginning of November, right when my life was falling apart. It had been a while since I'd spent time with her, and even now, I could appreciate that the visit wasn't what it should have been. I'd tried to be happy, to be strong, but in truth, things hadn't been so great in my personal life when she'd come to New York. The breakup had affected me in ways I tried to cover but couldn't.

I'd wanted life with Jed to work out so badly. I'd seen visions of the family we could have, the family I desperately longed for. I thought I'd found my forever, the uncondi-tional love like my parents had—the Sunday morning strolls through the park, the cute restaurants on weekends, and random, romantic getaways. The white picket fence and a few children running around keeping us exhausted but still in love. I wasn't alone anymore when I was with Jed, which I'd needed after losing so much. He'd promised me I'd never be alone that first night we kissed—and I'd believed him. I think maybe he believed it too.

I was caught up in what I thought was a whirlwind romance; it turned out to be a tornado of deceit, and I didn't know how I'd rebuild my trust in love, the future, or anything at all.

Along with the sadness of the breakup had come a lot of regrets. I hadn't spent as much time with Grandma as I would have liked since moving to the city. After my parents died, I swore I'd learned my lesson and would prioritize family. But the city, romance, and dreams made me lose sight of what mattered most. I hadn't been to Star Creek often in the past year. Guilt sank in that it had taken a disaster for me to get back to her. I knew family was the most important thing. I knew that more than most people. How had I let myself forget? I swiped at my tears. Never again, I promised.

As if she'd read my mind, Serena shook her head. "Don't even start feeling guilty that you weren't there or that this is somehow your fault. The important thing is you're going back now. You're going to be there when she needs you."

I nodded. Serena always knew what I needed to hear when I needed to hear it. She'd been a blessing and helped me through the second hardest time in my life.

"Are you sure you don't mind me borrowing your car?" I asked. Serena's parents had gifted her a car at graduation, a luxury I definitely couldn't afford. The parking alone would kill my budget.

"Of course not. It's kind of a waste having it in the city anyway. I'm glad it's being put to good use." In truth, the car was rarely used since neither of us had time to leave the city, and public transportation was easier. It was coming in handy now, though, and I was thankful for such a generous friend.

"Thank you," I said, hugged her again, and then beelined for the apartment door.

Before I got it open, she shouted, "Wait, one more thing!"

I paused and turned.

"When you come back, bring me some of those cinnamon rolls your grandma makes," she said, smiling.

"Of course," I replied. Still, as I headed to the parking lot to hop in Serena's car for what would be a long drive, I worried that cinnamon rolls were nowhere in my grandma's future. I silently prayed the entire way to Pennsylvania that Grandma wasn't sugarcoating anything—that it really was just a hiccup.

The trembling in my hands took me back to that horrible day four years ago.

I'd lost so much these past few years—and these past few weeks, in truth. I'd sworn to myself that this holiday season would be different, that the ushering in of Thanksgiving and Christmas would mean a brand-new version of me. It would be a time for achieving my writing goals and finding myself. Life would fall into place.

As my car plowed through the snow on the way to my grandma's tiny town, trepidation intensified in my heart. The farther from the city lights I drove, the more certain I became that my life was about to forever change. I just hoped I was strong enough to handle it.

TWO

Five hours later I arrived at Willow Bend Hospital as darkness descended on the snow-covered town, guilt residing in my weary bones. I hurriedly found a place to park, hoping I was actually in a spot since the lines were hidden.

I opened the door, the wind whipping through my travel-worn hair. The Willow Bend Hospital, which was one town over from Star Creek, towered above me, a few of the rooms' lights shining like beacons in the night. The town had already started their holiday decorating; they were always quick to get into the holiday spirit. Twinkling lights lit up the lampposts on the way to the front door, and wreaths placed sporadically marked the season. I didn't have time to revel in the details, though. I ushered myself through the front doors and took a deep breath. Hospitals always gave me the creeps.

The receptionist at the front desk directed me to the correct floor, and I hopped in the elevator. I tried to calm my frayed nerves on the way up to floor five, terrified of what I might find when I got to my grandma's room. It was hard to imagine the vivacious woman who still rode her bicycle every single day and wore red lipstick being down for the count. I had naively assumed she would be her young-at-heart self forever. As the elevator doors opened, I said a quick, silent prayer.

When I found the room, I smiled at the sight of Grandma sitting up in her bed with a murder mystery blaring on the ancient television mounted to the ceiling. She was arguing with Herbert Groves, her neighbor who was close to her age, about something on the show. Engrossed in their friendly dispute, they didn't hear me knock.

"Are you two causing trouble?" I teased, announcing my presence with a louder voice.

Grandma turned, her smile widening on half of her face. My heart jolted at the sight of her face noticeably distorted. She looked tired and weak in ways that were alarming. Still, I sighed in relief as I noticed she wore her red lipstick, even here.

"Lucy, I told you not to come here. What are you doing driving all this way just to come see me rest a little?" she said slowly, her words sounding labored.

I hurried across the room and wrapped her gently in my arms as I inhaled the familiar scent of cinnamon and flowers. I was relieved to find that the woman I'd seen earlier in the month was the same woman in this hospital bed, even though there were clearly signs that all was not well. Despite the tubes and beeping machines, Catherine Easton hadn't faded completely in the time since I'd seen her. That gave me comfort.

"I'll give you two some privacy," Herb muttered, standing slowly from his chair. He and his wife, Scarlet, had been friends with my grandparents for twenty years. Herb's wife died three years before Grandpa, and now he and my grandmother kept a friendly eye on each other. Herb's name came up more and more frequently in our daily conversations, so I suspected, even though they wouldn't admit it, something was blooming between them. Perhaps it had always been just under the layer of grief. Herb leaned over now to pat Grandma's shoulder. "I'll be right outside."

"I told you to get yourself home. I'm fine," she argued. "That chair can't be comfortable on the bones. Plus, Edmund is certainly lonely."

"Edmund is just fine. I was there a few hours ago. But I'll go check on him again if it will make you feel better."

"Thank you, dear," Grandma said, trying to wink but struggling. Love might not have been my forte lately and I was worried about Grandma, but I couldn't help the warmth in my heart at the sight of them.

"Has he been here all day?" I asked after Herb left and I took his seat. Grandma was right—the thing wasn't comfortable for the bones, the behind, or really anything.

"On and off. He's been carting himself back and forth between Edmund and here. He doesn't want to leave me alone. I feel bad, all of you fussing over me for a little heart hiccup. I just needed a little rest, some TV shows, and to put my feet up is all. I'll be out of here in no time."

As if on cue, the doctor walked into the room.

"You must be Lucy Carter. I've been hearing a lot about you."

I stood up. "All good things, I hope."

"Mostly," Grandma confessed, chuckling.

I shook my head.

"How are you feeling this evening, Ms. Easton?" he asked as he approached the bed with her chart.

I stepped aside to allow him space and grabbed the remote control to turn off the blaring murder mystery. I reminded myself to be patient and not hound the doctor, although I wanted to ask five million questions.

"Good as new. When can I go home?"

He sighed. "We've discussed this. I want to keep you at least a night for observation."

She groaned. "I know I'm good to look at and all, Doc, but I have a business to run."

He put aside the chart and eyed me.

"I know, I know. You're not telling me anything I'm not aware of," I replied even though he'd asked no question. My hands were up in apology. I knew exactly what he must've been dealing with the past few hours. Grandma was a firecracker, even at the age of seventy-nine. She didn't slow down. Ever. It was scary to see her hooked up to all those tubes and machines. Still, I couldn't help but smile at her larger-than-life personality that the doctor clearly understood firsthand. He looked like he'd been put through the wringer.

"And what exactly is it that you know?" Grandma asked, raising an eyebrow.

I inched closer, kissed her cheek, and said, "You're a little sassy sometimes. And stubborn."

"Oh really? Am I the only stubborn one?"

I shrugged. She had a point. I'd been accused at times of being stubborn—and a bit of a perfectionist. And a scheduler. We all had our downfalls.

"In all seriousness, Doctor, what can you tell me?" I asked in a quieter tone. He was jotting notes in his chart.

"And in English, Mr. Smarty Pants," Grandma chimed in.

The doctor shook his head with a smile. "Of course. So your grandma's neighbor brought her in this morning. She was a little dizzy and had some numbness in her left side.

We immediately did some testing because that can be a sign of a stroke or heart attack."

My stomach dropped. "A stroke? Heart attack? Oh my gosh."

"See, now you scared her for no reason. Darling, it's nothing. Look at me. Red lips and all. I'm fine," Grandma said, waving her hand.

I sighed. Usually, I admired Grandma's strength. She'd once broken her arm and hadn't cried a single tear. Now, though, her strength felt scary and false.

"The tests did show that your grandma had a stroke," the doctor said, reclaiming the conversation, "although it was relatively minor. We'll want to keep a close eye on her, especially with some of the ongoing symptoms. She's doing well, and we confirmed that she doesn't have any blockages. Still, we need to watch her closely. The road to recovery isn't going to be easy. She'll have lingering effects from the stroke with some facial paralysis, potential memory loss, difficulty with some speech, and also fatigue. We need to make sure she's taking it easy and taking care of herself, especially with her age."

My heart sank. A stroke. That wasn't good. My mind started to race with terrifying scenarios.

"My age? Who are you calling old?" Grandma asked, but she was smirking.

"Definitely not you. In all seriousness, Ms. Easton, you're in great shape."

"Then why did this happen?" I asked. "And will it happen again?" Fear overpowered all rational thought and Grandma's attempts at humor. This was serious. Thank goodness Herb had had the sense to take her to the hospital. What if he hadn't been there? I shuddered to think of

Grandma being alone, of what could have happened. I couldn't lose her.

Flashes of the city's intense pace came to mind. Maybe I'd pushed her to do too much during her visit. The museum, the food trucks, Central Park. Maybe it had been too cold for her. Or maybe she wasn't eating right since she was on her own. I really should've been there for her instead of wrapped up in my own life.

"Now, before you start worrying too much, Lucy, know that there's no real answer. These things do happen, especially as we mature," he said, leaning into the last word.

Grandma gave him a nod of approval.

"With that being said, we do need to monitor the situation, especially for the next few weeks and months. I'm going to put you on some medications, Ms. Easton, to help make sure this doesn't happen again. And I would demand that you take it easy, especially for the next few weeks. We want to keep stress down. I know this might be a strange concept for you, but I want you to relax. No sixty-hour weeks in the bakery. No packing your days with seventy different charity events and activities. Rest. Relaxation. Feet up with the soap operas playing kind of relaxing."

I suddenly wished I had a notebook to write down his suggestions. Making lists always made me feel better. But the bottom line was Grandma needed to take it easy. I could ensure that... maybe. Keeping such a headstrong woman on the couch would be challenging. The doctor had only had a taste of who he was dealing with.

"And how do you expect me to do that? You do realize there's less than a month until the Star Creek Holiday Bake-Off. Do you think I have time to rest and relax? There are hundreds of things to be done."

"Ms. Easton, I'm sorry, but your health comes first."

She scoffed, shaking her head. "Tell that to the entire town who has looked forward to this tradition now for thirty years. Tell that to all the bakeries who come to town and bring tourism to our community, which helps every single business. The hotels, the restaurants—everyone benefits. Not to mention the fact that the festival is essentially responsible for creating the holiday spirit in the town. We're just supposed to cancel it because I got a little dizzy?"

"Grandma," I said firmly, "we aren't playing around with your health. This is serious."

"And you think canceling the event I look forward to every year is going to help my well-being?" She was seriously despondent. Her lip quivered. I knew what the festival meant to her, especially with Grandpa gone. It had been *their* festival, a celebration that brought the whole town together every single year.

I'd attended the Star Creek Holiday Bake-Off many years as a child. My parents would bring me for the festivities. I had so many beautiful memories from it, ones I cherished a little extra now. The bake-off wasn't only about cupcakes. It was an entire day of the town coming together, of celebrating, and of being a community as we prepared for the holiday. In truth, Christmas just didn't feel like Christmas without the tradition. It set the stage in every way, the whole town joining in celebration.

Grandma was right. The town needed their tradition, and Grandma did too.

But the doctor was also right. Grandma's health mattered.

It mattered more than a manuscript I was supposed to be writing and sending to my agent. It mattered a heck of a lot more than happy hours or shopping trips or lights in the city I loved, the city that had become home despite the difficulties. And it even mattered more than the plans I had for the beginning of January.

Before I could think too much about what it meant or how underqualified I was to take on such a task, I said what needed to be said.

"I'll take over," I announced, interrupting the doctor and Grandma, who were bickering. "I'll do it." I put on a brave face, knowing what I was committing to—and knowing it would be a big challenge. I'd survived challenging things, though. I'd moved to a new city, chased my publishing dreams that felt impossible, and survived an unthinkable tragedy. I'd handled all sorts of disappointments and difficulties. I was strong, even though I hadn't felt that way in the past few weeks. Maybe it wasn't a trip to a new country that I needed; maybe the bake-off would be the challenge that would remind me exactly what I could do. Still, I tried to calm the fears rattling within. The bake-off wasn't a mini festival or a one-day undertaking. It was a massive event, a huge administrative undertaking. Plus, there was one other major problem.

I couldn't bake to save my life. At all. Ever.

But for Grandma, I would sort that out later. I would have to.

"I can do it," I said again, more for myself than for Grandma.

"What?" she asked slowly.

"I'll take over and make sure the bake-off happens. And I'll make sure you rest through it all. I'm staying in town."

"You can't do that, Lucy. You have your life in New York," Grandma argued.

I thought of how hard I'd fought to make the dream of living in the city come true. But that could wait. It would have to.

"And I have my life here too. *You*," I replied.

She opened her mouth to argue further, but I interrupted her. "Didn't you just claim I was a stubborn woman too? You should know then that once my mind is made up, it's done. I'm staying. I'm taking over the bake-off arrangements. And there's nothing you're going to say to change my mind."

The doctor eyed me. He eyed my grandma.

"Well, it seems it's settled," he said. "My work here is done for today."

"Well, about going home—" Grandma started again.

"Nope, no way. We're not going there, Ms. Easton. One night, a test in the morning, and then we'll talk. You know that's the rule. There are three stubborn people in this room," he said, lowering his chart as he nodded at me then stepped out of the room.

I glanced at Grandma, gauging her reaction to the news. "Don't think I'm changing my mind."

She sighed. "I'm mad I'm holding you back from the life you have in the city. But if I'm being honest, Lucy, my heart is happy you're staying for a while. I've missed you. And, who knows, maybe the Star Creek charm will help get you back in the saddle again."

"I hope so," I replied, thinking of that blank document on my computer I just couldn't add the right words to. Writing romance novels and breaking up with my boyfriend just as the holiday season was approaching wasn't exactly a walk in the park. "My agent has really been on my case, and I need the money from this deal she has worked out."

"Oh, I wasn't talking about writing. I know that will come. I was talking about getting back in the saddle for dating."

"Grandma, it's only been a few weeks," I replied,

shaking my head. "I'm not going there." *Not ever*, I thought, the memories of that painful separation still stinging in my chest.

"Give it a few more weeks in our cute little town and you won't even remember that guy. Trust me, there are all sorts of new changes in town."

I shook my head, afraid to ask what that meant. We talked for a little bit, and then Herb returned.

"What did I miss?" he asked, bringing a coffee for me and a bottled water for Grandma, much to her disdain.

"Oh, just that Grandma is going to be relaxing for the next few weeks, taking it easy, and not arguing with me," I replied.

Herb laughed out loud. "Good luck with that one. I don't think Catherine knows what the word *relax* means."

"Oh hush. Now how is Edmund?" she asked.

"Running circles around me, as usual. I told him you'd be home soon."

I smiled, thinking of the larger-than-life dog my grandma had adopted last year from the pound.

"Lucy, why don't you head to the house? I don't want Edmund being alone all evening, and I'm sure you could use some rest after the long drive."

"I don't want to leave you alone," I argued.

"You're not. Herb's here. We've got to finish our conversation about that show we were watching. Hand me the remote, please."

I found it on the side table and passed it to her. Her hand reached out shakily, and it took her a moment to clutch the remote. I could already see what the doctor meant by lingering effects. I tried to assuage my fears. It would be okay. *She* would be okay.

"Are you—"

Grandma shushed me as she clicked the On button. "Yes. Now listen, you've already made up your mind you're staying, so we'll have plenty of time to catch up. But I won't get to rewatch the end of this murder mystery, and I have to prove Herb wrong. I know it was the husband."

I smiled as the two started bickering. Just like an old married couple, I assessed, knowing they would both get grumpy if I said that aloud. Still, I thought it was sweet how Herb had stuck by her side, watching out for her. What would it be like to have that kind of love? Grandma had known that love for decades—she'd been married to my grandfather for fifty-one years. And even though I knew she missed him, it warmed my spirit to see her with Herb, her heart still open to the possibility of connection, even if she couldn't see it.

I leaned down and kissed her cheek again.

"I love you, Lucy. Thank you for being here," she said.

"I love you too. And there's nowhere else I'd be," I replied, meaning it.

I was where I needed to be. Star Creek was going to be home for a while. This would be my change of scenery. At the thought, an image of the passport in my desk drawer flashed in my head, but I shoved it aside along with the disappointment.

That was another lifetime ago, another woman. After all, I could plan all I wanted, but life really could change in the blink of an eye.

THREE

As I walked up to the familiar red door of Grandma's cottage-like house, I inhaled as if the rose bushes were still in bloom. Even though it was the dead of a Pennsylvania winter, if I closed my eyes, I could imagine the vibrant red buds I always loved as a girl. Grandpa would pick one from the bush for me when I was leaving after a visit, winking and imploring me not to tell Grandma. It was always our little secret, although, looking back, I'm sure she knew. Now the bush was snow-laden and barren. Still, with the key in the door, I could conjure the memory of those roses, of him, and of the past.

A loud, soul-splitting bark from inside jolted me back to reality. I braced myself for the explosion of fur, slobber, and paws that was about to hit me at a million miles an hour.

I threw the door back, and Edmund, Grandma's Great Dane, exploded into a frenzy of tail wagging, excited barks, and clumsy clomps around the entryway. Desperately avoiding being mowed down by one hundred and fifty pounds of black fur, I kicked off my snowy boots.

"Hi, buddy," I said when he finally calmed to a level where I could pet him.

I looked around the cottage. It was still the home I remembered from my childhood, where I had visited with my parents once a month, making the trek from New Jersey. It was the home I came to for a week over the summers, with Grandma and Grandpa taking me to all my favorite places. We would go to the nearby lake for a picnic and to the movies. Mr. Barbary's candy store was always a favorite stop for sweet treats. And my favorite place of all: the Star Creek Bookstore in the center of town. Grandma always took me and let me browse the shelves for hours. It was where my love for books started and where my dreams of writing started too. The magic in that shop, the connection I felt talking to Mrs. Beesworth, who passed a few years ago, had stirred in me a love for books and stories. Nostalgia settled into my chest as I thought about how much had changed.

As if to remind me of the most important change, Edmund barked again, jumping up at me.

"No, no, Edmund. If you jump up on me, I'm going to be out of commission too." I still didn't know how my sweet grandma handled the Goliath of a dog.

When she'd gone to the humane society last year to get a friend to abate the loneliness, she fell in love with a slob- bering, panting black puppy who had the biggest paws imaginable. They tried to warn her he would get big, but she just said she liked big dogs. When she called to tell me the breed was something called a Great Dane, I'd spit out my espresso in the café. She was already in love with the wild, ever-growing pup when I helped her understand exactly how big he would get. She kept him, against my keen advice.

That was Grandma, though. Handling everything. Making lemonade out of lemons—and making friends with a dog that was bigger than her. I hoped this emergency wasn't the end of an era. I shoved the fear aside. She was a strong woman. She would get through this, and the prognosis was positive. She had just been going a million miles an hour for too long. I would help alleviate some of that stress, and she would be perfectly fine.

Once inside the living room, I stopped to look at my favorite wall of photographs. In the center was a childhood picture of my mother, bright blonde hair shimmering in the summer sun as she ran through a sprinkler. Her toothy grin radiated joy, and it made me smile just to look at it. Pictures of my mother at all stages of life filled the wall, including one of her with my father on their wedding day and a picture of her with an infant version of me. It was a tribute wall, in a way, a recognition of how my mother had always been the center of Grandma's universe. Even now, that was clearly still true.

Sadness crept in, but Edmund nudged my hand. I ushered the dog into the kitchen and decided a cup of tea was in order. Grandma didn't disappoint; the tea bar was brimming with options. She always believed a cup of tea and a good cookie could fix everything. There were no freshly baked cookies on the counter, due to the day's events. It made me a little sad to think about the bakery without Grandma in it. I could probably count on one hand the number of times Grandma had missed work. The Star Creek Bakery was not just a business: it was her passion.

Edmund settled on the couch with me after I'd made my tea. We snuggled, family photographs all around. Sitting in the house devoid of those faces, sadness overtook me. I didn't know how Grandma lived in the shell of what her life used to be. Guilt surged again at the thought that I hadn't visited enough. Maybe I hadn't done enough. I'd gotten swept up in an image of Jed, of a life I thought would abolish the loneliness I'd felt for so long. I abandoned her for what turned out to be misplaced hope. I'd taken a risk, something I didn't like doing. And after the dust had settled and my heart had shattered, I was left confused, guilt-ridden, and more alone than I'd perhaps ever felt.

"You're here now," I told myself aloud, startling Edmund. And I was. I was here, and I was staying.

The thing was, as I sat on that brown couch, plaid and inviting, I understood staying in Star Creek perhaps wasn't all about Grandma. Being in that house, in that town, was arguably what I needed to heal as well. New York City had been my dream growing up, but in light of everything that happened, maybe I needed re-centering in a way I hadn't imagined.

All around the city were reminders of who I was with Jed. The food truck he took me to on our third date for gyros, the club we went dancing in on weekends. The sidewalks we walked down hand in hand, talking about our future. It was too much, no matter how strong I thought I was. After living for someone else, I needed to remember who I was again. Maybe Star Creek could help me do that.

My cell phone buzzed in my pocket, and I pulled it out to see Serena's name, a welcoming beacon in an existential sea of despair.

"Hey," I said, and Edmund wagged his tail. He laid his agonizingly heavy head back down on me after a moment, and I rubbed his ear.

"Lucy? How's your grandma? How are things going?" Serena asked.

"She's okay. She had a stroke, but it was minor. She's

going to need some recovery time, but she'll be okay. I'll make sure of it."

"Oh, thank goodness. Is she giving the doctors attitude?"

"Don't you know it." Serena had visited my grandma with me a few times in the past couple years and even helped me show her around the city when she visited. Serena and my grandma were in many ways cut from the same cloth—right down to the red lips.

"Well, there's a care package coming in the mail for her. I picked up a new red lipstick I thought she might like."

I smiled at how sweet that was. "Thanks, Serena. How are things?"

"Busy. As always. Jeff called me into work because of a missing file, but I found it. I think he was impressed."

"Good," I said, thrilled things were falling into place for Serena. She had fit right into the life she'd built for herself. Sometimes I felt like the foil to her life's smoothness, but I was glad for her. She deserved it.

"So how long are you staying?" she asked.

I sighed. "I think I might be here a while, actually. Grandma needs to take it easy, and with the bake-off coming up, I know she won't. So I'm planning on staying for that, to help her organize it and get it running. Plus, then I can keep an eye on her and make sure she's taking care of herself." I thought about her shaky hand, the droopiness of her face, and the tired look in her eyes. She couldn't jump back into it all. I needed to be here for her. "What about your car? I feel bad keeping it so long."

"It's fine. I don't need it, truly. But I have to ask. What about your plans for the new year? Are you still going on your trip in January?"

Edmund was snoring and putting my leg to sleep. I ran

a hand through my frazzled hair and peered out the front window of the living room at the snow flurries coming down again.

"It'll have to wait. Grandma needs me right now." I couldn't think about January or my plans. There was no way I could just up and leave Grandma like she was. I couldn't be so far away from her.

"I get it. I just wish there was another way. You've been talking about those plans for weeks. It was going to be your big year."

It was true. I had sworn that no matter what, I was reclaiming my life. I was going to do something big, something just for me. Something my careful, planning self normally wouldn't do. And even though it had cost me basically all my savings and was arguably unwise, I'd made the decision to do something adventurous, scary. Something to help get my writing mojo back. I was going to do something uncomfortable—take a risk. But this risk was for me, not for him. And that felt like exactly what I needed. I'd done my research. I'd weighed the options and consequences carefully. It felt like the right leap of faith.

But now, it was all on hold. I tried not to focus on the disappointment seeping in.

"Family comes first," I said. And even though it was true, that familiar pang of guilt rocked me again. Because if family really came first, maybe I'd have been there before Grandma got into medical trouble.

"You're right, of course. Guess I'll have to wait a while on those cinnamon rolls you promised, huh? And it looks like movie marathons solo again," Serena said, interrupting my gloomy thoughts.

"Hey, you can come join us anytime," I offered.

"Jeff would be the one in the hospital if I up and left for

a month. I guess I'll just maneuver the city on my own again," she said, sighing dramatically for effect.

"I'll miss you," I admitted.

"Hey, well, maybe the change of scenery will still do you some good. Doesn't every romance start in some sappy little small town?" She was not a fan of the genre, despite being best friends with me.

"Ha-ha. Well, honestly, it's worth a try. I'm desperate to get this book written and get Anna off my back. And another payout would be nice." I'd spent a lot of my savings already on the trip and desperately needed to replenish my funds. I'd quit working at the coffee shop down the street last year when my book royalties started to roll in, but now I was wondering if that was a foolish mistake.

"You know I've got you if you need it."

I did know. Serena's family was very wealthy. Still, I would never want her to give me money. Even when things were tight when we lived together, I refused to let her pay my part of the rent.

"Seriously, Lucy. It's okay to lean on others. But keep me posted, okay? On your grandma, on Star Creek, and on any love stories that crop up there."

"Well, the last part will be a short report, but I'll do my best. Love you. Miss you."

"Love and miss you too. Take care, okay?"

I hung up and settled back on the sofa. It was official, sealed with a phone call. Star Creek was my new home, at least for a month. I sat in the silence for a moment, the only sound Edmund's chainsaw-like snoring. No honking taxis or rushing pedestrians. It was quiet. Peaceful, even.

Maybe I could get used to it.

WHEN I WENT to the hospital the next morning, Grandma had her bag packed, her red lipstick carefully applied to her lips, and her hot pink pants and sweater on. I didn't even get through the door before she ushered me out, walking slower than normal but still in a rush.

"Let's go before they change their minds," she demanded, hurrying past me like a woman who had her sights set on running a marathon, not one who had just been in the hospital because of a stroke and was supposed to be taking it easy.

A nurse was down the hallway with a wheelchair, insisting that my grandma stop, but she wasn't having it.

Herb was behind her, shaking his head, exhaustion painted on his face. I hadn't heard his car pull into the driveway next door last night, so I was pretty sure he'd stayed all night with her.

"Is she actually allowed to leave?" I asked, worried Grandma was pulling one over on me.

"Oh, yes. The doctor cleared her. You ask me, they just got worn down by her," he teased. "Who doesn't, though?"

I laughed. Herb was no stranger to my grandma's bossy ways. Maybe her love life should be the topic of conversation instead of mine. Herb held her elbow and turned to wave an apology to the nurse, who had clearly given up on hospital protocol at this point, shaking her head.

Grandma eased herself into Serena's car with my help and thanked Herb for spending time with her.

"I'll bring you a box of cookies tonight. What kind do you want?" she asked.

"You know," he said, smiling.

"Don't you ever get tired of plain old chocolate chip?" she asked as he hovered outside her passenger door.

"Classic never gets old," he murmured, and Grandma's

cheeks flushed. Herb smiled, waved at me, and then shut her door. I rubbed my hands together as I started the car, the chill in the air making me question why we didn't both just move down South like Dad had always wanted.

"If we get going now, I should be there to help finish up the cupcakes before the lunch crowd," she said, staring at me expectantly. Her face was still distorted, the left side drooping visibly. My heart sank at the thought that her recovery might be harder than she hoped.

"You aren't seriously thinking you're going to the bakery today, are you? You just got out of the hospital. You heard your doctor. You need to take it easy." I looked at her incredulously, hoping against all odds she was just teasing. The stoic look on her face told me she wasn't.

"And what, sit around and let the bakery fall apart? The bakery is my life, Lucy." Her words were slow but articulate. "You know that. I'm not going to let it disintegrate because some strict doctor is overly worried about nothing. My face is a little droopy, and y-yes, my hands are a bit shaky. But I'm fine. Honestly. I think the facial situation makes me look more interesting."

"It wasn't nothing, Grandma. It's your health. It's everything. I'm not letting you go to the bakery. You need to kick your feet up, watch some mysteries, and drink some tea. No arguing. Trust that I'll help make sure the bakery is fine."

I put the car in Drive and pulled out of the parking lot, expecting more arguing from Grandma. She had been obsessed with the bakery since the beginning.

I understood her passion.

As I drove down the one-way street toward her house, I considered driving past the bakery, which was closer to the town center, but I knew that would only add fuel to the fire.

"If you're not going to let me go to work, then I need

you to do me a favor," she said, arms crossed. I felt bad she was so upset, but it couldn't be helped. It was tough love for her own good.

"Anything, Grandma."

"I need you to go in and make sure everything is okay at the bakery. Besides, you need to get acquainted with him, our recipes, and how it all works behind the scenes for the bake-off. Will is there, but I just like to have a set of eyes on the place."

"Is Will the one you were telling me about when you visited?" She'd mentioned something about a new baker and told me he was from the city too. She'd also said he was quite handsome, but Grandma was known to say that about pretty much any man she thought I might be even remotely interested in, so I always took her assessment with a grain of salt.

"Oh, yes. Will Westerly, the one I told you is just gorgeous. I'm sure you'll think so too," she said, smirking with her mischievous grin.

"What's that supposed to mean?" I dared to ask.

"It means he's quite a looker, you're newly single, and so is he. I think the two of you could be the chocolate to each other's chip. If you could get him to talk, that is. He's been pretty quiet since he started. I can barely get him to say two words to me some days. But he's a good worker and, like I said, good to look at. So that's what really matters."

"Grandma, I'm not looking to fall in love. I'm sort of over it."

"You can't be a romance writer who doesn't believe in love," she argued. And although she was right, I had the urge to change the subject.

"And you can't pretend you and Herb are just neighbors," I added with a smile.

"But we are. He's just a good friend is all. No one falls in love at my age."

"Don't be so sure," I added as we pulled into the driveway.

"And don't be so sure you're done with love, either," she replied.

I sighed, not wanting to think about love, romance, or anything of the sort. My mind was weary from traveling and worrying about Grandma—but also from the entire Jed situation that had unfolded like I was in some horrifying romantic drama. It was no wonder my writing was suffering; even the word *love* made me shudder.

I got Grandma settled on the couch after finally calming down Edmund, who was ecstatic she was home. Grandma gave him a few of his homemade treats and asked if I would bring more home from the supply at the bakery.

"You make dog treats now?" I asked. "Since when?"

She shrugged. "Since Will. He said they sold a lot at his last bakery. Now, enough questions. You need to get over there. The cupcakes don't ice themselves," she said with a smile. "And unless you've traded your writing for baking school, I feel like you have a lot of catching up to do."

I sighed at her lighthearted jab. I couldn't argue with that statement. Still, I felt bad leaving her.

"Are you sure you're okay?" What if something happened while I was gone? I didn't like the idea at all.

"I won't be if you don't keep my bakery running," she said.

I hesitated, studying her. She did seem more herself than the day before, but she was still not one hundred percent. I worried that they'd discharged her too soon, that something terrible would happen.

"You need to swear you'll call me if you feel even

remotely dizzy or tired or anything," I said, checking to make sure the phone was right next to her. I crossed the room and picked up the receiver just to make sure it was working. "And I'm not going to be gone long. I'll be home as soon as I can."

"I promise." She nodded her head toward the door, ushering me out.

"Okay, okay. I can take a hint. And besides, I'm sure Herb will find a few excuses to come over to see you." I still didn't feel great about it. But maybe Grandma was right; it would be worse for her to be stressed.

She shook her head as Edmund settled in on the couch beside her. I sauntered out of the house again and drove straight to the bakery after making Grandma promise yet again that she would call if anything felt amiss at all.

I was excited to see the bakery. It had always felt like coming home, the coziness of the place coupled with all the memories. I could almost taste the freshly baked cookies straight from the oven and smell the haze of sugar on my way over.

When I walked through the door and heard the familiar ringing of the bells, it wasn't just the sight of all the amazing baked goods that made my heart drop.

FOUR

He couldn't know. There was no way he could've known.

When I walked through the red door of Star Creek Bakery and heard the song he was singing, my stomach plunged into the ground. It had been my song with Jed, the one we'd danced to on our second date when he told me he loved me.

When the bells rang, the man behind the counter turned around and, thankfully, stopped singing. Still, the shock must've been visible on my face because the first words the handsome, dark-haired man with a killer smile said to me were, "Are you okay?"

The true answer was no, I was not okay. The relationship I thought was my forever had ended in flames of epic proportions before the holiday season, my career felt like it was in shambles, the one plan I had to get my life back on track had been postponed, and my grandmother had had a stroke. I was not in any way okay.

Looking into the dark eyes of the man in front of me, I saw a genuine concern that made me feel slightly better somehow. And although I would never admit it to my grandmother, she was right in her assessment of his looks. He was downright gorgeous, jaw-dropping even.

"I think so," I replied shakily, not sure what else to say.

An awkward pause ensued. I tried to continue staring while pretending not to stare—which never really works out.

"Can I get you anything?" he finally asked.

"Um, some dog treats," I replied, not wanting to forget them for Edmund.

He raised an eyebrow, peering around me as if to see if there was a dog in my car. "You came in just for dog treats?"

"No, sorry. Not just treats."

He paused and studied me again. I didn't elaborate.

I walked closer to the counter and set my purse down. Only one couple was in the shop, sitting at the little bistro table in the corner. They'd stopped eating their cupcakes to look over at us, openly eavesdropping on our conversation.

"Okay, good. Because you'd be the first person to leave without baked goods." His words were stiff, formal. He seemed a little distant. Grandma's assessment of his quiet nature seemed correct—although he'd said more than two words to me, so that was something.

"And what if I didn't like baked goods? Would that be so bad?" I probed.

"You do know where you're at, right? The most famous bakery this side of the Mississippi."

I laughed at that. Star Creek Bakery was something I was very proud of, and don't get me wrong, it has always had the reputation of being a top-notch bakery. But the most famous? This side of the Mississippi? Even I knew that was a stretch.

"Did Grandma pay you to say that? Or did she just tell you that in training and you believed it?" I teased, leaning on the counter.

"Grandma? Oh, you're—"

"Lucy. Yes. And you're Will. Grandma told me about you."

"Oh, sorry. Your grandma showed me a picture last week, but it was from when you were younger." He looked apologetic at the confession.

"That's mildly embarrassing." And something Grandma would do. Living in the past. I couldn't blame her. The present wasn't always the best place to be, despite our admirable collective efforts.

Will put down the dog biscuits, wiped his palm on his apron, and shook my hand very professionally. It was a warm but soft grip, and I fought the urge to shiver. I averted my eyes, his dark gaze inciting me to shift my weight to my left leg. He pulled his hand back promptly.

"How's she doing? From what she said, she never takes a day off."

"That's the truth. She had a mild stroke, and she definitely is going to have a bit of a recovery. She needs to take it easy. The doctor is concerned if she keeps pushing herself like she has been, we could have a different outcome next time. She fought with me, but I wouldn't let her come in today."

"No way. She needs to rest. We've got this." He nodded toward me, and I looked around, realizing he was all alone.

"Are Rita and George off today?" I confirmed.

Rita and George were an adorable middle-aged couple who joined the bakery team when Grandpa died. Grandma didn't want to give up the bakery, but she couldn't manage doing all the baking and running the front of the place, which had been Grandpa's job. She'd hired them, two Star Creek lifers, to help her with the business. They'd been a godsend and were part of the reason I didn't worry so much about being far away. Rita and George were family in essence, and they always made sure the bakery was running smoothly. When Grandma had told me to come help, I'd assumed that was why.

"Didn't your grandma tell you? Apparently they retired to Florida. That was why she hired me."

"When?" I asked, struck by my lack of knowledge and saddened at the news that they were gone.

"July, I guess." His answers were very to the point, formal even. I waited for him to elaborate, but he didn't. Despite his charming looks, a tension had formed in the air, a chilliness coming from him. I didn't understand why, but it made me feel—uncomfortable? I stuffed it down, telling myself he was just nervous to meet the boss's family.

"July?" I said incredulously. The elderly man in the corner of the bakery coughed because I'd said it so loud. "Why didn't she tell me?" I assumed she'd hired Will to have extra hands in the bakery, which was a good thing. I'd thought she was just slowing down a bit, which was understandable. But to find out she'd been going at it all alone for so many months... A pit formed in my stomach. Suddenly, I felt very out of the loop.

"Oh, that's easy. She was worried you'd feel the need to come rushing here if you knew. And she said she never wants you to give up your dreams. That's what she talks about when she mentions you. How you're a dreamer, like she was."

This softened the blow of the news a little bit. I smiled. I liked to think Grandma and I were cut from the same cloth. Her dream had been this place, this beautiful little bakery she'd run for all these years. And mine—well, writing of course, but I was still working out the details. Sure, I had royalties coming in, but they weren't enough for me to coast on forever. If Grandma could start a bakery from scratch and keep it going all these years, certainly I could get over a little writer's block. Oh, and a disdain for love. I'd have to work on it.

"I'm glad she hired you then," I said, sighing. At least Grandma's business was on the right track. And at least I was there to help sort it out while she recovered.

"Yeah, she said she needed help. I'd like to think it's because I'm such a baking genius, and she couldn't let my talent go to a rival." He smirked then, and I softened a bit. At least he wasn't being so icy. Just as I was getting ready to let my guard down, he took off running toward the oven in the back as a timer went off.

"Cookies!" he shouted.

I followed him.

"So if Rita and George aren't here, I'm guessing you really do need help with the baking?" I asked as he pulled some heavenly toffee crunch cookies from the oven. I inhaled deeply, unashamed by my obsession.

"Isn't that why you're here? To help with the baking?" he asked.

That was exactly what I needed—to pour myself into work, no emotional attachments or expectations. Just physical work to keep me busy and to keep my mind off the dozens of disasters imploding in my life.

"Yes. Grandma is worried about the bake-off, so I said I'd help with that."

"The bake-off?" he asked, tilting his head slightly as he put the cookie trays on top of one of the ovens.

"The Star Creek Holiday Bake-Off? You know, the event the whole town shuts down for on December 23 every year? Less than a month away?" I asked as he leaned on the counter space behind him, wiping his hand on the towel hanging over his shoulder. I inhaled deeply, the sweet smell of the cookies wafting my way. I didn't remember Grandma having this recipe. I was dying to get my hands on one of the cookies.

"I don't know what you're talking about. I've mostly been baking a lot of things," Will confessed, shrugging.

I studied him then, confused once more. "Grandma has you doing all the baking?"

That was absolute news to me. Grandma always did the baking. No one else was even allowed in the kitchen. It was her domain, her passion. Grandpa had done all the administrative duties for the business and run the front counter. Sure, sometimes he would carry ingredients in for her, and he certainly was always willing to be the taste tester. But the actual baking was Grandma's area of expertise. Even when the bake-off came around every year, Grandpa was only allowed to help with the basic tasks, like running the mixer. Rita and George had taken over for him when he died, as far as I had known. I was surprised things had changed so much.

"Yeah. She said she'd run the front. She wanted me to do all the kitchen work."

And with that, I knew. I knew Grandma hadn't been feeling well for a while. That was the only explanation. My stomach churned at the thought of how far out of touch I was with Grandma's life, with Star Creek. She was my only family, and I had let her down. How hadn't I seen it all?

"So what's this bake-off?" he asked, and I pulled myself out of my thoughts.

"It's basically the heart of Star Creek during the holiday season. We open up the festival to any bakery from across the country. Each bakery brings two bakers with them. There's a three-hour competition for them to create the best cupcake using a random supply of ingredients we provide. We have all sorts of booths and festival-like activities for the town during the baking. At the end, judges pick the best cupcake. The winning bakery gets a trophy and a prize and has their cupcake featured on Grandma's menu for the next year."

"Sounds like a lot of work."

I sighed. It was. And I had a feeling I didn't know the half of it but was about to find out.

"It is. And if you didn't know about it, I'm thinking Grandma hasn't done the usual prep work. Which she typically starts in about September. She really hasn't mentioned it?"

"Not a word," he said, leaning on the baking counter with the kitchen towel still draped over his shoulder.

She definitely wasn't feeling well. The bake-off was her baby, her prized undertaking. She always started early so she could make it bigger and better every single year. No wonder she'd been worried about it.

"Well, Will, it seems we have quite a lot of work on our hands if we're going to pull this thing off."

"And we've got a bit of work to do around here too. I hope you don't have a lot of plans this next month, Lucy. Because baking is about to become your entire life," he said matter-of-factly. "We're going to be spending a whole lot of time in this kitchen."

"There's just one tiny little problem with that," I offered, my face reddening as the tall, handsome man standing before me took a few steps closer.

"What's that?"

"I can't bake to save my life," I admitted, shrugging and hoping against all odds he was not only handsome but patient as well. Because dreams and ambition might run in the family—but my grandma's talents for baking most certainly did not.

FIVE

Throughout my time with Will that morning, I had to remind myself that he had only been working for Grandma for a few months because the way he smoothly handled baking, the register, and cleaning all at once made it seem like he'd been there for years. He was mostly quiet while he worked, not really going out of his way to talk to me or the customers. I tried to start a few conversations, but he was focused, giving me only one-word answers.

In truth, it was driving me a little crazy. I mean, would it be so hard to be friendly? To make conversation, especially since we'd be spending so much time together? Grandma had told me how wonderful the guy was, and sure, he was great at his job. But his communication skills left a lot to be desired.

As I struggled to mix the batter he'd made, all the buttons on the stand mixer may as well have been buttons on a rocket ship. However, he effortlessly maneuvered the world of the bakery in a way that helped me understand he was made for this role.

"So, what made you come to Star Creek?" I ventured, tired of the quiet.

Will was icing some complex-looking cupcakes. "Work," he replied without looking up.

"Do you have family here?" I stepped closer to watch him work his magic, pouring some kind of fancy filling into a pastry bag.

"Yes," he said. Another one-word answer. I let the silence sit between us, hoping he would fill it.

He didn't. I tried again.

"So do you have a favorite cupcake? I love chocolate with peanut butter. Oh, and there's a special almond one I really enjoy…"

He looked up at me with a serious face and gave me a single nod. Great, we'd lost even one-word answers.

I walked back over to my station, trying to figure out how to read the recipe he'd given me and told me was simple. *Is that teaspoon or tablespoon?* I couldn't tell. I considered walking back over to him and asking for help. Instead, though, I stayed planted. I watched him, stoic and cold, working in a bubble. It was like I didn't exist, like he couldn't make eye contact with me. What was wrong with me? I'd been friendly, hadn't I? Why had he pulled so far away after realizing I wasn't just a random customer?

Perhaps the song he was singing when I walked in had been a bad omen or a warning. His coldness, the way he made me come to him and be the one to talk first was frustrating. I wouldn't be that woman again. I wouldn't bend and stretch myself into being a cheerful, try-hard woman just to get his attention.

With Jed, I always put in the effort to make conversation, to keep us connected, to open communication. I tried to convince him to put his phone down at dinner in the final months to talk to me. I went on wild ski trips and hikes and did things I didn't like just to keep our relationship exciting. I had changed. I had bent. I had put in the effort—and he'd ended up scorching my heart anyway.

I wouldn't be that woman again. I would be who I was and say forget it to love.

Not that love with my grandma's new employee was even in the cards, I reminded myself. That was crazy. I glanced over at him, hating myself for doing it. I put my head down and focused on my work—the cupcake recipe. I'd sort it out on my own. I didn't need Will Westerly, Jed, or any other man for that fact. I would be just fine on my own, my heart preserved in its own glass case with a sign that distinctly read *Not for sale.*

AFTER THE LUNCH rush had died down and I was working on another batch of Grandma's famous strawberry ganache cupcakes, I stopped stirring the batter to look at Will, who was intensely focused on the poinsettias he was making for the cupcakes from earlier.

"So what happens if I accidentally mixed up baking soda and baking powder? Is that an issue?" I bit my lip as I stared at the enormous batch of batter I'd just mixed. I kept my words serious, cutting back on the friendly vibes I had tried to offer earlier.

"Um, yes. Quite," Will said, pausing from his work.

"Oh." I looked down at the huge bowl of batter I'd messed up.

"I'm guessing that wasn't just curiosity talking?" he asked, putting down the piping bag. It seemed like the most emotion he'd put into his words so far. But that was because work was involved. Which was just fine. Work. Professional. Just like I wanted.

The towel was still draped over his shoulder, and I wondered if he'd forgotten it was there or if it was a permanent part of his uniform. I was guessing the latter. He wandered over and stared into the bowl with me.

"You weren't kidding about baking not being your thing, huh?" he asked in a pointed voice.

"I did warn you," I replied.

He didn't smile, though. I wasn't sure if he was actually mad. Which made me sort of mad. In truth, it was my own fault. I'd come to help him and essentially just made things worse. Throughout the lunch rush I had managed to drop a glass, which shattered everywhere, mislabel the cupcakes in the front case, and burn two batches of chocolate chip cookies.

"You did. Maybe we should keep you out front," he said. I wondered if he just wanted to get me out of his kitchen. It might not be a bad thing to get a break from him.

"Well, out there, I mislabeled the cupcakes."

"I meant out front, out front. Like maybe holding a sign? How are you at sign flipping?" he asked, cracking a smile for the first time but quickly squelching it like he didn't want me to see it.

"Okay, I'm doing my best here, Mr. Know-It-All. It hasn't really helped that you're giving me nothing to work with, just being all silent over there."

"I was just teasing," he said. "I'm sorry." His words were softer, and after scrutinizing him for a moment and deciding it was a harmless comment and maybe not totally unwarranted, I softened too. He flashed me his teeth, perfectly white and straight, of course, and I found myself smiling back, despite it all.

"How have you been managing all of this by yourself?" I asked, shaking my head. I'd shoved my tangled brown locks into a tight ponytail. It swung side to side.

He shrugged. "You just do what you have to do."

The timer went off, and we returned to our tasks, me dumping the batter and starting over while he checked the other batch of cupcakes.

After a few more hours of work, we were ready for the next day, and the evening rush of moms buying bake-sale cupcakes had slowed. We cleaned the tables out front, and I smiled, thinking of how when I was a little girl, I'd go to work with Grandma and Grandpa. They would pay me with my favorite cookie, which happened to be Mom's favorite too. I'd wipe down tables, and they'd present me with my snowball cookies at the end of the day. It was a happy time. I loved working in that bakery, the smell of sweets all around me and the feeling of warmth radiating not just from the ovens, but from Grandma and Grandpa as well.

But after Mom... Grandma stopped making those cookies, and I stopped eating them. It hurt too much.

"So how long are you staying?" Will asked, interrupting my thoughts. I was glad for it.

"Why, are you ready to get rid of me?"

"You can never have too many hands in a bakery. Even if they aren't skilled," he said.

"Until the bake-off. And then we'll see."

"You're a writer, aren't you?" he asked. "Your grandma talks about you a lot."

I was certain she did. I was actually shocked she hadn't jumped on the chance to mention even more to me about him.

"I was," I answered as I tidied up the ingredients in my area.

"I don't think that's the sort of thing you just stop being, even if you want to."

"Well, when you're a writer who doesn't write, you can."

"Well, then write," he said, shrugging as if it was no big deal.

"It's not that simple."

"Seems simple to me. You love writing. So write."

It made sense. Nevertheless, as he stared at me with his big smile, I grew angry. It wasn't that easy. Life wasn't easy.

He turned his back to clean the counter beside the stove and started singing again. He was singing the song that took me right back to that ugly place with Jed and New York and a broken heart.

Even the strawberry ganache cupcakes weren't going to save me from all of that.

I'D CALLED Grandma at least four times to check on her during my time away, but it wasn't necessary. Herb was set up at her house, waiting on her hand and foot. When I returned from the bakery, Edmund jumped on me, as had become our custom at this point. I was covered in flour, exhausted, and more than a little emotional.

"How's the bakery? Did you bring me the cookies? Edmund's cookies?" Grandma sprang up from her seat on the sofa.

"Sit down, you," Herb ordered, pointing at the couch. Grandma rolled her eyes.

"I've never taken orders from a man, and I'm not about

to start now, Herbert Groves. Thank goodness you're home, Lucy. This man is driving me nuttier than an almond short-bread cookie."

"And this woman is driving me nuttier than an almond itself."

Although I was exhausted, I grinned as the two in-denial lovebirds started bickering about how their analogies didn't make sense and about the show they had been watching—and about everything.

Still, I noticed a bouquet of flowers on the counter that Herb had brought over as well as Chinese takeout containers from her favorite restaurant. A piece of me worried because the doctor had given Grandma a stricter diet to follow for her heart, but I decided it was a moot point. I was glad Herb was there making her feel better. It was clear he was smitten—and so was Grandma. I could see it in her eyes. She looked at him the same way she used to look at Grandpa.

"Anyway, how was Will? Isn't he quite the looker?" she asked, winking at me.

I took a seat on the recliner near the couch, and Edmund dropped his head in my lap. "If you say so," I answered noncommittally. I made sure to keep as much of a poker face as I could muster.

"Oh, come on. Admit that he's cute. And he's good at baking, which is saving my world."

"Grandma, why didn't you tell me about him?"

"I did."

"Why didn't you tell me he's doing all the baking now?"

Grandma took a deep breath and averted her eyes. "I didn't want you to worry. It's not a big deal, dear. I'm just slowing down, and, in truth, Will is more talented than me.

It seemed like a waste to put such an expert baker in front of a cash register."

"You know I would have come to help if you had asked," I said, guilt still haranguing me at not knowing Grandma was struggling.

"Which is exactly why I didn't. I'm doing fine here, Lucy. And it's a good thing, Will being here. As I said, he's quite the catch."

"Again, if you say so," I replied as Herb chuckled.

"I mean, I must be honest. I wanted to gush about him more, but I needed to save him for real life, when you visited. I knew I couldn't do him justice over the phone and that live phone book thing on the computer was acting up so I couldn't send you his picture. I just didn't realize you'd be coming so soon."

I smirked. Grandma had tried to get in on the newest technology, but it wasn't really her thing. I'd tried to show her how to set up a web page and social media profile for the bakery. That was a disaster.

"And what did you think would happen when I saw him in real life? Did you picture a whirlwind romance, me jumping into his arms? You know I'm not looking for someone right now. Besides, he's icy at best. Which is fine," I added hurriedly before she got any ideas. "Professional is exactly what I need."

"Well, he's not looking either, or so he says. He's all about work. But you two are both young and beautiful. And you're both successful. It doesn't hurt to explore. I think you two have a lot in common. You could help each other."

"Is there another reason you didn't tell me about him?" I asked, serious now.

"No, I just don't like to bog you down with details about my boring life," she said.

"You sure don't mind bogging *me* down with details," Herb said, teasing, as he sat on the sofa beside her.

She poked him in the ribs but giggled despite the jab.

"Grandma, Will also told me Rita and George left for Florida in July."

She looked away again and interlocked her hands.

"I hate that you feel like you have to keep things from me."

She looked over at me, and I could see the weariness. "I'm just getting older. But it's not for you to worry about. You have your city life. And as much as I would selfishly love for you to come live in Star Creek, I don't want you doing that because your old grandma has tired hands."

"But I want to be here for you. You're my family."

"And I want you to be happy," she said. "Really happy. You deserve it, Lucy. You worked so hard to get to the city, to be a writer. You always talked about doing that when you were little. You need to enjoy the life you've built."

Now it was my turn to look away. Because was I really happy? I'd moved to the city, my dream growing up, at twenty-two. Serena and I had done the New York thing, had explored and found the energy thrilling. And it was a good life, full of fun places, happy hours, museums, art exhibits, music, and just constant things to do. I'd been energized in the city, my writing flourishing. I had a writers' group I loved and bookstores I browsed weekly. I'd found who I thought was the love of my life, and I'd pictured a life of writing, marriage, mortgages, kids. The whole thing. I'd pictured a life of unconditional love, of never being alone.

After Jed broke my heart and with my writing plummeting, a thought had been worming its way into my mind —what if the city wasn't making me happy anymore? What if I needed a new dream? What if it was never supposed to be my dream after all? I could write anywhere, couldn't I? Maybe it had been foolish and naive to think the city was where I had to live.

That was why I'd bought that ticket to Paris after the breakup. That was why I did something drastic, something that might bring me back to life. I needed to get away, to think. I needed to sort out who I was and what I wanted now that I was alone again. And in truth, the thought of being alone scared me. I needed to feel alive again.

But those plans had changed. I was in Star Creek, the tiniest, sometimes sleepy town, but a town that had been the foundation of my childhood, of my family. Even just sitting in Grandma's house, I felt a connection I'd been missing in the cold, stark city streets. I felt close to my parents in a way I hadn't since they died.

Was it enough, though? And what did it mean for my career, for my life?

Grandma started asking more specific questions about the bakery, the customers, and how many cupcakes Will had made. Her eyes lit up when she talked about it, and I realized how sweet it was that she'd always known who she was and where she was supposed to be. From the time she married my grandpa, she knew Star Creek Bakery would be her passion, her pride and joy, and the center of her world— along with her family. She'd made it into the legacy it was, and she had something beautiful to leave behind.

Thinking about my empty notebook and the blank document on my screen, I worried that I'd never be able to say the same thing. Maybe I'd never settle into who I was and where I belonged—or who I belonged with. Maybe the best parts of my life were already behind me, a thought more depressing than the dreary winter night swirling outside.

SIX

The next day was Sunday, and the bakery was closed. It was a required day of rest according to Grandma. After the traveling, working at the bakery, and all the worrying about Grandma, I wanted nothing more than to sleep until noon, tucked under the guest room quilt.

Two things ruined that possibility.

The first was that I'd forgotten to shut the guest room door and at promptly six in the morning, I was startled awake by a lumbering presence. I opened my eyes to see Edmund's droopy face over mine, his four paws straddling my body.

The second was my blaring ringtone. I'd turned my phone volume up in case Grandma needed me while I was at the bakery and had forgotten to switch it to silent before bed. The noise startled Edmund, who jumped up and landed on what I thought was my kidney. I groaned, which scared him again, and he finally jumped down and went bolting out of my room, just in time for me to click Answer on the phone.

"Lucy, are you okay?" Anna's voice asked as I choked and sputtered a hello.

"Fine, fine," I said, still holding my side where the Great Dane had bounced off my body. "How are you?"

"I'm good. I just needed to check in on those chapters. How's the story coming? You know I love a good romance, so I can't wait to get my hands on some pages. And Sophie from the publisher is also anxious. The deadline's coming up, and they're really excited to see some chapters so they can start preparing some marketing. When do you think you can send me the manuscript? Or even just the first few chapters?"

I could picture Anna sitting in her office, her curly red hair standing up in many directions as she tapped her bright purple pen on the desk. She was a bulldog of an agent, going after aggressive deals and making so many of my dreams come true. And she never slept, from what I ascertained. Sunday, holiday—it didn't matter. The literary world never stopped, she liked to remind me.

I didn't want to let her down. This would be my third book, and she'd pulled a few strings and talked me up to get this contract. I couldn't fail her. I had to make it work.

"A couple weeks?" I asked vaguely, not telling her whether I meant chapters or the manuscript.

"Okay, okay. I'll make that work. I trust your process, Lucy. Just don't let us down, okay?"

And with that, she clicked the phone off. I plopped back on my pillow, groaning again. This time, the reality of my blank screen and my writer's block caused the noise, not my enflamed kidney—although that was still throbbing.

Eventually, I found the energy to get out of bed. There was no sense in pretending I could go back to sleep after that phone call. I needed an idea. I needed one yesterday. The pressure was daunting. When I emerged from the hallway in my pink pajamas, Grandma was already up and making coffee.

"What are you up to?" I asked, seeing her move around the kitchen slowly.

"Just getting ready to make some breakfast, dear."

"You're supposed to be relaxing."

"Cooking is relaxing," she said. "I'm not going to just sit on the sofa like an undercooked biscuit. I can make us some breakfast. We have to eat, after all. Besides, Herb will be here soon. It's tradition."

I couldn't say no to tradition with Herb, especially since I was rooting for the two of them. I settled in at the table but kept a close eye on Grandma. Her hands were shaking and her movements were slower than normal. It worried me, but she looked happy, despite her facial paralysis hampering what was usually a big, wide smile. Before I could verbalize my fears, Edmund galloped to the door as it opened.

Herb wandered in, and I felt sort of awkward sitting at the table in my pajamas.

"What are you doing cooking? I came over early so I could make the meal. You're supposed—"

"To be relaxing. Yes, everyone keeps reminding me how fragile I am. Just sit down. My granddaughter has already given me the lecture. I'm going to make breakfast, then I'll go sit on my behind like you all seem to want."

Herb sat beside me, shooting me a wide-eyed look.

"Keeping her calm is going to be a full-time job," I whispered to him, and he chuckled.

Grandma turned around from the skillet of pancakes, spatula raised. "Are you two conspiring?"

"No," we replied in unison.

"Sure," she said, but her face had a half smile painted on it. She knew she was difficult. She prided herself on it.

"So, Lucy. Your grandma is always telling me about your writing. Are you working on anything right now?" Herb asked. It felt like the universe was hounding me.

I sighed, burying my head in my arms for a brief, childish second. When I came back up for air, I shrugged.

"Not really. I'm under contract, but the words just won't come to me. In truth, an idea won't come to me. And I'm sure Grandma told you my boyfriend and I broke up at the beginning of the month, so writing about love just doesn't seem truthful right now."

Herb shrugged. "Love is never easy, huh? It's always a gamble. But it's worth it. That's what my late wife always said. Love is a gamble but worth it. She was big on bingo and poker."

"Her name was Scarlet, right?" I asked. She was a gorgeous redheaded woman who seemed to always be in a flashy, bright dress with her curls perfectly arrayed around her head. She brought lemonade out to all the neighborhood kids when we were playing. She died a few years before Grandpa. Perhaps that was what brought Grandma and Herb together. I would have to ask, but I knew Grandma wouldn't admit to any of it with Herb around.

"How did you meet?" I asked, hoping I wasn't prying too much.

He smiled. "She was jumping rope down the block from my house. We were both ten. I knew from the moment I saw those shiny red pigtails bouncing in the air I was going to fall in love with her."

"That's adorable," I said, practically squealing.

"It was and it wasn't. It took us twelve years to find each

other. We both dated other people, and the timing was never right. I thought I wasn't good enough for her, and she thought I wasn't interested. We finally admitted the truth to ourselves and each other when we were twenty-two, sitting in the diner with dates neither of us truly liked."

"Do you ever regret not saying something sooner?" I asked, my mind twirling around ideas. Grandma was still working on the pancakes, but she was quiet and listening as well. I wondered if she was thinking about her own love story with Grandpa.

"Things have to take their natural pace, you know?" Herb said. "I was a welder in my day, and it was the same thing. You couldn't rush the welds. Slow and consistent. You had to be really devoted to keeping it steady and letting it come to pass in its own time. I think that's the problem these days. Everyone is pushing to reach a deadline, a milestone, an ending. Just sit back and let it flow. We came to each other at the time we were meant to, and we built a beautiful life from it all."

"Ha! Spoken like a true man. 'Let it flow.' You know the only reason you can let things flow is because there's a woman somewhere behind the scenes working her tail off," Grandma said, finally breaking her silence and jumping on the chance to argue with Herb.

"Probably true. But I still don't think you can force love," he countered.

"And I don't think it hurts to hurry it along sometimes. We aren't vampires. Sometimes you have to set the timer and help things move at a reasonable pace," Grandma argued as she stacked the pancakes on a plate, and I suddenly wondered if we were still talking in hypotheticals. I smiled regardless, thinking of some ideas to put in my notebook. It was something, I supposed.

Herb and Grandma kept talking in cookie analogies. How long until they finally opened up about where they stood? Would it ever happen? I hoped so.

You can't force love, but you also can't sit back and let someone else do the work for you. That was what they'd made me consider.

It wasn't a book, and it wouldn't keep Anna off my back, but it was something. In writing, if you have something, you often can find inspiration from there.

I excused myself to go jot down a few notes in the notebook I kept on the side table by my bed. After scratching down a few phrases Herb had said, I returned to the kitchen. Grandma and Herb were laughing about some inside joke. They both lit up in the kitchen, pouring syrup over pancakes and talking about some old-time mystery show.

They weren't forcing anything. And they still had plenty of time. If only I could make them see it.

"Grandma, if you're okay, I'm going to go do some thinking for my book. Can I take Edmund for a walk around the neighborhood?"

At the magic word, the black dog barreled from the recesses of the hallway, jumping at least four feet in the air as he emitted an excited bark that practically rattled the windows.

"Dear, rule one of dog ownership: We don't say the 'W' word unless we are fully committed. There's no going back now, even if you wanted to."

"You can say that again," Herb added, but he was looking at Grandma, not at us. I obliged Grandma and scarfed down one pancake as Edmund zoomed in circles around the entire house.

When I finished, I clipped on Edmund's leash after

wrangling him into his bright red Christmas sweater Grandma insisted he needed to wear. His leash was also, of course, covered in Christmas trees. Shaking my head at the spoiled dog who had an entire wardrobe, I bundled up in all my winter gear, sweating from dressing the dog, and headed for the door. Edmund was already challenging my arm strength.

"Watch out for squirrels!" Grandma yelled from the kitchen, but I didn't have time to respond because, thanks to Edmund, we were off before I could even close the door.

My arm was aching about two blocks into the walk, and even though it wasn't actually snowing, the blowing snow from the ground created quite the winter wonderland. Mercifully, squirrels didn't seem to be a concern because I didn't think any would be coming out in the miserable winter weather.

We walked on, the quiet of the street lulling me into the perfect state of mind for brainstorming for my book. I inhaled the freezing air, my lungs feeling spicy but awakened. I always thought the energy of the city was what I needed for my creativity but the simplicity of this little town had me wondering if I was wrong. The empty streets seemed like a welcome mat for my mind to wander, for my thoughts to sort themselves out. For the first time since Jed and I broke up, I felt like a story was buzzing just below the surface. Maybe I could reclaim my writing.

Still, as my mind danced over thoughts about love, I couldn't help returning to the love I'd had, the hope I'd felt about romance in the beginning. It had been beautiful with Jed. He'd been there for me, reminded me what it was like to count on someone. He'd been the strong arms holding me when times were hard, when the sadness of what I'd lost was too much. He'd been the strong rock I needed to lean on and felt like I could.

Why had it all gone wrong? Why hadn't I been enough for him? And most of all, why had I been such a fool not to see the truth? My hand ached from Edmund yanking on the leash to sniff every single road sign and mailbox, but my heart ached worse. I hadn't seen it coming. Shouldn't I have seen it coming? I was a romance writer. I should have known the signs.

But looking back, there really weren't any. Not at first, at least. We were happy. We'd complemented each other, both go-getters chasing big dreams in New York. He was the wild to my cautious. He loved to talk about how my list-making made him more organized, and how his spontaneity was good for me. I brought the planner to the relationship, and he brought the element of surprise. We were a good match, opposites attract and all that.

Until, suddenly, it seemed like that wasn't what he wanted at all. He was annoyed by my constant planning. He felt held back when I didn't want to go skydiving with him or jump off a waterfall. He liked to take risks in business and in his life. But I loved him. I was crazy about him, and he loved me too. In his arms, I felt a safety from the world I hadn't experienced. So I did what I had to do—I met him halfway. Or so I told myself.

I went on the skiing trip that terrified me, trying to be brave and act like I was having fun as we flew down the mountain. I went on the fishing trip with him even though I hated being on a boat and got seasick. I went dancing at a club on a Tuesday even though I wanted nothing more than to stay in and watch television. I told myself I was living and that, more importantly, my parents would want that for me. I would fit in all the life they couldn't—and I would do it holding the hand of the man I loved. It was beautiful, magical. It was exactly what I was supposed to want. And it was worth it for love. Love was sacrifice, I told myself. Love was bending.

And then, in recent months, the shine faded. The flowers halted a few months ago, and his job often got in the way of romantic dates. He stopped talking to me. We stopped talking about the future.

I thought of that first time in the coffee shop when he'd walked in, loosening his tie slightly as he ordered a chai latte. I'd stared at him with his dark hair, his confident walk, and I'd been magnetized. They didn't make men like that back in my hometown in New Jersey.

To my surprise, he'd turned and noticed me too. When the barista called my name, he grinned, stepping forward to introduce himself.

"I'm Jed," he'd offered without any introduction or smooth line. He didn't need it. The guy oozed charisma from every single pore. One thing had led to another. First, we sat together and talked over our coffees. Then, by the time I left, he'd asked for my number. And within two weeks, he was kissing me under a lamppost, telling me he had never felt like that about someone.

It was the thing of romance novels. Picnics in the park, bouquets just because. Sweet, tender moments where he promised me forever. He exuded a strength and confidence about his life I hadn't yet discovered. A year went by like that, the magic blossoming. I thought he was my happy ending at a time in my life when everything had fallen apart. After my parents' deaths, I didn't think I'd ever find happiness again.

Jed changed my mind. I saw a future with him, his hand in mine, and I felt like I could face anything. I thought we'd move to the suburbs, get a golden retriever named Baxter, and have the white-picket-fence life I'd always envisioned for myself. I saw images of him commuting to his banking job every day while I stayed home, minding the kids in between writing romance novels loosely based on the love that was still wildly flowing between us. We'd go into the city on weekends for drinks. We'd go to Europe once a summer without the kids just to reconnect. I saw my fairy tale playing out before me.

And then, as the bitter wind whipped through my hair, he said the words that froze me from the inside out.

"I THINK we're better as friends. I don't want to do this anymore." All the magic of the season shriveled up, just like it had that first year without my parents. The magical glow of the holiday season was gone, and in its place was confusion, loneliness, and darkness.

"Why? What did I do wrong?" I asked. I thought of all I'd given, of how I felt like a shell of who I was—did I even know who I was anymore? I racked my brain, trying to detect how I hadn't been enough.

"I met someone else."

"What?" Even though I'd read my share of romantic dramas and watched all the movies, it hadn't crossed my mind that this could happen to me. It wouldn't happen to us.

He didn't meet my eyes.

"How long has it been going on?" I half whispered, wanting to know but not wanting to know.

He exhaled. "It doesn't matter."

"It matters," I demanded, stepping forward. Flashes of

the past few months came to my mind. I thought of all the magazine articles I'd read, the advice I'd asked Serena for, the fancy dinners and sexy nights out to get him to see me again. I tried to pinpoint the moment our relationship changed.

"Six months."

"*Six months?*" My mind flashed to half a year prior. Where were we? What were we doing then? Six months before, we were definitely still happy. Weren't we?

"You've been cheating for six months?" I asked again, incredulous. I didn't know what I hoped the outcome would be. That he would laugh and say he was just kidding? Or say no, he calculated wrong?

"Look, Lucy, I'm sorry. I didn't mean for it to happen. I didn't. But I just think it's for the best if we end this. We just don't fit."

"What doesn't fit?" I asked, hating myself for still standing there, for still giving him the time of day. But I'd given up so much, changed so much—and it still wasn't enough? I wanted to know everything about her, this woman who had taken him away from me. And at the same time, I wanted to know nothing about her. I wanted it all to be a bad dream.

I didn't want to be alone again in the difficult world.

"Us. You. You're just not what I need."

And there it was. The phrase that would replay over and over and over. Because somewhere deep inside I was still the teenage girl who just wanted to be needed, loved unconditionally. The twenty-two-year-old version of me, who was orphaned and felt so, so alone, who wanted to be part of a family again. But with his words, the picket fence was chopped down and Baxter, the dog we didn't yet have, took off into the woods. The kids vanished from my hopes, along with the hand-holding and sweet moments that would take us into rocking-chair sunsets with sweet tea.

I didn't say another word to him. I simply turned and left. I didn't look back. In truth, I didn't know who Jed was anymore. But that wasn't the worst part.

The worst part, I realized, as I rushed back to Serena to cry on our sofa, was that I didn't recognize me. I'd lost who I was, and with that fact, I'd lost all faith that love was what I needed.

EDMUND WOOFED, bringing me back to the present just as tears started to tug at my eyes. I refocused, taking in the car slowly passing by. Edmund was pulling on my arm, trying his best to chase it. I swiped at my eyes as I tried to get better control of the Goliath dog.

I'd lost control with Jed. I'd lost all control of my heart, of our story. I couldn't imagine ever doing that again. I couldn't imagine believing in love again, which was problematic since my book was due in basically three weeks. I had nothing.

Perhaps I could switch to a career of writing horror, but that made my stomach churn. Although I knew what the villain's name would be. That part was easy, thanks to Jed. I smirked, despite everything.

I was in the process of telling myself to get it together as we walked by the tiny park a few blocks from Grandma's house. I considered sitting on the bench and letting Edmund sniff around in the fallen snow. As we neared, I made the mistake of moving the leash from my right hand to my left. As the switch-off was happening, my mittens a little slippery against the texture of the leash, disaster struck.

Edmund yanked the leash out of my hands.

Which would have been okay, except that the exact same second, a black cat decided to dash right in front of our path, zooming toward the open park. Edmund didn't blink, didn't look at me for guidance, and he certainly didn't hesitate. His long, racehorse-like legs flung him forward with such velocity, I had no prayer of catching his leash.

"Edmund!" I shouted, but a black cat was much more interesting than a semi-sniveling, heartbroken woman. I ran after the dog into the park, but it was no use. The snow was deep, my shoes were not made for that kind of running, and Edmund was at least three times as fast as me on my best day.

"Edmund, please!" I implored. If I lost her beloved dog, my grandma might, in fact, suffer a heart episode there would be no recovery from.

Just as I was ready to sink into the snow with Edmund zooming all around me, the cat's whereabouts unknown, I heard a voice behind me, my saving grace.

"Cupcake!" the male voice yelled at the top of his lungs and, as if under an enchanted spell, Edmund stopped in his tracks and dashed toward the caller.

I turned to see Will Westerly grabbing the leash and wrangling the giant dog under control. Great. Just what I needed. Mr. Few Words to save the day with literally one word.

"You're a lifesaver," I admitted, happy I wouldn't have to spend hours chasing Edmund. I stamped through the snow, making my way to Will and Edmund, who was now sitting and drooling, apparently waiting for the cupcake.

Will shrugged. "Your grandma told me he comes running if you say *cupcake*. I didn't realize that tidbit of information would come in handy."

He gave me the leash, and I took it with both hands, wrapping it tightly around my mittened fingers. "Well, I'm thankful. Truly. He got away from me so fast."

"It's not the first time Edmund has gone for a run, according to your grandma."

"Still, I didn't want it to happen under my watch." A thought struck me as my heartbeat slowed and the panicked feeling dissipated. "What are you doing here?"

He shrugged again. "I live right there." He pointed to the white house on the edge of the park. It used to belong to a woman who always came out on hot summer days and gave all of us kids who were playing ice cream.

"What happened to Helen?" I asked, feeling saddened. So much had changed in Star Creek. How had I slipped so far out of the loop?

"The woman who lived there before me? She went to Florida."

I was relieved the news wasn't worse, but I was still taken aback.

"Why is everyone around here going to Florida? Is there a bus or something that takes you straight there? Are there a lot of commercials for Florida playing on the news stations?"

Will smiled. "Maybe. But the timing worked out perfectly for me. Her family is renting the place for now, which helped me immensely when I suddenly came to town. I love my family, but I didn't think I could handle living with them again. Let's just say they're a bit of a loud crew." He was opening up a little bit. Maybe when he was at the bakery, he was just focused. Maybe I'd misjudged him.

"Has your family always lived here? Did you grow up here?" I asked as we started walking back toward my grandma's house. I kept a death-grip on the leash, mentally tracing the name Westerly in my memory bank. Certainly, since it was Grandma's hometown and not mine, I didn't know every single person. Still, it was a small community, and the Westerly name didn't ring any bells.

"Sort of. My grandfather grew up here, actually. My dad moved away for work but eventually found his way back with my mom after I moved to the city. They were looking for some peace and quiet, I think. And Grandpa was living with them by then. He wanted to come back to the town where he grew up, and my parents obliged. They live on the outskirts of town now in a little two-story house."

"Oh, wow," I said, thinking about how adorable it was they'd moved back here for his grandpa.

"I love them to death, but it's just a lot. Grandpa is a firecracker, sort of like your grandma. They have a wild golden retriever, and there just isn't a lot of space in the house. I go there for dinner a lot, though."

I smiled, picturing Will with his family. "I'm sure they're glad to have you in town."

He sighed. "Yes. Mom was so devastated when I moved away."

"How long did you live in the city?"

"Five years." His voice quieted at the admission. I could sense the walls coming back up.

I shook my head. "I've been there about four. Although I'm sure Grandma told you that."

"She did."

I could see despondency written all over his face, an undeniable shift in mood at the mention of the city. I hesitated but decided curiosity wouldn't allow me to stay quiet. "You said you moved here for work, right?"

He looked at me, his dark eyes clearly roiling in pain.

"Yes." He put forth zero effort to open up more.

"But I'm sure there was work in the city," I pushed.

He looked away from me, clearly uncomfortable. "It's not something I like to talk about."

"I'm sorry."

Hands in his pockets, he looked straight ahead. "Me too. But I'm thankful to have a job at your grandma's bakery. At least I can still work in the field I'm passionate about. And Star Creek Bakery really is top-notch."

"So baking, huh? Is that what you always wanted to do?"

"Yes. I studied culinary arts in the city, but I always wanted to have my own bakery. When I got done with school, I stayed, tried to make a go of it. But New York is easy to be swallowed up by."

I smiled at that assessment. "That's the truth. But there's also something inexplicable there you can't find anywhere else. It's a weird concoction of chaos and excitement. There's nothing else like it."

His eyes looked wistful, and I regretted my statement. "But there are good things about being here too," I hurriedly added, trying to make light of a tough situation.

"Yes, like walking in the middle of the road," he said. We had moved from the snow-covered sidewalks into the barren roads.

"And the price of rent, I'm sure," I added.

"You bet."

We were at my grandma's house then, and even Edmund was shivering despite his escapades.

"Thanks for walking me home," I said, looking at him.

"You bet," he repeated. "See you tomorrow?"

I nodded. "You bet," I parroted. And even though the

walk had clearly taken us both to dark memories we'd rather leave behind, I saw him crack a smile.

"You bet," I whispered into the chill of the air as he walked back down the street, the silence of the town settling in again.

The smell of apple pie and the sound of Herb and Grandma's laughter invited me inside, warmth radiating onto the freezing cold stoop.

SEVEN

I walked into the bakery way earlier than the time I considered myself functioning. The moon was still in the bitterly cold, darkened sky, along with dots of stars. I considered snapping a photo of the bakery under the starlit sky, a perfect backdrop for the Star Creek Bakery, but I couldn't bring myself to pry my fingers out of my red mittens long enough to do it. Plus, I desperately needed coffee.

The bells on the door jingled as I let myself in. I'd expected silence to ease me into the morning. Instead, rock music blared from the kitchen, making my head pound. I wandered straight back to where Will was headbanging to the song as the mixer whirred.

"Hello?" I shouted. Nothing.

I walked closer. He was still jamming out, in his own little cupcake world. Finally, after shouting over the music to no avail, I tapped his shoulder. He nearly leaped out of his skin before whirling on his feet, ready to attack. I put my hands up. Hand to his heart, he laughed.

"You scared the life out of me!" he yelled over the music.

"Can we please turn that down?" I shouted.

He nodded, dashing over to the sound system. The silence felt deafening after he turned it down. My ears still buzzing from the beat of the music, I exhaled.

"Where's the coffee?" I groggily asked, not even trying to make friendly conversation.

"Not a morning person, I take it?" he asked, smiling. He looked fresh and wide-eyed, like he was made for this shift. And perhaps I was imagining things, but he seemed a little friendlier today. Maybe the whole Edmund escaping situation had softened him.

"Not at all."

"There's a fresh pot out front. Hope you like dark roast."

I didn't care if it was tar at this point. I needed some caffeine. I trudged out of the kitchen, Will still running the mixer and singing to himself.

After retrieving my coffee, the mixer mercifully stopped. I wandered back into the kitchen to watch him at work, grabbing the stool from the corner and plopping myself on it. He moved through the kitchen in an elegant dance, making the art of cupcake baking look graceful in a way that was magnetizing. This was undoubtedly his ultimate passion. It was written all over his face. I remembered a time when others might have said the same about my writing, about how the light in my eyes was different when I was on my laptop, immersed in my fictional worlds. I missed that feeling. I hoped someday soon, I could find it again.

"How's your grandma?" he asked as he scooped the batter into the cupcake pans.

"She has a doctor's appointment today. I was going to take her, but she informed me there are exactly twenty-six days until the Holiday Bake-Off, and she has an entire notebook full of things that need to be accomplished before then. So she demanded I come in today to work through some details and, at the very least, work with you on the cupcake plans for the festival. Herb volunteered to take her to the appointment and keep her occupied in a calm state for the day, bless him."

"So what do you need from me for this bake-off?" Will asked, wiping his hands on a towel.

"Well, there are a lot of moving parts. Essentially, we have a baking competition, where other bakeries attend to create a new cupcake flavor. The winner gets their cupcake on our menu. But in addition, we have an all-day festival full of booths and holiday fun. Our bakery creates new, special flavors each year, and Grandma said we sell a lot of them. So that is really a priority—creating new flavors."

Will smiled. "I was actually working on new flavors right now, just for fun."

"Perfect," I said, nodding, watching him mix up some frosting. I decided to venture on. "When I was ten, the cupcake of the festival was named 'The Lucy.' I remember how proud I was that year—and how many of those cupcakes I ate."

"What flavor was that one?"

"Well, it was a mixture of my favorite cookie that my mom would make and the whims of a ten-year-old. My mom used to make these little almond-flavored cookies called snowballs, and I was obsessed with them. No one else liked them because they were a weird sort of shortbread flavor. My great-grandma was Polish, and it was one of her traditional recipes. My cupcake was a play on that. It was an almond cake with a light, airy frosting, drizzled in a caramel sauce and sprinkled with powdered sugar. And there was, of course, a candy cane on top for good measure."

If I closed my eyes, I could almost taste that cupcake. I'd forgotten about that memory.

"I love it. We should bring those cookies back to the bakery. You know, in honor of the family."

My face fell. "No, we can't do that. Grandma took the snowball cookie off the menu when my mom died. She said it was too hard for her to make them. Too many memories with my mom."

"Oh, I'm so sorry," Will said, putting down everything and wiping his hands on the towel over his shoulder.

I looked down and to the right, trying to steady my gaze so I didn't cry.

We stayed in awkward silence. It looked like Will wasn't the only one to clam up and build walls when hard topics arose. I sighed. A long pause passed. Finally, he broke it.

"What happened?" His voice was quiet, and he walked closer to me. I held my cup of coffee, the warmth not strong enough to combat the frostiness in my blood at the loss of my sweet mother. I missed her every single day.

"A car accident. It's been four years." Every single time my phone rang, my stomach fell, reminding me of the horrible Tuesday when I received the phone call that changed everything. It was the day I became an orphan, the day I realized how quickly life could change.

"It can't be easy, even after a few years have gone by." He was standing right across from me, and I looked up to see the concern in his eyes. A comforting nature came from his presence, and his strong stance made me feel protected, safe. I couldn't explain it, and it seemed contradictory to his hardened stoicism I'd witnessed so far. But looking into his eyes, I felt like I could fall apart and he would make sure I got back up.

For a long moment, I thought I might fall into his arms. I thought maybe I could lean my head on his shoulder and feel his embrace. But he cleared his throat, seemingly also sensing where the moment was headed.

I stood abruptly to find something to busy myself with, and as I did, he tried to scurry away, and somehow we both headed the same direction. It was like a bad movie scene in slow motion. The paper cup I'd failed to put a lid on fell from my hand as his shoulder bumped into me. The hot liquid splattered through the air as I naively tried to grab the cup and save it. Coffee rained down on the kitchen floor as Will also tried to be the hero of the scene, and we collided, falling into a tangle of legs, arms, and coffee stains on the kitchen floor.

Stunned and wrapped together, we stared at each other, our faces closer than we'd ever been. My heart felt like it was in my throat as we both paused for a long moment, the feel of his hand on my arm sending electricity through me. We hurriedly disentangled ourselves, a clumsy mess of limbs, apologies, and sensations neither of us was looking for.

"I'm so sorry. I'll clean this up," I muttered, scrambling to get my feet under me.

"It's fine. It happens all the time," he said, handing me the towel from his shoulder. I took it, wiping at the coffee on my shirt before tackling the floor.

"Really? Girls spilling their sad life stories *and* their coffee in the kitchen all the time? I admittedly don't know much about the bakery business, but that doesn't seem like the best business plan. I should really talk to Grandma about that."

He smirked and quickly headed back over to his cupcakes.

Another long pause followed, but after cleaning up the mess, I looked at the batter he was dropping into the tins.

"What's the flavor you're working on?" I asked as I walked closer to his work area. Cupcake flavors seemed like safe territory, all things considered.

"It's going to be a red velvet cupcake with a chocolate ganache filling and a chocolate-covered strawberry on top. I just need a fun name for it."

"Oh, that sounds amazing. How about Berry Christmas?"

"I love it. Perfect. See, this is why we need a writer around."

Even though it was just a silly cupcake name, it felt good that I could contribute.

"Now we have to see if they taste as good as I'm hoping they do."

"I'm sure they will. Grandma said you've been bringing new flavors in that the customers keep asking for."

"I'm glad. It's been fun getting to try out new ideas."

He talked for a little bit about some of the flavors he was planning, and I was impressed by the creativity that went into the work. We were from two different worlds in many ways, yet we weren't. It was exciting to see someone passionate about creativity like I once was. I felt invigorated in a new way, like maybe my writing prowess would return.

I helped Will get ready for business, wiping tables, stocking cookies in the front case, and flipping the sign before the regular customer rush. I helped run the register, smiling as I heard him singing in the back throughout the day. It was a nice day of customers, easy conversation, and watching Will doing what he loved. We even sat down at lunch and worked on a few details about the festival, including the cupcake flavors we'd be featuring. I'd have to let Grandma help me with ordering inventory because I had no clue how much we'd need of everything. Still, it was sort of fun to be out of my element and learning new things. I could see why she loved this place, why she refused to sell it or give it up. There was an element of challenge and satisfaction when I saw the customers happy. And being surrounded by delicious baked goods certainly wasn't a downside.

"Let's make this bake-off one to remember," I said to Will before leaving for the day. "I don't want to let Grandma down."

"I agree. We've got this," Will said, smiling at me. He'd replaced the towel on his shoulder. It felt like we'd come to some sort of mutual understanding, which felt good. Two co-workers who had one goal in mind. It felt safe, reassuring. Planning for the bake-off was just what I needed to get my mind off all I'd been through.

At the end of the day, we cleaned the kitchen and prepared to lock up. He gave me a box of the Berry Christmas cupcakes to take to Grandma to taste-test. I left the bakery that evening exhausted, covered in flour somehow, but also excited.

I would pour my creative juices into making the thirty-first annual Star Creek Holiday Bake-Off the best the town had ever seen. It was intimidating, but I knew with Will's baking genius we could pull it off. At least, I really hoped so.

With a new sense of purpose in my step, I made a decision as I got in Serena's car. On the way back to Grandma's, I made a quick stop.

EIGHT

The sign for the Star Creek Bookstore was exactly the same as it had been when I was a little girl—a pile of books with a buzzing bee flying around the words. I was glad to find the lights were still on, a few townsfolk milling about the stacks when I walked through the door. I was sweaty, flour-covered, and probably not fit for bookstore browsing—but I didn't care. Inside it was as if I'd stepped back in time, when life was simpler. The smell of books wafted through the space, and I inhaled deeply.

When Mrs. Beesworth died five years ago, the store had shut down. But Grandma told me during her visit that it had reopened and Mrs. Beesworth's granddaughter had taken over. I was glad to see life back in the place where my dreams had taken flight.

I looked to the counter, half expecting to see Mrs. Beesworth with her huge, blonde hair smiling at me and rushing over to give me a book recommendation. That wasn't possible, of course. The thought saddened me.

"Can I help you?" a voice said from across the bookstore. I looked to see a younger woman in a hot pink skirt, sparkling black shirt, and blonde hair.

"I'm sorry. I'm kind of a mess. I'm Lucy, Catherine Easton's granddaughter. I'm in town for a while, and, well, this place was my inspiration for becoming a writer."

"Oh, how blessed! I'd heard you were in town. Come here, I have to show you something."

The woman pulled my hand as if we were old friends, and I followed her. She pulled me to the fiction section, where a small table was set up. I took in the sight of my picture, name, and a pile of novels.

"Mrs. Beesworth was my grandmother. I'm Carissa, by the way. She always talked about you, Lucy. She looked forward to your visits and talking books. She used to say you were going places, and that when your books got published, she'd set up a table. We put this table here with all your books. They're quite popular with the locals, although that's probably because of your grandma telling everyone about them."

Tears welled as my hands ran over the covers of the books I'd published. I thought about how it had all started right here in the Star Creek Bookstore. I glanced around, seeing the books, thinking about the little girl who had come into the store holding Grandma's hand, dreaming of being an author.

I'd done it. I'd made it happen. Mrs. Beesworth would be proud.

"We really should do a book signing sometime. Do you have any new books releasing soon?" she asked.

I turned and smiled at Carissa, seeing the resemblance to Mrs. Beesworth and feeling a bit of shame. "Not right now."

"Well, anytime you want to come have a talk or signing, just let me know."

I nodded and thanked her. It was a beautiful moment to see my childhood dreams come true in this place. But it also made me sad. What if this was it? What if I never wrote another book? What would I do? I couldn't live off my nearly non-existent savings forever. I had to sort out my future. And soon.

I sighed and headed over to the romance section to browse for a few new books that had come out recently. I purchased one book and assured Carissa I'd set up a book signing soon.

I was heading out the door, anxious to get back to Grandma, when I bumped into someone.

"Sorry," Will said. One word, as if we hadn't been working together all day. I raised an eyebrow. We were going backwards, it seemed.

"I didn't know you liked to read." It was a stupid statement, though, because I didn't really know anything about him at all.

He shrugged, looking somewhat embarrassed.

"Well, have a good night," I said and watched him walk through the door as I wondered what type of books he was into. I'd have to ask him the next day. Hopefully, I'd get more than a one-word answer.

NINE

"Gosh, if I was a few decades younger, I'd marry that man. His cupcakes are divine," Grandma said slowly as we taste-tested the Berry Christmas cupcakes. They were, inarguably, the best cupcakes I'd ever had.

"And the name is perfect. S-see, you two are a great team. I was worried about not going into the bakery and having to rest, but I think it's in good... hands," she said slowly, her voice shaky but her spirits seeming bright. I could see the wheels in her head spinning about Will and me making a good team—beyond work partners—but I beamed with pride anyway. It felt good to be successful at something again.

"He's amazing in the kitchen. I don't know how he stays so calm and gets all that baking done."

"He's a steady one. Reliable. And handsome, if I haven't said it before." She smiled.

"You've definitely said it before. A few times," I replied. We were sitting at the kitchen table while Edmund happily gnawed on the bone Herb had bought for him. Herb had gone to his own house, needing to spend some time with his cat, Sylvester. Sometimes, I thought it might be easier to move Sylvester into my grandma's house since Herb was always over here, but Edmund and Sylvester were sort of rivals, apparently. Nevertheless, I had to admit it was nice to get some one-on-one time with my grandma.

"You know, he's single too. And he lived in New York. You two have so much in common," she continued as I got out the notebook of things to discuss with her for the bake-off.

I set my pen down. "Grandma, I'm not looking for someone to date. I just broke up with someone a few weeks ago. And I'm too busy with the festival to consider it. I don't want to get involved with anyone, let alone the baker we need to pull it all off."

"Well, what better time to fall in love than the holiday season? Plus, it couldn't hurt your writing to heal your heart a little."

"It's too soon. I thought Jed was the one, and I was clearly way off base. I don't think I ever want to go through that again." Emotions started rising in my chest. I'd thought love would be the answer, the missing piece to my life. But I'd completely misjudged Jed. And I'd lost every part of me that mattered—my writing voice, my focus on family, and even the way I prepared my coffee. I'd lost so many details of myself. I wanted to believe I'd heal, but could I really? How could I trust another man after the lies Jed had told me? How could I trust myself not to let love completely change me?

I refocused on the notebook, looking at the immediate to-do list I needed to tackle, such as talking to the mayor about blocking off the designated streets and reaching out to vendors with information.

Grandma shakily reached over and grabbed the notebook. She slid it across the table and flipped it over. I stared at the table, and she gently grabbed my chin and forced me to look at her. Her face was still drooping, and it would for a while according to her doctor, but beyond her physical symptoms from the stroke, I saw the sweet, kind woman who, behind her sassy and sometimes bossy nature, would give anything for me to be happy.

"D-darling, listen," she started, her words a little broken. She paused, and I patted her other hand, letting her know it was okay. She could take her time. Her lingering symptoms obviously frustrated her, and she coughed before continuing. "You're so young. Too young to give up on love. I know what it's like to have your heart broken, truly."

I appreciated Grandma's attempt, but she had been with my grandpa practically her entire life. There was no way she could understand what it was like to feel so lost, so unsettled. She couldn't know what it was like to pour your heart into a relationship, to adapt for a man, and then be cheated on. She just didn't know. It had taken everything for me to risk my heart and fall in love, and there was nothing left.

"I met him in a coffee shop," Grandma said. "I was sitting there with a cup of coffee and a cupcake talking about fashion or something with my best friend when he walked in. He was tall, dark, and handsome, and he just had a strut that caught my eye."

Chills went through my body because her story reminded me of Jed.

"I was seventeen and smitten from the first moment he touched me. I would have married him right there if I could've."

I hadn't heard this story before. I listened, not wanting to interrupt as nostalgia was so clear in her eyes.

"We dated for four years. My mother wanted us to get married as soon as I turned eighteen, but he wanted to wait until he got established in his career. He was traveling a lot, a salesman of sorts. I naively sat back, dreaming of our wedding and the life we would build. He always told me we'd move to Maine after we got married. I had visions of raising a family near the coast, of being the perfect housewife."

"I'm confused. I didn't know Grandpa wanted to move to Maine. I thought he always wanted to stay here, which was why you did."

"Oh, yes. Your grandpa did. But your grandpa wasn't my first love. The tall, dark, handsome man I met at the coffee shop was Benjamin Wilson. And he broke my heart when I was twenty-one, four years after we met, when he told me he'd met a better match during his travels. For four years I'd built up this vision of our life together. I wasted those years because it wasn't meant to be. Or at least he didn't think so."

I was stunned. I could feel the emotion radiating off Grandma, even after all these years. The pain in me felt the heartbreak in her. Four years. I was so hurt after one year with Jed. I couldn't imagine.

"How did you do it? How did you get over it?"

"I cried, a lot. I stayed in my bed wallowing, wondering where my life was going. And then, finally, some of my girlfriends told me I needed to get out. They helped me pick out a dress, put on some red lipstick, and made me go dancing with them. I was a storm cloud that night, not wanting to do anything but cry over a man who was out with someone else. I thought maybe I'd be a spinster like Emily Dickinson, living in my parents' attic, writing sad poems or something.

"But that night, I met your grandfather. He was sitting at the bar drinking a beer when I walked in. And it was sort of like the movies. He locked eyes with me, and even though I wasn't looking for someone new to love, there was safety in him. A sense of protection when I looked into his eyes. I stood still for a long moment at the door as the jukebox played a song. He wouldn't stop staring at me, and finally, he walked over. Time stopped as he reached out and asked me to dance."

"Weren't you scared after Benjamin?" I asked, trying to picture a younger version of my grandma and grandpa in a bar.

"Of course. I almost said no. My head told me to say no. But the song was different, the man was different, and when he led me to the dance floor, the way he held my hand told me it was something else. I knew in that moment I'd love again, that this man would help mend my heart. I didn't see the life on the coast with a family. I didn't know what I saw, in truth. He was rough around the edges, less polished, and less certain of what he wanted in life.

"As we got to know each other, I realized a life with him would be a life we'd have to figure out together. He had dreams of owning a business, and I didn't know what I wanted. But three months later, when he asked me to marry him, I said yes without quavering. Because I just knew. I somehow just knew. And although you never forget your first love, darling, sometimes the second's even better."

I felt emotion welling up in me again as I could feel the love radiating from Grandma as she recalled the tale. I thought about the sweet life she'd built with my grandpa, how at a time when women really weren't supposed to have dreams outside of the house, he'd helped her follow her vision of starting a bakery. He'd made it his dream, his life's work as well. Together, they'd made Star Creek Bakery a staple in the community. Their love had made a life that allowed me to have the life I did, no matter how messy. She'd found a way to be who she wanted and live her dreams but also love Grandpa. They'd built a life together that was both their own individually and together. All because two people were in a bar and decided to take a risk.

Grandma's story was magical, inspiring, and healing. It also felt like a fantasy that could never be mine. I wasn't Grandma, not even close. I never would be.

"I'm telling you this because even if you don't know it, your heart will heal too. Someday, that Jed character will just be your Benjamin—a blip on the radar to becoming who you're meant to be. To being with who you are meant to be with. So don't hold on to that broken heart too tightly, and don't be afraid to see a wonderful thing that might be right in front of you. Put on your red lipstick and get out there. When it's meant to be, when the right person comes along, you'll know it. You'll feel it. Even though you might be broken, when you find him, you'll feel inexplicably safe."

She patted my hand, and then got up from the table to walk back to her room. I sat still, thinking about her story. Could she be right? Could I find safety again? It felt impossible. It felt like too much of a risk after all I'd been through. Maybe there was a happy medium. Maybe with Jed, it had been a risk that hadn't paid off. But would it pay to be too cautious? Would that really lead to happiness? It was a complex, whirling mess that I didn't have the energy to work out—at least not for myself.

Sometimes the best way for me to work out something complex was to write about it. So I slid the notebook back toward myself from across the table, flipped to the back, and started jotting down notes for the love story I knew I would write.

As the ideas flowed from my fingers onto the page, I couldn't help but think about that protected feeling I'd inexplicably felt when Will Westerly looked into my eyes.

The Second's Even Better, I wrote at the top of the page of notes, and then I sent an email to Anna, telling her I finally had my working title. Now, I just had to write the book.

TEN

Buckets of coffee. That was what was required the next morning as I stared at my computer before the sun came up, trying to get the words out. Even Edmund was still snoring as I sat at Grandma's kitchen table, the cursor on my screen taunting me.

I'd thought about Herb's and Grandma's stories and considered what kind of book the publisher would want, what kind of meet-cute would make for a good story. Still, my heart felt dull and uninspired. My mind just wouldn't focus.

I wanted to tell myself I was stressed about the bake-off and just thinking about my to-do list. I told myself the words wouldn't come because Jed was on my mind, and he'd hurt me so badly. In truth, though, other thoughts clouded my brain that I really didn't want to admit to myself.

Like Will Westerly.

I kept thinking about how he'd saved the day with Edmund and how even though I barely knew him, a warmth seemed to follow him. The way he smiled, the way he listened to what I had to say, and even the way he sang.

I took some notes that probably wouldn't help with the story and avoided my email because I knew Anna would be checking in. I sipped my coffee as the kitchen slowly brightened. Eventually, Grandma rose from her slumber and stumbled to the kitchen in her baby-blue bathrobe. With curlers in her hair, she looked like a woman from a cartoon.

"Morning, early riser. Are you working at this time of day?" she asked, peering over my shoulder.

"I wish. The words aren't coming."

"Pancakes might help," she offered.

"Only if they're chocolate chip," I replied. That was always our breakfast when I visited as a little girl.

"That's the only kind this skillet makes," she replied, getting out the familiar pan and starting the batter.

Grandma shuffled about, and I stared at the screen. Eventually, I turned around to see a bowl of batter big enough to feed the whole town.

"Grandma, I'm not that hungry."

"No, but Herb will be."

I smiled as I looked at her, raising an eyebrow. She pointed the spatula at me.

"Don't say anything," she said, the spatula shaking slightly.

"What would I say?" I asked innocently, twirling a piece of my hair.

"I know what you're thinking. We're just friends who help each other through hard times. That's it." She put the spatula down and leaned on the counter, looking as if she were tired.

"Grandma, sit. Let me finish the pancakes." I leaped up and walked over to help. She needed to be resting.

"I'm fine," she said, holding up the spatula. She wasn't

fine, but I knew better than to argue. I stood near her in case she needed to lean on me.

She flipped a pancake.

"Herb seems to spend more time over here than at his own home," I said, returning to our conversation.

"I enjoy his company."

"I noticed. Grandma, there's nothing wrong with admitting you have feelings for him."

She scoffed at the idea. "I'm too old for that sort of nonsense," she replied, rolling her eyes as she flipped another pancake.

As if on cue, the door opened and Edmund groaned awake in the back bedroom and plodded to the front door. He emitted a few happy barks at the sight of Herb.

"He doesn't even knock. Interesting," I said, and Grandma reached over and tapped me on the shoulder with her spatula.

"Smells good," Herb said as he carried the newspaper into the kitchen. He wandered close to the stove, and Grandma blushed. It was adorable. Why couldn't they admit what was so obvious?

Herb tried to tell Grandma how to flip the pancake— *Wrong move, buddy*. I studied them, how close they stood, how love clearly had blossomed between them. Still, I understood why they'd held back. To love and break up was hard. But to love, really love like they both had, and then lose your love—that had to be impossible. Love was always a risk, whether it turned out good or bad. There was always that eventual, inevitable heartbreak.

I thought of my grandpa and how beautiful his relationship with my grandma had been, how I'd often thought there would be no way I could find that kind of connection. I envied them, and so did the entire town.

Suddenly, my fingers started flying on the keyboard. I couldn't stop myself. Noticing my concentration, Grandma quietly slid a plate of pancakes to me and led Herb to the living room to eat, shushing him. I didn't say anything. My writing muse had kicked in and, even if it was just for a morning, I didn't want to let it go.

TWO HOURS LATER, I felt like I finally had somewhere to go with my book. I felt inspired and happy for the first time in a while. I finished my chilled pancakes, put the dish in the sink, and strolled out to the living room.

"Did you get an idea?" Grandma asked.

"I did. I think. But I don't want to talk about it until I get it all hashed out."

"Well, it might kill me to stay in the dark, but okay. As long as you're writing, that's all that matters."

"Are you two ready?" I asked, looking at the clock on the wall and realizing Will was probably wondering where we were. We were already half an hour late.

"When you are, dear," Grandma said, rising slowly. Herb reached over to help her. "I'm just happy you two are letting me out of this house, letting me contribute."

"Whoa, don't get ahead of yourself," I said, hand out. "We agreed to let you come along, but only if you have a seat, kick your feet up, and take notes. No hard work or stress."

Grandma rolled her eyes. "Honestly, you two are driving me bonkers. I'm fine. No problems at all."

"Yes, but the doctor still said you should take it easy."

"I'll take it easy when I'm dead," Grandma replied. "Until then, I'll keep doing it my way."

Herb exhaled. "You're exasperating sometimes, Catherine."

"Right back at you," she replied, rising from the sofa and giving Edmund a dog treat before we all headed out to my car. The bickering continued the whole way to the bakery, and I took mental notes.

Losing at love the first time was hard. But what about the second? Or even the third? Did the first love help you realize love was worth the risk? Or did it make you scared to try again?

I'd have to talk to Grandma about it all, do a little research.

And, in time, perhaps I'd have my own experience to go off. Regardless, I felt like I was back in the game, which was an exciting place to be.

ELEVEN

When we got to the bakery, Will was singing a song about sunshine—even though it was still a frosty winter wonderland outside. It was a good day for us to plan on working on the bake-off details because we probably wouldn't have many customers thanks to the snowy day. Most people in Star Creek would tuck in with a cup of coffee. Still, we could count on the regulars, and there was a lot of baking to be done.

We decided Herb would join Will in the kitchen to get the cupcakes and cookies prepped for the day while I claimed a corner table with Grandma to handle the bake-off details. This would also keep her off her feet. I tried not to take it personally that I was picked to stay out of the kitchen, although I assumed everyone decided it was for the best. It stung a little that Herb, a retired welder who could barely make grilled cheese for himself, according to his stories, was deemed a better baking assistant than me.

Armed with my laptop and a mile-long to-do list, Grandma and I got to work. I took notes on the event's regular attractions and must-have booths. I glossed over the event booth names that Grandma couldn't remember, not wanting to upset her. I also threw out a few new ideas and beamed with pride when Grandma said they were excellent additions.

"A photo booth? That sounds fun but also potentially dangerous," Will said half an hour later when he brought Grandma and me a new cookie recipe to try. It was a chocolate snickerdoodle and, although interesting, it wasn't my favorite. I politely ate it, though—which was no real feat, because even though the recipe was not my cup of tea, it was still scrumptious. Will could probably make an anchovy cookie that would be palatable.

"Dangerous?" Grandma asked.

"Yes," he said, looking at the list over my shoulder. "I mean, you get a handsome, overly good-looking guy like me in there, and it just sets the bar so high for everyone else. They'll feel sad about their pictures, and it will be a whole thing."

Grandma rolled her eyes, playfully jabbing him in the ribs. It was fun to see him loosening up. I could see the more playful side of him I hadn't really seen yet. I was glad he was feeling comfortable.

"Such a hard life being handsome," I said, and then blushed as I realized what had come out of my mouth. Grandma smirked, winking at me. I groaned internally, knowing she was never letting that go.

Will cleared his throat but didn't say anything about my comment. He thankfully returned to the kitchen before I could again put my foot in my mouth, and I started listing supplies we would need for the pin-the-nose-on-Rudolph game booth we planned for the kids.

"Looks like someone else was maybe glowing a bit," Grandma teased, winking again.

"Grandma," I groaned, feeling like a sixteen-year-old girl again instead of the twenty-six-year-old I was. I shook my head, focusing on my computer. Out of the corner of my eye, I saw Will jovially stocking the front counter display. He glanced over, perhaps feeling my eyes on him. I quickly returned to my work, my stomach dropping when I was caught.

"No one can blame you, dear. Look at the man. He's... oh, shoot. What's the word?"

I looked at her, waiting. She leaned her head in her hands.

"Oh, man. It's another word for... um..." she huffed.

I reached across the table to pat her hand. The doctor had told us she might have good days and bad, that sometimes words and memory loss were part of recovery.

"Handsome?" I offered. She looked at me, still frustrated with herself. But then half of her face turned into a grin. I missed Grandma's big, full smile, but it made me happy to see her face alight.

"You said it," she said. "Twice."

"Because you couldn't think of the word," I replied. "Don't get any ideas."

"I could think of the word. I'm fine." She was quiet, though, and I could tell it was bothering her.

"Grandma, it's okay. Not every day will be the same, and sometimes—"

"Don't. Don't make this about the stroke. I forgot a word. It happens to everyone." Grandma glowered with frustration, something that usually wasn't a hallmark of her personality.

I nodded, deciding to change the subject. "Okay, we have so much work to do. Let's stop focusing on my love life and focus instead on these forms for the competition. Now, we have about twenty entries."

"Twenty? That's terrible! Usually by this time I have about fifty. Oh dear, I've really dropped the ball." Grandma's face reflected sheer panic. She fumbled with her hands, wringing them as she looked out the snowy window beside us.

I reached across the table and patted her hand. "Grandma, it's okay. We still have a little over three weeks. I'm going to work on our social media campaign, and I'm sure I can get that number up."

Grandma groaned. "I don't like social media. We've always done word of mouth. I don't want to be doing those crazy dances or anything."

I laughed. "We don't have to do videos. I just think we need a social media presence. I'll take care of the details. And if we need any dancing, we'll make the guys do it," I assured her.

We looked into the kitchen to see Herb bobbing his head to Will's singing. He looked like a fish out of water in the kitchen, standing awkwardly as Will moved feverishly about in his element. Herb hadn't caught on to the elegant dance, but he was keeping Will company and handing him kitchen equipment when he asked for it, so that was something.

We all had a lot to learn from Grandma.

We did some more work on the details of the venue, the booths we would have, and made a list of who we would still need to contact. Grandma was a wealth of knowledge, covering details I wouldn't have even thought about, such as parking and making sure we had enough hot chocolate cups. She was frustrated she couldn't remember a few details, like the name of the vendor she'd used last year for the cups and the name of the street where we'd put extra parking signs. I skipped over it, trying not to worry about it too much. She'd been through a lot, that was all. We just needed to keep her calm.

"You were made for this," I said a few hours later.

She smiled. "It just comes with time. Once you find something you're passionate about, it's easy work. And your grandfather also played a part. We figured it out together."

I smiled at the mention of him. "Did you two ever doubt yourselves?"

"Every day. Especially in the beginning. There were plenty of times we thought about throwing in the towel. Like the year that fancy cupcake bakery opened up a town over and our sales plummeted. And there were years when it was just all a lot, when we fell into a routine and felt like the romance died."

"How did you make it?" I asked, thinking about my writing instead of the festival.

She shrugged. "Just love. We loved each other enough to work through the hard times and to believe they would pass. There really isn't any secret. If you love someone, if they make you a better person, then the rest sort of just works out, even during the challenging times."

I smiled. "I hope I'm lucky enough to find that someday." The words were out before I could think about them. It startled me. I'd convinced myself the past few weeks that love wasn't for me, that I didn't need it. Maybe a small part of me, although terrified, still believed it could happen for me. Perhaps that was the scariest part of all, knowing I would someday have to take the risk once more.

Will chose that exact moment to deliver us two cupcakes.

"I have a new flavor that needs a name," he said,

explaining the red velvet cupcake with cream cheese icing and a red poinsettia on top. It looked like a work of art, and I hated to bite into it. I groaned when I did, though. It was amazing.

"This one's a winner," I said, and he smiled wide. "I could eat these every single day. What if we called it Christmas in Bloom?"

"That's good," Will said, nodding. "Do you just keep cupcake names in your back pocket or what?"

"She's skilled, that's for sure," Grandma concurred, and thankfully, before I could be too embarrassed by the accolades, Will rushed back to the kitchen as a timer beeped and Herb yelled for help.

"Christmas in Bloom. I think it's the perfect sentiment, don't you, Lucy? It sort of has a ring to it. Things blossoming, even in the dead of winter. Flowers, love, you know," Grandma noted with a smirk.

"Grandma, don't."

"Why do you fight it, Lucy? He's a great guy. He's from the city too. And you would have delicious baked goods every day. Doesn't sound like a bad life to me."

I sighed. "One, we're just co-workers. That's all. Here to get a job done."

"Well, that's boring," Grandma said, shaking her head.

"And two, he's cold with me still. Distant. There's definitely a story, and I wonder what it is. He seems really sad when he talks about it. I mean, I know New York didn't work out for him. But I wonder what happened." I almost hated myself for playing into her hands, for asking questions and showing interest. But I was curious. He'd clammed up when he mentioned the city during the Edmund debacle.

"I'm not sure. He doesn't really like to talk about it. I've definitely noticed. The Westerlys moved here years ago, and they seem like a nice crew. Herb knows Will's grandfather from the bowling league he plays in on Thursdays. Nice family for sure. But I've also seen a change in Will in recent days. He's opening up more. I wonder why that is."

I sighed and glanced over at Will, who was heading out of the kitchen, stretching his back. The towel was once again draped over his shoulder, his signature look. He smiled at me, offering a little wave. I waved back, feeling foolish and a little surprised by his friendliness. But maybe Grandma was right. He did seem to be letting his guard down at times. That gave me hope—and I wasn't sure why.

Still, I wondered why he seemed so broken. There were difficult memories there, I was sure. I just wondered if eventually I'd get to hear them. I also wondered if I carried that obvious badge of broken on me as well.

TWELVE

The next morning, the sun's rays bounced off the snow that covered every inch of the ground. The flurries had stopped for the time being, and I imagined the white snow dissipated, giving me hope for spring, even though it was a long way away.

I'd taken more notes on my laptop and even started a rough outline for my romance novel. I was feeling vibrant and optimistic, the words slowly starting to flow and the bake-off coming together.

When Grandma got out of bed, the table was covered in my attempt at scrambled eggs, toast, and bacon. I wanted her to stay off her feet and to actually rest. I was glad she'd slept in—being at the bakery yesterday had clearly taken a toll. She'd fallen asleep immediately after returning home.

I was still worried about Grandma's recovery. We couldn't be too careful, and I saw things the doctor didn't. The subtle shift in the way she moved, the way her face didn't quite smile fully, the moments of memory fog. It all painted a picture that scared me more than I wanted to admit.

"It smells wonderful," she said as she walked into the kitchen.

"The bacon is a little extra crispy, but I did my best." The meal looked anemic compared to what Grandma usually made. But she smiled as if I'd cooked a feast worthy of royalty. Grandma kissed my cheek as I led her to her chair and, right on cue, Herb came through the front door. When he got to the kitchen, a smile filled his face, almost as bright as the sun shining off the white snow.

"Bacon? Your grandma never lets me have bacon."

"Because you eat too much of it, and it isn't good for you."

I winced. "Sorry, next time I'll get turkey bacon."

"In that case, load my plate up," he announced, smirking.

We settled in and passed around the platters of food, Edmund begging at my feet for bacon. I slipped him a piece as Grandma turned to the fridge for some orange juice.

"Grandma, I have great news," I said. "A bakery from New York saw my advertising on our social media and applied. They're a big deal too. It will bring in a lot of attention."

"That's amazing!" Grandma said. "What are they called?"

"M&K Bakery," I said. "Reviews online rave about their cookies. I'm sure they're not as good as yours, of course."

Grandma smirked. "Thank you, Lucy. But it's okay to like other bakeries. That's the whole point of the bake-off: to support other businesses like ours."

When I was old enough to understand the festival, I always appreciated that about Grandma. Most entrepreneurs saw other businesses in their industry as competitors to be slayed. Not Grandma and Grandpa. They saw their bakery's success as an opportunity to support others, and I loved that the Holiday Bake-Off gave bakeries of all sizes a chance to participate. No one was turned away, and I thought that was such an admirable thing. The community also appreciated the tourism the festival brought in, so it was a complete win-win for everyone.

"Well, today I think we should start working through some more of the to-do list. I put in an order last night for some of the supplies. It should be here at the beginning of next week," I said. A countdown clock was constantly running in my head now, and the list of things we needed to do was still a mile long.

I expected Grandma to leap into a conversation about what I should focus on next and remind me how many days we had left. I was certainly counting.

But Grandma didn't say anything. She looked at Herb, then back at me. She winced.

"I know I dropped the ball on the festival, but honestly, with your help I'm feeling really good about it. I know it's going to be a smashing success. So, if it's okay, Herb planned on taking me into town today to do a little Christmas shopping."

I tried not to let my jaw drop to the ground. A date. Grandma was going on a date—and I couldn't be happier. I didn't care if I had to stay up for seventy-two hours straight to get things ready for the festival—I was thrilled for her.

"That's awesome! Go, and don't think twice about any of it."

"You know, when I was younger, I thought taking a break was for the weak. But I don't know. The older I get and with this heart hiccup, maybe taking a break isn't so bad."

I eyed her, taking in the wistful look. My stomach

dropped a little bit. Was she feeling worse than she was letting on and trying to cover it? Panic started to swirl and take me to a dark place—a place where people could be ripped away at any moment.

Grandma seemed to sense my concern and patted my hand from across the table. "I'm fine, Lucy, really. You can call my doctor and confirm if you don't believe me. I'm not going anywhere for a long time if I can help it. But I'm just saying, it's healthy to take a break, to make memories. Don't get so wrapped up in your work you forget to live. Okay?"

The words struck a chord in me. I'd been feeling so guilty for the little work I was doing on my book, but Grandma's words helped me fling away that feeling. It was okay to take a break. It was okay not to meticulously plot out my life like it was a novel. I inhaled the thought, trying to store it away to remember for later.

Grandma and Herb insisted on clearing the table, so I went upstairs to change clothes and get ready to go to the bakery. I wanted to work on some of the details for the festival even though Grandma was taking the day off. There were a lot of phone calls I could check off the list, and it would help to be in the bakery in case Will needed support. As I was saying goodbye to Grandma, she leaned back to take in my outfit.

"Adorable. Perfect," she said, and I wondered why she was so interested in my jeans, boots, and red sweater.

"Thanks," I said, shrugging it off.

"Have a wonderful time," she shouted as I left.

I turned back, pausing in the doorway as the frigid air smacked into my face. I squinted at her suspiciously, but she turned quickly back to the dishes. Something was up, and I didn't think it had anything to do with her health.

What had she planned? What was I walking into?

I strolled out the door and headed to my car. As I drove toward Star Creek Bakery, I wondered what she knew that I didn't.

***

WHEN I PULLED up to the bakery, Will was standing outside, wrapped in a scarf and winter coat. His hands were casually in his pockets as he leaned against the door, which prominently displayed the *Closed* sign. On each side of the door, two Christmas trees were strung up with lights. They hadn't been there the day before. Holiday lights also covered the edge of the roof, and gorgeous electric candles glowed in the windows.

Will looked as if he'd been waiting for me. I got out of the car, confused and expecting the worst.

"What's wrong? Was there a water main break or something?" I asked.

He shook his head as he walked toward me. "We're closed today. Official orders from your grandma were that you needed a break after working so hard yesterday, and that I'm to show you around the town." He shrugged. "I tried to tell her we were busy, but it was the boss's orders."

He seemed a little shy about it all, and I wondered if he even wanted to go or was just doing it out of obligation. It definitely seemed like the latter. Leave it to my grandmother to turn the bakery into her own version of the dating game by coercing her employees to date her granddaughter. I would need to talk to her about human resources and policies.

I shook my head. "She tricked me."

"I sense that's something she does frequently?"

I smiled. "You're catching on."

"Anyway, I have to obey orders from the boss, so looks like we're stuck with each other today. I've got it all planned." His words were soft and teasing, not cold and callous like the first day. That was progress, but I was still nervous about spending a day with Will, who rarely said more than a few sentences unless it was about cupcakes. It might be a long day.

"Did you decorate?" I asked, sidestepping the conversation about the day.

He nodded. "I stayed behind a little last night. I thought with everything going on with your grandma, it would be helpful to cross that off the list. I found the decorations in the storage room."

I smiled at his thoughtfulness. With the red door, Star Creek Bakery definitely gave off holiday vibes.

"Thank you."

"Of course," he said, shrugging as if it was nothing. But it wasn't nothing, not by a long shot.

"I appreciate the sentiment about taking a break. But the festival is coming up. We have so many phone calls to make, details to work out."

"I know. My mother is calling the mayor today about the parking situation, and my grandpa is going downtown to work on the floral arrangements and Christmas trees your grandma wants for the festival. I didn't want us to get behind, so those two things are taken care of, and I think I have some ideas for the cookie recipes your grandma wanted to add to the lineup. We're going to be fine, truly."

"Your family is willing to help? That's so sweet."

Will nodded. "Yes. They're loud and a lot to handle sometimes, but they do rally together for a cause they believe in. Your grandma's bakery is something they all care about—especially when I deliver cupcakes weekly. Now, come on. We've got quite the list of stops to make."

Grandma's words made so much more sense now. She was prepping me because as I followed Will to his car, I thought about all the things I should be doing. But as I climbed into the passenger seat, the blue scarf wrapped around his neck brought attention to his gorgeous, dark eyes, and I couldn't help but be excited to have a day to just forget about it all.

And to be honest, despite the awkwardness that still lingered between us, I was excited about who I was adventuring through Star Creek with.

IT WAS fun to see the town I'd known since I was a little girl from a newcomer's eyes. I probably should've been the one showing Will around because many of the haunts from my childhood were still landmarks in the small town. But I let him take the lead and fed off his excitement for the spots and local favorites he wanted me to experience.

He was opening up in new ways, and being out of the bakery was letting me see him differently. He was less serious, less closed off outside of work. I was starting to realize he had a good sense of humor as I spent most of the morning laughing so hard, tears were ready to burst from my eyes.

Although some of the stops were places I'd been, it was like experiencing them for the first time with Will. He brought a childlike enthusiasm to everything we did, which was unexpected—and wonderful. It was so different from Jed's constant black tie, always trying to impress others. With Will, it was more natural.

Not that there was a "with Will" to speak of, I reminded myself.

Our first stop was the Route 22 Diner, where Will ordered chocolate chip pancakes and snickerdoodle French toast for us to share. I didn't have the heart to tell him I already ate breakfast, but it wasn't really a punishment to eat more. I promptly made room once I smelled how delicious the breakfast was.

"So do you think you're going to stay in Star Creek?" I asked after taking another bite of the pancakes.

Will glanced out the window. "Well, when faced with the prospect of leaving city life for the quiet suburbs, I wasn't so sure. But honestly, it's starting to feel like home already. There's a quiet peace here, and even though I haven't been here long, it just seems like a place where everyone's connected. I like that. Plus, I mean, these pancakes are the best I've ever had. How about you? How are you adjusting?"

I sighed. "Well, growing up, New York was my dream. I always wanted to be a writer, and the city seemed to have the energy I needed to pursue that career. Plus, most publishers are there. I moved into an apartment with my best friend, Serena, and honestly, after growing up in the New Jersey suburbs, it was an adjustment. I loved it, though, and it energized my writing. But lately, I don't know. The thing with writing is I can do it anywhere, and sometimes I sort of feel like maybe it's time for a change."

I took a sip of my coffee and glanced out the window. I thought of my passport in my drawer and the date I was supposed to depart looming.

"That's the thing they don't always tell you, huh? Dreams definitely change sometimes," Will said, and I turned back to him.

I shrugged. "And maybe that's not a bad thing."

"Maybe not. Even though leaving my New York dreams behind wasn't easy, I don't know… A part of me feels like this was how it was supposed to happen. I feel like maybe leaving the city and coming here is leading me to bigger dreams in some ways," he said, his vulnerability coming through his eyes.

"I'm sure your parents are happy to have you back too."

"Mom cries every day. They're tears of joy—at least, I think. I'm an only child, so when I moved far away, it broke her heart."

"Where did you grow up?"

"North Carolina. We lived near the beach. But I'm really starting to like it here. My parents find it peaceful and charming."

"Yeah, it's a nice town. I used to come here a lot as a child to visit my grandparents and stay with them. There's just something homey here."

It hit me then. Since leaving the city, I'd settled into a sense of comfort I hadn't felt for a long time. I still had my worries for the future and about Grandma, but somehow, Star Creek seemed to say, *I've got you.* I didn't feel so alone in the middle of it all.

"Can I ask you something else, sort of random?" I broached, deciding to take advantage of Will's walls being down.

He nodded.

"What were you getting at the bookstore? What kind of books?"

"Just a few things I had to pick up," he said and took a bite of pancake. It was odd that he wouldn't tell me what he was getting. But I decided to let it go. Will Westerly was a man of mystery, apparently, and I had pushed it this morning. I didn't want to risk him clamming up again.

We finished our breakfast, paid, and Will announced we were heading to the next activity.

"I hope it doesn't require too much exertion because I'm so stuffed, I can barely move."

"Me too. I will say, moving to Star Creek might not be great for my waistline. I mean, New York has some great dinner spots—but they've got nothing on this town."

"Agreed," I said. As we drove to our next spot, we talked about our favorite hotspots in the city, our favorite restaurants, our favorite food trucks. The conversation flowed easily, and I couldn't help but think how perfect it was—two city dreamers, settling here in the small-town life. I had a sense of camaraderie that couldn't be ignored, and it felt good to have someone who understood.

I eyed the sign for the Star Creek Consignment Shop as Will slowed the car. It was a place I'd actually never been before.

Will shrugged. "I didn't bring very much from the city with me, so this place has been my best friend when stocking my house. And they get some pretty nifty things in sometimes. I've been coming almost every weekend since I moved here."

I followed Will into the store and spotted a familiar elderly man standing behind the counter.

"Lucy? Is that you?" he asked, and I immediately smiled at an old friend I hadn't seen in years.

"Mr. Barbary? Oh my goodness, I had no idea this was your store," I proclaimed as he came from around the counter to hug me. His signature polka-dot bowtie was still in place, just as it was in my childhood memories.

"What happened to the candy business?" I asked,

saddened to realize I hadn't been in town enough in the past few years to notice the disappearance of the town staple, at least from a child's perspective. I could still conjure images of the magical, brightly colored polka-dot door that always stirred dreams of faraway lands when I walked through it.

His expression saddened. "There just isn't a market for penny candy anymore. So I had to change it up. I bought this place from Mrs. Goodson a few years ago. Consigned furniture is still fun, I suppose. I like watching adults find treasures. Speaking of which, Will, you should check out the hand mixer I got in. It's an antique, so it might be a fun collectible for your kitchen."

He led the way for Will, and I followed, studying the cluttered aisles of furniture, décor, and all sorts of knickknacks. Still, it saddened me to see Mr. Barbary here instead of in his little candy store.

Will perused the mixer with fascination. The phone rang, pulling Mr. Barbary to the front desk.

"This place is fun," I said, looking around at all the unique pieces. "But I'm honestly so sad about the candy store."

"What did it used to be called?" Will asked.

"Mr. Barbary's Candy Bonanza," I said with a smile. "He had a really fun polka-dot door that stood out on Main Street. It beckoned all the kids in. There were stuffed animals everywhere in that whimsical place, and there was also a huge glass counter that seemed miles long. All the children would walk the length, pointing to penny candy he would load up in a paper sack. And he always threw in a free lollipop for good measure. It was such a thrilling place as a child." Nostalgia filled my chest as I thought of some of the candies I used to love, most of which were now obsolete.

Will smiled. "Your eyes light up when you talk about it. I wish I could've seen it."

I nodded.

"Well, we can't bring the store back permanently... but what if we brought it back for a weekend? What if we had a candy booth Mr. Barbary could run at the festival? It would be really fun for the kids—and I suppose for the nostalgic adults as well," Will suggested.

My heart lit up at the prospect. "That's an amazing idea! Oh my gosh, I love it, and I know Grandma will too."

Back in the day, Mr. Barbary would sometimes supply candy for Grandma's more adventurous cupcake concoctions. I knew it would be like having an old friend back if Mr. Barbary agreed.

On our way to the counter to present the idea, Will grabbed my hand and yanked me back. I collided into his chest, and he caught me.

For a split second, we stayed melted together, me taking in the intoxicating scent of his cologne and the feel of his strong, rigid body holding me upright. But then the second passed as we realized how close we were. We stumbled away from each other, and I cleared my throat as Will stumbled through an apology.

"Um, sorry. I... Look, this is awesome for you. Not practical, but awesome." He pointed to a teal-colored typewriter. It was worn, the letters practically rubbed off. Whoever used it had done a lot of writing, which I found charming and inspiring.

"Maybe it would be good luck, help me get my writing mojo back."

Will picked it up without even looking at the price tag as Mr. Barbary wrapped up his phone call.

"Mr. Barbary, we'll take this and the hand mixer today," he said.

"Oh, good choice. I can't tell you who because I'm sworn to secrecy, but let's just say someone pretty famous in the writing world owned that at one time."

This confession piqued my interest. Even though I rationalized that Mr. Barbary was just being a good salesman, I liked the idea of the tale being even remotely true.

"Can you give me a hint?" I implored.

He shrugged. "Let's just say it might have something to do with the father of American free verse poetry."

"Wow," Will said.

I just smirked as I perused my mind for the literary knowledge I'd stored there. No, the dates didn't really align. Still, I humored Mr. Barbary. It could bring good luck regardless.

"I'll take extra good care of it," I promised.

I reached into my bag, but Will waved my hand aside. "I've got it."

"No way, I'm not letting you pay."

"If a good man wants to buy you a gift, let him," Mr. Barbary said, winking.

As he punched the amounts into the cash register that could also be an antique, I brought up our idea.

"Mr. Barbary, we were thinking. We're trying to add some new booths to the Star Creek Holiday Bake-Off. What would you think of running a candy booth for the children? We would provide all the candy, and you could keep a cut of sales to compensate you for your time."

He paused, his finger ready to punch in the next number. His eyes lit up, a wistful look as if he, too, were walking down that glass case in his memories.

"Are you serious?" he asked, his voice soft and solemn.

"Completely serious," I assured him.

He grinned the biggest grin I'd seen, and I thought for a moment a tear might come to his eye. It was as if we'd just offered him a mansion instead of a booth at the town's annual festival.

"Yes, I would love to. Oh, I would love to."

He rushed around the counter to wrap me in another hug, and I could feel his happiness radiating. When he finally pulled back, he did have tears in his eyes.

"I've missed my business so much. This truly means the world to me. You can't imagine."

"I can," Will said, also solemn. Then he added, "Well, who knows. Maybe reintroducing the candy store will ignite some interest for a reboot."

My fingers were crossed. A man like Mr. Barbary deserved to live out his passion.

"The typewriter and mixer are on me," he said then, canceling the sale on the register when he crossed back behind the counter. "Merry Christmas to you both."

"No, Mr. Barbary. No way," Will and I simultaneously argued.

"Nonsense. What did I just tell you? When a nice guy gives you a gift, you accept it. End of story. You're giving me a chance to revisit my dreams. Hopefully the mixer and typewriter will keep your passions close by as well."

"Thank you," I said as Will shook his hand.

We left the consignment shop with our new décor—but also a new sense of what the bake-off meant—could mean— to the town.

BY THE TIME we got to our last stop, snow flurries had returned, but Will assured me that was a good thing.

We pulled up to the town center where the gazebo created a charming, picturesque scene that was the backdrop to so many Star Creek events. At the Spring Fling festival, the mayor always gave a speech in the center of the pristine white gazebo while the town gathered around. On the Fourth of July, it was the spot where the annual BBQ cook-off winner was announced and where the fall festival soup contest took place. Between the holidays, the gazebo was a romantic staple in the town where proposals, engagement photos, and just the special, everyday kind of memories happened.

Now, the town's Christmas tree sat in front of the gazebo, having been lit the Wednesday before Thanksgiving at the tree festival I hadn't been to in years. Still, if I closed my eyes, I could taste the hot chocolate, hear the excitement bustling through the town as everyone gathered shoulder to shoulder to count down to the magical moment. Poinsettias perched on the snow around the structure, and twinkle lights covered the gazebo in a glorious presentation. With the snow piled around, it felt like a scene in a snow globe.

Will purchased two hot chocolates from the drink cart run by a recent high-school graduate in the park. We claimed seats on the benches that lined the interior of the gazebo and warmed our hands on our cups, taking in the scene of the busiest street in town. Most of the town's shopping was on this street with stores selling everything from candles to purses to pottery. It was a quaint section of town that always caught the eye of tourists, and it would be the central location for the bake-off festival's events.

In a few weeks, we would stand here in the gazebo at the end of the bake-off and crown the winner the day before

Christmas Eve. We would look out into the crowd of people and see how my grandma's bakery had brought everyone together for the day as we prepared to celebrate the holidays. Even though planning the festival was exhausting, even though my trip to Star Creek had rocked my plans for December and beyond, sitting in the gazebo with Will reminded me how special it was. To have this time to slow down, to visit this town that felt like home, and to be close to genuinely good people—perhaps it was just what my spirit needed.

"Beautiful, huh? I think this is my favorite part of the town," Will offered as he pulled out his phone and did something completely surprising and unexpected.

He held out his arm for a selfie, and I leaned in with my hot chocolate. He demanded I yell "cupcake" before he snapped the photo. Even though I was cold and still full of pancakes, I had to admit, there was a glow about me, about both of us.

"There's something about this place that you can't find in the city, even in Central Park. There's just a quiet familiarity. Like coming home," he said. He was talking about the city without melancholy in his voice. That was a good sign.

"Yes. Like coming home. I'm glad I'm not the only one who feels that way," I agreed.

We sat in silence for about half an hour, both lost in our own worlds yet lingering in the comfort of being together. There was no need to speak, to fill the space. No need to have a purpose to our sitting there. No rush to dig into each other's pasts or uncover more about who we were. We simply sat, relaxing in the gazebo and in Star Creek. Most importantly, we were both fully present in the moment; it felt like a more intimate moment than I'd ever shared with anyone. It was different. Will was different.

After a while, we headed back to the car, and Will tossed an impromptu snowball at me on the way. I returned the favor, although my snowball embarrassingly missed him and hit close to the hot chocolate cart. After profuse apologies, I tucked my frigid self into Will's car, and we laughed about my throwing arm as he drove me back to the bakery. When we got there, he put the car in Park.

"I had an amazing day with you," he murmured, staring at me.

For a long moment, we gazed into each other's eyes. I thought he might kiss me. I thought I might want him to. I saw him move a fraction of an inch forward, but then, just as quickly, he pulled back. He ran a hand through his dark hair, the snowflakes that had speckled it now melted. I cleared my throat and got out, claiming my typewriter from the back seat.

"Thank you for everything. I'll see you tomorrow bright and early so we can work on the cookie recipes."

He looked back at me, but I could tell something was plaguing him. I paused, wondering if he would add something, but he didn't.

"You bet," he said and then added, "I had a great time today."

"Me too."

I waved and stood with the car door open for an awkward, pregnant pause.

Then I turned to Serena's car. Will waited until I started the ignition, then waved, and drove away. I exhaled, thinking about the day we'd had together as Will's car grew smaller in the distance.

THIRTEEN

Grandma was slumped back on the sofa half asleep with a
Christmas movie on TV when I returned. She didn't leap
up when the door shut like she usually did, ready to pepper
me with questions. My heart sank. But Edmund, who had
been asleep in front of the fireplace, rustled awake, which in
turn stirred Grandma.

She slowly came to, the weariness visible on her face. I
asked where Herb was, panicked that she'd been alone
while I was out frolicking. She said Herb had gone home to
spend some time with his cat, Sylvester, and assured me she
was fine and taking a cat nap. I assuaged the bubbling fear,
letting her answers satisfy me for the time being. I brushed
off the snowflakes after setting the typewriter on the
counter and then took a seat by Grandma.

"You tricked me," I teased. "Did you and Herb go
shopping?"

"No, it was just a cover to get you to the bakery alone.
You deserved a day off, and I knew you wouldn't take it
unless I did. We spent the morning watching television and

eating, mostly. Which was way better than shopping. But enough about my boring day. I want to hear about yours."

I smiled. "We got a typewriter and a mixer from the consignment shop. Oh, and Mr. Barbary and I made plans for a candy booth for the festival. It was Will's idea."

"Uh-huh," Grandma said, motioning for me to continue. "And…"

"And it was nice. We went to the diner and got pancakes. We went to the gazebo and had hot chocolate. It was a great day, but I feel guilty for not working on the Holiday Bake-Off."

"I mean, how were things with Will? We can talk about the festival and the candy booth, which I love, later. I want to know about your date. You seem radiant. Did you have a good time with him? Did you get to know him better? Did you both open up more? I never see him act so happy except around you, which I think is a good sign."

I sighed. "Grandma, was this your elaborate matchmaking plan? To send him as my tour guide? And by the way, it isn't a date if you don't agree to go."

"I disagree. And anyway, did it work?"

"He's a nice guy and all, but we're friends. That's it. I just got out of a relationship. I'm not ready for love, and I doubt he is either."

"No one ever is. But that doesn't stop it. I see the way that boy looks at you."

"He's hardly a boy, Grandma. He's twenty-eight."

"He's a boy to me. But, Lucy, I just think he could be good for you. Both from the city, both creatives, both driven. He's a good one. Don't close your heart off because of that first love. Sometimes the second's better."

I glanced out the window, staring into the darkness. It

was such a hopeful, light concept. But my heart still ached from Jed's betrayal, and I didn't understand how anyone could open themselves up again. Jed had been everything I needed. He'd been a good man—until he wasn't.

Today, I saw a different side of Will, a side that was kind and lighthearted in ways I could appreciate. But that didn't mean he couldn't break my heart or wouldn't. That didn't mean he wouldn't expect me to bend to his will, to abandon who I was and what I wanted. And I wouldn't do that again. Not for anyone.

Which brought me back to the most important topic: writing.

"Grandma, that reminds me," I said.

She clicked the television off.

"I wanted to talk to you about my new book idea. It came from the story you told me about your first love, Benjamin. That idea of the second love being even better— well, it inspired me."

"Did it?" she asked.

"I want to write a book loosely based on you and Grandpa. With your blessing, of course."

Once the words were out, my nerves kicked in. I didn't realize how anxious I would be until the question was out. What if she hated the idea? What if it saddened her? Fears swirled in my head as Grandma sank back into the sofa, exhaling softly. Her expression seemed melancholic, despite the starry look in her eyes. I thought tears were getting ready to fall. She reached a quivering hand up to her face and wiped at her eye, confirming my suspicion. My heart sank. This was a terrible idea.

"If you don't want me to, I can come up with something else. It's just, your love story is beautiful, something everyone would want to read about. And I would change your names, of course. It wouldn't be exact. But if it makes you uncomfortable..." The anxiety poured out of me.

Grandma reached out slowly and touched my arm. She cleared her throat. "Lucy, stop. Of course you can write about us. It just—wow, I never thought anyone would care about our love story. Or want to write about it. And to have you write it—what a treasure. I know your grandfather would be proud."

Tears started to build in my eyes. I exhaled all the worry I'd been entertaining.

"Thank you," I said.

"I'm assuming you might need some more details?" she asked slowly, the words coming out laboriously. I worried that the memories, the whole concept had pushed her too far. Maybe I should've waited until she was further along in her recovery.

"I don't want to pressure you, Grandma. Especially if it's going to be hard on you to remember all those moments with Grandpa gone."

She was solemn and looked away for a moment. "It's never easy thinking about him, but that doesn't mean I don't. I think about him every day. And to have our story put into printed words, well, I think that will be a beautiful way to honor what we had."

I patted her hand, nodding. I was determined then to do her proud, to make their love story shine. I had a new sense of purpose behind my writing—and a lot more pressure. I had to get it right.

"If it's okay, I have a list of questions. Let me grab them from my room," I said.

"How about if I put some tea on? We can meet back at the kitchen table in a few minutes?" she suggested.

"Perfect. Thank you, Grandma."

"Me, little old me, in a fancy novel. I can't believe it." She was shaking her head as she carefully stretched her body and got to her feet. I offered my arm for her to pull herself up, and she accepted. She shuffled to the kitchen, leaning on the walls on the way. I made sure she got there safely before heading back to the guest room.

In my room, I grabbed my notebook, feeling new motivation to make this the best book I'd ever written, to do my family proud. As I was heading back toward the kitchen, my cell phone vibrated in my back pocket. I pulled it out to see Serena's number and paused in place while I answered.

"Hey, you," she said. "How's Star Creek? How's your grandma? Are you learning to make cupcakes?" She fired questions before I could process them all.

"So good," I answered, unable to hold back my smile. "I just got back from a day of exploring the town. Grandma organized a day off for me and Will."

"Will? Tell me more," she urged.

"Baker Will. He's from the city, but his family is here so he moved back and is basically running Grandma's bakery. He took me out to show me around today."

"Uh-oh."

"Uh-oh, what?" I asked, heading back inside the guest room to look for my laptop and charger.

"I can hear it in your voice. You're a smitten kitten."

I groaned. "First, I thought after Jed, we agreed you wouldn't be using that term. And second, no. Just no. He's a friend, a co-worker really, who was just being nice."

"And is this co-worker slash friend who is kind also handsome?"

"I don't know," I replied, rolling my eyes. "Some might say so, I guess."

"I can hear the smile in your voice. He is. Oh, Grandma

Catherine, good job, girlfriend. She hired him for you. I know it."

"Don't get ahead of yourself. We're really busy with the bake-off and then, once I know Grandma's okay, I'm coming back. So there is no Will in my future."

"Oh, I think there *will* be. See what I did there? Who says lawyers aren't funny?" She laughed aloud at her own joke and despite my eye roll and annoyance, I laughed too.

"I could say something, but I won't."

"Well, I can't wait to meet him during the festival," she said.

"You're coming?"

"Of course I am. First, my best girl is running the show. And also, cupcakes? How can I resist. Oh, and then there's the bit that my holiday season currently looks like a few holiday movies on repeat and a frozen dinner with Gary. And yes, I've kept your little plant alive. But honestly, it all sounds incredibly sad, even by my standards."

"You know, while we're turning the subject to my apparent love life, how about you? What's going on with Noah?"

Noah was a new attorney at Serena's firm. He had a surfer vibe going, which, when coupled with a suit, was exactly Serena's type.

"We had coffee yesterday to talk about a few documents and a cease and desist we were preparing."

"Romance is alive," I teased. "But seriously, that's good."

"We'll see," she murmured, but I could hear the levity in her voice.

"Maybe you'll have a holiday date after all."

"Well, only if he's willing to go to Star Creek for cupcakes. I miss you. I don't know if I can wait until that weekend to see you."

"You know you're welcome anytime. Just say the word and Grandma will have a buffet of breakfast foods and pastries at the ready."

"I love that woman, truly," Serena said. "Well, I'll let you get back to your small-town love story. Wow, that romance novel should be flying from your fingertips, huh? Who knew little old Star Creek would be such an inspiration?"

"If you say so," I replied, but in truth, it had been. Not because of Will as Serena was suggesting. Although, if I were being honest with myself, there was a jolt when I was with him, something I wrote about frequently but had never really felt before. Sure, Jed and I had been madly in love in the beginning. But looking back now, I never had those proverbial butterflies around him, not even in the beginning.

I'd told myself it was love, that he excited me. I convinced myself that was just what love felt like. I'd thought perhaps all of the butterflies, the electric feelings of love were just falsities; they were a pact among romance writers, a creative licensing of untruths that no one really felt in the real world. I'd convinced myself with Jed that I didn't really need them, that happiness, stability, and companionship were so much more than those fleeting feelings.

But Will made me realize maybe the butterflies were real. Will made me understand, too, that maybe I did, in fact, need those feelings. Did that mean I could consider risking it all again after it had gone so, so wrong?

I shook off the thought as I brushed my hair back into a ponytail and grabbed my laptop. I needed to put Will out of my head and focus on the story. As if it was a sign, my phone started buzzing. It was Anna. Rather than avoiding her call as if she were a telemarketer, I answered.

"Anna, great news! The novel is flowing, and I've got a solid sense of direction. I think this one's going to go big places," I said. After a short conversation where my agent literally exhaled for thirty seconds in relief, I hung up, sought out Grandma, and got to work.

FOURTEEN

"I see you've recovered from your day of excitement yesterday. I heard a handsome man showed you around town," Will said when I got into the bakery the next morning. It was still dark outside, my frosty breath billowing in the morning air on my way in the door.

Will looked like he'd been in the kitchen for hours already, his energy and progress on preparing cookie ingredients almost maddening. A rock song was blaring, and he was bobbing his head to it as he talked. I couldn't help but notice his overly happy mood. The brooding, quiet man seemed to have been replaced with a new, chatty Will. I liked it—but I wasn't reciprocating his mood because I felt like I was barely awake.

"I still might be full from those pancakes yesterday. And I also think my arm hurts from that snowball, so I doubt I'll be able to help with any dishes."

"Convenient," he teased. "Are you sure you're ready for this?"

We'd set today as the day we would work on cookie recipes for the Holiday Bake-Off. Traditionally, we had a cookie-decorating station with sugar cookies, but Grandma also created new flavors each year for the festival. The town always had informal bets on what the flavors would be. Will was taking over the challenge this year and had asked me to help. I was honored he'd deemed me worthy of having a spot in the kitchen, even though it wasn't really deserved. It was something, though. Besides, by helping, my plan was basically to taste test.

"So I have a few ideas I want to try out. Here, I got you an apron," he said, passing me a folded, pink heap of fabric.

I eyed him. "I thought I was just the taste tester." I tried to give him a look of innocence, one I hoped he couldn't turn down.

"Not today. Today, you're learning how to make cookies. It's no fun just watching."

I beg to differ, I thought, and then blushed. I needed to keep it professional, platonic. We needed to stay focused.

In a complete change of pace, Will began walking me through different dough ingredients and tips and tricks for the perfect cookie. We'd definitely turned a corner since that first day when he barely gave me the time of day.

"So, what flavor do you think? Go wild," he said.

I sat on a stool, pondering the question. I had never invented a cookie before. It seemed next to impossible.

"Just be creative, like when you're writing. How is that going, by the way?" he asked as he worked on his own bowl of dough.

"Mercifully great. I got an awesome idea for my new book, and the words are flowing." It felt good to say that aloud, I realized, as I kneaded the dough in my bowl. I'd missed the days when writing came easily.

"That's good news, Lucy. I'm happy for you. So take that creative energy and pour it into the cookie."

"I have no clue what I'm doing," I admitted, staring down at the ball of plain dough in my bowl. I couldn't imagine it being anything other than the basic chocolate chip at this point.

"That's the fun of it."

I looked at the counter where Will had set out a mass of different potential ingredients. I felt as if I were on one of those baking shows—one I had no business being featured on. Nevertheless, I decided to embrace the challenge and run with it.

Will and I agreed that for our first batch, we'd just give it a try and not talk to each other about our choices. We'd wait until the taste test. Where silence had lingered only a few days ago, laughter and storytelling now filled the kitchen. Will told me about growing up in the South and one of his favorite fishing memories. I told him about the time my mother decided to sign me up for soccer, thinking team sports would help me be less awkward. It had backfired. I'd scored a goal for the other team and been promptly removed from the soccer league.

"That's terrible," he said. "They kicked you off for scoring a goal?"

"Well, technically I ruined the team championship for everyone with that goal," I said. "But I was glad. I didn't really feel the illustrious soccer career in my blood. Mom and Dad, although they'd never admit it, would sort of hide on the sidelines when I played, trying not to claim me because that goal wasn't the first issue I had on the field. I was a bit of an embarrassment."

"I can't even imagine that," Will said, and I peeked over to see he was loading up a cookie sheet. I was still debating on my flavor.

"What were your parents like?" Will asked, stopping

what he was doing. I could tell he was treading lightly, nervous to ask.

Usually, I didn't like to talk about them. Sure, I thought about them every moment of every day. I missed them, ached for them. But to talk about them was to speak in the past tense, to admit they were gone. Still, the way Will asked the question, soft and still, I felt like I wanted to answer him.

"They were the best. Truly," I said, tears coming to my eyes as we both paused from our work. "Dad worked in marketing, but he always wanted to be a writer deep down. He was the one who encouraged me to chase my dreams, no matter what, and told me I could achieve anything I wanted. Mom was a financial planner. She commuted to the city every day from the suburbs of New Jersey. She's the reason I wanted to live there because she would bring back stories from the subway, from the food carts by her office. It sounded so vibrant and exciting. She always made time for me, even though she had a big job. We would go into the city on Saturdays once in a while to see a Broadway play and get lunch. Those were my most magical days."

"Sounds amazing. I've always wanted to go to Broadway," Will confessed.

I raised an eyebrow. "You lived in the city. Didn't you ever go?"

"No," he said, shrugging. "I didn't have anyone who would go with me, and I was so busy with my business." He sighed.

"I'm sorry things didn't work out there," I said, feeling like since we were talking about vulnerable topics, it was okay to say.

"It's fine. I'm here now," he replied, and then turned the conversation back to the bake-off.

I was glad to open up about my parents—but I felt like Will wasn't comfortable yet to do the same about his past. It hurt a little to think he didn't trust me. But I tried not to take it personally. Everyone healed in their own time and had their own process. He would come around and share when he felt like he could.

At least I hoped that would be the case.

<hr>

"ONE, TWO, THREE," Will said as we both bit into his cookie recipe first. Immediately, from the first bite, it was a taste of heaven.

"This is phenomenal," I said, taking another bite.

The cookie was a play on cheesecake with a soft cream cheese center, a few berries drizzled on top, and some crushed chocolate cookies sprinkled as a finishing touch.

"Not too bad. I'm thinking we call it Elvish Delights?" Will ventured, clearly nervous to put his name forward.

"That's a pretty good name for a man who claims he isn't good at creative writing," I teased. I finished the cookie and then retrieved my plate from the counter.

"So it's probably not going to be as good as yours, but I'm pretty proud of myself, I won't lie. I didn't even burn them, which is a win. I'm calling this one The Naughty List."

He laughed at the name, shaking his head. I shrugged, and we both took a bite. I studied him carefully and was thrilled when Will's eyes lit up.

"I like the texture. That's innovative how you mixed so many elements together, but it works. And I like the name."

I smirked. "Basically, I built the recipe with my stomach. Everything looked good."

I'd used about six different kinds of candy bars and broken them into little pieces along with some pretzels. The result was a very texturized cookie—but it was a chocoholic's dream, for sure.

"That's two winning cookies. I'd say we've been successful," Will said.

I boxed up a few of the leftovers. "We've just got one more set of tastebuds to impress, and these are officially on the menu," I announced, holding up the box with mock fanfare.

Will pretended to bugle, and we both broke out laughing.

It was getting close to lunch time, so we put aside the joking and hurriedly cleaned up our areas. Will had prepped some cupcakes and cookies for the regular customers before I'd gotten there—I swear, the man didn't need sleep. I put on another pot of coffee and headed to the front counter to help.

Grandma was supposed to come in at noon because she wanted to help out, but I got a phone call around eleven.

"Dear, I'm so sorry. Herb has tempted me to play hooky again today with lunch at the diner. Are you two okay? I don't want to leave you hanging."

"Is this another setup?" I asked, eyeing Will suspiciously. He was finishing up some final icing touches on the cupcakes.

"No, no. Nothing like that, I promise. I just know things are in good hands and, well, I could really go for a salad from the diner."

I was thrilled that Herb was getting through to Grandma and succeeding at getting her to relax. Still, as I hung up the phone, a part of me worried. Grandma was definitely backing off from the bakery. I could still see the lingering effects of her health issues—how tired she was, her facial expression, her shaking hands, her need to lean on things to walk across the room. It had shaken her more than she wanted to let on, and the effects were taking a toll. It worried me.

I tried to tell myself that maybe with me in town, she finally felt like she had the freedom to step back a little, which was a good thing. She deserved to enjoy some time off after working so hard her entire life, and I was glad I could provide that relief. But I shuddered to think about what might happen when I left. Was Grandma done with the bakery? Was she too tired to run it? And what if her health got worse? She clearly needed me. How could I go back to the city? Still, the thought of abandoning that life also made me shudder. New York was where I belonged, where I'd always wanted to be—wasn't it? It was all so complicated.

"Are you okay?" Will asked after I rang up the next customer and turned to get myself a cup of coffee. "You look worried."

"It's just Grandma. She isn't coming in," I said.

"Isn't that a good thing? She needs to be resting."

"It is, it is. And don't get me wrong, I'm happy she trusts us to keep things going. But it scares me to see her stepping back. It's just sort of a reminder she won't be here running the bakery forever, and I don't know. After losing my parents..."

Will put a hand on my shoulder. "Hey, listen. Your grandma, as far as I can see, isn't going anywhere anytime soon. She's still a firecracker. I just think maybe with you in town, she feels like she can step away and focus on herself, which is such a good thing. If anything, that's going to make her healthier. And I think Herb might have something to do with it."

"You've noticed too?" I asked with a widening grin.

"Of course. The way those two interact, it's like they're already married. I don't know what they're waiting for."

I shrugged. "Love is scary," I admitted.

"You're telling me," Will replied, and I wanted to ask him to elaborate, but at that moment his phone rang.

"Excuse me," he said, stepping into the kitchen. I wiped down the counters and refilled Mrs. Stella's cup of coffee. She was sitting in her usual spot by the window, her canary yellow sweater bringing a sense of sunshine in the middle of the dreary winter day. We talked about her dog, Precious, and her plans to go to bingo over the weekend.

When Will returned from the kitchen, he stood by the register. I could tell he was waiting for me, so I wrapped up my conversation with Mrs. Stella and wandered back over to him, my heart fluttering. Phone calls always made me so nervous.

"That was Mom," Will said, hands in his pockets. He rocked back and forth on his feet as if he was anxious, and my heart started racing.

"Is everything okay?" I asked, docking the coffee pot.

"Yes, yes. Fine. But she was wondering if you would like to come over for dinner tonight. She's making meatloaf, and she wants to fill you in on those phone calls she made."

"Oh. Well, um, sure," I agreed, shrugging. "Of course I'll come and chat about the bake-off. It's coming up, so if there were issues with the calls she made, I definitely want to take care of it." *Keep it professional. Platonic*, I told myself. Internally, I was already scoping out what I was going to wear and panicking about meeting Will's family.

"I'll be honest with you," Will replied. "I doubt she really has anything life-changing to share about the phone calls. I'm pretty sure she just wants to meet you." Now it was Will's turn to redden. He looked down at the floor. By admitting that, he was basically confessing he'd talked to his family about me.

"Oh," I said, considering. Will *must* have been talking to his parents about me. And if he was talking about me—No. Of course not. It was simply that they were curious about me and the bakery.

"Sure. I mean, since we're working together and everything. She probably wonders about the family who owns the bakery," I said, trying to act calm.

"Right. I'm sure that's it," Will hurriedly added. "Can I pick you up at seven, then?"

"Yes, sounds great." I could hear my voice coming out like a robot, as if that would cover up the awkwardness instead of making it worse. I felt the gangly teenage girl hiding inside of me emerging and tried to quiet her.

"Okay. And come hungry. Mom doesn't take no for an answer when it comes to filling your plate. And refilling it."

I smirked. "Well, I think by tonight, the pancakes from yesterday will have worn off. But I'm going to have to constrain myself from eating more of the Elvish Delight cookies. They're to die for."

Will beamed. "I'm glad you like them."

We stood strangely then, and I wasn't sure how to disengage from the conversation. My head was swirling with thoughts about meeting Will's family, meatloaf, and what he'd told them about me. Mrs. Stella raised her hand like a school child, and I was thrilled to have to deliver another scone to her.

The rest of the day passed in a whir. Grandma eventually stopped in after the diner to see how the recipes were coming. She gave both cookies her stamp of approval and swore she couldn't tell which one was Will's recipe— although I knew she was just being kind. I told her I was going to Will's for dinner and not to make a big deal of it. She immediately made a big deal of it, asking if I had anything to wear and if she and Herb should go pick something up at the Dresses and More Boutique that just opened.

"I think it's casual," I said.

"Oh, dear. Meeting the parents is never casual. Remind me later and I'll tell you about when I first met your grandpa's parents. It ends with a tablecloth lit on fire."

"We're just friends," I said, deciding that loudly proclaiming that statement since we were in earshot of Will was more pertinent than my innate curiosity at the comment about the tablecloth. I made a mental note to check in on that story later because it sounded like great book material.

"We'll see," Grandma said, and my jaw popped open. Before I could argue, she was whisking Herb away to Dresses and More, promising she'd find something appropriately stunning.

Will had overheard the conversation and was chuckling. "Why do I have a feeling you might be coming to dinner in a ballgown when your grandma is done?"

"I'm sorry. She just gets ahead of herself when it comes to me and my love life." And then, after saying "love life" in reference to Will and his family, I froze. I wished I could retract the words. Will, though, just carried onward with the conversation.

"Don't they all?" he asked. "Trust me, I'm sure my mother will embarrass me at least a little. Or a ton. If she gets out old photo albums, you have to swear to me you'll deny them."

"I'll do no such thing," I said, wondering what toddler Will looked like.

The rest of the day went smoothly, although my nerves were growing. I was meeting his parents, and, regardless of our situation, it would be nerve-racking.

I remembered meeting Jed's parents for the first time. He took me to their country club, where everyone was dressed like corporate CEOs. Not understanding their country club dress code, I had shown up in dark-wash jeans and a blouse and felt humiliated. His parents barely said three words all night, and I kept struggling with what fork to use on the immensely decorated and complicated table setting. It was disastrous, perhaps a premonition of where Jed and I would ultimately end.

This was different, I reminded myself. Will and I were friends. Co-workers. Nothing more. This was just some friendly, homemade meatloaf and a discussion about the bake-off.

Still, when I got home and Grandma presented me with the inarguably gorgeous, chic black dress Herb had helped her pick out for me, I couldn't help but feel like maybe this was more important to me than I wanted to admit.

Because even though we'd just met, something in my gut was telling me Will and I were much more than co-planners for the bake-off. Something else was marinating between us. I just hadn't decided yet if it was worth the risk for either of us or if he even felt it.

FIFTEEN

Will was at the door a few minutes early, and I had to admit to the butterflies, now a familiar sensation, fluttering in my stomach when I heard the doorbell. Edmund, of course, galloped to the door before anyone else could consider approaching it. I walked into the living room in time to see Edmund not only slurp Will's face but also try to grab the two bouquets of flowers he was holding.

As the commotion died down and Will handed Grandma a bouquet of yellow roses, I felt myself twirling my hair, which I'd decided to curl. He turned to look at me and was still for a moment. I considered that I'd gone too far overboard with the hair, makeup, and sleek black dress featuring rhinestone beading on the cap sleeves. I suddenly felt like a wannabe prom queen instead of a twenty-six-year-old writer going to a semi-business meeting with a semi-co-worker. Things had certainly gotten complicated in Star Creek.

"You look beautiful," Will announced, crossing the floor to hand me a bouquet of white roses.

"Herb picked the dress," Grandma whispered from

across the room, steadying herself on the back of the sofa. "She's a knockout in it, huh?"

Jed and I had gone out hundreds of times in fancy clothes, and he'd complimented me frequently. But there was something different about the way Will said it with a quiet sense of comfort, like he was stating a fact, not like he was checking off a box on a list. It made me feel like I could stand taller, and I stopped worrying if I'd gone over the top.

"It's just the first time you've seen me without a ponytail and sweating in the bakery," I teased, realizing it was true.

"Hey, you look beautiful then too. Even when you're burning my cookies," he joked, and Grandma snickered.

"That was one batch." I could feel my cheeks warming.

"Three so far, Ms. Carter, if I'm counting correctly."

I rolled my eyes but crossed the living room to put the roses in a vase Grandma was already getting out. My hands felt sweaty because this most definitely was seeming more like a date than a friendly business meeting with meatloaf. Will even wore a collared shirt. And he'd brought flowers. This was starting to feel like something else entirely.

"You two have fun," Grandma said, ushering us out. Herb was on his way over with Chinese takeout.

I considered scolding him because Grandma really was supposed to be eating healthier according to the doctor. But that could be a conversation for another time. I smiled, thinking about how good it was that Grandma wasn't alone. We had a few weeks left until the bake-off, and it was good to know that even when I returned to New York, she would be more than okay.

I brushed thoughts of New York aside. I was here now, in Star Creek, getting into a car with a handsome baker who was making me laugh as he sang along with the radio as soon as we took off. I felt a little nervous, but those feelings were assuaged by his easy demeanor and charming conversation.

I was hooked, if I was being honest. And although that scared me, I knew that was part of the territory.

DÉJÀ VU KICKED in as Will opened the door and a big dog immediately galloped toward me. His parents had a golden retriever, but he was gigantic for his breed. Stanley, as they called him, immediately took a running jump onto me, and I stumbled backward into Will.

It wasn't quite the greeting I had envisioned with his parents. The Westerlys wrangled Stanley off me and then panicked when they realized muddy pawprints covered my brand-new black dress.

"I'm so sorry," Will apologized, enunciating each word carefully. "Let me get you a towel."

I smiled, pushing back my hair and laughing as I examined the distinct muddy marks all over my dress.

"It's completely fine. I'm used to Grandma's Great Dane, so it's nothing new, truly. This isn't even that bad. Hello, everyone," I said, realizing in Will's flustered state, he hadn't had a chance to introduce me. Everyone smiled, a collective sigh of relief passing among us as we realized the pressure to be perfect had gone by the wayside. An elderly man, who I decided was Will's grandfather, then wandered out with a cane. He eyed my dress and the situation and shrugged.

"Looks like a trendy new dress pattern if you ask me," he said, and Will's parents shook their heads. Will's grandpa hobbled forward, shooing the large dog away.

Stanley clearly respected the man and moved out of his path and sat calmly. The man patted the dog on the head and then, when he reached me, outstretched his hand.

"I'm Grandpa John. It's good to finally meet the woman Will won't stop talking about at family dinners. You're right, Will. She is quite a looker," he shouted. Grandpa John warmly shook my hand, and I felt myself blush. Will had been talking about me and not just platonically, if Grandpa John was to be believed.

Returning from the kitchen emptyhanded, Will groaned, and his mother chuckled.

"I'm sorry, it seems in the confusion, Will forgot to introduce us. I'm Cindy Westerly," Will's mom said, stepping forward to hug me. I hesitated due to the mud, but she didn't think twice.

"And I'm Levi," his dad said, giving me a little wave.

"Enough formalities. Why don't we gather around the table? Dinner's almost ready. Lucy, would you like a change of clothes?" Cindy asked me.

I looked at the muddied dress, shrugged, and said, "I'll be okay. Just a towel will do."

Will promptly smacked himself on the forehead. We all flinched. "Shoot, I'll get that. Oh my goodness, this dog has me frazzled."

"Or maybe it's the pretty girl you brought home," Grandpa John said with a chuckle, nudging me in the ribs before sauntering to the dining room. Stanley trailed him.

I followed Will to the kitchen, where he handed me a towel. I wiped at the pawprints, which promptly smeared, making the problem worse. I shook my head and laughed.

"I'm so sorry again," he said, and I realized as I studied him that I'd never seen him so flustered.

I put the towel on the counter, figuring it was a lost

cause. "It's really fine. I love dogs, so I don't care. As long as you don't mind sitting next to a muddy woman at dinner."

He shook his head and, putting his hand on the small of my back, led me to the dining room. We settled around the table, and Cindy retrieved the meatloaf from the oven. We said grace and then passed around enough food to feed a small army. Cindy had clearly gone overboard, but the food looked amazing.

"Lucy, I wanted to update you on the phone calls I made for the festival. Everything is set as you needed. But before we get to business, I just wanted to get to know you. Will says you're here from New York for a while?" she asked, jumping right in. I was happy she wanted to learn more about me. She'd already surpassed the word count of Jed's mother on our first meeting.

"Yes, I'm from the city. I recently moved back in with my best friend, Serena. She's a lawyer."

"I see," Will's dad said. He'd mostly been quiet through the earlier fiasco, but now he smiled at me. "I also hear you're a romance novelist with quite an impressive talent. Will said you're a beautiful writer. I'm not a romance kind of guy, but I'll take his word for it."

I turned to look at Will. "You read my books?" My mind flashed to that night I passed him going into the bookstore.

Will blushed again. He was definitely wearing his nerves on his sleeve tonight. It was charming. "Yeah, I did. I'm not much of a reader, but I thought it was pretty cool to be working with a writer and I wanted to check them out. I hope that's not weird."

"I mean, it's always terrifying as an author to know someone is reading your work. But I appreciate it."

"Well, let me tell you, Will isn't a reader, but he liked them so much, he passed them on to me, and now I'm basically your author page's stalker. You're talented, Lucy. What made you decide to live in New York?" Cindy asked.

"It was just something I always wanted to do. Before she died, my mother worked in the city. As a little girl, I always loved watching her go off to work in her heels and her suit. She'd come home with stories about singers and the sky-high buildings and the coffee shop she loved on the corner. There was just so much energy there. I wanted to be a part of that, and I felt like it would inspire my writing. Plus, my best friend, Serena, was going to the city for law school, so it felt like a perfect opportunity."

"I'm sorry about your parents. That can't be easy. I lost my mom when I was in my twenties too." Cindy was seated across the table from me. She reached over to pat my hand. Usually, I hated feeling like people pitied me. But looking in her eyes, I saw a motherly concern, almost as if my own mother were seated across from me. It brought tears to my eyes.

"It's been hard on me and on Grandma. But she always reminds me we're strong. Or tough cookies, as she would say." I grinned. "She loves a good baking pun."

"Well, Will here is lucky to have a job with her. I told him those hoity-toity bakeries in the city were overrated. And I told him from the beginning he shouldn't trust a girl like his ex," Grandpa John chimed in.

Will's dad cleared his throat, and an awkward energy took over. I glanced at Will to see him pushing his potatoes around.

"We're thankful your grandma hired him," Cindy said, trying to redirect the conversation to positive territory.

I followed her lead. "Well, it's easy to see why Grandma snagged him up. He's amazing at what he does, truly. I'm glad he's in Star Creek, and I know my grandma is too."

He looked at me then, and I saw some of the melancholy fade away. It was a moment worthy of a sweet, romantic scene in one of my novels.

Sadly, that was the exact moment Stanley decided the meatloaf looked scrumptious. He jumped on the table near me, creating a scene of chaos, spilling wineglasses, and scarfing up the remaining meatloaf. Screaming ensued, and Grandpa John said some choice words that were not appropriate for the dinner table.

When the dog had finally been removed from the dining room by Grandpa John's stern voice, we all stared at each other. Potatoes, meatloaf, and wine were strewn everywhere. The dining room table looked like a tornado had hit, and my muddy dress was no longer the biggest mess to contend with. We all sort of looked around, not sure what to do, the monstrosity of the mess breathtaking in all the wrong ways.

And then Will's dad started laughing. Not a quiet chuckle, but an out loud, mouth open guffaw. That was all it took. Soon, we were all giggling so hard we were crying. When Grandpa John returned from putting Stanley outside, he stopped in the doorway and stared at us.

"What's happening now?"

No one answered him. We just kept laughing, me in my muddy dress, the whole family covered in bits of food. After a while, we got to work cleaning up, doing dishes, and wiping down remnants of Stanley's fiasco from the floor. Cindy was singing while she washed dishes, and Will joined in. I could see karaoke ran in the family.

Levi busted out another bottle of wine and retrieved the family tradition—Pictionary. We gathered in the living room near the enormous, perfectly decorated Christmas tree. We formed teams, Grandpa John playing with me and

Will. I almost spit out my wine when Grandpa John asked if Will had learned to draw from Stanley.

The night flew by. It was messy and chaotic, but overall, it was the kind of night I had craved. Friendship, laughter, and nothing too serious. Cindy eventually brought out the baby pictures to accompany the cheesecake and eggnog she'd made, and I smiled my way through Will's childhood. I took special note of all the ones of him in the kitchen, a little boy with the widest grin. With Cindy's cheesecake, it was easy to see where his inspiration in the kitchen came from.

When it was finally so late that Grandpa John started nodding off, I decided, begrudgingly, to call it a night.

"I had the best time," I said, hugging Cindy and Levi before making my way to Grandpa John.

"You come back now. And let us know if you need more help with the bake-off. We're glad to help. Although, Grandpa John might eat more cupcakes than he helps make," Cindy admitted. We had never really gotten to anything else related to the business part of the night, but that was okay. Everything was in place, and I wasn't feeling worried about it at all.

After we'd said our goodbyes, we turned to leave, Will's hand on the small of my back once more. It felt natural.

"Son, she's loads better than that other girl. Nothing like her in all the best ways," Grandpa John whispered, but it was loud enough for me to hear. I tried to pretend I hadn't, but I couldn't help wondering what the story was—and if Will would ever fill me in.

Whatever had happened in New York had clearly done a number on him and perhaps on the whole family. I could see that behind Will's comedic, warm personality was a man who was dealing with his own battles and heartbreak, probably not so different from mine. I hoped someday he would see that he could trust me with the story. And maybe someday, I'd feel better about unloading mine on him.

"I had a wonderful night," I said to Will as we stood on the doorstep of his parents' house. I wrapped my coat around myself a little tighter. The night was warmer than it had been recently but still cold. Our breaths made puffy clouds in the air between us, mingling together in abstract shapes.

"Thank you for coming. Sorry it was so chaotic."

I shrugged. "Let's call it energetic instead."

"Sounds good to me."

We stood there for a long moment. I stared up into his eyes and, the way he looked at me, I thought maybe this was the moment. This was when it would all change for us.

But he turned and looked at his car.

"You must be freezing," he said, nodding toward it. I followed his lead and got into the passenger seat, shoving down the disappointment that was slight but perceptible as he drove me back to my grandma's house.

Still, thinking back on the night and his family, I couldn't help but smile.

SIXTEEN

The countdown was on as the calendar flipped to Friday, December 1. Although we had checked off quite a few tasks from the to-do list, my heart was racing looking at all we still had to do.

Grandma had convinced me she should come back to the bakery to help again on Friday. After a lengthy questionnaire to make sure she was feeling okay and a pinkie promise that she'd tell me if she started feeling dizzy or tired, I drove us into the bakery. Herb had a bowling league tournament that morning, so he was busy anyway. I didn't like the idea of Grandma being alone and wanted to keep an eye on her. At least at the bakery, I could accomplish that.

On our short drive over, I asked Grandma to elaborate on the tablecloth story she'd mentioned. She glowed at the thought of the tale, and she was so excited, the story just flowed out of her as if it had happened yesterday.

"After the night in the bar where we danced, we were basically inseparable. I was working as a secretary then, and your grandfather had taken a job in the coal mines. We were both exhausted at the end of the day and, quite frankly, not living the life of our dreams. But after his long shift, he'd come and pick me up. We'd go out for coffee or to the local bakeries. He hadn't grown up in Star Creek like me, so I used to tease him that he was a transplant. He had moved to town for his work a few months before I met him. He was a city boy at heart, which was why I think your mother always had dreams of New York. We spent those next two weeks exploring the town. It was wonderful seeing it from his point of view. My family met him and, of course, loved him. And then, two weeks in, he wanted to take me home to meet his parents."

I followed the story, imagining the younger version of my grandparents that I'd seen in pictures.

"His parents lived in Richmond, Virginia, so it was a four-hour drive. It was a scenic trip, and I should've been excited, but I was sweating through my clothes. He'd prepped me that Ruby Easton was a difficult woman to please. She was from a generation where women were seen and not heard, for sure, and she didn't understand this new wave of women who were working. In truth, I didn't like her even before I met her, but I tried to stay open minded."

"Sounds like a gem," I said sarcastically.

"Well, she didn't welcome me with open arms, but his father *was* a gem. Even then, baking was my passion, so I brought the family a box of cookies. Ruby promptly stowed those on the counter, not wanting her own dessert to be outshined. Throughout dinner, your grandfather held my hand under the table as Ruby Easton peppered me with questions about my past and about what a good girl like me was doing in a bar the night we met. Things just weren't going well, and I was feeling hot and sweaty. I started to think it had been a mistake, that as much as I was falling for your grandfather, I couldn't marry a man with a mother like her. I wouldn't let my dreams be crushed. I was thinking about how horrible it would be to have my heart broken yet again when your grandfather leaped up from the perfectly set dining room table."

We'd pulled into the bakery, and I put the car in Park, but neither of us moved. I had to hear the rest.

"What happened?" I asked.

"He let his mother have it, which, according to the rest of the family, was unprecedented. Even his father never spoke back to the unthrottled Ruby Easton. But in that moment, he told her how it was going to be. He told her she would respect his future wife, and that he loved me. It had only been two weeks at that point. Looking back, it was crazy. I'm surprised I didn't go running regardless. But, in truth, I was feeling it too. And when he stood up to his mother, the woman he loved and respected the most, to protect me, I knew beyond a doubt. He would go to the ends of the earth to love me. I knew he was it for me. Most of all, I knew I could be brave enough to love again."

"That's so sweet," I said, smiling at the thought as my heart warmed.

"Oh, it was. Until your grandfather slammed a hand on the table, which caused one of the many pillar candles to topple over. The precious tablecloth caught on fire, screams ensued, and the dinner literally went up in flames. His dad had to rush to get water from the kitchen to put the fire out, which he mercifully did. If firetrucks had to show up at my first time meeting the family, I'm not so sure the wedding would've happened."

She shook her head, smiling—but then her face grew more serious. I could tell that reliving the past was more difficult than she was letting on. She turned her head to look out the window and sighed. We sat in the quiet for a long moment, my grandma pulled into a different time, into the memories that were entertaining but probably not easy to revisit. I could understand that. Because sometimes the memories reminded you with a stabbing in your chest exactly what was lost, of the people who weren't in your life anymore.

"Did Ruby ever accept you?" I asked after a long moment when my grandma cleared her throat and turned back to me with a soft smile. She wiped at a rogue tear running down her cheek, and I scolded myself for pushing her too much, for making her relive the memories. What if it was getting in the way of her recovery?

"Yes, actually," Grandma replied. "Because in that moment, I think she saw how crazy your grandfather was about me, and vice versa. We never had an issue after he almost burned down the entire house with his flailing hands. However, the family did relentlessly tease me about bringing flames to dinner for the rest of our marriage."

I patted Grandma's hand. "I'm sorry."

"For what, dear?"

"Making you relive the memories. I know it's probably hard on you."

"Darling, I'm always reliving the memories. Now, I just get to share them with someone who understands the loss a little bit. I'm okay. I am," she reassured, patting my hand.

I smiled but wondered if she was telling the truth. My grandma and grandpa had such an epic love story spanning so many years. I couldn't imagine what it was like—to lose your other half.

Slowly, we peeled ourselves out of the car, and I made a mental note to remember every detail of the story. Because that was what love really was. It wasn't perfect. Sometimes things even caught on fire. Still, it was having someone who was willing to go to the ends of the earth to protect you and love you. It was having someone you would risk everything for. Someone you would replay memories for even when it was painful to do so. In short, it was beautiful.

Will was singing loudly in the bakery, already at work, of course, when we went in.

"There you two are. I saw you in the parking lot and thought there was a staff meeting I wasn't invited to," he teased as he rolled out some sugar cookie dough.

"We were just strolling down memory lane," Grandma said. "Do you ever sleep? You know I don't expect you to live here, right?"

He shrugged. "I love coming in and getting a head start. I work out emotions on the dough."

"Reminds me of someone else I knew a long time ago," she murmured, her eyes looking teary. She joined him then, washing her hands and getting a chunk of dough to roll out. They started talking about cookie dough thickness and ingredients. I could see Grandma was right—Will had the same passion for Star Creek Bakery that she'd always had. It was a moving thing to witness someone's dreams come true.

I didn't know what had happened in New York, and I felt sad for him that things hadn't worked out. But as I watched him in the kitchen with Grandma, he seemed to be exactly where he belonged. He'd found a new version of his dream, which wasn't always a bad thing.

I thought of my book then, coming along slowly but not perfectly. It had taken getting out of New York to find my muse. I was writing a book I'd never considered—but it was turning out to be a book I was so proud of. Maybe I was right where I belonged too.

And then, I thought about the plane ticket. I'd been so certain traveling was the answer for me, the dream to pursue. When I bought that ticket, I felt my whole body come alive. I'd felt the moroseness of my post-Jed world lift free as I felt re-energized again. But standing in the middle of the bakery, I thought for a moment that maybe my dream had transformed. Maybe going abroad wasn't what I needed after all—which was a good thing, because as the days went by, I was pretty certain Paris was getting further and further away from possibility.

Mom and Dad's tragic car accident had thrown me for a loop. It made me question everything. The one thing it taught me, though? Family was everything. Making memories was everything. And being back in Star Creek with everyday interactions with Grandma made sense.

"You look lost in your own world," Grandma said after all her cookies were on the pan.

I snapped out of it, realizing I'd just been standing there frozen, thinking.

"A little. I was thinking about Mom and Dad," I whispered, and Grandma nodded.

"There's not a day that goes by that I don't think about them. I'm sure it's the same for you. It's so hard, isn't it?" She wiped her hands on her apron and walked over to me. We embraced, and being in Grandma's arms somehow assuaged the pain. I inhaled the familiar cinnamon and floral scent of her perfume and leaned into the moment. Moments were precious, after all.

"Do you ever wish you'd spent more time with Mom?" I asked, tears flooding down my face. The stabbing pain from that day four years ago rushed back. Sure, time had dulled the edges slightly and crumpled the center, but the pain was still there. It was always there, I'd learned. Grief was relentlessly willing to rear its wicked visage at any moment. It was something I had learned to exist with.

Grandma studied me. She knew what I was asking. "Your mother knew you loved her. She was so proud of you, Lucy. She was thrilled that you were out living your dreams. That's all a mother ever wants for her child. Do we fantasize about our children staying put in our town forever, working with us, spending every waking minute with us? You bet. Because to us, you're always our lifeblood, our entire heart. But we also know you have your own life to live, and your mother knew that. She was happy knowing you were brave enough to go after your dreams, even if they took you away from her."

We headed to the corner table out front where we'd been sitting to do our festival planning. I had my laptop with me and set it on the table. Grandma's words tried to sink into my heart, but the guilt was still overflowing. When my parents died, the weeks after were a blur. Grandma helped me through, of course, with everything from the estate to funeral plans. She'd come to New York for a few weeks and stayed with Serena and me as I navigated the grief. However, the predominant feeling that kept bubbling up along with the deep melancholy was guilt.

I hadn't spent enough time with Mom in her final months. Caught up in my novel writing and, in truth, the vibrancy of the city, I'd ignored her phone calls sometimes. I'd shrugged off making it home to see her and Dad as often as I should have. I'd used "I'm so busy" as an excuse to reject her offers to come into the city for lunch or dinner. She was a ferry ride away, yet I could count on one hand our interactions in those last months. I assumed, like we so often do, that there would be time for that. I would have years and years to make up for the moments I was missing. So I lived my life and ignored hers. And then, all of a sudden, it was too late.

Grandma had been a proponent from that very first day that I had nothing to feel guilty about. Even though she, too, was drowning in sadness over the loss of her daughter and son-in-law, she'd been the pillar who supported me in the darkest hours of my life. She'd helped me get to a place where I could celebrate the memories, the lives they lived, instead of just mourning what was missing. Still, every now and then, the grief and the shame crept back in.

"Your mother would want you to keep living the life you want, Lucy. That's the biggest way you can honor her memory. Live the life you want, no matter what that looks like. She was never afraid to do that."

I nodded, swiping at the tears. "It's so hard," I whispered.

"Life is hard. But if you're lucky, you find a few good people who can lead the way through the difficult times and help you come out the other side."

I smiled, appreciating I was lucky in that sense. I had an amazing best friend, Serena, who would do anything for me and vice versa. I had Grandma, who was sometimes sassy and a little bit nosy, but also an amazing column of strength. Her love for me radiated in every word she said, and her kindness was something the whole community appreciated. It was part of the reason she'd started the Star Creek Holiday Bake-Off. She'd wanted to bring the town together, for everyone to feel a sense of love and family during the holiday season, whether they had loved ones or not.

"Let's talk about some of the things left on our to-do list," I said, wiping away the tears and desperately wanting to switch the topic.

"I've been thinking for a few days about adding a new tradition to the festival," Grandma said as Will delivered us both a cup of coffee.

He leaned on the back of my chair for a moment, listening to Grandma's idea. His nearness made my stomach flutter, but I focused on her words.

"I want to have a way to honor all those we have loved. I'm thinking we could make a memory wall somewhere at the festival, where everyone can write a message for someone they have loved and lost. A memorial wall of sorts, maybe with holiday lights. Just a way to let people know it's okay to grieve, and it's okay to still love those we've lost, especially during the holiday season."

"I think that's absolutely beautiful," Will said, patting me on the shoulder as I nodded.

Without thinking, I reached up and covered his hand with my own, the feeling of warmth pulsing through my body in an undeniable fashion.

Grandma didn't wink or make any funny comments. She just smiled that smile that said it all. I didn't fight it; I was too lasered in on how touching her idea was and how much my mother would have loved it.

"I adore the idea," I admitted, and then reached down to type into my laptop, adding the concept for the wall. "We should work on the festival map so we can release it to the newspaper. Do you have last year's?"

Grandma nodded and headed to the back office to find it. I was glad she seemed to be getting around better today, only leaning on every other table on her way to the back. Will took her seat across from me as he waited for the cookie timer to go off. He leaned back in the chair.

"Are you ready for your first Star Creek Holiday Bake-Off? You've never been before, right?" I confirmed.

He shook his head. "No. My family has, but I was always busy the days leading up to Christmas. It's a pretty big day in the baking world."

"Did your bakery have a big event last year?" I asked, feeling like this was neutral territory.

Nonetheless, his face tightened. "No, not really. We were too busy celebrating. But this festival sounds amazing."

I thought about last Christmas. I hadn't made it to Star Creek because Jed had whisked me away to the Rocky Mountains for a romantic getaway. Grandma said she understood and had literally forbidden me from coming to the festival.

"Our cupcakes can't compete with a romantic getaway, even if they are the best in the state," she'd said.

Jed and I had a great weekend, but I'd missed the Star Creek Bake-Off. I'd missed seeing Grandma in her element and the entire town gathering to hear the winner at the gazebo in the town center. I missed all the companionship of the neighbors joining together, the excitement buzzing in Town Hall as every corner of the building was jam-packed with joyous people celebrating Christmas and all its traditions. And now that I was understanding just how much planning went into the festival on Grandma's part, I felt horrible I hadn't offered to help in the past.

"Your grandma's such an amazing lady. This bakery is a staple in town because of what she's accomplished here. It's really inspiring, I think. It makes me feel like maybe I could do something this great someday," Will said, leaning forward. "It reminds me why I wanted to start a bakery in the first place."

"You could do it, Will. I know you could. You're a natural here."

He exhaled. "Well, I don't know. I had my own bakery already, and it didn't go so well. I ran it with a partner, and things didn't work out like I'd planned."

This was news to me. I knew he'd had a bakery in the city—but not that he had a business partner. I was starting to piece together the story, or at least starting to make inferences. I assumed this partner was probably more than just a business associate. That would explain a lot.

"I'm sure it wasn't your fault," I offered, not really knowing what else to say.

He shrugged. "It depends on who you ask. But I was so glad your grandma gave me a second chance at my dream. Most people won't hire a failed business owner."

"Most people aren't as wise as me," Grandma said, returning with a file in her hands. "Business is tricky. Just because you have one that doesn't take off for one reason or another doesn't mean you can't be successful somewhere else. I was lucky that when I opened this place, there wasn't any place like it around. It helped me get off the ground and build myself as a feature in this town. New York is such a densely packed market. Plus, if you don't have the right business partner, you're doomed."

The timer went off, and Will returned to the kitchen after thanking Grandma for her kind words. She passed the festival map over, but I was staring after Will.

"What happened?" I asked in a hushed whisper.

Grandma shrugged. "I don't know. He doesn't like to talk about it, so I don't press him. I just know he left the business, and the partner kept it going. Apparently, it has a new name and everything now."

"Doesn't that worry you? Didn't you check into it? Or call his references before hiring him?" Suddenly, I realized Will Westerly wasn't someone we knew all that well. What if the reason the business hadn't worked out was something really scary or criminal?

Grandma smirked. "Darling, my instincts have never

failed me yet in this business. When people told me I should've done more research before buying this building, I told them I just knew in my gut it was right. And it's worked out. So many times over the years, I've let my intuition guide me. When Will Westerly strolled into this building asking if we were hiring, I knew from the second I saw him he was a good fit. And he has been. He's here early, he's great with the customers, and he's an even better baker than me, if I'm being honest. We all have a past, and we all have a laundry list of failures. I care about character. I care about having someone who is passionate."

"I'm not sure modern human resource policies would align with your hiring practices. But you're right, he's great at what he does. I'm glad he's making your life easier."

"And he doesn't seem to be making your life any harder," she said, raising her eyebrows. "Now, let's look at this map and see what changes we need to make."

Grandma was laser-focused on the festival, and I didn't stop to argue or turn the conversation back to Will. Still, she was right. He was part of the reason it wasn't so hard moving to Star Creek, even if it was temporary. He'd made things so much easier on me, and not just when it came to the festival. A few weeks before, I'd been crying myself to sleep over Jed. Now, I found myself inspired, happy, and feeling hopeful about the future.

It was crazy. I'd only known Will a little over a week. But maybe Grandma was right. Maybe I really should trust my gut. It seemed to tell me every time Will Westerly was close that he was exactly the kind of guy I needed.

SEVENTEEN

Grandma had planned on going to the bakery with me to help with some details again, but the Pennsylvania winter had other plans. A snowstorm blew in the night before, and the weather took a major turn. By the time we woke up on Saturday morning, it was clear we weren't going anywhere.

Grandma sat at the kitchen table with a cup of tea. Edmund got up and strolled to the front window. I peeled back the curtain.

"It's still coming down. We have about a foot already." The snow was beautiful and gleaming, although I knew the aftermath of the storm wouldn't be. No one posted pictures of the reality of the cleanup on social media—like matted, sweaty hat hair or the aching back you get from the loaded shovels of snow.

"Looks like we're stuck in for the day. I think I'll make lasagna and maybe some Christmas cookies. Maybe we could decorate this place for Christmas too? I wouldn't mind putting up some of the décor. Do you want to help?" Grandma asked.

"I don't want you overdoing it," I said, knowing she would shrug it off.

"A little holiday cheer and baking isn't going to kill me," she said.

"Okay, but you're getting help." I thought about my looming deadline, as my laptop stared at me from the kitchen counter. "Do you mind if I do some writing first? I'm making some progress and want to keep it going."

I'd been writing every night, even when the bakery and the planning of the bake-off had me absolutely exhausted. The words were flowing faster than I could keep up with. Grandma's love story had sparked the muse, and the town was giving me plenty of filler information as well. From the laundromat downtown where the elderly women gathered to gossip, to the Route 22 Diner, I had so many cute locales to draw from and some charming characters. Really, Star Creek itself made a perfect character, its charisma and quaintness brimming everywhere I looked.

Grandma's story was the springboard, but now the creative juices were unstoppable. I felt like I was turning my grandparents' love story into something universal that would strike a chord with so many readers. In short, I didn't yet feel like trashing the entire manuscript, and I was already about a quarter of the way through. It was progress even my agent would be happy with.

"Of course! You go write your heart out. I'll get started on the lasagna and then maybe later you can take a break to help with cookies and decorating?"

"Sounds perfect. Thank you. Yell, though, if you need anything. And take breaks."

"I don't want to interrupt your flow. I might actually take Edmund over to visit Herb; that way you'll have some quiet."

"Please be careful. The snow is deep. Do you want me to shovel first?" I looked out at the precariously high snow drifts. The last thing Grandma needed was a fall on top of everything else, and with the way Edmund ran through the snow, the chances were pretty high.

Grandma peered out as well, saying, "Oh," when she saw how deep it was.

I was just getting ready to say I'd pile on some snow gear and head out to shovel when I saw the outline of a person trudging down the sidewalk. The figure was bundled up tight so only a nose peeked out and some eyes. Winter boots, gloves, and a red shovel accessorized the look. I wondered who it was and where the person was headed in this weather when they stopped in front of Grandma's house, leaned on the shovel for a moment, and then got to work.

"Looks like our snow hero is here," Grandma said.

I squinted, trying to discern who it was. We stared in silence, both perhaps trying to figure out the same mystery, when, as the person shoveled, a song erupted from his mouth. It was muffled due to the scarf and us being indoors, but there was no mistake.

Will Westerly had come to dig us out.

"I knew he was a perfect gentleman," Grandma excitedly announced, shaking my arm. "I'm going to thank him and invite him in for tea when he's finished."

"I've got it. I don't want you falling," I said, grabbing my coat and boots from beside the door.

"If you say so," she replied, winking.

I trudged out the front door into the blustery snow.

"I CAN'T BELIEVE you walked all this way," I said once the shoveling was finished. I'd stayed outside to keep Will company as he worked. He refused to let me lift a finger. My insistence on helping seemed to offend his masculinity, so I stopped asking—although I wasn't much help in the heavy snow removal department anyway. My back was thankful.

"I figured your grandma and Herb would need digging out, and this snow is so heavy. I also knew if you were out shoveling, your grandma would never stand for that, and I didn't want you and Herb having to battle her to keep her inside."

We took off our wet coats and winter gear inside the door as Edmund rushed to greet Will, nearly knocking him over. The black dog leaped up, standing on his hind legs. His front legs were draped over Will's shoulders, and he still towered over him.

"Oh, Edmund," Grandma said, rushing out with a wooden spoon in her hand, an apron covering her clothes. The dog turned, saw Grandma, and quickly got down. I laughed at the enormous dog who definitely outweighed my grandmother respecting her enough to listen.

"Come in, come in. Herb is on his way. I made a full breakfast to warm everyone up." Grandma ushered us inside, and the warmth of the house enveloped me along with the hearty smells coming from the kitchen—bacon, pancakes, and coffee. I wished Grandma would take it easy, but my stomach grumbled at the heavenly scents.

"Do you just have a fully stocked fridge and pantry at the ready in case a moment like this arises?" I asked, thinking of my apartment with Serena stocked solely with wine, chocolates, and maybe an occasional Greek yogurt.

"You can never be too prepared. I sent Herb for some things last week."

A few moments later, Herb arrived. "Bacon again?" he asked delightedly as he calmed Edmund down and approached the table. "I love having you two around."

We smiled as Grandma scolded him about salt and the ration he was allowed while pointing the wooden spoon at him.

"And I believe you've met your quota for work today," Herb replied, gesturing toward the table.

"Cooking is not work, as I've said before. And I still have a lasagna to make as well as some cookies."

We settled in around the feast Grandma had prepared, the frigid day warmed by the comfort food around us. Edmund received a piece of bacon, and everyone was truly cozy in the conversation. I smiled across the table at Will, thinking of what a good man he was to show up when he did. After breakfast, we all helped clear the table.

"Do you need help with your lasagna? I've never been much of a cook, but I'm wanting to learn," Will offered.

"You can't cook even though you bake things worthy of royalty?" I asked, seriously thrown off.

"We all have our flaws, I suppose. I'm sort of relieved, Will, that you have one. At least we know you're human now. I would love the help if you aren't busy," Grandma said.

"I only had a day of binge-watching TV planned, so I'd enjoy the company, honestly," he said. I knew I didn't conjure the obvious look he shot my way. Maybe it wasn't just snow removal and a cooking class keeping him around. I felt my cheeks warm as I carried a plate over to the sink.

"You," Grandma said, pointing a finger at me. "You get back to that room and write. Don't even think about butting in on our lasagna making. As much as I would love to spend time with you, I will not be the one in the way of your writing."

"But..." I said, fully planning on using the turn of events as an excuse to avoid my manuscript.

"I'm serious. You get back there for at least two hours. If you do a good job, we'll consider letting you come help with the cookies."

"You're right," I admitted, sighing. I was thankful she had ripped my excuse away. I was on a roll and needed to keep it that way.

"She's always right if you ask her," Herb teased, taking his tea over to the couch to sit with Edmund.

"Of course I am. I see you've finally learned," Grandma replied as I headed to the guest room. Grandma starting bossing Will around as soon as I turned away, telling him where to find ingredients and lecturing him about the seasonings. Every step toward my room was a little painful.

I wanted to be in the kitchen watching Will work. I wanted to spend the afternoon getting to know him more.

But Grandma was right. I needed to stay focused and motivated. There was no use in getting distracted this late in the game.

PERHAPS GRANDMA'S bacon and pancakes really did have magical powers, as Herb often suggested. The words flew from my fingertips, and I hit a new word count record in the two hours I spent in my room. I could hear Will, Grandma, and Herb laughing and singing as they worked, but it only seemed to add to my concentration, not take away from it. When I finally emerged from my room feeling productive and empowered, they all smiled my way.

"Did you get some quality writing in?" Grandma asked. She was sitting on a chair at the table, and I could tell she was tired. I offered her a weak smile, not wanting to make her upset by fussing over her.

"I did. I hit a new word count goal and wrote the adorable first kiss scene and even a horse and carriage date scene!" I exclaimed, beaming with pride.

"Is a horse and carriage really the epitome of romance?" Will asked. "Because they look good in the movies, but is it really that fun freezing your fingers off while a horse poops in the street?"

Grandma burst out laughing.

"Hey," I scolded, even though I, too, was wearing a grin at his brutal honesty. "I will have you know that horse and carriage scenes are the height of romance. It's just beautiful and quiet. A big gesture."

"Have you been on one?" Will asked.

"Well, no, but I'm telling you. It's romantic," I admitted, sort of thrown by the fact I hadn't ever been on one even though I wrote that scene into almost every single story. It was a little embarrassing. I should probably think about that.

"We had a horse growing up," Herb said. He was seated at the kitchen table with a fresh cup of tea—or a very cold one from earlier. "It was a nasty old thing. Loved biting kids' fingers and refused to do anything it was told. We called it Marshmallow."

I grinned at the name and pictured Herb as a young child with an untamable horse. Perhaps he was used to working with creatures with wild spirits and that was why my grandmother's spunky attitude didn't bother him.

"Well, some beings don't wish to be tamed," Grandma said as she inspected the lasagna that was cooling on the stove. Perhaps she was thinking the same thing I was.

"That smells amazing," I said, eyeing their work.

"Thanks, dear. We had a team meeting while you were gone and decided lasagna dinner will commence at 6 p.m. followed by decorating and a Christmas movie marathon."

"Movie marathon?" I asked, my interest piqued.

"Yes. The weather isn't letting up, and we decided there was no use in us all sitting at home bored. So, after dinner, we're going to put up a few decorations that Will has graciously agreed to pull down from the attic. Then we'll watch two movies. One is a classic the boys settled on, and one is a movie I picked for us. I'm betting once we start watching, you'll be able to discern which is which," she said, rolling her eyes.

"I like the sound of this. It's a perfect night for movies." I was also happy Will was joining us, although I didn't say that out loud.

"Well, I'm going to head home for a while to be with Sylvester. I do wish he and Edmund would get along better so I could bring him with me." Herb headed toward the door.

"They're getting better. It'll just take some more time," Grandma said as she walked Herb out. "I'll see you at six."

"I'm counting on it," he said, smiling and turning to wave at all of us.

After he was gone, I smirked. "Introducing your pets to each other? That's something a couple does when they're trying to consolidate households."

Grandma groaned. "You and your little match-up schemes. You used to accuse me of meddling in your dating life."

"Yes. And now it's my turn. But in all seriousness, I think you two are adorable together. You glow when he's around, Grandma. There's nothing wrong with another chance at love. That's what some wise people told me a few days ago."

She softened at the words. "Thank you, dear. I do enjoy his company. It's nice not to feel so alone in this world, you know? It's comforting to have companionship. I appreciate it more and more the older I get."

And I did know. I knew what it was like to sit in a cold room alone, feeling like there was no one out there for you. I knew all too well what it was like to love and lose. I knew what it was like to crave companionship, connection.

"Companionship is perfect, which is why I'm glad for the invite tonight," Will interjected from the kitchen. I'd almost forgotten he was there and was a little embarrassed he had overheard my lofty sentiments.

"Of course, Will. Anytime. We owe you more than breakfast and lasagna for saving the day with the snow removal," Grandma said, turning to him.

"By the looks of it, I might need to do a touch-up. I'll come back around five, if that's okay, to see to the walkways."

"You don't have to do that," I said. "I'm capable."

"I know. But I don't mind doing it at all. There's nothing wrong with a second chance at love..." he began, and my heart skipped a beat. "And there's nothing wrong with accepting help for a snowy walkway."

I felt foolish. Had I thought he was confessing his love to me in my grandma's kitchen over a pan of lasagna? Did I even want that? It hadn't even been two months yet since Jed stomped on my heart and shattered my visions of the future.

There was nothing wrong with a second go at love—but that didn't mean I was ready for it.

Did it?

AT FIVE, Will returned with another surprise up his sleeve —or, more accurately, dragging behind him.

A Christmas tree.

Grandma held Edmund back as I opened the door, the snow-laden branches leaving a trail in the yard.

"A tree?"

Will shrugged. "I walked to the lot in town. Turns out Mr. Carlson was there despite the weather. Said a lot of people had the same idea, so I figured we could maybe add it to the night's activities if your grandma is up for it. She mentioned there were quite a few antique ornaments in the attic, so I thought it could be fun."

I was a little worried it might be too much for Grandma, but I turned to see a childlike glow on her cheeks and knew it was perfect. Despite the snow and needles littering the carpet, Grandma exclaimed how beautiful it was and how thankful she was. After letting Edmund go—he promptly tried to tackle the tree—Grandma showed Will to the attic stairs so he could retrieve the base and decorations.

The snow had softened to a lighter pace, the flurries flitting precariously on the winter wind. After Will had retrieved the decorations, Herb arrived. He helped Will settle the tree into the base and into a good spot in the living room, and I helped brush off the snow and clean up while Grandma finished some prep in the kitchen. Will insisted on touching up the sidewalk, removing the layer of snow that had accumulated since he'd left. Herb popped open a bottle of wine and a bottle of non-alcoholic sparkling cider for Grandma since she wasn't supposed to drink alcohol on her new meds. I was impressed he'd had both in stock in his pantry. We abandoned the tree to eat, deciding we'd return to it after our stomachs were full.

"You know, back in the day, I would have been so upset about having to close the bakery today for the snowstorm. I would have been panicking or using the day to get ahead on cleaning the kitchen. I might have even cross-country skied to the bakery if I had to. Now, though, it's been a blessing, hasn't it? I'm loving that we got to spend today tucked away, making memories." Grandma held her glass of sparkling cider in the air, and we all followed suit because her words felt like a toast.

"To making memories in the snow," I said, and everyone clinked glasses.

The lasagna was unsurprisingly amazing, and we all went back for a second slice. We agreed there would be no "shop talk," instead trading fun winter memories and nostalgic stories. Will shared about the first time he went sledding and knocked out his front tooth when he didn't know how to stop. Grandma shared a beautiful memory of making snow angels with Mom, and I swore to myself I would only smile, not cry. I shared about my first snow in the city when Serena and I had traveled through the unusually barren streets for an impromptu, desolate photo shoot at some famous spots. Herb's memory was of his wife during their first snow as a couple, when she'd made her famous potato soup and they'd snuggled up in front of the window.

We all had moments from the snow, memories we'd like to live inside. We'd experienced heartbreak and loss. Still, as we shared tales and laughter around my grandmother's table, there was not a stoic face to be found. That was the beauty of love and memories. You always had the moments to return to. You could always relive those feelings and smiles when you had moments with those you truly loved. They never died, living on in those photographic stories we remembered.

After dinner, we gathered around the tree, which did look lovely. It was just the right size for my grandma's cozy living room. Will and Herb expertly pulled out the string lights, which we were happy to discover still worked. They wrapped the tree as Grandma carefully unwrapped ornaments, tears welling in her eyes at a few handmade ones from my mother and a few Grandpa had bought her. We carefully gathered around, placing ornament after ornament as Grandma walked down memory lane. Some of the ornaments were ones I had made, and Will got a few jabs in at my dilapidated bird and my toothy grin on a self-portrait.

When we were finishing, Will reached into his pocket.

"I have one more, if it's okay," he said. He held out a cupcake ornament to my grandma. "I bought this for you as a holiday gift, but I thought today seemed like a good time to give it to you." It was a gorgeous, delicate ornament made of crystal and gemstones.

My grandma eyed it and could not stop staring. She held it up for Herb to see, and then handed it to me for closer examination.

"Thank you," she said. "It's beautiful."

"And thank you, for welcoming me into your baking family and your home." They hugged, and I smiled at the sweet gesture. I was glad Grandma had Will to help her and to keep an eye on her, and I was glad Will was feeling more comfortable.

"Thank you," I said when Herb and Grandma headed back to the kitchen to refill their drinks. I helped Will carry boxes to the attic. "I appreciate all you've done for us today and for my grandma."

"Of course. She's done so much for me. I know I haven't been here long, but it's starting to feel like I belong here."

"I'm impressed you shopped for the holidays already," I said, smiling. I was usually the organized one, the work-ahead kind of person. I hadn't even thought about holiday gifts yet under the circumstances. I tried not to let the thought worry me, but the next day I'd need to make a list of items to purchase.

We finished carrying the boxes to the attic, and then we all met back in the living room. We claimed our seats; Herb and my grandma perched on one sofa, while Will and I settled in on the other—and then Edmund jumped between us. Grandma couldn't stop laughing as she teased us that there would be no touching between us with Edmund chaperoning. I'd usually be annoyed Grandma was bringing up Will and me in that way, but I couldn't help laughing because Edmund did look so ridiculous, towering over us like the jolly giant he was.

Grandma decided we would start with the guys' movie pick so we could "get it over with." The action movie with slight holiday elements was somewhat interesting, but it just wasn't my cup of tea. Will and Herb all but created a secret handshake as they slapped their knees and looked at each other after pivotal scenes. At least someone was bonding over it, I supposed.

Next was the movie Grandma had picked for us, a classic romance set in a winter wonderland of a small town just like I loved. There was the meet-cute and the first kiss scene that made Grandma and me gasp. There was the tearful breakup and the happy reunion. In short, everything I loved in a romance story. I didn't peel my eyes from the screen the entire time, and I was pretty sure even Edmund was watching. When the final credits rolled, I glanced over to see Will swiping his eyes. I leaned around Edmund to get a better look.

I thought about teasing him, but judging from the despondent look on his face, they weren't just rogue tears at a happily-ever-after. They seemed like more. I let him have his moment, returning to my side of the Edmund blockade.

"Well, the night is still young, I suppose," Grandma said, although Herb was yawning. "At least it is for those of us who are still young."

"You're older than me," Herb replied, leading to a bit of a bickering session over age, emotional age, and the like.

"Regardless," Grandma said, interrupting her own fight, "is anyone up for some cards? I could really go for a game of poker. Your grandfather and I used to play poker when there was a snowstorm like this. We'd sip some hot cocoa and play for cash, although I always won, so it wasn't really a contest." At the mention of my grandfather, I noticed a subtle shift on her face. She cleared her throat, glancing over at the portrait on the wall of the man she'd loved for decades. It couldn't be easy, even after all this time. It couldn't be easy living around the constant memories of the beautiful life you once had together.

"I have no idea how to play poker," I admitted, hoping to bring Grandma out of her sadness. It worked because the three others in the room gasped.

"How can you get to twenty-six and not know how to play poker? Where did you grow up?" Will teased, and I was delighted to hear his steady voice showing no signs of sadness.

"Sorry, it just wasn't at the top of my list of priorities."

"Well, it's at the top of my list of priorities to teach you.

No granddaughter of mine is going through another day of life without understanding the most basic game out there. Now come on."

I looked at Will, wondering if we were unfairly monopolizing his night. He seemed enthused, rushing after my grandmother and animatedly telling a poker story from his culinary school days. Herb and I shrugged and followed the two leaders out to the kitchen. I helped Grandma prep the hot chocolate as Herb and Will got the deck ready.

We spent the next several hours in the world of poker. I learned the basic rules, we drank a lot of hot chocolate, and Grandma did her winning dance quite a few times. Finally, when the clock was nearing an absurdly late hour, the yawns around the table were impossible to ignore. Even Will looked exhausted.

"Well, I think it might be time to call this snow day officially over; what do you all think?" Herb asked, yawning before he got through the entire sentence.

"You just don't want to lose another hand," Grandma teased, but she, too, couldn't fight the yawn.

Will started cleaning up mugs and cards, and we all pitched in. Edmund had long since fallen asleep on the sofa, his snores echoing through the house.

"Will, let me give you a ride home," Grandma offered.

"I'm fine. I don't mind walking," he replied.

"Nonsense, it won't take but a few minutes."

"I like walking in the snow. It's peaceful, and it'll help me clear my head before I go to sleep," he replied, the look on his face wistful. I was getting ready to insist I drive him home, but with his hands in his pockets and his face in a stoic line, I could tell he was mulling over some things. I imagined the movie choice had stirred some strife in him. Maybe that was what he wanted to work out. I could understand that. So many times, walking had been my saving grace, my best therapy after all the dark times in my life.

I led Will to the door as Grandma followed, leaning on Herb's arm. They were chatting about poker and the movies.

"Thanks for everything," I said to Will. "I'm glad you were here. I had fun."

He turned to me at the doorway as he put on his coat. "Me too. This is probably my new favorite snow memory," he admitted, smiling. I could still see the cloud of uncertainty in his eyes and hints of something else—a lightness that came from our time together.

"Me too," I replied. "See you on Monday?"

"You bet," he said, nodding.

"You bet," I parroted.

He nodded again, and then headed out into the night air to go home. I watched him walk down the street until he was a tiny figure, hands in his pockets.

"He's a good bloke," Herb whispered behind me.

I jumped.

"Sorry, didn't mean to scare you. But he is a good one. Great family. And his grandpa John bowls with me. John says Will is really liking it here in Star Creek."

"I wonder why that is?" Grandma asked dramatically, and I turned to see her winking at me, tapping her chin with a gusto that told me exactly what she was getting at.

"See you tomorrow," Herb said to Grandma.

"I'm counting on it," she replied, smiling and waving as he left. We watched closely, making sure Herb made the short trek across the yards to his front door. Then we closed the door on the cold night and headed inside.

"That was a great night," I said as I helped Grandma lock up for bedtime.

"It was. I didn't think Will would ever want to leave," she teased.

"Same with Herb."

We eyed each other from across the kitchen.

"It was almost like a double date," Grandma said cautiously, studying me to see what I said.

I thought about it and shrugged, also looking back at her. "It kind of was, huh?"

We both nodded, neither arguing nor fighting. We were both thinking about the night, about how cozy it felt being there with Herb and Will.

I went to bed thinking maybe it wouldn't be such a bad thing if the evening was labeled as a date. I was also thinking that perhaps my favorite snow memory had shifted too.

I wasn't thinking about what that meant for the future or how scary it was. I wasn't worried about Grandma's recovery or the details of the bake-off—or thinking about the trip I was supposed to be taking. Worry, in short, had slipped away, replaced with something else. Because as I drifted off with the comforter tucked around me, I thought of how peaceful the day had felt with Will close by.

EIGHTEEN

On Sunday, after a full day of writing, I asked Grandma if she minded if I went out for a little while. She had plans to watch some game shows with Herb over at his place and was thrilled when I confessed my plan to her.

"Are you sure you don't need a new dress?" she'd asked as she studied my jeans and baby-blue sweater. I'd swept my hair up into a loose topknot and only swiped on some lip balm. Sundays were always my day to go easy on the makeup and hair—self-care Sunday and all that.

"It's fine, Grandma. We're not exactly going anywhere fancy," I said, smirking.

"A date is a date," she replied.

"It's not a date," I answered.

"There's no backtracking."

I groaned. "Fine. It's a date. Are you happy?" I asked, half teasing her. In truth, despite not going all out with my appearance and the fact that Will didn't know I was popping over, it did feel sort of like a date. The two of us going out after spending the whole day together yesterday.

The butterflies dancing in my stomach. My sweaty palms and constant second-guessing if I was acting like a fool.

It certainly felt like a date.

"Very happy," she replied. And with that, I headed out the door and got in my car.

When I got to the house at the edge of the park, I started to second-guess myself. He just spent the whole day with us yesterday. What if he was busy? Should I have called first? I pulled into the driveway and debated whether to go forward.

It was a ridiculous idea, I decided. *I should be writing all day, not out frolicking.* I was getting ready to put the car in Reverse when Will stepped out his front door onto the huge, Victorian-style front porch. Hands in his pockets, he studied me for a moment, realized who I was, and waved.

There was no going back now. I put the car in Park, internally scolding myself for being so foolish. I peeled myself out of the car as elegantly as possible—which was not elegant at all considering the bulky coat I was wearing. I kept telling myself not to fall in the driveway and make matters worse.

"You didn't lose Edmund again, did you?" Will asked, gesturing toward the open park.

I smiled, shaking my head. "Not this time."

I walked closer to the porch, not wanting to scream from my car but also afraid to get too close in case he turned me down and I needed to bolt. I didn't want him to see the embarrassment on my face.

"So I wanted to thank you again for shoveling yesterday. I thought if you were up for it, I'd take you to my favorite spot in town for dinner. But, you know, if you're too busy or you don't want to... I'm sorry, I should've called first," I rambled, my words whirring out a mile a minute. I paused, shifting my weight to my left foot, waiting for the verdict.

"I'm always in for food. Do you want to come inside while I grab a few things?"

I nodded, walking forward and traversing the wooden steps in front of the charming house. I'd always loved this house as a child, the Victorian, scrolling structure just looking like a house out of a big, romantic movie. All that was missing were two rocking chairs on the porch for sipping coffee and watching the setting sun.

I walked inside Will's home and couldn't stop myself from peering all about. I could tell he hadn't quite settled in yet, but in fairness, it hadn't been that long since he'd moved in. A couple of boxes were still in the corner of the living room. Nonetheless, as Will headed upstairs, I walked up to the gorgeous fireplace and noted a few pictures on the mantel of his family.

I smiled at the photo of Grandpa John and a younger Will holding up a fish near a river. There was a picture of Will at what looked like his culinary school graduation, and a photo of him in a bakery. I walked down the mantel, studying the life of the man I was slowly unwrapping, smiling at his huge grin in each one. His vivaciousness came through the photographs, and for a moment, I wondered who he was before life changed him—before the losses he'd experienced in the city shifted where his life was going. Was he a different version of who I was seeing now? It was impossible to know, and as the thought crossed my mind, I started to wonder if the same could be said about me.

"I haven't had much time for decorating, but I did manage the mantel so far," Will said, startling me as he walked in the room.

"This house is gorgeous," I replied, peeking around at all the details. It had a historical charm to it combined with a modern, eclectic mix of décor. I spotted a few whimsical pieces of furniture around the house as well and assumed they came from Mr. Barbary's shop, which made me smile.

"Come see the kitchen. It's obviously my favorite room," he said, and I followed him through an archway into the adorable kitchen, complete with black-and-white checkerboard tiles on the floor and an island.

"I love this house. Helen used to offer us ice cream on her porch, but there was such a big group of us kids playing at the park when I would visit, we never came inside."

"It's a great house. I was drawn to it immediately, and not just because it was available. A big part of me hopes maybe the family eventually decides to sell it. I would love to buy it."

I nodded. "It would be a great place to live. Sounds like you're really liking Star Creek if you're planning on putting down permanent roots."

He nodded. "Yes, I'm enjoying it very much. When I first came here, I wasn't sure what I was doing. I thought maybe I'd just pass through until I got my life together. But now, I don't know, is it weird it feels like home already?"

"Not at all," I said. Because it was true. I hadn't been back in Star Creek for very long, but something about the place just embraced me. Maybe sometimes our hearts needed a reprieve from all the noise, from being a number in a sea of people. Maybe we all needed to go somewhere we could be known, accepted, and welcomed. If I was being completely honest, I was also thoroughly enjoying the company I was keeping.

"There's just one thing missing here. I would like to get

a cat eventually," Will confessed, snapping me out of my Star Creek reverie.

"You're a cat kind of guy, then?"

"Yes, for sure. We had one growing up, a fluffy white male. His name was Pancake, and he was my best friend. He passed before I went to culinary school, and then I got so busy in New York, I didn't get another. I miss having a cat, though."

"Pancake. That's adorable. We had a cat growing up too. Mine was named Hamlet," I said with a grin.

"Always a writer at heart, even then," Will observed.

"So why don't you get another cat now that you're here?" I asked.

"I will. I just haven't had time with settling in and the bake-off and everything. Once things calm down, I will."

"Do things ever calm down in adult life? I haven't seen proof of that yet."

"You're right," Will offered. "Shall we?" He led me out the door, pretending to be a formal gentleman, rolling his hand in a *you first* gesture that made me laugh. We headed out to my car. Will offered to drive, but I assured him I wanted to.

"So where are you taking me?"

"Just the best place in town. Grandma basically lives there."

"The bakery?" Will teased as I pulled out of his driveway.

"Okay, a place she visits a little less frequently than the bakery," I said, turning down the lane and heading to our destination.

"I PROBABLY SHOULD HAVE ASKED if you like Chinese food," I admitted as we pulled into the Red Dragon Buffet. It was Grandma's favorite place for takeout, but they also had a wonderful buffet that was so big, no one ever left hungry.

"I love Chinese," he said, practically jumping out of the car.

"Have you been here yet?" I asked, hoping I'd found a spot he had yet to discover.

"Your grandma brought me lunch from here once, but I've never had a chance to annihilate the buffet like I'm about to. I'm actually starving, so you had perfect timing."

I smiled as I led the way, excited to be part of Will's first Star Creek Chinese buffet experience. It felt like the perfect place to take him—it was casual but delicious. It didn't scream romance, which was perfectly fine, of course. It was a thank-you dinner for shoveling the snow. Sure, it might feel a little like a date, but it wasn't a full-blown, candles and roses kind of place that would make us both question where the line in our relationship was.

Friendly. Egg rolls. Platonic. Buffet lines.

There was no chance we'd get carried away there, right?

After we settled into our booth, we immediately hit the buffet and loaded up. Our growling stomachs influenced our food choices, and I returned to our table with food heaped high on my plate.

"This place is my new favorite, and I haven't even tasted the food yet," Will said, sitting down across from me.

"Well, when you do, that will just seal the deal."

We both dug into our piles of food, and I savored every bite of the wonton, my favorite. Will raved about basically everything on his plate. After retrieving a second round, we finally slowed down enough to enjoy conversation with each other.

"So tell me, Lucy Carter, what's the big dream?" Will asked before taking a bite of crab Rangoon.

"Writing," I said, shrugging. "It's what I always wanted to do since I was a little girl. I struggled to make friends when I was younger. I was quiet, shy. Books were my refuge, and I always wanted to create that for someone else. I would write these little mini books and make everyone in my family read them. I think Grandma still has a couple, actually. I wrote one about a crow named Sven one year that I was pretty pumped about."

"Sven? That's quite the name for a crow," he said between bites.

I nodded. "I had quite the imagination. I think you have to as an only child."

"I agree," Will said. It was another thing we had in common. "What else is the dream? You've published a few novels now. What's next?"

I stared ahead, thinking about what the answer would have been a couple weeks ago. I thought about the ticket I'd bought.

"I don't know," I admitted. "I mean, I feel like I've achieved my dream, sort of. I have books published. But I'm just always worried my career is drying up, like it's not going anywhere. It's so hard to stay inspired, especially because the sales on my last book sort of slumped. I always wonder if this is it for me or if maybe it was a childish dream to think I could make a career out of writing." Even saying the words made me sad. I thought of the younger version of me coming to Star Creek, tiny hands running down the rows of books as Mrs. Beesworth told me about authors she thought I'd like. I recalled the magic I found in the pages, of how I dreamed of seeing my name on the cover of a book. And it had happened, which was thrilling. But what if this was as far as it went?

"You're too young to give up on your dreams. Come on, what's your wildest dream with your writing? Like, sky's the limit?"

I realized I had never told anyone that because it was too embarrassing. Jed was a realist. He had always tried to keep my feet on the ground when I even hinted at bigger dreams. I looked at Will, knowing I could trust him.

"I want to write a book that millions read. I want to be a household name. I want to be on a book tour that goes international. And I want to inspire at least someone else to chase their dream too." Just like that, over a plate of chicken and broccoli with lo mein, all of my writing dreams poured right out.

Will didn't look shocked or skeptical. Instead, he nodded. "Then make it happen. You'll do it. I know you will."

He didn't know my whole life story or every nuance of my writing career. He barely knew me at all in some ways. There was no reason for him to believe in me. There was no reason I *should* believe his words.

Yet I did. With every ounce of my body, I felt like I could trust not only Will's faith in me, but in my dreams as well. Suddenly, even though I'd sidestepped my plans a bit, the passport in the drawer didn't feel so out of reach.

"I also want to go to Paris for a while to work on a book. I think the City of Love would do wonders for my writing." The words flew out of my mouth. Other than Serena, I hadn't told anyone about my plan, not even Grandma.

"I've never been but heard it's gorgeous. I love all these dreams you have. You light up when you talk about them."

"Okay, your turn. What about you?" I asked, pushing food around on my plate as I was getting full. I needed to leave some room for almond cookies, and, of course, a fortune cookie.

He sighed. "Well, my dream was to run a New York bakery that was world famous. Now, I don't honestly know. I think I would like to own my own bakery again, but not in the city. I think it's too painful there. But starting a bakery anywhere else feels daunting. I guess I'm sort of scared it'll be a failure."

It was the first time I saw Will bare a part of his heart, show his vulnerability. I wasn't ready to let that opportunity go. "Can I ask what happened?"

A frosty look filled his eyes. He glanced away, and I wondered if it was too much to ask him. But then, he turned back, took a breath, and began talking.

"Mostly it was my business partner. Things got complicated, and it wasn't working with us for a lot of reasons. When things fell apart, I ended up here, confused and stressed. I felt like a failure. But your grandma had a 'Help Wanted' sign in the window, so I decided to give it a try. I'm glad I did. Now, I don't know. Maybe a city bakery wasn't what I really wanted anyway. I love that Star Creek Bakery is such a pillar, a legend almost, in the town. I love how the same customers come all the time and you get to know them—not just in the bakery, but in daily life. I love to get their feedback and make new recipes. I didn't always have that in the tourist-laden city."

"I think your dream is a good one too. I think you'll own your own bakery again. You're so talented. It would be ridiculous if you didn't."

"We'll see, I guess. That's both the downfall and excitement of life, isn't it? You just never know what's around the corner."

I concurred, and we both agreed to head to the buffet one last time for a few small desserts. We left the Red Dragon Buffet stuffed but satisfied—with both the food and the company. At the register, Will tried to fight me and insisted on paying.

"No way, pal. This is a thank-you for shoveling snow."

"Is it just a thank-you?" Will asked, sounding slightly downtrodden. He studied me, and I felt myself flush. The owner of the buffet cleared his throat at the register.

"Because, call me old school," Will said, reaching into his back pocket for his wallet, "but I believe a gentleman pays on a date."

Now my face definitely flushed. I didn't argue. I just stood there trying not to look rattled as Will paid for our dinner. As we left and got in my car, he didn't say anything more about the date or the label or anything else. He just started talking about a new cupcake he was planning and acted casual and collected.

Internally, I was excited, anxious, and thrown. These past few days, I kept playing the maybe, maybe-not dance with myself. I could easily convince myself Will and I were just building a friendship, a working relationship. That was all.

But tonight, I had confirmation that he was, in fact, feeling things as well. The butterflies I had when I was around him were obvious because he hadn't been afraid to boldly call our dinner a date.

Still, although a part of me was thrilled, I was also feeling anxious. Because if he was calling it a date, and I felt like it was a date—where did that leave us?

We were engulfed in planning the bake-off with a

romance brewing that neither of us probably needed right now—but both probably wanted, at least a little bit.

I felt the walls of my heart crumbling as I drove Will home, thinking about the possibilities. I thought about what it would mean for his dreams, for mine, and for both of our bandaged hearts. But I couldn't shove away the thought that we were falling for each other—and I was excited about that, which was, inarguably, the most terrifying fact of all.

NINETEEN

When Monday rolled around, we were back to being busy. Grandma came along to help with recipe details while I worked on finalizing bake-off applications. I spent most of the day reaching out to participants with details about parking, nearby lodgings, and rules of the competition.

Essentially, each bakery could bring two bakers with them. There would be a three-hour competition to create the best cupcake using a random supply of ingredients we would provide. The competition kicked off at five o'clock with the winner being crowned at nine in the evening. This gave everyone the day to enjoy the festivities, food trucks, and booths before the competition got underway.

All bakeries would receive basic ingredients such as flour, sugar, and other necessities. There would be a table of random ingredients ranging from candy bars to fruit that could be used on a first-come, first-served basis. Three judges were present, and they would crown the winning flavor. The winning bakery would receive a trophy, a small cash prize, and have their cupcake featured on Grandma's menu for the entire year with a prominent sign on the wall about their business.

It was a fun competition, and the bakeries that came always brought their A-game. Thanks to the social media campaign and despite our late start, we were up to forty-three bakeries attending. It was a massive undertaking that required a lot of coordination. Finding oven space had been a struggle, even in the first years when only a dozen participants came. Residents of the town volunteered their kitchen spaces for the baking. Contestants would gather at the town center, where we read the rules, and then each team received huge bins to put their ingredients in. They would do an ingredient grab at Town Hall and then be driven to their assigned kitchens to complete the baking. They were not allowed to use any extra ingredients.

It was a hodgepodge of a competition, but it worked for the small town. Perhaps that was the true charm of it: the basic, simple elegance of the whole thing and the fact the community really had to come together to make it work.

After I reached out to the bakeries with instructions, I also had to verify with the volunteers who had offered their kitchens for the contest. We had a few on standby just in case someone had a last-minute emergency preventing them from participating. All volunteers were required to be in the parking lot by Town Hall at promptly 4:30 p.m. to escort their assigned bakery team back to their house.

It was a monumental task, but I was thankful Grandma had been so organized over the years. She had impressive systems in place despite her hatred of technology and had given me so many tips. I was thankful to be a part of the planning, no matter how hectic it felt, because it gave me a chance to learn the ropes. I already knew that next year, I would at least be stopping by on weekends to help her with the organizing leading up to the festival.

As I put the final touches to the day's work, and Will and Grandma were in clean-up mode, my mind wandered to next year. Where *would* my life be by then? It was crazy to think of how up-in-the-air everything felt. A few months ago, I was standing on solid ground in New York. My career wasn't exactly where I wanted it to be, but it still felt stable. Now, being here in the bakery, I realized that Star Creek fit, too, somehow. It felt right. I guessed that was the fun and the trauma of life. You never knew where it would end up.

I sent the last email of the day and checked in on Grandma and Will. Grandma was resting on the stool by the counter. After a day of baking, she looked tired, and panic set in. I'd been so wrapped up in my work, I hadn't paid attention to how hard she was working.

"Grandma, are you okay?" I asked, thinking about the doctor's orders not to let her overexert herself. Herb was at an eye doctor's appointment and running errands for the day. I'd come to rely on him to keep an eye on Grandma. I had gotten too used to him being around.

"I'm fine. It felt good to be in the kitchen." Her words were labored, and her breathing was heavier than normal.

We had plans to head over to Town Hall as soon as we were done with the bakery work for the day. We needed to check out the venue and make sure everything was arranged as far as table space and outlets for our needs. Town Hall would also be the location for several of the booths, including the candle booth and the Humane Society booth. It had been my idea to invite the local shelter to bring some adoptable dogs and cats and hand out free dog treats, which Will was going to make.

After Town Hall, we also had an appointment at the

Humane Society to check in on some details and verify which animals they were bringing. Grandma wanted to put up printed photos of all the available pets to encourage adoption, so we were also picking those up. In short, it was a busy night after a busy day. But looking at Grandma, I knew she needed to rest.

"Grandma, why don't you let me take care of the errands tonight? Honestly, I don't mind, and I'm sure Will would probably be willing to help too," I said, nearly certain that Will would be happy to help.

Will was finishing a final wipe-down of the counters, and Grandma wouldn't go home without a fight. I didn't want to upset her, so I changed my tactic.

"I wouldn't mind spending some time with Will, if you catch my drift," I whispered, shrugging.

That was all it took. Grandma winked. "Oh, I get it. That's fine. Herb should be finished with his errands, so I'll have him pick me up here."

"I can take you home," I said.

"You're not the only one with a Monday night date. Herb wanted to go to the Red Dragon, but I said I was busy. I'll just call him and tell him there's been a change of plans and my schedule is free for takeout and a movie."

"Are you sure you don't want a ride?"

"No way, dear. You two have a busy schedule. Herb and I can handle our Chinese takeout."

"Well, we'll wait until Herb gets here," I offered, and Grandma didn't bother arguing.

I headed to the bathroom in the back of the bakery to try to salvage my hair and dab on a little makeup. I didn't want to look completely unprofessional at the meetings.

A few moments later, Herb arrived. "You three look exhausted," he said when he walked through the door.

"Sorry I couldn't help today. I'm all yours the rest of the week."

"Well, you better make sure you fuel up because we have quite a bit of work to keep you busy. You might regret offering to help," Grandma said as he led her out the door.

"Never," he replied, smiling down at her. I noticed his hand was on the small of her back, and she wasn't fighting it. My heart warmed at the sight.

She leaned heavily on his arm, and the two walked very slowly. Still, Grandma lit up when Herb was around. It made me feel better. I knew he would take care of her.

"They're so good for each other," Will said, standing beside me as I watched Herb open the door on his yellow Volkswagen Beetle for Grandma.

"They really are. I'm glad Grandma's opening up to the idea," I replied.

We both stared in silence as the car drove off, perhaps both lost in our own versions of the tormented memories of love destroyed. After a long moment, Will broke the silence.

"I guess we better get a move on. We've got two stops to make, and I don't know about you, but I could go for a burger too. I'm thinking the Route 22 Diner might have to make our list of errands. You know, just to make sure they're up to par for the tourists who will be coming."

"Of course. Only official business," I replied, smiling. I was not one to disagree with a burger run, so we quickly locked up the Star Creek Bakery and got in my car.

THE TRIP to Town Hall was smooth because the mayor's assistant, Trina, had been involved with the Star Creek Holiday Bake-Off since its inception. She was a pro at all the details and checked off more than was on my list. The supplies we needed were already organized, and we reviewed the map I had planned. She even had signage ready to put outside and the numbers for the volunteers to hold up that corresponded with their assigned bakers.

We finished early enough to make our stop at the Route 22 Diner for the burger Will was craving—and me too, now that he had put the idea in my head.

After we had properly sustained ourselves with sky-high burgers and milkshakes—Will insisted they were a diner must-have—we headed to the outskirts of town where the Star Creek Humane Society was.

"Why do I feel like we aren't leaving here emptyhanded?" Will asked as we pulled up to the barking menagerie of kennels. Some of the dogs were outside, tails wagging, and I felt my heart in my throat seeing all the homeless babies. I'd been a cat person growing up since that was all Mom would allow us to have with our busy schedules. Seeing a gorgeous lab in the front kennel as we walked through the door, I knew I was a dog person too. If I ever had my own house, a dog was definitely on the list of must-haves.

Inside, Ms. Wanda Sensing greeted us as though she'd been waiting all day for celebrities to stroll through the door. She gave me a huge hug and told us how thrilled she was with our idea to add the Humane Society to the festival events.

"This just means the world to us, and I'm hoping with your help, we can clear the shelter during the festival. Now, can I get you all some tea?"

Ms. Wanda, as she told us to call her, was a sweet woman with short, curly hair and a bright dress that certainly brought some life to the dreary December weather. She'd told me over the phone she was a transplant from Georgia and was passionate about all things animals. When I'd pitched my idea for a shelter dog mistletoe kissing booth for the festival, she was happy to oblige, already listing off dogs who would be perfect for the event.

We followed Ms. Wanda back to her office, and then she headed to the break room to retrieve the tea we said we didn't need but she insisted we did. A few minutes later, she reappeared, teacups in hand. She plopped into her wheely desk chair so wildly, I thought she might wheel right out of the office.

"So, first, here is the stack of flyers your grandma asked for. These are photos of every adoptable animal available. She wanted to make a sort of wall of animals outside of Town Hall. We're running a holiday special the whole month of December and January, where adopters get twenty-five percent off adoption fees. I want to find all our sweet animals a home."

"I would love nothing more," I said, taking the stack and handing it to Will.

"Here's the list of dogs I think would be perfect for the mistletoe booth. I wish we could take them all, but we only have so many hands, and plus, I think there are a few who would be too anxious with the crowd. But our hope is that even having the five we picked will bring more people into the shelter. The free dog treats are such a sweet idea. Thanks, Will, for dropping off samples last week. All the dogs went crazy for them," she said, eyeing him now.

I turned to him. "I didn't know you did that. Grandma didn't mention it." That was shocking because Grandma was always looking for ways to remind me of how amazing Will was.

He shrugged. "I did it on my own, after bakery hours."

My heart melted a bit, and Ms. Wanda let out a little

whimper as she slapped the table. "I always love a man who has a heart for animals. Honey, if I was about forty years younger, I'd be asking for your number."

Will flushed, still looking through the photo stack.

"We've got some donation jars and also some cute Christmas T-shirts for our stand as well, if that's okay," Ms. Wanda continued.

"Of course. I want you to make the most of it, so anything you want to do is great. And Will's dad is actually working on building the kissing booth out of plywood. He's going to paint it next week so it looks super cute. It will be a great photo spot for festivalgoers and hopefully boost your reach on social media as well."

"Oh, that's perfect! I love it. You two are amazing. Thank you for everything you're doing for us. It's a rough road sometimes, but people like you make it so much better."

We went over a few more details while Will flipped through the handouts in his possession. I was getting ready to check in and see if he had anything to add to the conversation when he interrupted us by holding up one of the flyers. I peered at Joey, an all-white fluffy cat who was pictured on the flyer.

"Is Joey still available?" Will asked.

"Sure is. He's back in the cat room."

"Can I meet him?"

And with that, Ms. Wanda sprang into action as if we were prepping for the president to arrive. "Follow me," she said with a huge gesture, rushing through winding hallways so fast, we could barely keep up. There was nothing like a potential adoption to energize the already energetic Ms. Wanda.

When we got to the room, a few cats were out in the

open room, meowing and playing. Others were in rows of cages along the wall. I smiled, taking in the sight of kittens, older cats, and all different colors of fur. It was easy to see why Ms. Wanda was so passionate.

Right in the front playing with the other cats was Joey. He knew exactly what he was doing, for sure, because he strutted straight up to Will and rubbed his leg.

"Oh, he knows. Boy, does he know," Ms. Wanda said.

"This guy looks just like a cat I had growing up," Will said.

"Well, Joey is our longest resident. He is ten and came to us about a year ago when his owner passed away. He is a cuddle bug, but let me tell you, he also has a sassy side. But he would be a great companion."

By this time, Will had crouched down close to the floor, and Joey was jumping up on his lap. The two looked bonded already, and I knew Will's initial reaction to the shelter was right—we weren't leaving emptyhanded.

"Should I go ring the adoption bell?" Ms. Wanda asked, rubbing her hands together.

"Yes, you should," Will said.

Ms. Wanda jumped into the air, pumping her fist. The cats didn't even flinch, perhaps used to the woman's energy. She went to get the paperwork from the front office, and we followed. But first, important business had to be done—we had to ring the bell she had out front.

"This is our fifth adoption today. Hot dog! At this rate, we might not have anyone for the kissing booth."

"That wouldn't be a bad thing," I said, and she agreed.

After taking some photos of Will and Joey for the adoption wall, we removed the flyer from the stack of adoptable animals and headed out, assuring Ms. Wanda we'd keep her in the loop about Joey's new life.

"Well, I did say this would happen," Will assessed, taking the cardboard carrier Ms. Wanda had hooked us up with out to the car. "Now we just have one more problem: I have zero cat supplies at home."

"Oh shoot, I didn't think of that."

"Neither did I. Of course, I didn't plan on adopting a cat today when I woke up this morning."

"Well, I'm glad you did it anyway."

We drove off to the pet store to get some supplies.

BEFORE TAKING Will home after the pet store, we had one more stop to make. Luckily, Joey seemed to be pretty cool with the car because he wasn't making a single peep.

"He's a sweetheart," I assessed. Will had his finger poked through the holes in the box to pet him. I could tell he was in love, and it made me smile to see the two of them.

"He is," Will agreed. "I'm really happy."

As we pulled up outside of Grandma's house, I thought I was too. I really was. A few weeks ago, that sentiment felt impossibly out of reach. But as Grandma and Herb popped their heads out once I honked and came rushing to the car, I thought about how Grandma, Herb, and Will had all embraced me in a way that made me feel welcome. At home. Accepted. And most of all, like I could conquer the world, just as I was.

Grandma went straight to Will's window.

"What's wrong?" she asked.

"Big problem," he answered, handing her the flyers. "There's one flyer missing from this stack for your adoptable animals wall."

"Oh?" she asked, eyeing the cardboard carrier and perhaps catching on. "Why is that?"

"Because little Joey here is staying with me." Will retrieved Joey's flyer from the car's dash. We'd kept it as a memento.

"Oh, how sweet. Just in time for the holidays too. What a lucky cat! Herb, come here! Will got a cat." She opened the car door and peeked through the holes to get a look.

"You'll have to stop by later this week and see him once I get him settled in," Will offered.

Herb pushed in to get a look, too, although it was tough to see Joey through the box. "Oh, that's great, Will. Cats are the best."

"Well, let's not get carried away here. I think dogs are pretty amazing too," Grandma said. "But I'm happy for you and Joey. He's got a good home lined up—and more cat toys and towers than I think one cat can play with. Did you leave anything for the other cat owners?"

I grinned, turning to see the mountains of cat supplies Will had bought. We basically bought out the entire cat section at Frank's Pets and More. Will said we needed one of everything to give Joey the best life.

"He's one lucky cat, that's for sure," Herb added. "If you need anything, let me know. Oh, and I'll talk to Doc Wilson next time Sylvester goes for his checkup. I'll see if I can get you on his patient list in case you need anything."

"Thanks, Herb. I appreciate it," Will said. "I guess we should probably get Joey home. He's been a good sport for the shopping trip, but I'm guessing a bathroom break might be in order soon, and I don't really want that happening in Serena's car."

"Oh, good point," I said, thinking about the disastrous consequences of that potential event. Serena was nice enough to loan me her car, but I thought that might be pushing our friendship. I waved to Grandma and Herb and stepped on the gas as we pulled away.

At Will's house, I helped him carry Joey and the million cat supplies inside, then I stayed and assisted him, designing the perfect cat area for Joey.

"Wait," I said, freezing as Joey jumped on the cat condo. "Oh, no."

"What?" Will asked, rushing to make sure Joey was okay.

"No, it's just... did you check with the landlord? Are you allowed to have a cat?" I didn't know why, but the thought hadn't occurred to me until that very moment.

"Oh, no!" Will shouted. "Oh, no. I forgot. I didn't even think of it. What will I do now? Where will Joey go?"

"I'm sure Grandma can talk Helen's family into letting you keep him. And if not, don't take him back! I'll take him. Grandma or Herb will take him. We'll figure it out. He can't go back now," I said, feeling teary as I watched Joey happily kneading the carpeting on the cat tower.

"I'm kidding," Will said, putting a hand on the small of my back. "Helen's family told me when I moved in I could have a cat or a dog, they didn't care."

I turned and looked at him. "Are you serious?"

"Completely," he said, smiling. "I mean, I might be young and a little out of it when it comes to adulting, but give me some credit."

I poked his ribs. "I can't believe you tricked me. I was over here practically weeping at the thought of Joey's great home being ripped out from under him before Christmas."

He grabbed the hand that poked him in the ribs. I fought against him, poking him again.

"You better watch it," he said, a smile on his face, but I didn't give in.

I kept poking. "Apologize for getting me all upset," I said, smirking.

"Never. I'll never admit defeat," he shouted, although he was laughing and seemed ready to beg for mercy. The tables turned, and soon he was tickling me. I was giggling and screaming like a child, flailing about.

"Wait!" I shouted, and Will promptly stopped. I turned to look at Joey to make sure he was okay. I didn't want to traumatize the poor cat after just bringing him home. But he was happily curled up on the condo, ignoring our antics.

I waited a moment, and Will asked, "What?"

Then I turned and struck.

The tickling fight ensued for an embarrassingly long time. Still, it felt good to laugh, to joke around, to play. Walls crumbled with our laughter in ways I hadn't felt before with him—or with anyone else. Finally, when we were both out of breath, Will flopped onto his sofa, and I plopped down beside him. We were both gasping for air.

"I think we're too old for this," Will said, looking over at me. My hair had to be a frizzy mess, but it didn't matter.

I smiled, leaning my head back on the sofa. "I agree."

We sat in silence for a moment, the comfort of Will's couch and the adorable quality of his home making me not want to leave. Eventually, I thought of the manuscript sitting on my computer.

"I better get going. As much as I want to stay and watch Joey all night because he's so cute, I need to get some writing done."

"Ah, okay. You better get to it then. You can visit Joey anytime, and once that book's done, you can sit with him for hours on end. But I won't let him keep you from your writing."

He stood and walked me out. It wasn't that he wanted rid of me, I didn't think—although I had won the tickle fight, clearly. It was that he didn't want me to lose focus. He knew how important finishing the book was.

Jed had always made me feel so guilty when I had to write. He'd do just about anything to distract me or beg me to spend time with him watching a movie instead of writing. With Jed, I found myself writing at weird times, sneaking to my computer when I had a chance so he didn't guilt trip me. It was stressful to be up against a deadline, and looking back, my creativity definitely suffered. But in the moment, I never thought it was odd or bad.

Seeing how Will rooted for my dreams and fought to keep me focused on them was beautiful. It was something I didn't even realize I wanted or needed. Or maybe even deserved.

After a quick discussion, Will assured me he would just get his car from the bakery the next day—he didn't mind getting in a long walk later.

"I'll see you tomorrow?" I asked at the front porch.

"You bet," Will said.

He stood at the door watching until I got in my car and then waved from the porch. As I drove by, I thought about how I really could picture those two rocking chairs on the porch—and maybe a tiny one for Joey too. I could picture sunrises and sunsets and everything in between right there.

I went home and wrote more words than I thought possible in one evening.

TWENTY

Grandma had a doctor's appointment Wednesday morning, which Herb drove her to. Will and I got to work early and prepped cupcakes for the day before tackling a few more small to-do items on the festival list. Around noon, Grandma strolled into the bakery, smiling at the sight of customers filling all the tables. She stopped to chat with a few regulars, and Herb beelined for the kitchen to give Will a hand.

"How did things go?" I asked when Grandma was done talking to Mrs. Stinson in the corner of the bakery. I was brewing more coffee for the afternoon crowd.

"Perfect. The doctor said everything is looking great. He said my heart sounds good, and he can tell I'm less stressed," she said, beaming.

"Well, I'm glad. But I hope you don't take that as a sign to overdo it."

"I won't," Grandma said. "Truth be told, I've been enjoying stepping back. Before all of this happened, do you know how long it had been since I went to lunch on a weekday? Or took a day to watch mindless daytime television?

It's been a nice reprieve. I guess I just didn't realize how tired I was until I took a pause. I love the bakery, but I didn't realize how hard it's been on me with your grandfather and Rita and George gone until now. I honestly don't know how I've kept up this pace so long."

The usually joking Grandma I was accustomed to was uncharacteristically serious, and my heart panged to hear her words. I wished I lived closer so I could be more help. I wished I had at least come home on weekends these past couple years.

"And don't go getting crazy ideas in your head that you should've helped more," Grandma said, her intuition clearly leading her to exactly what I was thinking. "This isn't your responsibility. I love having you here, I do. You and Will have been a godsend. You've saved the festival. You've pulled off what seemed impossible, and I really think it's going to be the best bake-off the town has seen. But this bakery isn't your responsibility. Besides, Herb has really enjoyed helping. He told me it's nice to have purpose again."

It made me feel better to hear that. I could tell Herb and Grandma were finally heading down a path of admitting what they were feeling. I was so happy Grandma had someone to rely on, someone to fill her days with laughter and connection. That made the thought of returning to the city in a couple of weeks more bearable.

Still, as I stood in the doorway to the kitchen watching Will and Herb work as they shared a funny story, I realized how much I would miss it all. The four of us, a unit, working toward a common goal. Will's smile and singing voice. Random dinners and adventures with him. The sweet, small-town vibe of Star Creek. Snow days tucked away with lasagna, movies, and good company. Poker games and diner trips and all the warmth that had filled my freezing cold days recently. A town I had come to really know in a short amount of time. The orders of our regular customers I had memorized. I'd settled in so quickly to a routine I'd come to love. Could I really just up and leave it all once the festival was done?

I thought of my days in New York, sitting in the apartment alone working on my writing while Serena was at work. Random cocktail hours but no one to look out for me or care if I was writing or not. Thousands of people standing beside me on the sidewalk, but no one knowing my name. The city had always felt so energizing to me. Now, thinking of those blustery, bustling streets, it felt cold and isolating. I was never alone yet always lonely in a stark, undeniable way.

"Ms. Catherine, the delivery truck is here. Do you think you and Herb can take over the kitchen and front end? Lucy and I can work on organizing the bake-off supplies if that sounds good to you," Will announced.

Grandma nodded, and Herb gave a mock salute before reaching for an apron.

"No way, mister. You're not making cupcakes or cookies or even boiling water without supervision. I remember that time you took over pancake making at my house," Grandma teased. The two started bickering about what constituted burned pancakes. Will and I shook our heads.

"Hope no one is desperate for a coffee refill anytime soon, because this argument might take a while," Will said as we headed out to the supply truck to get to work.

We fell into a rhythm of stacking boxes in the storeroom, trying to keep the supplies relatively organized. It was a lot of back and forth, so neither of us talked much, mostly because we were out of breath from lugging the supplies and moving boxes around.

After all the boxes were finally unloaded and I signed off with the driver, Will and I stood in the stock room staring at the crowded space.

"Let's take a break. Grandma and Herb are probably still bickering, so we won't be missed for a few minutes," I said.

Will didn't argue. He cleared off a sturdy box for us both to have a seat. Surrounded by storage, we rested our weary legs and arms, staring into the cluttered room.

"Herb said your grandma is doing well, according to the doctor," Will said.

"Yes, thank goodness. I just hope she doesn't take it as a sign that she can do more work. I worry about her overdoing it." It was a pressing concern on my mind because although Grandma's words about enjoying her time off were hopeful, I also knew her. She was a go-getter. She couldn't help herself—sitting still felt like failure to her.

"Well, I'll always keep an eye on her and make sure she isn't doing too much."

"That's not your responsibility," I said.

He turned to look at me as if he was offended. "No, but I want to. Your grandma is a wonderful woman and an inspiration. She chased her passion. That really motivates me to chase mine. I see how happy she is and the beautiful legacy she's built in this community. To some people, they're just cupcakes. But I love seeing how my creations can take someone's so-so or even horrid day and turn it around, even if just for a moment. I love that there's a sense of family at the bakery, that Mrs. Stinson and Mrs. Stella come here every day, not just for baked goods but for community. No one has to feel alone thanks to Star Creek

Bakery. That's such a beautiful thing, and I'm thankful to be a part of it."

His words made me feel not only relieved but reverent toward him. He was a good one, truly.

"Well, I appreciate that. I'm glad Grandma has someone who shares in her love for the bakery. And also, I think Herb will be sticking around. Grandma said he has really been enjoying helping out."

"He's a good guy. And he's crazy about your grandma," Will said.

"That's for sure. Hey, how's Joey doing?" I asked, turning the conversation as I remembered the sweet white cat.

"He's good. He sleeps with me now, his paw on my shoulder all night like he's afraid not to be touching me. And he is really enjoying all the toys we bought. You'll have to come over and see him again sometime."

"I'd love to," I replied immediately, and then worried it came off as a little too enthusiastic.

"There's only one problem. I no longer can wear anything black. I swear he climbs into my dresser and my closet hunting out black shirts to sleep on. I either need to change up my closet color choice or get a very big lint roller."

I grinned, picturing Joey hunting out Will's black shirts —which he had a lot of, I realized.

"I guess it's a fair trade. Maybe it's time to mix up your style," I teased.

"Yeah, I think I've come to realize change isn't always a bad thing," he said. And I couldn't have agreed more.

With that, we got up, our legs sufficiently rested. Plus, we were a little worried Grandma and Herb were still arguing about burned food and cooking skills.

Sure enough, when we went back to the front, Mrs. Stella flagged me down for a refill on her cup of coffee, and Joseph Regals, the town's most successful realtor, was waiting at the counter. I jumped in right away, and Will headed back to break up the argument that was still going. We got everything quickly under control. We were a good team, I considered as I put another pot of coffee on. As the day ended and we prepared to clean up, Will popped his head out of the kitchen.

"Hey, can you be ready at six tonight?" he asked.

I eyed him suspiciously. "It depends. What do you have in mind?" I grinned.

"It's a surprise. But I think you'll like it. Consider it research for your writing. And dress warmly." He tucked his head back into the kitchen.

Grandma, who had been wiping down tables, looked at me. "Another hot date, huh?"

"And what are you and Herb doing after work?" I asked as I wiped down counters.

"Herb is cooking tonight. He has some pasta recipe he wants to try. He said being in the kitchen has inspired him. I'm a little terrified, actually. I think he just wants to make up for the burned pancakes."

"They weren't burned!" Herb shouted.

"Oh no. Not this again," I said. "You two are going to be banned from saying *pancakes*."

We finished up, and I had to admit, I moved a little faster than normal. I wanted to get home in time to shower and put on a few swipes of makeup. If we were doing something research-worthy, that clearly meant something romantic.

Grandma and I headed home, both in an excited mood to get ready for an evening with our favorite men. I felt a little guilty about my manuscript when I saw my laptop on my desk, but there would be time later. I dug out my warmest sweater, and dabbed on some makeup just in time for Will to appear at our door at six.

Grandma, too, had put on her red lipstick and a sparkly black top.

"Look at us," Grandma said as she headed to answer the door. "Two hot dates for two hot women, if I do say so myself."

I smiled at the sentiment, both because she'd called us hot and also because the *date* word wasn't something either of us avoided anymore.

As Will greeted me at the door with red roses this time and yellow roses for Grandma, I smiled at how much things had changed.

The thing that didn't change, though? Edmund still jumped on Will's shoulders, almost knocking him over. It wouldn't be a date without that, I realized, as we finally wrangled the dog off Will, and I headed out the door for whatever adventure awaited.

TWENTY-ONE

The drive to the ice-skating rink a few towns over took an hour. I'd been there once with my grandfather as a little girl but was too afraid to go out on the ice. We'd sat on the sidelines, and I'd watched the beautiful skaters whirl by as we drank hot chocolate on the bench. It had been before Christmas, and gorgeous pine trees were lit up with delicate, twinkling lights and a perfect night sky had lined the ice. It was a magical moment.

There was no sitting on the sidelines now, and I was glad for it. I'd spent my life sitting on the sidelines in some ways, too afraid of getting hurt. With Will by my side, I felt braver. Not skydiving kind of brave, but it was a start.

Will rented us both skates, and I precariously followed him out onto the ice. Thankfully, the rink wasn't packed since it was a weeknight. Still, my stomach fluttered with nerves. Will sensed my anxiousness as I crept onto the ice holding his mittened hand. The brave girl routine wasn't fully mine to claim.

"You *have* been skating before, haven't you?" he asked.

"No," I confessed, shrugging.

"But you said you were here before with your grandfather. And it was also a scene in your first book. That's why I brought you—I thought it must be something you liked doing since you wrote about it so vividly."

I smiled at the fact that he'd not only read my book but remembered that scene. "I have been here with my grandfather, but we didn't actually skate. I was too afraid."

He turned backward as if it was as natural as walking. He got in front of me, holding both of my hands as if I were a child. I tried to glide, but it wasn't as easy as it looked, and I was terrified of the date ending with a broken arm or leg for me. This only made my movements worse.

He skated backward, pulling me slowly along, checking every now and then to be certain he wasn't about to plow over any children or wayward skaters. At the speed we were going, I doubted it would matter if we did—someone could walk out of our way in time, let alone skate away.

"So let me get this straight. You are a sweet romance writer who has never been in a horse carriage or ice skated? Your scenes feel so real. I thought for sure those were things you'd done."

I smirked. "I just have a good imagination, or so they tell me."

"Thank goodness I brought you here. You can't be a romance writer who hasn't ice skated," he said, still towing me along. My nerves calmed, and I felt like with my hands in his, I would be okay. He wouldn't let me fall. As I gained confidence, my skating got a little smoother. We were still going very slowly around the rink, but at least I was gliding my feet in a way that I no longer looked like a newborn giraffe.

"Well, I'm not sure if this level of awkwardness would make for a good romance scene, anyway. I think I'll stick with the sweet, charming scenes from the movies."

"What fun is that? I think these moments are where the real romance is," he said, and he wasn't grinning. It was something my ex never would've said. To him, romance was something to post on social media about—envy-worthy, picture-perfect moments.

But Will was right. We finished our first lap around the rink. The messy moments were the ones that made me feel like it was real. The moments when the pancakes were burning or the coffee was spilling. When the flour was in a dust plume over every surface and we were laughing together at the mess we'd made, telling stories as we cleaned it up.

The real beauty was in the moments that weren't movie-worthy but just real-life us. When those moments happened, I knew we trusted each other enough to let them. We weren't trying to be something we weren't. We weren't trying to be impressive or picture-worthy. We were just being together. Wasn't that what everyone craved, deep down? Wasn't that what love really was?

We started on the second lap, and I thought about the word *love*, how it had come to mind. By that point, I wasn't so terrible on my feet, and Will skated back to my side, holding only one of my hands. We were still going at a snail's pace, but we were skating, and I wasn't relying on him as heavily. Still, I clutched his hand tightly, not wanting to let it go for more reasons than just safety. He'd given me the support I needed to make it around the rink but then stepped back little by little until I was managing it on my own. Wasn't that what a true partnership was?

After a few laps, my legs were aching, so we left the ice. We found a bench to claim, and Will grabbed some hot chocolates. We sat in silence for a little while as we warmed our hands on the cups and watched the rink.

"It's beautiful here," I said, studying the couples whirling about, the trees sitting around the edges of the rink with their Christmas lights shimmering.

"It really is," Will said.

"So it seems like you've been skating quite a few times, judging by how good you are," I observed.

"No, I'm just a natural-born talent when it comes to the ice," Will said, but I could tell he was joking.

I lightly punched his arm.

"Okay, okay. You're right. I always wanted to play ice hockey, but there weren't a lot of opportunities down South and my mom worried I'd get hurt. After culinary school, I joined an adult hockey league in the city. I really loved it for the year I played."

"Why did you stop?" I asked, intrigued to picture Will as a hockey player.

"My ex didn't like me playing. She said it took away from the business too much."

I froze as he entered unfamiliar territory.

He hadn't opened up about his ex at all. I didn't even know her name. Will had been open and warm about almost everything since he'd let me in—except this. He'd been guarded about his past. It was an obvious pain point for him, one he preferred to shove away. In truth, it had scared me to think he was hiding something about his past. Maybe we were taking more steps forward tonight.

"I'm sorry to hear that. So this ex was your business partner for the bakery, I'm assuming?"

"Yep. I met her in culinary school. We opened the

bakery together two years later. It was tough, of course. Really tough. We didn't agree on a lot. She didn't like to give up control of anything. She pretty much just delegated me to the counter. But when I started playing hockey, she didn't like that it pulled me away from work one night a week, so I quit. Looking back, I realize I gave up a lot for that business and for her." There was a heaviness about him now, and I felt bad for him. Still, I wanted to hear more, to understand.

"How did she end up with the business? What happened?"

He let out a heavy sigh and glanced away. A long pause followed, and I thought maybe he wasn't going to answer. But then he turned back, nodded as if to give himself permission to continue, and began explaining.

"The business wasn't doing well at all. We were bleeding money. I tried to convince her to experiment with the menu and offer more options. She didn't want to hear me out. Finally, we came to a tipping point and, after all we'd been through, she told me one night she didn't love me anymore. She told me running the business with me made her realize she didn't want us anymore, didn't think we'd work. And if we didn't work romantically, she didn't want to work with me either."

"Why didn't you get to keep the business? Or at least half of it?"

He sighed. "Because I thought she was the one. I really did. Looking back, I can see it wasn't a healthy relationship. I can see how she clipped my wings, held me back from being my best self. But at the time, I was heartsick and heartbroken. I didn't want to hold things up, and I didn't want to continue with a dream that felt broken. I tried to get her back for a while. I begged her not to leave me.

"She offered to buy me out of the business, and I thought it would make her happy, so I agreed. I spent a few months living on savings and trying to figure out what to do next. I considered finding a new bakery to work for, but nothing felt right. I considered starting my own bakery in the city, but that didn't feel right either. Then, two months after we split ways, I found out she had a new partner—in business and in love. He was another student from our culinary school I'd always suspected she was interested in. She pulled him into the business, and he filled my shoes right away. They changed the business name, their recipes, everything pretty much. But even then, I wasn't ready to let go."

His eyes started to water, and I could see the shame in them.

"I clung to her like a desperate man. Maybe I was. I tried everything to get her back. But the bakery started doing better. It was like proof that I'd been holding her back, which hurt. At that point, I'd had enough. I couldn't stay in the city and watch this new guy live out my dreams. My parents suggested I come to Star Creek, so I decided to give it a try. That was when I heard about your grandma's bakery, and it seemed like a good way to put distance between me, the city, and my ex. I had to get away from her so I wasn't so focused on getting her back—because I finally accepted she wasn't coming back."

"I'm sorry that happened to you. She sounds awful. But I'm glad you're here now." I put my hand on his knee and leaned into him.

"Me too," he said, but the story had left him emotionally drained.

I stared out at the rink, my head on his shoulder. "Do you still love her?"

"No," he replied quickly, in the way someone says it when they're trying to assure themself they don't.

My stomach dropped a little bit. "It's okay if you do. You were together a long time. You were building a life together."

He softened, pausing for a long moment. "I think I miss the idea of the life I thought we would have together, you know? For a while, there was this big, exciting dream we were living out together. And now it feels like someone took my place."

I thought about how I would feel. Losing Jed was hard. But it would've been even harder if our dreams had been wrapped together like Will and his ex. Or if I had to see my replacement roll in. I shuddered. I'd never met the woman he left me for, and I was sort of glad for that—although I had, of course, done my share of unhealthy social media stalking after the breakup.

"That makes sense. About living out the big dream. My ex, Jed, was my first love. I had visions of us building this beautiful life together. I was blindsided when he told me he'd met someone else. Months before. So for months, while I was trying to make it work, he was out with someone else." The memories stabbed into my chest as if I were still standing in front of him, hearing the news that gutted all my dreams.

Will squeezed my knee. "I'm sorry. He sounds like a fool."

"It's okay. Looking back, even though it's only been a little over a month, I can see that he wasn't perfect for me like I'd tried to convince myself. He didn't get my writing dreams, didn't really support them. I never quite felt like myself around him either. Everything had to be picture-perfect in his world. Appearances were everything, not true happiness. I don't think I would've actually been happy if we'd stayed together. I don't think I *was* ever truly happy with him, to be honest. I just convinced myself I was because I didn't want to be alone." I took a deep breath. It was a hard confession, and my eyes stung.

"I understand that as well. I've had time away from her, and now I can see she wasn't it for me. She didn't light me up or support my passions. She took but never gave. That's not the kind of love I want."

With my head still on his shoulder, I thought about his assessment and about Jed. Will and I had both been through the wringer when it came to love. Yet here we were on the other side, sitting at this ice rink with hot chocolate and the warmth between our bodies.

"I think Grandma might be right. I think sometimes love is even better the second time around. By then you know who you are. You know what you want and what you don't. Even if it doesn't work out, that first love is valuable. It teaches you who you are and what love means to you so the second time when it comes, you're actually ready," I said, the words tumbling out. And I believed them. Suddenly, Jed and the hurt from what he did to me seemed smaller.

I sat up and looked at Will. His dark eyes perused mine.

"You might not have horse carriage or ice-skating experience, but it sounds to me like you know a thing or two about romantic wording. That was beautiful."

"Thank you," I said before taking a sip of my hot chocolate. "Now, how about we get back out there and give this skating thing another go before we head home?" I stood up precariously, almost falling with the hot chocolate in my hand.

Will smiled before he stood and joined me.

"Yes, let's go again," he said, leading the way to the trash can to dispose of our cups before we headed out onto the ice.

The second time, we were both so much smoother on that ice, gliding around like a weight had been lifted from both of us.

TWENTY-TWO

My legs ached for the next two days, which made organizing the Holiday Bake-Off supplies even more strenuous than it would have been. I was handling a ton of emails from vendors, volunteers, and contestants. That coupled with working on my manuscript in the early mornings and evenings had me exhausted. Still, when Friday arrived, I was re-invigorated thanks to an exciting opportunity I'd managed to snag for Will.

So far, he'd been surprising me. It was nice to be in the driver's seat now. I'd cleared everything with Grandma to make sure she didn't need me Sunday and that she would be okay with Herb for the day. She'd assured me she'd manage, especially when I told her what I had in mind. I felt a little nervous because it would be the first time I was going so far away since I'd gotten the phone call about her stroke. But I knew Herb would keep an eye on her.

"I must admit," she'd said, "I'm a little jealous. That's such a fun trip you have planned."

"You don't think it's too much?" I asked. After I'd

snagged the tickets from a friend in the city, I was terrified of just that very thing.

"No way. He'll love it. You two will have a blast."

Emboldened by Grandma's words and the fact that I couldn't return the tickets anyway, I waited for the perfect moment to fill Will in on his upcoming surprise. The morning was crazily busy, especially when an out-of-town bus tour pulled into the parking lot mid-morning. Herb, Grandma, Will, and I didn't get a moment to breathe let alone talk until the early afternoon. Then Will was finalizing inventory lists with Grandma for the recipes we had planned for the festival. With the influx of tourists expected, we'd have to bake a whole lot more cookies and cupcakes than we would for a normal weekend, and it took a lot of coordinating.

By the end of the workday on Friday, things had finally slowed down enough for me to talk to Will.

"So I wanted to see if you have any plans on Sunday," I said, feeling suddenly shy.

"Other than sleeping all day and eating bags of potato chips in front of the television? No, not really."

"Good. Save the potato chips for another weekend because if you're up for it, I have a surprise for you. It's going to take all day."

"I'm game. What should I wear?" he asked, and I was relieved he had zero hesitation.

"Wear a heavy coat, but other than that, just jeans and a nice shirt."

"Okay, sounds good."

"Well, that was easy. No other questions? No trying to probe out of me where we're going?"

"Nope," he said, wiping his hands on the towel over his

shoulder. "It's kind of nice to be surprised sometimes. When it's a good surprise."

"It's a good one, for sure."

"Well, I'm glad you agree about surprises. Because I have a surprise for you as well. Luckily, it's for tomorrow night at eight. Hopefully that works for you."

It was my turn to be intrigued. "Really? A good kind of surprise?"

"Of course. Make sure you dress warmly. Looks like we've got quite the busy weekend planned."

Grandma heard him and smiled.

"I'm glad for it," she said. "Lucy has been burning the candle at both ends. She needs a break from all the work."

It was true. I'd been pouring a ton of effort into my manuscript, but it was paying off. I was about seventy-five percent finished. This was the fastest I'd written a book yet —and it was also probably the proudest I'd felt of a rough draft. Still, all the work was catching up with me, and I was looking forward to kicking back this weekend—especially with Will.

"Since it's going to be a busy weekend, we better make a plan for all the tasks we need to finish for the festival so we can tackle them in the time we have," Will said. I agreed that was a good idea. We finished cleaning up the bakery and made a plan for what work we needed to finish on Saturday in order for the festival plans to be at a place we were all happy with.

I couldn't stop thinking about Saturday night or the surprise I had planned for Sunday. I was excited to see what Will had planned for us, but more than that, I was anxious to see how surprised he would be with the tickets I'd purchased. It was the first time in a while I was exhilarated about the weekend to come. That was a nice surprise by itself.

When I got back to Grandma's house, I promptly called Serena to tell her the good news.

"Guess what?" I asked. "Are you busy Sunday, say around five?"

"Other than a hot date with some legal briefs, I'm free. Why?" she asked excitedly.

"Because I'm swinging by the city and wanted to see if you would like to get dinner."

She let out a squeal that told me she was in. "Of course! That's so exciting. What are you coming back for?"

"A surprise. For Will."

"Wait, is Will going to be with you? Am I going to meet the stud who has been stealing all your time?"

I smirked. "Yes, against my better judgment perhaps, especially after that comment."

"Oh, I'll play it cool. You know I can. I'm just so excited to see you. And to put a face to the name I keep hearing."

We spent some time catching up, but every few minutes, Serena would again mention how excited she was. And, in truth, I was too. It would be nice for Will and me to be back in the city, a place we called home not so long ago. And I was also excited for my best friend to meet Will and get a feel for him. She knew Jed, and she'd seen the red flags before I was willing to admit to them. I trusted her judgment, and I wanted to see what she thought of Will and if she saw anything I hadn't.

If I really cared what my best friend thought about him, then I definitely cared about him more than I'd admitted up until that point.

I fell asleep thinking about Sunday, about how

surprised Will would be, and about how excited I was to experience it all with him by my side.

TWENTY-THREE

Dressed in a red-and-black plaid sweater, my favorite red jacket, and a black hat, I waited anxiously by the door for Will to pick me up Saturday night. Grandma and Herb had planned an impromptu pizza-making date, and I'd scarfed down a slice they offered me in the interim of getting ready and waiting for Will for the surprise.

"Do you know what he has planned?" I asked Grandma.

"No, he didn't tell me. And even if he did, I wouldn't tell you. That's the fun of surprises," she said. Edmund had his head resting on the table as he stared at the pepperoni pizza with pure love.

A few minutes after I fixed my lipstick from the unexpected pizza slice I devoured, Will knocked on the door. Edmund went into a frenzy, but Will was ready for him as he jumped on his shoulders. They embraced, as was becoming their habit.

"Are you ready?" he asked after telling me I looked beautiful. I brushed off the compliment—I was only in a winter coat and hat, after all. Still, it felt good to be noticed.

I said goodbye to Grandma and Herb, who were heading to the living room to watch their weekend murder mystery program with the remnants of their pizza dinner. I followed Will outside to his car, the night crystal clear in the way only a winter night in Pennsylvania could be. I looked up and spotted the stars in the sky, which served as a gorgeous backdrop to an evening date with Will.

"Are you going to tell me where we're going?" I asked, anxious about what we were doing but in the best of ways.

"You'll see." He, too, wore a heavy wool coat and scarf as well as a black hat. We drove through town, and Will animatedly told me about Joey's latest antics with a pair of his boots. It made me smile to hear him light up when talking about his cat, and I listened intently. I was paying so much attention to his story that I didn't realize where we were until he parked his car on Main Street, near the gazebo. I wondered if maybe we were doing a replay of the hot chocolate date, which was fine with me. At night, the twinkling lights took on an even prettier aura.

"Okay, we're right on time. They should be here any minute," Will said, ushering me over to the gazebo. He had a gift bag in hand, and my curiosity was definitely piqued.

"Who will be here?" I wondered if maybe his parents were joining us, and I smiled at the thought.

But a few minutes later, the clomping coming down the street and the appearance of a gorgeous white carriage told me everything. My mouth opened wide and instantly curved into a smile.

"Is that what we're doing?" I asked, afraid to assume but knowing it couldn't be a coincidence.

"You bet," he said, scrunching his nose at me in a way that was endearing. "I figured it was about time our resident romance writer got to ride in a horse-drawn carriage."

"But I thought you said it wasn't really romantic," I said, perusing him.

He shrugged. "I figured it was worth you giving it a try and seeing for yourself."

I turned to take in the sight of the gorgeous black horses walking toward us. The driver was dressed in a suit and a top hat and stopped right in front of the gazebo. I stepped up into the carriage and felt like royalty. I couldn't believe he'd gone to these lengths to give me this experience. Tears threatened as a wave of emotion overpowered me, but I smiled through it, truly excited to experience this with him.

After we were settled, the carriage took off through town, and I got to see Star Creek from a new vantage point. As we rolled through the place I'd come to know and love, I turned to look at the man I had come to know and love it with. Will Westerly, the man who had changed my mind about ice skating, baking, and men in general, was now taking on horse carriages.

As we plodded forward, I realized he hadn't changed my mind about the carriage.

"This is, for sure, the epitome of romance. I stand by my assessment and my romance scenes," I announced, turning to him. We snuggled closer under the throw the driver had provided, the chill of the air biting through my clothes. Sidling up to Will's warmth alleviated the cold in my body —and my heart.

"Well, I'm glad. If I'm being honest, it does seem more romantic than I first thought. I guess it's also about who you're with and not just the carriage." His words were a soft confession, his dark eyes perusing mine as if to ask if that was okay to say. My heart fluttered as I stared up at him, and he stared back. I was certain it was our moment. I was sure our entire present and future would shift in that exact second. I was sure he would kiss me.

"Oh, I almost forgot!" He leaned down to retrieve the bag on the floor of the carriage. I was thrown and a little disappointed but temporarily distracted by the bag he set on my lap. "This is for you. I hope you like them. And I hope it's okay I took the liberty of asking your grandma about them. She seemed more than willing to share, but I don't want to interfere or make anyone sad. But... well, just open it."

I gingerly pulled back the tissue paper and found a bakery box in the bottom. Uncertain what I'd find, I put the box on my lap and carefully peeled back the top.

When I saw the contents, my heart fluttered, and the tears fell without warning. I raised the box up to my nose, closed my eyes, and inhaled deeply, the memories swirling through my mind. I was no longer in the carriage with Will. I was back in my mother's kitchen, the aroma of her snowball cookies tantalizing me as I sat down after school with her.

I opened my eyes and looked from the cookies to Will. I had no words for what he'd done. It was a beautiful gesture, one I'm sure he second-guessed after I'd told him Grandma and I hadn't made the recipe since Mom died. For him to go out on a limb not only to get the recipe but to make them for me—it meant everything.

"Is it too much? Are you upset?" he asked, and I realized I'd been sitting in reverent silence for a while.

"No," I said, shaking my head vehemently. "No, it's perfect. I can't believe you did this for me. I can't believe it. I love them." I swiped at my tears. I didn't realize how much I'd missed them, needed them in my life, until that very moment. It was like a piece of Mom was still in my present world. It had been a mistake to shove the recipe aside, foolish even. Will had reminded me it was okay to live in the happy moments of the past.

I rested the box back on my lap, then studied the gaze of the man who was so caring and supportive in every single way. And then, I took matters into my own hands.

I leaned in, tilting my head to the right slowly, not wanting to go too fast or scare him. Will followed my lead, and our lips met in the back of the carriage. We savored the sweet kiss for a long moment, our lips joined and welcoming each other with hesitancy and certainty. It was clear we both wanted this kiss but were also afraid. Still, at the meeting of our lips, my heart felt as if it were on fire in all the best ways. I'd come alive. It just felt right. When we gently pulled back, tears were still streaming down my face.

"I'm falling for you," Will whispered, a confession from the depths of him, a vulnerable admission I never would have seen coming that first day we met. I couldn't hide the smile that spread on my face.

"I'm falling for you too," I replied, breaking out of the chains of fear. I stopped worrying if it was too soon to fall again or how it would end. I simply basked in the fact that it was confirmed. There was no more hiding from the truth. Sure, we might still be terrified of what it meant for us. We were both broken from a shattered past with hearts that had been cleaved by others. Sitting in the carriage, though, with the cookies on my lap and Will by my side, I knew that whatever came, we'd figure it out. The future was uncertain, but that was life. We could never be sure of what the future would bring. We could only continue clomping down the path, rolling slowly but together through the familiar lanes, hoping we could hold each other in the carriage if we hit an unexpected bump.

I looked back down at the cookies, my mouth watering at the sight. I removed a mitten and reached in, handing one to Will. I took one as well and paused to study it for a moment. Will clinked his cookie against mine and we laughed at our cookie cheers. Grandma would definitely be a fan. We bit into our cookies at the same time. For me, it was like going home. The tears threatened to well again.

"They're perfect. Thank you," I whispered through cookie crumbs.

"You bet," he replied through his own mouthful of cookie.

We turned the conversation to lighter topics, but when the carriage dropped us off at the gazebo, we asked the driver to take our photo. It felt like a monumental night, one we'd want to remember. When we were heading back to the truck, Will paused for a moment by the gazebo with an arm around me.

"You're right. Those carriage rides are the height of romance," he said.

And we kissed once more under the twinkling stars and lights of the gazebo, our lips tasting as sweet as the cookies we'd just devoured.

When I got back to Grandma's after our carriage ride, my fingers flew on the keyboard. I wrote the best carriage ride scene I'd ever written, moved by real-life inspiration and two kisses that made me believe I could love again.

TWENTY-FOUR

I woke up bright and early Sunday morning. Grandma had groggily pulled herself out of bed in the total darkness to see me off and give me warm cinnamon rolls for the trip—and for Serena. I'd insisted she stay in bed and rest, but she wouldn't hear of it, so I humored her.

My growling stomach was happy for the food. As I finished packing up supplies, she sat down and leaned her head in her hands, which gave me pause. But it was extra early, even for her. I kissed her cheek and thanked her for the road trip snacks, then made her promise to call if she needed anything. Herb popped over before I was out the door, which made me feel a lot better about being gone for the day.

Armed with the cinnamon rolls and coffee in to-go cups, I pulled into Will's driveway. He'd been watching for me and immediately dashed out the door. I was thankful I didn't have to get out of the warm car and traverse the freezing cold temperatures again.

"All ready?" I asked as he climbed in.

"Yes. Do I smell cinnamon rolls?" he asked as he buckled up.

I handed him his coffee. "Yep. Grandma got up extra early to make us some road trip breakfast."

"When I was growing up, road trip breakfast was candy from the gas station. This is quite the elevation."

I pulled out of the driveway, and we were set, the GPS directing me on the already familiar trip. I planned on grabbing lunch before heading to Broadway, and I was excited to show Will around the city. Even though he'd lived there, too, I wanted to show him *my* version of New York.

He begged me to tell him where we were going, but I didn't give in. I had put my phone in the console so he couldn't see the address we were heading toward. The suspense was killing him. Still, he passed the time by turning up the radio and serenading me with today's hits, making me laugh so hard I had to tell him to stop so I didn't have a driving mishap.

We covered dozens of topics on the drive—everything from what the best documentary series currently was to the best cookies for the holidays ranked in order. The conversation was light, and we were both in a jovial mood. The kiss the night before had loosened something between us— perhaps an even wider freedom to be at ease, to be ourselves. I relished the connection and the comfort.

Eventually, he caught on that we were going to the city. I sensed a slight shift as we neared the familiar tunnel and worried I'd made a mistake. I watched him glance longingly out the window at the skyline and realized this might be his first time back since he moved to Star Creek. He was quieter the closer we got, more reserved. I felt the walls coming back up.

"I'm sorry if I've made you sad coming here," I said, deciding to clear the air as we sat in traffic.

He turned to me. "No, I'm excited to make new memories. I just didn't expect to be back so soon." His expression was solemn, and even if he was trying to cover it, I could tell it was upsetting to be here. Maybe this had been a terrible idea.

"Well, I guess the surprise is partly out so I can tell you what I have planned," I said, smiling at Will. His mood shifted again, lightening slightly. I was glad for that.

The honking and heavy traffic increased my anxiety. I had already grown accustomed to the easy driving in Star Creek. I waited another moment to build suspense.

"And?" he prompted.

"And you said you've never been to Broadway, which seems ridiculous to me. So I'm taking you to one of my favorite shows, *Sweeney Todd*. I think you'll love it." Everyone always thought it was odd that as a romance writer, my favorite musical was a bit of a dark horror. But something about the twists in the story fascinated me, perhaps because it was so different from my usual genre.

"Wow, are you serious? That's amazing," he replied, his smile beaming. He seemed floored by the gesture.

"An old friend was selling tickets, so I snatched them up. After the show, we're going to dinner with my best friend, Serena, if that's okay."

"Perfect. I'd love to meet her."

We inched forward in traffic, and Will stared loftily out the window. A few minutes later, he said, "I still can't believe you did this for me. It's amazing. Thank you."

And just like that, the heavy weight of his return to the city seemed to shift to true enthusiasm. I was thrilled we had the chance to make our own city memories together.

They would never erase the pain we'd both experienced here, but perhaps they would help soften the edges. With time, they may even overpower the sense of heartbreak we'd felt on the city sidewalks. And maybe, a piece of me considered, Will would someday think about returning to the city. But I was getting ahead of myself. We'd shared a few magical kisses, certainly. But that was it. Wasn't it?

We finally got to the apartment, but we were short on time, so I didn't have a chance to show him around. There wasn't much to show him anyway, as I'd packed up most of the sentimental items and relics in preparation for the trip I wouldn't be taking. Serena had texted that she had to go to the office for a little while and would meet us for dinner. I did pause to show him Gary, who was thriving thanks to Serena's green thumb. Next, I took Will to my favorite café just a few blocks down the street. We scarfed down a sandwich and soup before hailing a taxi and heading to the show.

On the ride over, he held my hand. I looked out the window, feeling lost in the sights I'd missed. Still, his hand rooted me to Star Creek and the newfound contentment in small-town living. I felt like, somehow, I was part of both worlds—the world of Will Westerly and the bakery, my grandmother and the empty streets, and the city with the stiletto-heeled dreams I carried from my mother. They both fit, and that was both magical and confusing.

We got to the theater and took our seats, and it was so special to see the place through Will's eyes for the first time. He was entranced from the moment we walked through the door. When the show started, he was glued to it, and I was glued to watching him make new memories. The early morning, the drive, and the money had all been worth it to experience this with him.

We left the play, and Will couldn't stop talking about how amazing it had been.

"I'm so glad you liked it," I said as we waited to hail a taxi in the matinee crowd.

"I loved it. Thank you so much," he murmured, and then he leaned in to kiss me in the middle of the overflowing city sidewalk. The lights, the honking horns, and the crowds of enthusiastic tourists melted away as we stood, lips touching, for a long moment. Gone were the fears and sadness. Instead, a feeling of comfort, of home took their place as Will put a hand around my waist and pulled me closer. I realized that whether we were in Star Creek or New York, I never felt lost with him. I was grounded in who I was. And that was perhaps the most magical feeling of all.

We jumped in the taxi and got to the restaurant at the perfect time to snag our reservation. We were led to the table, where Serena was already sitting. She leaped up at the sight of us and wrapped me in a hug that went on for ages.

"I've missed you," she said, and I thought she might be ready to cry, which made me almost cry too.

"I've missed you more," I replied, squeezing my best friend tight. We finally let go, and Serena gave Will a subtle but effective perusing.

"So you must be Will Westerly, the amazing baker I keep hearing about. It's wonderful to meet you," she said, leaning in for a hug. It was a brief, platonic hug, but Serena managed to mouth, "He's gorgeous," to me.

We took our seats and ordered drinks.

"How was the show?" Serena asked, and Will gushed about how exciting it was. Serena was all smiles as she listened. I tried to glance over the menu but couldn't focus. I was so proud that I'd arranged today, that it had been a hit with Will.

"Wow, you two are having an amazing weekend. First, the enchanted carriage ride and now the trip to New York. When's the wedding already?" she said, and I shot her a look as Will laughed, turning slightly red.

"Just kidding, you two. Sort of," Serena said, and I gave her a subtle kick under the table.

"So, speaking of relationships, where's Noah? I thought you were going to bring him."

At the mention of Serena's love interest, her face turned slightly red. The smile that spread at the mere mention of his name told me everything.

"He has a trial he had to work on tonight. He sends his regards. He'll be coming to the bake-off, though."

"I can't wait to get to know him," I said. Whoever was making Serena so happy must be a really great guy.

"Speaking of the bake-off, how's it all going?" Serena asked.

"Busy but great. We've got all sorts of fun plans. And thanks to social media, I've got some big bakeries coming, even a few from the city," I said.

"That's amazing! I'm so happy for all of you. But tell me, Lucy. Have you learned how to bake a cupcake yet?" Serena had seen some of my sad attempts at dessert from our time living together.

"I mean, she hasn't burned a batch of cookies or cupcakes in a week, which is good. And one of her cookie recipes is going to be at the festival," Will answered.

"It was only a few batches in the beginning that burned. I'm better now."

"I can see you're better, Lucy. In all sorts of ways," Serena added as the waiter came to take our order.

We spent the rest of the dinner catching up about our favorite shows and Serena's work. She asked Will a bunch of questions about his childhood, his plans, his life. He didn't seem to mind the lawyerly interrogation, answering honestly and even telling a few jokes now and then. Serena and Will got along swimmingly, and when we excused ourselves to the bathroom for a moment, she grabbed my hands in front of the sink.

"He's amazing. I like him, Lucy. I really like him for you. He's fun and witty but also seems so sweet and caring. He's everything Jed wasn't, if I'm being honest. He's a good one." Serena was serious as she stared into my eyes, and it made me want to cry. I was relieved that she felt that way. Ever since Jed, I'd wondered if my judgment was bad when it came to men and love. Her words reassured me I wasn't ignoring red flags or seeing something that wasn't there.

Will was the real deal, and we were headed on the path to being more than just a fling.

"I don't know what's going to happen with you, and I know you have to sort out how he might fit into your dreams, but I can say this—I've never seen you this happy. Truly. I miss you like crazy, but I think maybe Star Creek was exactly what you needed."

I sighed. "I'm happy with him. So happy. But I do keep thinking about how the bake-off will be over in a couple weeks, and I just don't know what to do. I can't imagine leaving Star Creek. First, of course, there's Grandma to think about. She has Herb now, but I know I'll worry being so far away with her still recovering. And it feels like home there. As scary as it is, Will does make me so happy. I don't know if we'll be able to grow our relationship sufficiently if we're long distance, and I hate leaving him with the weight of the bakery. But then, when I think about never coming back to the city, that stings too. Being back here makes me realize how much I've missed it all. And plus, there's the Paris situation."

After Jed left me, I'd gotten through the visit with Grandma, painting on a brave smile and showing her around the city. In the days after she returned to Star Creek, my heart ached as darkness settled in. I felt lost and dead inside. I felt like I might never write again. And that was when it hit me: Paris. I'd always dreamed of going to the City of Love for a visit. But what was stopping me from something bigger?

I was single. I had a job I could do anywhere, even if I felt more successful in the city. A change of scenery, a brave new adventure was what my soul needed. So I'd bought a ticket to Paris and planned on pouring my savings into staying there for the month of January. I'd explore, get inspired to write another book, and who knew? Maybe I'd even have a few flings with some hunky French men. Nothing serious, of course. I'd sworn off love at that point.

But then Grandma had called, and the bake-off required so much focus. I'd headed straight for Star Creek, putting the trip out of my mind. Now, though, I thought about my manuscript that was almost finished—truly my best book to date. I thought of how homey I felt in Star Creek, how my days were filled with purpose of all kinds. And I thought about Will. There was no French boyfriend out there who could heal my heart the way he had.

After I'd committed to staying in Star Creek, I told myself I could still make it to Paris.

But now, a huge question loomed—was that even what I wanted anymore? I'd planned on flying across an ocean to reconnect with my inspiration and passion. It turned out I'd found it in a little town I'd visited repeatedly throughout my life. This time, things had been different. This time, Will Westerly was there. And this time, arguably, I understood an important truth in a new way—family, making memories, and connecting with the community was the best way to feel alive.

Serena exhaled, blowing her bangs out of her eyes. "It's complicated, isn't it? Life? Dreams? Love? But you're smart, and you're passionate. You'll figure it all out. You'll find a way to make it work. I know you will. And whether you're living in the city or Star Creek or Paris or Antarctica, our friendship *will* work long distance. I'll make sure of it."

"Of course it will. I love you like a sister, Serena. Thanks for always being there for me."

We hugged again, both near tears.

"Okay, okay. I have to get back to the office soon to help Noah with the trial. And you have a long trip home and a festival to finish planning. Oh, and a relationship with that gorgeous man to explore. So let's get it together and go order our dessert."

I smiled, nodding. "Just don't tell Grandma we're eating dessert here. Oh, I have a box of cinnamon rolls in my car for you. Grandma sent them. They're not as good as when they are fresh out of the oven, but they're still great."

"In that case, forget dessert. I'll have Grandma Catherine's cinnamon rolls over this place's pretentious dessert any day. And yes, you can use that quote as a review for social media," she said, laughing.

We headed back to the table to gather Will and our belongings. As we approached the table feeling lighter about everything, I froze.

Will was standing beside the table talking to a woman with red hair. Her hands were animatedly flinging about, and I could sense the tension from across the room. Will was staring at her intently, focused on the conversation. I paused, taking in the stiff movements of her arms, the way he looked at her. It was as if it was just the two of them, the rest of the room fading away—including me. Their conversation was clearly heated, but it was also all-enveloping. My stomach sank.

Serena paused, too, taking in the sight. And then, before I could approach or sort out what was happening, the woman turned and left, rushing out of the restaurant right past us.

And so did Will.

TWENTY-FIVE

"Uh-oh," Serena said as we stood in the wake of Will and the woman. I was still frozen, unsure what to do. "I'll get the bill. You go take care of that," she said, nodding toward the door.

I opened my mouth to argue, but she shook her head. "Go."

Without another thought, I headed straight out the restaurant door, terrified of what I would walk into but too overwhelmed to consider it too deeply.

Once outside the door, I glanced right and then left, finally spotting Will leaning against the building. I exhaled slightly to see that he was alone. I meandered down the sidewalk, taking in the sight of him. He was clearly shaken, hands in pockets and jaw clenched. He was looking up at the city sky.

"Are you okay?" I asked gingerly once I got to him.

He looked at me, and I could see he was hurt, broken even. He shrugged. A long pause ensued.

I realized I was holding my breath and exhaled.

"I'm sorry," he said. "I didn't mean to ruin dinner."

"It's okay," I said. "Who is she?" I asked for the confirmation I didn't really need. I suspected already.

"My ex."

The two words hung in the air between us. He didn't say anything else, the tension building.

"I'm sorry," I said, even though I didn't know what for.

He didn't say anything. Cold, distant Will was back, off in another world. I closed my eyes, fighting back tears. I wondered again if my judgment was off because suddenly, I felt like I was back standing in front of Jed, cold and despondent.

"Are you two okay?" Serena asked, coming out the door a few minutes later.

I nodded.

"Everything's fine," Will said after clearing his throat.

Serena gave me a look but didn't say anything else. She hailed us a cab, and we headed back to the apartment. The entire way there, Will didn't say anything.

And his hand was kept strategically away from mine.

THE DRIVE to Star Creek was quiet. I wanted to think it was because we were both tired, but I knew that was a lie. It wasn't just the ex, the whole restaurant situation. It was the city in general and what it meant to us respectively.

For me, visiting the city had stirred a reminder of how broken I felt, how torn in half I was. And for Will, it had apparently been a very blatant reminder of what he hadn't yet overcome.

"Are you okay? After seeing your ex?" I asked eventually, unable to keep pretending everything was fine.

"Fine." A one-word answer. But in that single word it was clear that he wasn't even close to being fine.

I sighed, my head and heart telling me this was a mistake, that I should run. Things had changed so drastically, so quickly, and a part of me wondered if perhaps it was more than just bad luck. Out of all the restaurants, Will's ex had been at the exact one we were at. It was as if the universe was conspiring against me. Maybe it was.

We were quiet the rest of the way home, Will's walls fully up—and mine too.

I DROPPED Will off at his house after making the long trek back to Star Creek. We didn't kiss goodbye. He thanked me for the tickets, for the trip, but I could tell his smile was fake. I smiled back, nodding, but on the way back to Grandma's, tears fell. It had been a disaster, and not just because of his ex—but because reality had slapped me across the face. I'd thought Will and I were headed for something bigger, something stronger than what I'd had in the past. Now, I saw only heartbreak, uncertainty, and pain.

When I pulled into Grandma's driveway, I wanted nothing more than to climb in bed and forget about the day. I dragged myself into the house, expecting to find her and Herb cozy on the couch watching late-night movies. But the only movement in the cottage came from Edmund's galloping paws.

Otherwise, there was bone-chilling silence. I walked back to Grandma's bedroom. She wasn't there, and my heart started pounding. After yelling out "hello" several times with no response, I knew something was wrong. I pushed past Edmund to investigate, trying not to let my mind get away from me. Maybe she was over at Herb's. But that seemed unlikely.

Then I saw the note on the kitchen counter that made me go rushing right back out the door once more, forgetting my exhaustion and my fears about Will as adrenaline and horror surged.

TWENTY-SIX

I was out of breath when I dashed through the hospital doors, leaned on the counter, and asked the receptionist where I could find Catherine Easton. My mind was traveling to the worst places, and when she said Grandma was in the ER, the panic bubbled up even more. I followed her directions, my legs not moving fast enough as I blasted into the emergency wing.

It felt like forever until the nurses, after proper interrogations, led me back, making an exception for the number of visitors probably because of the sheer distress on my face. In a tiny, curtained-off area, I finally exhaled to see Grandma, Herb by her side. She looked tired, her color slightly off. But she was sitting up, talking quietly to Herb. She was alive. She was conscious. I let myself relish in that for a second before rushing to her side.

"Grandma, what happened?" I asked.

The note on the counter had been in neat text:

> *Your grandma is at the hospital. She's with me. She's going to be okay. Herb.*

ONLY NOW THAT I could see her with my own eyes did I slightly believe the okay part.

"Lucy, I'm fine, I'm fine. Tell me about your trip. I'm sorry to drag you back out into the cold. You really should have just called, you know," she said, and I could hear that her voice was shaky and weak.

"You should have called *me*. Grandma, why didn't you call?"

"This is why. I didn't want to ruin your trip for some silly fall," she murmured.

I turned to Herb, confused. He also looked tired, perched in a chair beside her.

"We were wrapping some holiday gifts this evening and watching movies. Your grandma got up to get some more tape, and I noticed she was unsteady and wobbly."

"I was just tired," she argued, rolling her eyes.

I turned my attention back to Herb.

"I was just getting up to help her when she tripped over the end table and fell. She had some scrapes on her, so I rushed her here."

"I needed a few bandages is all. I don't know why they insist on keeping me cooped up here in this unflattering gown."

"Grandma, you should have called," I repeated, teary and worried. I could see the bandages on her arm. I squeezed her hand, upset that I'd been in the city when this happened and worried about what would happen when I returned to the city for good. Would this be how it was? Me feeling out of the loop because Grandma didn't want to affect my busy life? Flashes of my mother came to mind too.

"You're always more important. Family is always more important," I said, tears falling.

"There, there," Grandma said, comforting me and squeezing my hand. "It's okay. I'm okay. I'm not going anywhere, not with the bake-off coming so fast. That is, if they let me out of here before then."

Herb chuckled. "You can see your grandma has been very cooperative," he said sarcastically with a grin. "I think they might discharge her just for some quiet around here."

Grandma shot him a look, which did make me feel better. She was still her sassy self, even if her words were slower and her voice breathy.

"They're running some tests right now. Dizziness and lack of coordination are all par for the course when you're recovering from a stroke. But they want to make sure there aren't any issues," Herb said seriously. "I demanded they do the whole works."

"Which is quite annoying, if you ask me. I'm fine. Now, more importantly, how was Edmund when you got home?"

"He's fine," I assured her.

"Your grandmother insisted I go check on him once we had her settled and the doctors assured me she was okay. That was when I left the note. I didn't want to worry you if you got home and found her missing. She threatened my life if I called and ruined your date."

"Herb, you shouldn't have listened," I said.

"Have you seen all of the baking equipment and kitchen knives that woman has? I wasn't taking any chances," he teased. "But she was okay. I was taking care of her. No need to worry you for no reason, I figured. And your grandma didn't want you speeding home."

I looked at her then, my eyes softened. I could understand that. We were both a little tense when it came to cars and speed for very good reasons.

"I'm glad you're going to be okay."

"Well, now if we could just get the doctor to get me out of here. We have an early morning tomorrow."

"No, we don't," Herb and I said in unison.

"You're resting tomorrow. And maybe all week," I said.

"You need to take it easy. The doctor wasn't happy with how much you've been doing," Herb added.

"He needs to mind his own business. Telling me he's heard from sources I've been working too much. That's just ridiculous."

Herb and Grandma started bickering about what the doctor said. I took that moment to exit the room and find the doctor that Grandma wasn't shy about dissing.

"Hi, I'm sorry to bother you. I'm Lucy, Catherine Easton's granddaughter. What can you tell me about her condition? Is she okay? I'm worried she's doing too much."

"Lucy, your grandma has told me all about you," the doctor said. It was a different one than we'd had the first day I'd come to Star Creek. "Your grandma is going to be okay. Lack of coordination is part of the recovery. But we do need to be careful. I'm concerned because her blood pressure was a little high, even with her medicine. And I can tell she's tired. I don't want to scare you, but she needs to take it easy. I know she loves the bakery and the Holiday Bake-Off, but do what you can to minimize her stress and work."

"I will," I promised. And I would. It would be my only mission.

"She's a firecracker, that one. But we all slow down as

we age, or we should. I just worry Catherine didn't get that memo. She needs to relax a little bit so we can hopefully decrease her chances of another heart incident."

I didn't like the way he said *incident*, and I didn't like the stoicism in his voice. It wasn't just a hiccup—it was terrifying. I'd been so wrapped up in my book, in the Holiday Bake-Off, and in Will that I'd been slacking on watching her health. I needed to do better.

I went to the vending machine to get some snacks for the three of us after the doctor said he needed to run a few more tests. I sat with Grandma and Herb until she begged me to go home to Edmund, which I begrudgingly did. Herb swore he'd stay with her. Still, on the drive back to the house, I couldn't help but worry. What were we going to do after the bake-off? So far, that had been the entire end goal. But it was looking like we needed to have bigger conversations about Grandma, about the bakery, and about me.

There were choices to be made, difficult choices that would impact lives. I crawled into bed, letting Edmund sleep beside me. I cuddled up to the big dog, tears falling on my pillow as I considered how messy the recipe for life really was. No one ever had it figured out exactly, did they?

TWENTY-SEVEN

I called Will extremely early the following morning to apprise him of the situation as I headed to the hospital. I felt bad putting all the prep work on his shoulders, especially since we hadn't had a chance to talk, but I wanted to spend the morning with Grandma. I kept the conversation concise and professional; he did the same. I didn't have the energy to think about it, though. I had other priorities.

Herb had called around one in the morning to tell me they'd admitted her for the night so she could have a bed. When I walked into the room bright and early, she was already sitting up with the morning news on. Despite a night in the hospital, I was relieved to see she looked better. The night of forced rest had done her good. She even wore her red lipstick, which she'd made Herb retrieve from her purse.

"Good morning, darling. Are you hungry? Maybe I can get the nurses to bring you breakfast. And how's Edmund?" Her speech was still a little slower than normal but more familiar. She even had some color in her cheeks. Herb was still in the chair beside her, right where I'd left him.

"I'm not hungry, Grandma. I'm fine. And Edmund is fine. Missing you, of course."

"My poor big guy. I can't wait to smooch his big nose. How much longer, Herb? Should we get that doctor in here again so I can ask him?"

Herb shook his head, eyeing me.

I raised an eyebrow. "Are you causing trouble again?"

"I'd like to think of it as going rogue from the recipe," Grandma replied, taking a sip of the orange juice in front of her. I claimed a chair by Herb and patted his arm.

"What's the doctor saying?" I asked him.

"Am I chopped liver?" Grandma asked.

"You're willing to say anything to get out of here. I know you," I said.

She shrugged in admission.

"After running some tests the doctor said she looks okay to leave. There wasn't another mini stroke or anything. But we do—"

"Have to make sure I take it easy. Yes, yes. But the bake-off is coming quickly, so we've got work to do that I can't complete from this bed."

"Grandma," I said as Herb said, "Catherine."

"I will prop my feet up afterward. You'll see. I'll be attached to the couch so much, you'll have to peel me off of it. I swear. New Year's Eve, New Year's Day, the whole lot of it, Catherine Easton will be perched on the couch watching soap operas. But until then, I'm helping. This festival is important to the town and to me. I will not miss it."

I sighed, looking at Herb. He looked downright exhausted, but he still managed to smile at my grandma. I loved him for that, for the way he was tender and patient with her. For the way he let her be her own, sometimes obtuse, self.

"Well, we're going to agree to disagree on what relaxation looks like. But you are not going to the bakery today. You will be doing some of the feet-propped-up couch sitting you were describing. We can talk again tomorrow."

"Someone needs to check on Will," Grandma said.

"I'll go in once we get you settled at home," I replied. "I'm sure Herb could use a break."

"From me?" Grandma asked, looking shocked.

"No, no. I'm fine," Herb replied. But he did not look fine. He looked like he could sleep for four days.

"I just mean a break from the hospital environment. Herb, why don't you head home and shower. Take a rest. I'll wait with Grandma until they discharge her and then settle her in."

"I don't want to leave," Herb said.

She patted his hand. "I'll be fine. You need to take care of yourself too. It's not like you're a spry chicken, after all."

He grinned and leaned in to kiss her forehead.

"Thank you," he said to me before stretching and then heading out the door. "I'll see you both later."

"I'm counting on it," Grandma replied.

Once Herb was gone and I took his seat, Grandma turned to me.

"Did you bring a notebook?" she asked.

"No, I didn't."

"Right. Okay, well, this napkin will do. And here's a pen I asked the nurse for last night when I wanted to take some notes. Get ready to write, missy. I've got a list of things I need you and Will to take care of."

"What happened to taking it easy?"

"Giving you a list isn't exactly difficult work."

"Easy for you to say," I teased, nudging her arm.

The list of duties took up two napkins. It was my turn to be tired. Still, as I watched her eyes light up over the planning and the list of necessities, the attention to detail, I knew why the Holiday Bake-Off mattered so much to her. It was her tribute to a man she'd lost, to a life she'd fought for, and to the woman she had once been. I could understand not wanting to lose that.

A FEW HOURS LATER, Grandma was settled on the couch begrudgingly, still adding to my list. Herb had showered, rested, and returned looking refreshed. He brought some Chinese food for all of us, which I thankfully scarfed down before heading to the bakery.

Armed with my list, I headed inside to see Will's mom behind the counter.

"How's Catherine?" she asked after she finished ringing up her current customer. She crossed behind the counter to give me a hug.

"She's fine. Just a little scared, but she's going to be okay. We just need to keep her calm."

"That's no easy task," Cindy said.

Will rushed out from the back and also asked about Grandma.

"She's okay," I said, hearing the relief in my own voice. "So much so that she sent us two lists of duties for the day."

Will smiled. Despite everything, he looked better today, more himself. Perhaps he was just putting on a brave face in light of the situation. He wiped his hands on the towel over his shoulder, flour sprinkled all over him. He also crossed from behind the counter to wrap me in a hug. I fell into his arms as his mom headed back to man the cash register.

"Your mom is helping out?" I asked.

"Yes, I didn't know if you'd make it in, and I wanted to make sure I kept things moving for the bake-off. I knew that no matter what, Catherine Easton wouldn't let us off the hook if a single detail was overlooked."

"She is particular."

"Are you holding up okay? I know it must have been scary," he said, squeezing my hand as he guided me to an empty table in the back corner of the seating area.

"I'm fine. I'm fine. It was just... terrifying." And with those words, the tears flowed out as if they'd been waiting for permission to fall. It had all come flooding back, being in the hospital with that nauseating feeling of terror all over again. I'd lost loved ones before, and I wasn't ready to lose one again.

But that was the risk of love, wasn't it? Whether it was a love you were born into or a love you chose, nothing was guaranteed. There was always the risk, the terror that one day, it would be ripped away from you. A medical emergency, a car wreck, a bad choice, an accident. Love was always precariously balancing on the precipice of disaster.

I looked at the man seated across from me. Patient and kind, he'd opened my heart again to the possibility. He had made me feel like my heart would be safe with him, that he'd care for it in ways Jed never could. Yet seeing him with his ex in the city, all the old fears had rushed back.

There were no guarantees, were there? Even if he tried to be the most cautious steward of my heart, he couldn't protect it from disaster or his own heart's whims. He couldn't protect our future from heartbreak or the haunting of the past. And that, perhaps, was the scariest part of it all.

A timer went off in the back, and Will excused himself to go get the cookies out. I sat still for a long moment, staring at a photograph on the wall of Grandma and Grandpa, thinking about how there was never enough time no matter how you looked at it.

TWENTY-EIGHT

By Tuesday, Grandma was anxious to get out of the house.

"I'm going to be more stressed if you make me sit at home and do nothing to help. And I'm tired of being cooped up. It was a tiny, clumsy fall. I'm fine."

Herb, Grandma, and I were at the breakfast table. Herb had come over early to make breakfast so Grandma didn't have the chance.

"Grandma, I know you want to help. Maybe we can have you make phone calls here with Herb."

"Nonsense. I'm fine. The doctor said to take it easy, not to curl up and die at home. I'm not running a marathon anytime soon. I think I can go on a few errands with you. If it makes you feel better, I'll even agree to mostly wait in the car while you hang up the signs."

We were supposed to hang up the festival posters on Monday, but with Sunday night's incident, it had been delayed. I had planned on going myself this morning and then helping at the bakery, but Grandma insisted that she was going too. It was one of her favorite parts of the planning, she argued. As much as I wanted her to stay on the couch and rest, I also hated the thought of her missing out on so much of what she loved.

I sighed, looking at Herb. He raised an eyebrow, silently asking my thoughts.

"Fine, Grandma. But if you start to feel dizzy or tired at all—I mean *at all*—you better tell me. And I will be doing all the major work. You're just along for the ride."

"That's the spirit!" she said, clapping her hands. "Let me go put on my favorite holiday sweater, and I'm ready."

Herb chuckled as he helped lead Grandma back to her room.

"And you're bringing the walker, no exceptions," I yelled. That had been another point of contention. The doctor prescribed her a walker to make getting around easier. Grandma said she wasn't an old lady and would not be using it.

"We'll see!" she yelled.

I shook my head.

"I'll put it in your car," Herb said. "She's feisty this morning."

"Isn't she always?"

"Nothing wrong with a feisty woman. Well, sometimes."

I smiled at Herb's comment. He appreciated Grandma for who she was, difficult parts and all. And that was something magical. It made me think about Will and me, how there was no pretending or pretense... at least that was what I had thought. We'd started out focused on the bake-off. And now... well, I didn't know what we were. I couldn't think about it. I had to focus on the work ahead and Grandma. After the festival, I'd sort it out.

As I walked Grandma to the car, making her lean on my arm against her insistence she was fine, I wondered if I really would sort it out. Grandma was a feisty woman, but so was I, I'd rediscovered these past few weeks. The question was, what would I fight for? Who would I fight to be? I had no clue and not much time to sort it out.

"And we're off," Grandma said as I pulled out of the driveway, brushing away the big decisions. Those were problems for another day.

***

GRANDMA AND I DROVE AROUND, and I stopped to put up flyers wherever she pointed. I also left stacks of maps around various town hotspots. We took a break midday when we hit the Route 22 Diner to get a cup of coffee and a bite to eat. Grandma was supposed to be following a strict diet due to her heart, but she always found a way to justify a "little treat." And who was I to argue? Burgers over kale any day, I always said. I couldn't blame her, although deep down, I did worry a little that it was a bad decision.

"I'm so glad everything is coming together," Grandma said as we waited on our burgers. I felt guilty taking a break while Will and Herb were probably still so busy, but Grandma and I both agreed we'd take them back some surprise lunch to make up for it.

"It really is," I said, thinking about how much we'd accomplished in the past two weeks. It had felt impossible, even to Grandma, when we set out to put the Holiday Bake-Off together so quickly. But here we were, a little over a week out, and it seemed like everything was going to be just fine.

"I don't just mean the festival, dear. I mean with you. I know when you first came here, things weren't going so smoothly because of Jed and the writing. But look at you. The book is coming along, and things with Will are progressing nicely. Star Creek has that effect, doesn't it?" She played with the straw in her water, eyeing me seriously from across the table.

I smiled. "Yes, I think Star Creek is exactly what I needed. The book is something I'm so proud of, but that's thanks to you, Grandma. I really couldn't have written it without all your help."

Hearing about Grandma's life had been more than just inspiration for my book. It was soothing to hear about how everything lined up, how her path, although rocky at times, led her to the life she had. It was a grand life indeed, and it was a grand love too.

"It's been really helpful for me, actually, sharing stories from our life together, especially our early life. If I'm being honest, guilt has been creeping in." She averted her eyes to the paper placemat on the table.

"Guilt about what, Grandma?" I asked, studying her with surprise. She traced a loopy word on the placemat with her finger, perhaps gathering the strength to tell me what was in her heart.

"Guilt about loving again after your grandfather. I know it's been years. I know he would want me to be happy, and Herb makes me so happy. But sometimes, when I'm with him, I just feel like I'm not being faithful to your grandfather's memory." Tears flowed from her eyes, and she looked up to study me, her glasses fogging. Pain was etched in every line, every crevice of her face. My heart broke to see her hurting. I got out of the booth and slid in beside her, putting an arm around her.

"Grandma, there's nothing to feel guilty about. You're right. Grandpa would want you to be happy. He would want to know you were taken care of and finding a reason to laugh. He would want you to explore and have adventures. He would want you to have a partner to lean on. And Herb is someone Grandpa liked and respected. That would make him happy."

"Maybe that's why I feel guilty. It's so weird to think about how Herb and your grandfather were friends, and now—I just didn't plan on this, you know? At first, we were friends in grief. And, I don't know, over time I just realized my heart was in love with him, even if my head was trying to deny it. I love him. And I think he loves me." She paused, inhaling deeply and averting her eyes as if pondering whether to say something. Then she turned back to me and admitted, "He kissed me yesterday."

I squeezed her tighter, smiling at this confession. I'd been waiting for the past few weeks for Grandma to say what I already knew, what we all already knew. Still, I understood her hesitancy. And I wondered if dredging up memories, good and bad, of Grandpa had played a part in her hesitancy.

"It's hard to love, isn't it? For so many reasons, it takes courage. The past always tries to creep in somehow. But, Grandma, one thing I've learned from coming to Star Creek, from Mom, from everything really, is that you have to appreciate the moment, whatever that looks like. You have to trust your heart to lead you to what's best for you. You're right. I was in a dark place with my writing and my heart when I first came here. But you know what? Those hardships led me here, with you, with the bakery, and with Will. I think sometimes you have to step back and ask what makes you happy. And then, you have to be brave enough to trust in it and where it takes you."

Grandma patted my arm. "You're right. Herb makes me

happy. I don't know what that means for our future. I don't know what will happen between us. But he makes me so happy, and that's what matters."

Our burgers came to the table then, and Dina, the waitress on duty, eyed us, confused. She hesitated and then set the two plates in front of us, both on the same side of the booth. We were a mess of tears at that point, but the burgers brought us out of it.

"Okay, enough sad talk. Let's live in the moment, like you said—and enjoy these amazing burgers before we have to get back to work."

I stayed where I was, beside Grandma, and we dove into the best burgers we'd ever had with a side of laughter over a joke Grandma had heard at bingo the other week adding to the fun.

THE REST of the week flew as we were all fully enveloped in festival planning. We ate, slept, and breathed the Star Creek Holiday Bake-Off. I prepped ingredients lists and made phone calls. Will finalized recipes and made a baking plan for the following week. We checked in with vendors and made more flyers. We contacted the mayor and arranged for security. All of this while running the regular bakery, writing my manuscript, fitting in holiday shopping, wrapping gifts, and tackling life.

Will and I didn't get much alone time that week, so we didn't get to discuss what had happened in New York. By the weekend, we were both exhausted, but we managed a simple night out at the diner while Grandma and Herb went to Christmas bingo at the firehall, complete with a visit from Santa. After dinner, we took Edmund for a walk through the park, Will holding his leash tightly as we admired the Christmas lights strung up all around town.

With the festival approaching, I breathed in the simple joy, the warmth that was the holiday season. Despite flashing memories of Will with his ex in New York, seeing him breathe in the simple joy, too, and look peaceful made me happy. I didn't want to ruin it. So I swept the situation under the rug, even though a nagging part of me said it wasn't a good idea. Flashes of my last relationship filled with secrets and walls sent a shiver through me.

Despite the fear creeping in about Will and the chaos of the bake-off, I felt hopeful for the holiday for the first time in a long time. There had certainly been Christmases that were hard and bleak, especially the first without my parents. But this year, Christmas didn't feel like a burdensome cloud hovering over the calendar, a reminder of who wouldn't be at the table. This year, I felt connected in ways I hadn't ever felt. I felt inspired and at peace, knowing that no matter what happened with the bake-off, I'd done my best to pull off a holiday miracle. And along the way, I'd bonded with Herb, Grandma... and Will. There would be no shortage of joy and connection at the holiday table this year, and I was glad for that.

Will seemed to be relishing in the excitement of the approaching holiday season as well. We basked in the simplicity of our time together, which seemed to be what we both craved. We talked about everything and anything that came to mind. We kissed. We laughed. We forgot about the past, at least for a little while, and focused on the moment in front of us. He didn't bring up New York, so I didn't either.

Despite the joy and excitement, troublesome thoughts were always just beneath the twinkling Christmas lights and gingerbread. As the festival inched closer, my head and my heart were in a bitter battle: What would I do after the weekend of the bake-off? Where would I end up? And whatever I chose, what would it mean for me and Will?

I exhaled as we strolled through Star Creek, the cloudy sky masking the stars I hoped were still shining brightly, even if I couldn't quite see them.

TWENTY-NINE

The final countdown was on, and the whole town was getting ready for the weekend. Monday morning opened with a sense of anxiousness for Will, me, Grandma, and Herb. We'd delivered decorations to Town Hall and the other spots where the vendors were going to be housed. We were fielding calls left and right, and Will had already prepped the baking schedule that would start on Wednesday.

I was trying not to panic as I worked my way through the to-do list in front of me. Grandma was reassuring me that everything would be great, especially with four of us tackling the list. And then my cell phone rang. It was Anna.

"How's it going, Lucy?" she asked, her voice chipper as always.

"Great. Really busy but great. What's up?"

"Just wanted to check in on the book and see how you're doing," she said.

"The book is going well. I should be able to finish the draft next week, and then I just need a few weeks for editing and proofing before I send it your way."

"That's fabulous! But about that schedule. Do you think maybe you could move all that up and, say, have a copy to me by Saturday?" she asked gingerly.

I froze, staring straight ahead.

"Um, why?" I asked, my brain screaming that it was impossible.

"Well, there is a significant opportunity from the publisher that has popped up. Something about a cancelled book. Anyway, they loved the first few chapters and synopsis I sent, and they would like to get your book on the schedule sooner than expected. In order to meet editing deadlines and production schedules, they would need your final manuscript in two weeks. Which means I would need your copy this weekend so I could turn it around to you in a couple of days with suggestions."

This couldn't be happening, not now. Normally, I would jump on the opportunity. Although it was a monumental task on a normal week, I would commit to it and get it done. I'd have to forego my usual proofreading from my trustworthy editor, but I knew Anna could take care of any typos I missed. I had gotten substantially better at grammar over the past few years too. Still, to whip the manuscript into shape by Saturday would be a Herculean effort.

And in the middle of the festival prep? Impossible.

"I wouldn't normally put this pressure on you, but they've offered to up your advance if you can deliver, and you would get a significantly higher first printing. With things being a little rough this past year, I thought it was a great income opportunity for you."

She was right. She was absolutely right. But looking into the kitchen with Grandma, Herb, and Will rushing about, I knew there was no way I could essentially be in two places at once—helping with the festival prep and writing my heart out.

I sighed. I hated that I had to pass up such a great opportunity. But family came first.

"I don't think I can make it work," I said. "I'm sorry, Anna."

"Listen, take today and think about it. I know you can do it, Lucy. You're a fabulous writer. Just think about it. Call me back later today and let me know if you change your mind."

Near tears, I hung up the phone. I rubbed my temples, trying to mitigate the panic in my chest. If I couldn't finish the manuscript when they wanted, what if they dropped me altogether? What if this was my opportunity and I was blowing it?

Then again, I couldn't abandon Grandma this week. I couldn't. I wouldn't. Grandma walked over, her sixth sense kicking in.

"What's wrong? Who was that?" she asked. She, too, dealt with phone call anxiety since Mom and Dad's accident.

"My agent," I said, trying to get rid of the anguish from my face.

"What did she want?" Grandma probed.

"It's not important," I said, heading to the case to rearrange the stock.

Grandma grabbed my arm. "It *is* important. What did she say?"

I looked at Grandma. She would know if I was lying. So I told her what the call had been about.

"Call her back now and tell her you are going to do it," Grandma demanded.

"I can't. Not with the festival," I argued.

Will and Herb both emerged from the kitchen.

"What's going on?" Will asked.

"Nothing," I said, but then Grandma filled them in.

"Oh my gosh, what a great opportunity! Lucy, call her back now and tell her you'll do it," Will said.

"It's not possible. I can't leave you all hanging."

"We've got this," Herb practically shouted as if he were rallying the troops. "You need to get that manuscript done. It's a great opportunity."

"But how will you all get everything done for Saturday?" I asked, feeling both thankful they were so supportive and guilty.

"My parents are retired. One phone call, and I'll have my parents and Grandpa John over here to help. I know they'll pitch in. We've got it covered," Will assured me.

"But I don't want to miss out on everything," I said.

"Why don't you bring your computer here?" Will asked. "You can work in the corner. We'll deliver you coffee and baked goods. Then, if you need a break or have a moment, you can join in."

"I don't know," I said, the daunting task now sinking in.

"You can do this. I know you can," Will said, stepping forward and grabbing my hands. He looked at me with such faith, such determination that I believed him. For better or worse, I actually believed him.

"Okay," I said. "You're right. I can do this. I'll finish by Friday so I can be at the festival, though. That's the only way this will work."

"Yes!" Grandma cheered, and the other two joined in. They all embraced me in a group hug for a moment, offering words of encouragement. I felt like I was off to the Olympics. In some ways, I was. It would be the most challenging week of my life—but it could also be the stepping-stone to my dreams.

I called Anna back and committed to having the manuscript to her by Friday.

"That's wonderful news! And I know you'll pull it all off. Your first chapters were great. I have no doubt in you," she said.

I had the support all around me—now I just had to believe in myself. I rushed back to Grandma's to claim my laptop, returned to the bakery, and set up shop at my table for the week.

It wasn't going to be easy, especially knowing how long the to-do list was. But within an hour, Will's family had arrived; the reinforcements were in place.

His mom, dad, and grandpa all swung by the table quickly to give me a thumbs up and to cheer me on before heading to the kitchen to be put to work.

It was a small town, Star Creek. It wasn't a publishing mecca like New York. But the one thing it had the city didn't? All this unbounded support, encouragement, and belief in the beauty of my dreams and my ability to carry them out.

I was right where I belonged. I put my fingers on the keys and got to work.

THIRTY

I spent the week feverishly writing in the corner, and my grandma spent her week busily making phone calls to finalize details for the festival from the table at the opposite corner. Herb kept a close eye on her and made sure she wasn't out of her seat too often. This annoyed her no end, and despite my earbuds, I was fully aware of several bickering matches.

Will's entire family jumped in to help, working overtime to get all the cookies and cupcakes baked for the festival. In addition to monitoring Grandma, Herb kept the front of the bakery running and answered phone calls from tourists confused about parking or vendors needing extra supplies. It was a team effort, and I was so thankful to have these people on my side in what felt like an impossible task.

Every time I was ready to give up, feeling like the book couldn't possibly be finished in time, Will seemed to sense it. He'd show up right when I wanted to call it quits with a cookie or a cupcake and a fresh cup of coffee. He didn't say a word, knowing perhaps how important it was for me to stay focused. I would nod, he would smile, and we would go back to our respective tasks. We barely spoke to each other all week, both focused on our work.

I did take breaks to eat lunch and dinner. During those times, when we were all gathered, Will's family and mine, it was a true stress reliever. Herb and Grandpa John would exchange funny stories, and Will's parents were always full of adventurous tales about Will growing up. Together, we all committed to making magic happen for the town. Together, we pulled through and by Friday afternoon, two things were clear:

1. We had enough baked goods prepared for the army of people we were expecting.
2. I'd made my deadline.

After the bakery hours were officially done and Grandma turned the sign to Closed, I headed home to do one final proof of the book while everyone else finalized plans for the next day. I'd been in the team meeting in the morning and had written down my schedule of events to check on and things to be in charge of. We'd divided the actual work for Saturday so we could all enjoy the festival as well. I was looking forward to it after a grueling week of solitude on my computer.

A few hours after leaving the bakery, I stood up at my desk, stretched, and then hit Send on the final manuscript. Overpowered by emotion, I stood in the pride of what I'd achieved for a moment longer, thinking about how this story really was a labor of love and reconnection. I'd reconnected with Star Creek, with Grandma, and, most importantly, with myself over the past few weeks. Without the trip to Star Creek, this book never would have come to be. That was pretty magical.

It was out of my hands just in time to enjoy the festival, and I couldn't be happier. I wandered to the kitchen to grab a snack when I heard an abrupt knock followed by Herb letting himself in... Edmund blasted off the couch to greet Herb, and I turned to the living room to look for Grandma.

Then I froze. Herb looked terrified, and Grandma wasn't anywhere to be seen.

My heart started to flutter because this time, the bad news hadn't come from a phone call or a note on the table. It had come from a knock at the door.

THIRTY-ONE

"Is she here?" Herb asked, frenzied and shaken.

"Who?" I asked, not believing what he was insinuating.

"Your grandma. Is she here?"

"No," I said, shaking my head.

At that, Herb held his head, exhaling loudly. I could see tears starting to form in his eyes.

"She's missing, then," Herb said. "And it's all my fault."

"Come, sit. Tell me," I ordered, hurrying him to a seat at the table but desperate for details. He was clearly distraught, and I didn't want something to happen to him, even though I was panicking. With Grandma's health, I certainly didn't want her lost in town. I told myself to breathe and to get the facts before I panicked, although it was definitely too late for that.

"We were finishing up at the bakery, and we both stepped out back behind the storage area to get some air. And, well..." he said, looking bashful now. He ran a hand through his thin, gray hair, sighed, and squeezed his eyes closed as he admitted his truth. "I told her I love her."

I studied him, seeing the embarrassment bubble up even now.

"And then what happened?" I asked. I wasn't expecting this to be the inciting incident.

"She told me she loved me too," Herb said. "But then she excused herself. I thought she went inside or was having second thoughts. When I went back in after regaining my composure, Will said she hadn't returned. I scared her away and now... who knows where she is? We looked all around the bakery, even at the café down the street. She's gone, Lucy. It's all my fault."

I sighed, rubbing a hand through my own hair now. Grandma couldn't have disappeared into thin air. Clearly, Herb's words had scared her, or more than that, maybe the fact that she'd said them back had upset her. I thought back to our conversation about love and her guilt for Grandpa.

"Stay here, Herb. You stay here just in case she comes back."

I grabbed my car keys and headed out the door. I knew exactly where Grandma was—and I knew why.

SHE WAS SITTING on the familiar bench when I got there. She'd had it installed by his grave a few years after his death, saying his headstone wasn't comfortable. She was lost in thought and only glanced up when my car screeched to a stop. Her hands were folded in her lap, and she looked at ease sitting there, despite everything.

I slowly approached and sat on the bench beside her. Snow was piled up all over the cemetery, but she'd wiped it off Grandpa's stone. The snow created a silent ambience that was peaceful in a soul-filling way.

"I miss him," I said simply, starting the conversation with a very real truth.

"As do I," she said, reaching for my hand.

I scooched over on the bench and leaned my head on her shoulder.

"I'm sorry if I worried everyone," Grandma said.

"You gave Herb a scare, you know," I said. "What happened? Why'd you take off?"

Tears flowed freely from her eyes.

"I don't know," she admitted.

"Don't you?" I asked gently, squeezing her hand.

"I do know. I felt guilty. Because I love him. I told him I love him, and I do, Lucy. I really, truly love Herb. I have for a long time. But saying it aloud, it just felt—it felt like I was being unfaithful to your grandfather. Our love was a story for the ages, as you know from the book you've been working on. All those memories, all those stories. How can I try to replace him? What would he think?"

I sat up straighter, reaching over to wipe at Grandma's cheek.

"First, there's no replacing Grandpa. No one thinks that's what you're doing. Not even Herb. But, Grandma, there's no shame in opening your heart again. Grandpa died, but you didn't. Your heart didn't. Your capacity for love didn't. Isn't that what you told me when you talked about second loves? That they're better because you know love and who you are at that point? I'm not saying your love story with Herb will be better or worse than your love story with Grandpa. It will be different. It will have its own ebb and flow. But if you could open your heart a second time and have such an amazing story with Grandpa, why couldn't you find something beautiful a third time? And don't you think Grandpa would want that? To see you happy?"

Her face had softened. She sniffled, looking at me. "I just don't want to stop loving your grandfather. I can't let that go," she said.

I put an arm around her. "I don't think you have to. I think you can hold space in your heart for both, and I know Herb understands. He's lost his love too. You're both heading into new territory, but it's together. What better man to navigate these complicated waters with than Herb, who has been through a similar experience?"

"You're right," she said, rubbing her eyes. "You're right."

"And I see the way you two are together. It's special, Grandma. You don't find that every day. I think you should stop worrying about appearances and what's right or what's honorable. Start thinking about what makes you happy, really happy. Start following your heart. The rest is just extra."

We sat in the quiet for a while longer. Eventually, Grandma was the one to stand up.

"Take me home. I need to finish my conversation with Herb," she said, standing taller and prouder. As we walked to the car, she turned and paused for a second. She blew a kiss to the grave. "Forever, my love. I love you forever."

We headed home then, to Herb and the future. I was the one who was teary on the drive this time.

THIRTY-TWO

Friday night felt like Christmas Eve even though it was only December 22. I could barely sleep from unquenchable anticipation. Still, as I tucked myself into bed, I told myself the festival would be great. We'd done all we could up until that point to prepare for the bake-off. The weather was only calling for a few flurries, and some of the contestants had already arrived in town. The festivities were about to begin.

I woke up extra early on Saturday, a ball of nervous energy. Grandma was already making breakfast in the kitchen when I got up at four in the morning.

"Grandma, what are you doing? We can just grab something quick at the bakery or on the way," I said.

She held up the spatula to shush me. "Trust me. It's going to be a long, busy day. It won't hurt to take time and eat a hearty breakfast. You'll thank me later, I assure you."

Obliging her, I sat at the table with my phone and notebook. I checked the bakery email, fully expecting disasters already. Grandma had warned me to expect at least two things to go wrong—they did every year. I was pleasantly surprised to find only one email asking for clarification on the address of the Holiday Bake-Off location. Maybe this was a good sign.

Herb came over as soon as the pancakes were finished, as if he had a breakfast sixth sense. Or as if Grandma had already texted him. They had still been talking when I was getting ready for bed the night before. They'd apparently overcome the whole love situation because Herb strolled over and greeted Grandma with a kiss, and she didn't shy away from it.

"Love is in the air for the bake-off," I said as I lifted a cup of coffee to my lips. Grandma pointed the spatula at me, but I just laughed.

We sat down and ate breakfast, Herb and Grandma radiating happiness. It was good to see that they'd worked everything out. I was happy for Grandma, so happy.

But there would be time for that happiness tomorrow. Today, we had to focus.

As soon as our pancakes were down, I got out the list and reviewed my notes for who was to be where and when. We were all starting off at the bakery to make sure Will had put the final touches on the cookies and cupcakes we'd need. Grandma and I were then going to travel around the festival sites through town to make sure the vendors had what they needed and to deliver complimentary cupcakes. After that, we'd meet back at the bakery.

Grandma and Herb had the early afternoon to enjoy the festival while I helped with things at Star Creek Bakery. She would kick off the competition in the early evening before returning to the bakery, and Will and I would have the rest of the evening to explore the festival, check up on vendors, and to see how the bake-off was coming along. We'd all be at the gazebo for the crowning of the winner.

If everything went as planned, that was.

We had extra hands on deck in case we ran into any snags. Will's family was coming around ten in the morning, and Serena and Noah would be in town by noon at the latest. They'd all offered to help out with shifts at the bakery or anything else we needed. It was comforting to see everyone pulling together.

The festival didn't officially kick off until noon, so we had a few hours to finish prepping. Still, it felt like the to-do list was never-ending.

"Does the list of tasks ever go down?" I asked Grandma when we got to the bakery and I flipped through my notes. She had actually reminded me of two more tasks I needed to add to the list on the way.

"It'll go down tomorrow, after the cleanup."

I groaned. "I didn't even think of the cleanup part."

"Well, luckily, the church down the street usually comes and pitches in. Pastor Rodney is a fan of our cinnamon rolls, so he'd do just about anything to get in my good graces and snag a few. It will be cleaned up pretty quickly once he gets the whole congregation out here."

That was a relief because by tomorrow, we'd all be in a sleep coma for most of the day.

Of course, when we got into the bakery, Will was already hard at work. He was putting some finishing touches on cupcakes and filling the front case when we arrived.

"Why am I not surprised you're already here?" I'd thought we might beat him. He had his towel draped over his shoulder, of course, a sign he was in work mode. He wiped his hands on it, walked over, and kissed my cheek. That would never get old.

"So how are we feeling? Ready for the big day?" he asked me as Herb and Grandma settled in.

"I am. Nervous, of course, but I know we did everything we could to make this whole thing a success. And we pulled in some big-name bakeries, so that should help us, especially with social media. I think today could be a big deal for us."

"I know it will. But we do have a tiny problem," he said.

"What's that?" I asked.

"We iced some of the Peppermint Paradise cupcakes yesterday too soon and they're a melted mess. I've already started a new batch, but we're going to need to make quite a few more in order to have enough. Your grandma said that one's a yearly staple."

My stomach dropped. "What are we going to do? We can't get off schedule. Grandma needs to do her check-in, so she can't help." I tried to tell myself to take a deep breath.

"I've got this," Herb said, strolling straight for the kitchen. He went to the corner and claimed his apron—Will had bought him one, apparently. "You and Catherine can go check in on the vendors. My man Will and I will get this taken care of. I'm a pro at the Peppermint Paradise ones."

"Except for the icing melting off bit," Grandma observed, grinning. She turned to me. "This will be perfect. Let the boys finish up in the kitchen."

I agreed hesitantly, going through a few of the checklists with Will before heading out. I was secretly happy, though, to get to go with Grandma. I did want to see how things were coming together—and also hopefully avert any other issues that might have already cropped up.

"Have fun out there," Will shouted from the back as he and Herb got to work.

"You bet," I replied with a smile, and then we were off.

WE STARTED AT TOWN HALL, where the memorial wall of lights was set up along with the Mistletoe Kissing Booth with the shelter dogs. It was also the central location for the ingredients for the bakers. Currently, with several hours until the festival officially began, it was essentially chaos.

A few other vendors were setting up their booths in Town Hall, and they were feverishly trying to get organized. The owner of Anne's Candles—Anne, no surprise there—was barking orders at her husband, who was lugging a precarious stack of boxes. The shelter volunteers were trying to set up their donation stand while tending to the needs of five very excited dogs.

Will's dad was putting the finishing touches to the actual kissing booth, and I gave him a wave. He was bent down to put some screws in the bottom corner of the booth, and a Pomeranian was jumping on his back playfully. I laughed at the sight, and Grandma and I wandered to the ingredients table. After we had verified quantities and items were exactly where they were supposed to be, Trina emerged with a clipboard.

"Hey, you two! How's everything going? Can you believe it's the day of the festival? Now, let's just go over my list and make sure everything's in order," she said, and began rattling off all sorts of questions. Grandma took over, answering them promptly. I was so relieved Grandma was having a good day and was feeling great. I really needed her help to make sure the festival went smoothly. Plus, I was happy she could be a part of the day that meant so much to her.

Since Grandma seemed to have the review of details handled, I wandered over to the memorial wall. There was a gorgeous, twenty-foot red banner covered in holiday trees and angel wings. On a table were hundreds of bright green sticky notes, tape, and several markers. Instructions on the wall said to hang a note to memorialize a loved one you were missing. On the wall, dead center, I noticed a single note already hanging. I walked over to read it.

To my forever love, Paul, for the beautiful life we shared and the legacy you've left. This festival wouldn't be happening without you, and I know you're here with us today. I love you forever, my love.
    Your Catherine

TEARS CAME TO MY EYES. I had no idea when she'd had time to complete the note. I was guessing she'd stopped sometime the night before or perhaps she'd written it when the idea originated and given it to Trina to put up. Still, the fact that Grandma began the festival with this keepsake, that even as she gave her heart to Herb, she didn't forget her love for Grandpa, moved me to tears. After a long moment of studying the note and thinking about all we'd both lost, an arm wrapped around me.

Grandma stood beside me, studying the single note. She didn't say a word, nor did she need to. We were both lost in the memories and also the realization that today was about so much more than Christmas and cupcakes. It was a day to celebrate the legacy our family had built, the love we had for each other, and the sense of community that had arisen from Grandma's bakery dream. She'd impacted so many lives with Star Creek Bakery. *They'd* impacted so many. That was their legacy.

After a long while, Grandma walked over to the table and picked up a note and a marker.

"I thought you would do the honor of writing one for your parents," she said, tears welling.

I nodded, smiling at her thoughtfulness.

Grandma patted me on the back and walked over to the Mistletoe Kissing Booth, perhaps needing some fur therapy. Or perhaps it was more about giving me the space I needed to grieve, to remember, and to conquer the sadness I spent so much time burying.

I stood for a long while, thinking about what to write. It finally came to me, how to capture my parents' love for me and each other. I wrote it out, studying the simple words, the letter to their memory.

And then, I put it in my pocket. It was not for others to see but for me. It was my processing of their legacy and how it affected me. I took another green note, a blank one, and wrote out a simple message.

Mom and Dad,
   Forever missed. Forever loved.
Love,
Lucy and Catherine

I TAPED the note to the wall right beside Grandpa's. Then I gathered Grandma and took her to the selfie station set up by a local photographer. We got a few photos together, and I placed the strip of printed pictures in my back pocket with the memorial note. They would be tokens of a day that meant so much more than I ever could've imagined.

Grandma's health was something I never wanted to change, but in a way, I was thankful for the chance to come to Star Creek and experience all of this with her. It had put so much into perspective.

TOWN HALL WAS one of several places on the map with Holiday Bake-Off vendors. Some of the in-town businesses were participating with special activities and discounts as well. We also had a kids' corner set up in the church on Main Street, and that was our next stop.

Mr. Barbary was alight with energy as he organized his candy booth at the church. I smiled at the sight of the gorgeous jars of candy he'd arranged. For twenty-five cents, kids would receive a red paper sack they could load up with candy from the bar. Underneath the tablecloth on his L-shaped tables were boxes and boxes of candy. I'd gone a little crazy with the ordering when Grandma told me to buy as much candy as I wanted, fully supportive of Mr. Barbary's return to his passion. She, too, was hoping it would ignite an interest in a new candy shop for her dear friend.

After ensuring Mr. Barbary had everything he needed, we also stopped by the Rudolph dart game at the church, which was coming along nicely, and the present pond, which was a play on the duck pond game at carnivals. Red-and-green tinted popcorn and white cotton candy that looked like snow were also available for the kids, which the local firefighters were handling.

A projector on the back wall of the church played some cute holiday movies, and beanbag chairs donated by a local school created a tiny movie theater experience for children who wanted to take a break from the festivities. In the same corner, a hot chocolate bar offered refreshments for kids and adults alike. The jars of marshmallows, candy, sprinkles, and various other hot chocolate add-ins were mesmerizing. Green-and-red streamers decorated almost every inch of the place, and faux snow covered the floor. In the far back corner, Santa sat on a rocking chair, prepared to take photos with kids as an elf stood nearby ready to hand out candy canes and books the community had donated. It was, in short, a magical Christmas wonderland.

"I love this," I said, looking around.

Grandma smiled. "It's all thanks to you, dear. I'm so glad you stayed to help. I feel bad you had to abandon New York for a while, but this wouldn't have happened if you hadn't. The community is going to have such a wonderful day today." She squeezed my shoulder, and I smiled as I stared at our handiwork.

The festival had been difficult to organize at times and exhausting. My ticket to Paris was supposed to be used in a little over a week. Suddenly, Paris didn't seem so important or even like a good fit. Standing in the basement of the church watching community members scramble to create a Christmas experience all the kids would forever remember, I knew being in Star Creek meant so much more.

We made a few more stops around town, ensuring everyone had what they needed. We delivered a few rolls of tape and permanent markers to some vendors. We got some change for a vendor selling leggings and another who was selling jewelry. We made sure everything was in place for the bake-off stage, and then, satisfied that in a few hours the contest would launch without an issue, we headed back to the bakery.

When we arrived, Serena was waiting for me, and I squealed when I saw her.

She was perched at a corner table with a handsome blond man. At the sound of my screeching, she dashed across the tiled floor, her blue scarf dangling around her neck and her beret almost falling off.

"I've missed you," she said, squeezing me tightly to her. The blond man approached behind her, hands in his pockets. Once Serena and I were finally done hugging and exclaiming our love for each other, she turned to him.

"Lucy, I want you to meet Noah. Noah, this is my best friend you hear about all the time, Lucy."

He extended a hand for me to shake, exchanged pleasantries, and I studied him while trying not to be too obvious.

A moment later, Will, Herb, and Will's mom emerged from the kitchen. We finished introductions, the bakery a bubbling cacophony of hellos, laughter, handshakes, and hugs. The energy was strong, and I was so happy to have all my favorite people in one place.

After a little while, Grandma said, "Everyone, can I have your attention?"

We all silenced and turned to Grandma, who was leaning against the front counter.

"I just want to say thank you," she said as we all gathered around. "Thank you for being here and helping make this festival possible. It means so much to the community, but it means even more to me. When my husband died, I didn't know if I'd be able to go on with this place without him. I especially didn't know if I could carry on this wonderful Christmas tradition, both physically and emotionally.

"But all of you being here with me today to continue the legacy means so much. More than you know. And I also want to say a special thank you to Lucy, my granddaughter. Your hard work these past few weeks has made miracles happen. Truly. I want everyone to have a wonderful day, and be sure to take a break and enjoy yourselves. You all deserve it."

"I should've brought champagne for the toast," Serena said, smiling.

"A girl from my own heart," Grandma said, winking. "I'm kidding, I'm kidding. Only hot tea for me these days," she added when Herb and I both gave her a look.

"Okay, only an hour to go. Let's get everything ready for the early afternoon rush," Grandma said, and just like that, it was all hands on deck as we prepared for the start of the festival.

THIRTY-THREE

The festival kicked off uneventfully at noon, but soon after, as Grandma warned, tiny issues started cropping up. For one, it seemed like every tourist wanted to stop at Star Creek Bakery for one of the specialty flavors. This made me happy since it meant my social media efforts had been worthwhile. However, when Berry Christmas was running dangerously low an hour into the festival, Will panicked.

Luckily, our reinforcements jumped into the kitchen to make more. Serena did a supply run for cherries since we were running low on those, too, for some of the other recipes. Noah and Will aproned up and started baking. Grandma and I ran the front of the bakery, which was sheer chaos.

The second issue was when the Rudolph game was unmanned, which we caught word of an hour and a half into the festival. Will's mother, a true champion, jumped in her car and headed straight for the church basement to get to work.

All in all, things were going well. I looked at all the customers coming into the bakery and saw nothing but smiles and heard jubilant chatter. Kids animatedly listed all the stops from the festival maps they wanted to visit, and couples languidly strolled in for some of the fun Christmas names. I could see why Grandma put in so much effort year after year. It was magical how some cupcakes and a holiday festival could warm the town, even on a snowy December day. The Christmas spirit was surging.

We made it through the initial rush of visitors, and the new batches of Berry Christmas were coming out of the oven like clockwork. With our supplies replenished and the lines settled down, we made a new plan of attack. Serena offered to run the front of the bakery while I went with Grandma to kick off the competition. Noah and Will kept baking—Serena was more than a little glad to see that Noah had natural skills in the kitchen. I think she was envisioning weekend cinnamon rolls in her future. Maybe Grandma would give them the recipe.

Herb had driven over to Town Hall already to assist with the Mistletoe Kissing Booth. I think he just wanted to scope out potential friends for Edmund and Sylvester as he was a true softy for animals, and apparently the shelter had brought over a few cats to join the fun.

Grandma and I hopped in my car to make the short trek to Town Hall, although the traffic in Star Creek was much more hectic than I could've imagined.

"What a rush," I said when we neared Main Street.

"It is, isn't it? It's exhausting and stressful. Every year, I feel like it's never going to come together. But when it does, it's magical. To see the town and all the tourists out and about, enjoying a blustery day. It makes it all worth it. And I've had so many people, old and young, talk about how they just don't feel like it's the holiday season until the Holiday Bake-Off happens. It makes people feel like they aren't so alone, and if that's the only legacy I leave behind, I'm happy."

"You're leaving behind a much bigger legacy than that. Your bakery has done such big things, Grandma."

She shrugged, never one to brag about herself. "We all have our strengths. I was just fortunate enough that this town embraced mine. And I've been lucky to have family and friends who support my dreams."

We got to Main Street a little before five. I found a parking spot as close as possible after dropping Grandma off and then made my way to the gazebo. The participating bakeries were already lining up at their designated spots. Each team held a banner so the gathering crowd could see who was competing.

Grandma, sporting her brightest shade of red lipstick, was heading to the microphone when I got there. I smiled at her encouragingly and let her shine as I stood to the side.

"Welcome, everyone. We're going to get started soon, so I want to say thank you to everyone who came out and made today possible, and thank you to our wonderful bakeries present today for the fun! We want to remind everyone to be back here at 8 p.m. for the judging. Bakers, when I say go, you will head over to Town Hall, where all the ingredients are laid out. Your basic ingredients such as flour, sugar, butter, eggs, and the like are already at your assigned home. You will have five minutes to pick any specialty ingredients you want from our tables in order to make your masterpiece. You cannot use anything else once you leave Town Hall, and you cannot omit any items you take. You must be back at Town Hall by eight, where you will submit your cupcakes for the judges. We will announce the winners at nine. Any questions?"

I looked out at the bakers, who all seemed nervous.

Some of the competitors were from well-known bakeries in New York. I couldn't imagine this would be that challenging for them.

The excitement in the crowd rose as Grandma got back on the microphone. "Let's talk about who our judges are," she said, turning to her left where the three judges were lined up.

"First, from New York, we have our very talented culinary instructor Michael Annison. He's a true powerhouse when it comes to all things baking and has a ton of awards to his name. We're honored to have a real expert in the house to help us make these difficult decisions. Let's offer Michael a warm Star Creek welcome."

The crowd cheered and I turned to eye the pastry chef Grandma had had me contact. He was an instructor Will knew in the city, and Will had given us the connection.

"Next, you all know him as the kindest resident in Star Creek. He grew up here and has been a staple in our community. Today, he is running the candy booth, and he also runs the consignment shop we all know and love, but I'm hoping maybe with a little encouragement, we can bring back the permanent Mr. Barbary's candy store for our future generations to enjoy. Bringing his knowledge of sweets and treats, let's welcome Mr. Barbary!"

Blushing, Mr. Barbary stepped forward. I knew it meant a lot to him to be asked to judge the contest, and I couldn't think of a more perfect person.

"And finally, well, it's me, Catherine Easton. I've been the owner and baker at Star Creek Bakery for over fifty years. Goodness, where has the time gone?"

Grandma got the loudest cheers from the crowd by far. She blushed, but I clapped loudly and let out a yell. She turned to me, shaking her head.

"We're getting ready to give you the go-ahead, but I would be remiss if I didn't mention this lovely lady. My granddaughter, Lucy Carter, has joined me for the past few weeks from New York to help organize this entire shindig. If it weren't for her hard work, well, honestly, the festival wouldn't have happened this year. Let's give Lucy a huge thank you."

Now it was my turn to step forward and blush. I waved to the crowd, knowing every phone call, every late night, every ounce of sweat was worth it.

"Okay, okay. No one should give me a microphone. Enough talking. Bakers, get ready! Get set! Go get baking!"

And with that, the ninety-eight bakers representing forty-nine bakeries in attendance dashed toward Town Hall as the crowd went wild. I didn't have time to bask in the sentimentality of it all. I rushed to the parking lot behind Town Hall to make sure every baking team knew where to go. I had my organized list printed, and I'd checked it at least twenty times. Still, I had a panicked feeling. What if one of the community members didn't actually show up? What if there was a miscalculation?

I exhaled the biggest breath of my life when all the bakers had found their cars and taken off. The area cleared out, and I took a quiet moment in the empty parking lot to thank my lucky stars I hadn't messed anything up.

Now, we had a few hours until the winners were announced. I returned to the gazebo to collect Grandma and head back to the bakery. Will and I were about due for our break to explore, and I was feeling like a giddy child ready to get out into the festival with him.

THIRTY-FOUR

When Will and I finally got a chance to break away from the bakery, it was nearing the end of the festival. I was worried we wouldn't get a full experience, but Star Creek never quit until the last moment. All the vendors and booths were still going strong, and the energy remained vibrant in the town.

We headed to Main Street, both exhausted but re-energized by the sights and sounds of the festival. We stopped briefly to take in the live nativity, but the donkey was a bit unhappy and the sheep was trying to make a run for it. We laughed, and Will stepped in to help calm the donkey. We walked on, catching up to a few strolling carolers who stopped and sang a Christmas song.

Will turned to me. "Do you want to dance?"

I eyed the bustling streets, snowflakes caressing us. We were both frazzled and sweaty from a day spent running around. It felt sort of silly, especially since it was a holiday carol. Nevertheless, looking into his eyes, I knew I couldn't say no.

He reached out his hand and led me to the middle of

the closed-off street. The singers stayed put, watching us as I leaned into him, resting my arms around his neck as his hands found my waist. We slowly swayed, and I couldn't stop staring at him, at the man who had opened my eyes and heart back up in just the short time we'd known each other. All my fears melted—our trip to New York that had ended awkwardly, the ex, my fear of getting hurt again. In his arms, I felt like it didn't matter. What mattered was being together in that moment.

A small crowd of festivalgoers gathered, and I heard so many "awws" that I knew I was blushing. When the song stopped, some of the spectators actually clapped for us, and Will spun me out and took a mock bow. I laughed and laughed, shaking my head at his showmanship.

"Come on, you show-off," I teased as I grabbed his hand and yanked him inside. The first stop on our list was the Mistletoe Kissing Booth. Will took pictures of me with an adorable pug I'd had my eye on at the shelter. As if on cue, right when the picture was snapped, the pug slurped the entire side of my face. The resulting photo was me laughing so hard, my eyes were closed. It was pure perfection.

Will and I stuck with the picture theme and hit the photobooth next, doing all of the required poses. We printed two film strips, and when I examined them, I couldn't stop staring. Happiness radiated from us in a way that was almost sickeningly sweet. Almost.

We made our way to the food truck section of the festival and got different meals so we could share. I snagged an order of street tacos, and Will went for the cheesesteak and fries. We ate until we felt like we might vomit, both obsessed with each other's entrée.

Then we reached the church and the games section.

"That one," Will said, pointing at a huge stuffed reindeer. "I'm winning that one."

I shook my head. The reindeer was enormous, so big I didn't even think Edmund could pick it up. To play, we had to throw darts at a picture of Rudolph and try to get the dart right on a tiny dot on his red nose. In order to win the extra-large prize, we needed three hits.

"No one has won it yet," I said, looking at the huge stack of prizes.

"Oh, I'm going to win," he assured me.

"Hope you brought a lot of cash," the familiar game attendee said, laughing.

"Mom, don't taunt the festivalgoers," Will replied, handing over a five-dollar bill for three darts.

"If you do win, people are going to say it was rigged," I said. Will's mom had been stationed at the Rudolph game all day. Will's dad had offered to give her a break, but she seemed happy running the booth. She was all smiles, even after so many hours of watching people throw darts.

"Oh, no way. Everyone knows I don't take it easy on my son," she teased.

"You can say that again," he replied, tossing the first dart.

Three darts in, he hit the nose twice—and had enough points to win a tiny toy duck.

"It's okay," I said, but Will was persistent. He handed over another five dollars and tried again.

I think the total was $55 when he finally threw the elusive third dart needed to equal the reindeer prize. He didn't mind since the money was being donated to the local food pantry, so it was for a good cause, as Will reminded me over and over. He insisted on taking a photo of his mom handing me the reindeer so he'd have proof.

"My hero," I said, kissing his cheek as I lugged the huge reindeer on my hip.

I didn't have the heart to remind him there was zero room for things like that in a New York apartment. I proudly carried the huge prize through the crowds while everyone stared.

We stopped for a hot chocolate and found a bench to sit on, the three of us. The reindeer was perched on the outside of the bench, keeping watch on the crowd as I snuggled into Will.

"This festival is even better than I could've imagined. Even being involved with it, I couldn't have pictured something this beautiful," Will said. He squeezed my hand with his free hand. "We make a good team."

"We do," I murmured, enjoying the warmth of his body and the feel of his hand on mine.

He let go of my hand and reached up to my face, cradling my chin. He looked into my eyes for a long while. "I'm so glad we both ended up in Star Creek. I'm so thankful we found our way to each other, even if it took some heartbreak. I'm falling in love with you, Lucy, and I can't wait to see where this journey takes us."

We kissed then, soft and sweet, the taste of hot chocolate lingering on both of our lips. When we pulled back, I stared into his eyes for a long while, thinking about how my book title was aptly named.

The second was even better. The second love. The second kiss. The second time Will told me he was falling for me.

It was so, so, so much better, I thought as we stood from the bench and headed back to Town Hall to see what was happening at the bake-off as it was winding down.

Nothing could ruin the moment, I was thinking to myself.

But then, as if I'd tempted fate, everything changed. Will locked eyes with the woman I'd seen in the city. A wave crashed into everything as if fate was stepping in, as if we were doomed to fail.

It was the redhead from the New York bakery standing with a tall, handsome blond man.

Will let go of my hand and whispered, "No way."

THIRTY-FIVE

"Will?" the redhead asked.

He stared ahead, not taking his gaze off her. It was like
the entire festival faded away and it was just the two of
them. Lugging the reindeer, which suddenly felt ridiculous,
I hesitantly followed Will to the table where the woman
and man stood behind their cupcakes.

"Marissa," he said icily. His entire body had gone tense,
and his hands were in his pockets.

There was a moment of silence between them.

"I didn't know you'd be here. I heard you moved out of
the city, but I had no idea it was *here*," she said.

He nodded. "And I had no idea you'd be here," he
replied and then turned to me.

I felt my stomach drop. How had this happened? In the
chaos of the festival, we'd never talked about the list of
bakeries coming. And now—this. I felt guilty for sending
Will into the lion's den.

"Oh, you remember Kevin, right," she said then, wrapping an arm around the man standing beside her.

Silence. Nothing from Kevin or Will. Just an icy stare.

"The bakery is doing really well," Marissa said, and I saw Will tensing his jaw.

"Fabulous," he growled. I'd never seen him so angry. "I have to get going back to the bakery and make sure the cupcakes are all good," he said then. He didn't turn to me, didn't introduce me. He spun on his heel and took off. Abandoning the reindeer at the table, I ran after him, my stomach in knots.

Thinking of the list, Marissa Lillith had enrolled M&K Bakery from New York. How? How hadn't this come up?

I followed Will down the snowy, dark street, a scene that was becoming all too familiar. My stomach dropped at the realization. Once outside, he leaned against the stone wall of the building, staring icily into the abyss.

I approached him. "I'm sorry. I had no idea. I don't know how I missed this."

"It's not your fault. You wouldn't have known," he said. "It's just a bad trick from the universe, I guess. A slap in the face yet again."

I leaned against the wall beside him, looking out into the festival that no longer felt so magical. We said nothing for a long moment, but I could hear Will's ragged breathing. He was enraged, thrown back into the headspace of the past. I could understand that. But as I stood there, thinking about his reaction in New York and now here, how he had clammed up, another thought crept in.

He still loved her.

He said he was falling in love with me, but he still loved *her*. I swallowed, my chest feeling heavy now.

"It used to be M&W," he said then. "M&W Bakery. My dream. We ran it together, and at first, it was spectacular. And then it wasn't. Then she fell for him. And suddenly, my dream was no longer our dream. My dream was dead. I see he's stepped right into my shoes."

I could hear his voice wavering. I reached for his hand. He held mine, but not tightly. His heart wasn't there.

"I'm sorry. I really am. It can't be easy."

He slapped his free hand against the wall. "It isn't easy. Because here I am falling apart, and there she is, having it all. She's not upset or rattled by any of it. She's better than ever."

I stayed exactly where I was but felt myself distancing from him. My hand was still holding his, but it didn't feel the same as it had an hour ago. A gap was widening between us once more, a gap I didn't know if we'd bridge this time. I was no stranger to being second choice, and the sting of betrayal from Jed wormed its way between Will and me. I'd done everything to be what I thought Jed wanted, and it still wasn't enough. Was I doing the same thing once more? Was I walking right into the trap again, being second choice? Tears threatened to fall from my eyes. I fought to hold them back. I let go of Will's hand.

"What did she say in New York? The conversation looked heated," I ventured, wanting to know but also not wanting to know.

He shook his head. "She was just telling me that she missed me, that I should stop by the bakery sometime."

"That's horrible," I said, meaning it. I could see the tears welling in Will's eyes. He didn't say any more. I felt myself pulling back. He did too.

Will decided he would go back to the bakery. He didn't want to be at the big bake-off reveal. I could understand that. But as I watched him walk away into the festival crowd, leaving me behind, I also felt frustrated. I could understand how seeing her might throw him for a moment.

But what about me? Wasn't what we had strong enough to alleviate that pain? Hadn't he, too, found something new? Wasn't he feeling better than ever? And if he wasn't, what did that really mean about what we were? Perhaps I was just a rebound, a distraction from his broken heart. Maybe, if I were digging deep, he was too.

Maybe there was nothing special about us together. Maybe we were just two broken souls thrown together by a coincidence that had come to feel like more thanks to a Holiday Bake-Off.

Maybe we were nothing at all, I thought as I glumly trudged to the gazebo, trying to paint on a smile I no longer felt.

THIRTY-SIX

"What's wrong?" Grandma asked when I smiled at her on the gazebo stage. We had a few minutes until the winners were announced, and the bakers, tired and overwhelmed, were gathering in front of the winner's circle once more. Mr. Barbary and pastry chef Michael were beside Grandma, both holding their stomachs from trying dozens of cupcakes to determine the winner. With the trophy behind us, a crowd was gathering in the street in front to see who would be crowned the grand winner. Herb was standing near Grandma, nervously shifting from foot to foot.

Serena and Noah were directly in front of us, and so were Will's parents. Everyone in the entire town had collected here to see who would win. Everyone except Will.

"Nothing," I replied to Grandma, my gaze scanning the crowd until I found Marissa and Kevin, snuggled up together. Her vibrant red hair looked magnificent, despite the baking challenge, and her ruby red lips were perfectly pouty. She was gorgeous, I thought, jealousy surging.

"Do not lie to me," Grandma said, grabbing my hand. "And where's Will?"

I sighed, looking at my watch. It was almost time for the Star Creek Holiday Bake-Off finale. I pulled Grandma aside.

"The girl from M&K Bakery from New York City, the big bakery I was thrilled about?"

"Yes," Grandma said, turning to look at the crowd. Her eyes landed on Marissa.

I turned, too, but luckily, she wasn't paying any attention. "That's Will's ex-girlfriend. The one who broke his heart and took the bakery from him."

Grandma covered her mouth with her hand, shaking her head.

"Oh no. He didn't see her, did he?" she asked after a beat.

"Uh-huh. With her new boyfriend."

"Oh dear."

"I didn't say anything because of everything going on, but we saw her in New York too."

"You're kidding? I thought the energy was a little off when you came back."

"Yes. And now she's here. Both times, it was clear he was heartbroken to see her. He clearly still loves her." My voice unexpectedly cracked at the confession.

"I hope you don't think this says anything about you," Grandma said, touching my shoulder. "I'm sure he's just shocked."

"But if he really was falling for me, Grandma, shouldn't he be fine with whatever Marissa is doing? Shouldn't he have at least introduced me to her or leaned on me for help?"

Grandma sighed. "A broken heart is fragile and unpredictable. Give him some space, and give yourself some too. It will all be okay. These things are never easy."

I appreciated Grandma's attempts at comforting me, but it wasn't working. It just felt like things had taken a turn—and not for the better.

"We'll finish this conversation afterward. I have to announce the winners," Grandma said. She pulled out her red lipstick and did a quick touchup as I held up my phone so she could use the screen as a mirror. When I gave her the thumbs up, I painted back on the fake smile as Grandma approached the mic.

"I'm so excited that it's finally time to announce the winner of this year's Star Creek Holiday Bake-Off! We had a really hard time making our decision."

Mr. Barbary, who was clutching the trophy with both hands, nodded in agreement.

"This year's winner is..." Grandma paused for suspense.

I looked out into the crowd of bakers. They all looked exhausted but anxious. I couldn't help but find Marissa in the crowd. She clung to Kevin's arm.

"The Minus One Bakery for their delicious, gluten-free Razzle Dazzle cupcake."

Pastry chef Michael was holding a silver platter. He pulled the lid off to reveal the gorgeous blue-tinted cupcake, complete with Razzle candies on top.

A cheer went up from two brunettes to our left. They were hugging each other and jumping up and down. The entire crowd was cheering loudly as the women approached the gazebo to claim their trophy and the $500 prize check.

"This cupcake will be available at Star Creek Bakery all year long and, I'm hoping, at the Minus One Bakery in New Jersey as well. I will confess, I've never understood the gluten-free cupcake trend, but you ladies changed my mind. I guess an old dog really can learn new tricks, so thank you."

Grandma hugged them, and the crowd started to disperse. I looked out one more time to find Kevin comforting Marissa. I couldn't help but be drawn to her, if for no other reason than to try to understand what she was to Will. Just as I was preparing to head back to the bakery, wondering what would happen next, there was a tapping on the microphone. Herb had walked forward to claim it from its stand.

"Hello? Excuse me?" he said way too loudly. A screech caused children and adults alike to cover their ears, but it served Herb's purpose; everyone froze in place. They all turned to see what was going on, and Grandma stopped mid-conversation with the Minus One Bakery ladies, confusion on her face. I studied Herb, wondering what he was doing. He shifted his weight to his other foot. One hand was in his pocket. He was uncharacteristically nervous.

"I'm sorry. I don't mean to interrupt this exciting moment. I'm so happy for you, Minus One Bakery. But I have one more announcement, if you don't mind. Catherine, will you join me?"

My heart pulsed with excitement. Grandma looked genuinely confused. She cautiously stepped forward and stood across from Herb.

"What's wrong?" she asked, watching him suspiciously.

I stepped closer, and held up my phone to video the scene. It felt like this would be a moment we'd want to relive, if things were going in the direction I suspected.

He exhaled loudly into the microphone. The crowd again gasped and held their ears.

"Catherine Easton, I've known you for many, many years. We've both gone through so many triumphs and tragedies as neighbors, living right next door to each other. But this past year especially, I've come to really get to know you. And the more I've come to know you, the more I've come to love you. From your breakfasts that lack bacon but not love, to our spontaneous movie nights, every day I get to spend with you is magical.

"You remind me that there's still so much life and laughter out there for me. You remind me what it is to have fun and to look forward to getting up in the morning. There's no one else I would want to spend my final years with. There's no one else who makes me feel like life is still so beautiful. I want to spend as much time with you as I can in whatever years I have left. I want to make more memories. Most of all, I want to stop having to walk across the sidewalk and go home every night. I want to build a home with you."

Everyone in the crowd was silent, and Grandma raised a hand on her chest. For a split second, I was worried this was too much. I tamped down the negative thoughts, though. This moment was too beautiful. I'd waited this whole month for something this big for Grandma and Herb. I wouldn't let fear usurp it.

Herb's legs creaked until he was on one shaky knee. He winced as he reached into his pocket. Grandma gasped. He pulled out a black velvet ring box, popped it open, and held it shakily up to Grandma.

"Catherine Easton, I know I'm not your first love. But I would love to be your last. Will you marry me?" he asked.

The crowd gasped, and some women shouted "aww" nearby. My own heart pounded. I angled the phone better to see Grandma's face.

There was a pause. I felt the entire crowd hold its

collective breath. Panic started to rise within me. Oh no. She couldn't possibly.

Her stoic face turned into a huge, relentless smile.

"Of course I will," she said.

Herb sprang to his feet like he was a man fifty years younger. Grandma kissed him slowly, sweetly, and the crowd exploded. Claps, cheers, and laughter rang out on Main Street. All of the bakers applauded, and Herb, wearing some of Grandma's red lipstick, pulled the ring out of the box and put it on Grandma's finger. He held her hand up for the crowd as if she'd just won a boxing match. In truth, it was Herb who had won perhaps the most challenging match of all. Grandma snuggled into him, and the crowd kept clapping. I reached up and swiped at a tear rolling down my cheek.

And then, as if on cue—and perhaps they were—fireworks we definitely hadn't planned exploded in the distance. Red, white, and green bursts of light illuminated the sky. It was beautiful. Grandma looked overpowered by emotion, and rightfully so. Her life had shifted so much in one night. Then again, so had mine. I stood to the side, watching the fireworks and thinking about how happy I was for Grandma.

A hand tapped me on the shoulder. I jumped, startled by the invasion. I turned to see Marissa, right in front of me.

"Be careful with him. He's complicated. He doesn't let go easily." Her words were punctuated with an iciness that chilled me to the core.

"What do you mean?" I asked, my stomach dropping.

"I mean that even after I told him it was over, Will clung to me like a sad little puppy. Begging me to take him back. Crawling to me saying I was the love of his life."

I glared at her, hating that she was trying to paint Will in such a pathetic light.

"He's moved on," I said, defending him, wanting my words to sound stronger than I felt.

She laughed. "If you say so."

I opened my mouth to reply—with what, I didn't know.

"He came by to kiss me before he left the city for here. Tried to convince me to take him back even then. I don't think those kinds of feelings die in a few weeks. He might say he's moved on, but he had to move to a different state to put space between us. You saw how upset he got when he saw me at that restaurant. Do you think if he were back in New York he'd feel the same about you? That he would be over it all?"

I hated the smug look on her face. I hated the way she talked about Will. I hated what she'd done to him.

But when I opened my mouth to reply, nothing came out. Because most of all, I hated that it felt like she was right.

Will said he'd moved on. He made me believe it. But a painful thought stabbed into my chest. Was he looking at me but thinking about her? Was I putting effort into building a relationship while his heart still pined for another woman?

Was I Will's fool just like I'd been Jed's?

Before I could think of something to say, Marissa was gone, weaving through the crowd as she clutched Kevin's hand. I stood there, alone, leaning against the side of the gazebo and wondering how things had gotten so messy.

THIRTY-SEVEN

On Sunday, I wanted to sleep the entire day away, but it was Christmas Eve. And the buzzing of my cell phone on the nightstand woke me up earlier than I would have liked. Still, my heart jolted even in the midst of grogginess when I looked at my phone. It was Anna, my agent.

"Darling, how are you? Happy Christmas Eve! I have wonderful news. Just wonderful news. The publisher loves the book! Absolutely love it. They think it's going to be a smashing success."

"Oh my gosh, really?" I asked, smiling despite my body feeling like it had been hit by a bus. "What about the edits?"

I'd expected to have some rewrites in the coming days from Anna.

"You wrote your heart out on this one. I felt like under the circumstances, it was in great condition to pass off to them. And it was. They love it."

"That's amazing, Anna." Despite my exhaustion from the festival and my confusion over Will, nothing else seemed to matter in that moment. I'd pulled off the impossible. I'd written a story they loved.

"There's more. They actually want to get a rush on production. That means their editing process is going to be a whirlwind. Also, they're wondering if you can be at their offices Tuesday, January second. They want to meet with you in person to talk strategy."

"That soon?" I asked in disbelief. How was this happening so fast?

"Of course," I heard myself saying, although as I hung up the phone with Anna promising to send more details later via email, I couldn't help but feel my heart sink.

I'd known this time was coming. The bake-off was over, and Grandma was doing well. I was worried still, of course, but she had Herb to keep a close eye on her. I knew she was in good hands. And Will was there to run the bakery. I hadn't planned on staying forever. I had my life in the city to get back to. Still, unexpectedly, I also had a life here now. How could I make both work?

I flopped backward in bed, the phone cradled on my chest. I thought of Will and what it would mean for us. Was there even still an us? I pictured the way he'd looked at Marissa and thought about what she'd told me at the fireworks.

Deciding I might as well get out of bed and get moving on the cleaning portion of the day, I peeled myself out from under the covers. We had a lot of organizing and tearing down to finish since we were too tired last night and had come straight home. I dragged myself to the kitchen and pulled out ingredients to get pancakes started. Grandma was still asleep, which was uncharacteristic for her. But she'd had a big day, even bigger than expected. I smiled, thinking of the look on her face when Herb proposed. It had been a beautiful moment that made me almost forget all my own love woes.

I texted Serena when the pancakes were in the frying pan. I kept making the pancakes, Edmund standing with his head resting on the counter. The smell of breakfast must have wafted through the house because Grandma came out then. She was moving very slowly, and I worried she'd overdone it at the festival. She was leaning on furniture more than she had been in recent days, her balance clearly off. Still, she smiled at the sight of breakfast.

"It looks amazing," she said, eyeing the plate of food. Her words were slow, her speech not as articulate as I would have liked. But it had been a busy day. It made sense she was tired, I reminded myself, trying not to panic.

"Can you help put out plates, Grandma? Or should I say Newly Engaged Grandma?" I smirked at her, and she rolled her eyes. She did dramatically flash her ring, though, as she set the table. "I'm so happy for you," I added.

"Me too. I can't even lie. Me too. And I'm glad you were there during the big moment, darling. It meant a lot to me."

"Can you put out two extra plates? Serena and Noah are joining us," I said.

Grandma nodded. "Will?" she asked, raising her eyebrows.

I silently shook my head.

Grandma put out the plates then walked over, hugging me as I flipped the next batch of pancakes. "Have faith, Lucy. You two still have a story of your own to write."

I shrugged, sighing. "I don't know if there ever even was a story at this point." I thought about the news I'd received from Anna. I needed to tell Grandma. But for some reason, I couldn't bring myself to tell her. I didn't want to overshadow the proposal by bringing up her story with Grandpa. Deep down, though, I think a part of me didn't want to face the music. New York was calling to me, Will and I were struggling—and maybe Star Creek wasn't home like I thought it could be. Still, she deserved to know. I thought about telling her—but at that moment, the door opened, and Edmund went running.

"Where's my soon-to-be wife?" a voice called out.

Grandma giggled like a schoolgirl.

"Soon? You think I'm organizing a wedding right after that whole festival?" she asked, teasing.

I smiled at how their breakfast greeting was now accompanied by a kiss. I thought if Herb had his way, the wedding most definitely would be soon.

The door opened again a few minutes later as I was finishing the last few pancakes. Grandma warmly greeted Serena and Noah. The house was filled with laughter, but one laugh was missing. I shoved the thought aside as the five of us sat down to breakfast.

"Where's Will?" Serena asked. I hadn't had a chance to fill her in.

"He'll meet us at the bakery for cleaning," I said, sipping my juice.

"Which reminds me. Noah and I are available if you need help. We're staying until the twenty-sixth since my family is out of town, so put us to work."

"Nonsense," Grandma interrupted. "There's not that much to do, and we have enough hands. The church is helping out, so it won't be that much, honestly. You two need to explore Star Creek and take advantage of the quiet. Route 22 Diner is an excellent place for lunch, and there's also the lovely park. Go out and enjoy the holiday spirit that's still alive and well. You've done enough work already."

Serena started to argue, but I jumped in. "She's right, Serena. We're fine. You two go enjoy your day. We can meet up for coffee later if you'd like. And dinner is, of course, at five tomorrow at the bakery." Serena and Noah were going to spend Christmas Day with us and then head to her family's the next day. Noah's family wasn't around, so they were happy to have dinner with us at the bakery, which was our tradition.

Since their first year in business, Grandma and Grandpa had started the tradition of hosting Christmas dinner at the bakery for friends, family, and anyone in the community who didn't have somewhere to be. Some years, the bakery was full. Some years, it was just the two of them. Grandma always made sure she had enough food for an army, which was shocking considering the proximity to the festival. I would be helping her prep the hams and sides later in the day, a task that felt monumental considering how tired I was.

"If you're sure," Serena said.

"Positive," I replied.

"Okay, okay. Besides, you have that hunky Will of yours to help, I suppose."

I just nodded. It was too complicated to get into this early in the day.

We finished breakfast, and Serena and Noah headed off to their day of small-town life. Before they left, Serena hugged me, leaning in.

"I know something's up. I can see it on your face. We'll catch up tomorrow? Are you okay, though?"

"I'm fine. Just a few complications. Nothing serious," I replied, thinking of the book news that should be exciting but also felt complicated.

"Okay, as long as you're sure. Call me if you need me before tomorrow," she said.

I nodded, appreciative to have such a good friend.

Grandma, Herb, and I cleaned up the dishes, got changed, and prepared to head into the bakery. There were odds and ends to tie up, supplies to put away, signs to take down around town, and some general cleaning up to do. I also wanted to update social media with pictures from the event.

My body was tired; my mind was tired. My heart was tired. But there was truly no rest for the weary, so onward we went, a newly engaged couple and a newly broken woman, ready to face the day. Or at least pretending to be ready.

WE WERE ALL LESS peppy than usual as we got to work. Will had done some cleaning the night before while we were all at the ceremony announcing the winner. I tried not to think about why he'd disappeared, but our interactions were definitely tense.

I flashed back to my first day when Will was cold and distant, as if he couldn't trust the new woman in the bakery. I was getting similar vibes from him again, which hurt. I wanted to shout at him that I wasn't her, that I wouldn't break his heart like she did. But I was too angry, too hurt myself to bridge the growing gap between us.

The radio played Christmas songs, but he wasn't singing. The familiar towel was draped over his shoulder, but it clung to him in a defensive way instead of the usual, welcoming style I was used to. Everything had changed.

As promised, the congregation showed up to help clean up Town Hall. I went with Grandma around town to collect signs and clean up some of the other areas. I tried to insist that Grandma should go home and rest, but she wouldn't hear of it. Despite being exhausted, she was on cloud nine. I tried to don a chipper mood for her and thought I was doing a great job, but after our last stop, when we pulled into the Star Creek Bakery parking lot, she put a hand on my knee before I got out.

"It will be okay. Talk to him. You two both have walls up."

I nodded. "It's just complicated, Grandma."

"What isn't complicated?" With that, she shrugged and got out of the car, as if there were no questions to be asked about it.

When we were finished and getting ready to go home and start cooking, Will walked up to me, uncharacteristically nervous.

"I was wondering if you want to get some lunch maybe?" he asked, averting his eyes.

My stomach actually knotted, and not in the butterfly kind of way.

"Sure," I answered, although I was terrified of whatever he was going to tell me, and more terrified of how I would react.

We agreed he would pick me up in an hour since showers were in order for both of us. As the water rushed over me and I shampooed my long, heavy hair, I tried to let the fear and negative vibes wash down the drain as well. But old habits stuck around like a plague sometimes.

WE SAT on the bench outside of the Taco Time! truck parked near the gazebo on Main Street. Bundled up on the bench, we ate our tacos and stared out into the desolate street. Everyone in town was prepping for their Christmas Eve traditions, the excitement of the bake-off perhaps fueling them for their own hectic schedules. It was weird to think how just one day earlier, this same street had been bustling with activity—and with Marissa.

"I'm sorry about yesterday," Will finally said. "And for what happened in New York. I'm sorry you got stuck in the middle of it." We'd been making small talk and discussing the clean-up of the festival, both avoiding the true topic we needed to discuss. "It just really threw me."

I waited for him to continue. But he didn't.

"I feel like there's still a lot between you two," I said, putting down my taco in the foil wrapper to turn and face him.

He sighed. "Yes. No. I don't know. The thing is, I don't love her anymore, Lucy. I know that. I know I'm done with her, that she's my past. But why does the past linger in your head so much—and your heart? Like seeing her there with him, living out the dream that used to be mine, it was so painful. And it just brought back all the good and bad times for some reason, a punch in the gut of memories and dreams that are gone now."

I breathed in a little easier, appreciating his vulnerability. At least he was letting me in now. That felt like an improvement. Still, it hurt to hear him talk about her. He said he didn't love her—but was that only because she wasn't a possibility? I thought about the restaurant, about the way she completely caught his attention at the bake-off. I shuddered, thinking about how maybe it would be a different story if she wanted him back. I thought about what it felt like when the man you loved was in love with someone else.

My heart couldn't take that again.

We sat for a moment in silence, both thinking. Then I spoke up.

"I just have to know. If she wasn't with someone else, would you be with her?" The knot in my stomach returned. If he said yes, what would that mean for us? Could I be okay with it? I didn't know if I would be able to move forward knowing that. But if he said no, could I move forward knowing that everything was about to change for us in a few days?

He set his empty foil wrapper on the bench. He took my hand in his and looked me in the eye.

"I'm interested in you and you only, plain and simple."

It was the answer I wanted to hear—but also the answer I was finding hard to believe.

"That doesn't answer the question. Would you be with her if you could?" I pushed.

He sighed. "It doesn't matter. She's moved on. I have too."

Tears welled. He loved her. Somewhere in that heart, he still loved her, didn't he? And was he really moving on if she could rattle him so much?

He had said he loved me, and I wanted so badly in that moment to believe him. I wanted to understand where he was coming from, to empathize with the hurt because I'd felt it. I wanted to believe our love story was true and real and possible. I wanted to have faith that we could win. But too many realities gnawed at my heart.

I wanted in that moment to confess my own heart to him, too, and to lean in and kiss him. I wanted the Marissas and Jeds of the world to fade away. I wanted to sit there by the gazebo forever, staring at Main Street and making promises to each other we would keep. But there wasn't just Marissa in the way of our hearts.

"I'm going back to the city on Friday," I blurted.

"Why?" he asked, one word that didn't even begin to capture all the questions lurking between us.

"I have a marketing meeting with my publisher."

"Oh," he said. "So then what? Are you coming back?"

I squeezed his hand. "I don't think so," I said honestly. It was the first time I'd said the words aloud, and I shuddered at the reality of what they meant. I was leaving—leaving Star Creek, leaving Grandma, and leaving Will. My heart panged. But it was better that way. I had my own dreams, and this thing with Will—it was a risk. It was safer, smarter for me to go back to my life and for him to settle into his, with Marissa or not.

"I see," he said quietly.

"I just don't know what that will mean for us, if I'm being honest, Will. I've loved being here with you. You've really been amazing, and I can't imagine not getting to see you every day. But this is so new, and I just don't know how it's going to work out long distance. We have such different dreams, you know? And I can tell you still have feelings for her. I just think it's too soon for whatever this is between us."

"So you don't believe me?" he asked, pulling his hand back. His words and eyes were still soft, but I could feel the cracking of his heart. That made me want to crack into pieces too.

"I saw how you looked at her both times, Will."

"You of all people should understand it's not so easy to move on," he replied. His voice was hardened, his eyes glaring.

"It doesn't matter, does it? Love her or not. Love me or not. We're going in two different directions. We have different goals."

"You're afraid. I understand that, but, Lucy, don't throw us away because of what the past did to you."

"I'm not," I retorted. Now it was my turn to get angry. "It's not about Marissa or Jed. It's about us. My dream is in the city, and yours isn't."

"Don't make this about our dreams. Because I don't know if our dreams are that different. We want to live out our passions. We want to be happy. I'm happy with you, Lucy."

"And I'm happy with you, Will. But I belong in the city, and you don't want to be there. And dreams don't build a relationship. I've learned that before. And I don't know, maybe we got caught up in the excitement of the bake-off and just got ahead of ourselves."

He stood up from the bench then. "No. I won't let you minimize this. I know what I feel, and I think you do too. You're going to New York. So what? It's the modern era. We have all sorts of ways to stay in touch. And I have a past. Who doesn't? If you don't want this, that's fine, and I understand. But don't let excuses get in the way of something that could be beautiful."

Now it was my turn to stand. The anger was palpable in my tone. "I'm not making excuses, Will. I'm being realistic. Love is a mess sometimes, and it doesn't always work out. This isn't some happily-ever-after novel. It's real life."

"And real life can't be a happily-ever-after?" he asked, arms crossed against his chest. We were now several feet apart, and I felt the distance growing.

"That's not what I'm saying. It's just... I don't know, Will. I don't know what I'm doing right now."

"Well, I know this. My feelings for you aren't going anywhere, even if you do. So let me know when you have it figured out."

"Will," I said, but he walked back to the car wordlessly. When he got there, he turned to me. I'd followed him.

"I'll walk," I spewed, pausing at the car door.

"I'm not letting you walk," he replied, his words softening. "Come on."

"No, I'm good." I turned to head down Main Street toward Grandma's house. It was only about a mile away. Still, with the cold and my already weary body, I knew I might regret it.

But pride takes precedence over cold, and a stubborn heart won't always admit the truth.

We parted ways. I wondered if I would ever see him again.

At that thought, my heart really did shatter.

THIRTY-EIGHT

I woke up on Christmas morning feeling anything but jolly. Sunday had been a day of clean-up, recovery, and prepping for Christmas dinner. Herb, Grandma, and I had settled in after our cooking was done to watch some Christmas movies. Still, I couldn't help feeling glum about how I'd left things with Will. I hadn't slept well.

I went to the kitchen, where Grandma had already laid out a breakfast spread. She looked good, was glowing even. It was partially because she was having a good day health-wise—but probably more because of the ring on her finger. I hugged her as she wished me merry Christmas. Herb was already there, sitting at the table waiting for his bacon and Christmas-tree-shaped pancakes. We ate, Edmund even getting a plate of his own since it was a holiday.

After the meal, we gathered in the living room to exchange gifts. I tried to smile and enjoy the day. A couple weeks earlier, I'd imagined Christmas with Will in the mix. I thought about the baking pans and recipe book I'd bought for him, now carefully wrapped in my closet. I didn't know if I'd ever give them to him.

Gifts were exchanged. Edmund got a new spring sweater, a dog bone, at least ten chew toys, and a blanket—Grandma insisted the entire time that the dog wasn't spoiled. Herb and I just side-eyed each other. Grandma bought Herb an indoor gardening set he had been talking about and tickets for a winery tour upstate. Herb bought Grandma a gorgeous diamond pendant, a few books she'd wanted, and a matching sweater set for her and Edmund, which she loved. Sylvester got catnip treats, which Herb promised to give him later.

Next, I handed Grandma a box. When she opened it, she gasped.

"How did you get this done?" she asked as she stared at the portrait of Edmund I'd had commissioned. I'd had to pull some strings with some friends in New York to get it rush ordered and delivered in time, but I was so pleased to see Grandma's tears. It was worth it.

Herb opened his next. A portrait of Sylvester. I was so thankful for the artistic community connections I'd made. He also couldn't stop staring at it.

And then, I handed them one more box with a grin. It had been a risk, but it had paid off. Grandma pulled back the paper carefully. In a golden frame was a painted portrait of Herb and Grandma. I'd borrowed a photograph she had on the fridge. In the picture, they were in a garden some-where, perhaps long before they'd even admitted to them-selves they had feelings for each other. Even though they stood apart, the way they smiled at each other—you knew just by looking at them that they were crazy about each other.

"You knew. You knew before we did," she said, tears falling as Herb thanked me profusely.

"This will be beautiful in our home," Herb said, and the

way he leaned into *our* told me he was more than happy with how things had turned out.

"Your turn now," Grandma said, handing me a stack of packages. I thanked them as I opened beautiful journals, antique pen sets that would be so inspiring, and a new laptop case. There were also scarves, new dresses, and a gorgeous necklace.

"You got me too much," I said.

"What are grandmas for? But here, there's one more. It's not from me, though," Grandma said. I looked down at the tag and saw handwriting that made my stomach plummet. "He gave it to me yesterday and asked if I would pass it along."

My heart nearly leaped out of my chest. I carefully pulled on the silver ribbon, peeling back the red paper to reveal a jewelry box. I was upset he wasn't there to give me the gift himself. Our future didn't look good, so in some ways, I didn't even know if I wanted a memento of what could never be. But when I opened the box and looked at the silver pendant, tears flooded. Two words were scrawled in the center: *Dream big.*

But it wasn't just the words that meant so much—it was the script. Because instantly, I recognized the writing. I didn't know how he'd done it, but it was my mother's handwriting. Those beautiful, scrawling letters that were unmistakably hers. I crossed the floor to show Grandma, and she gasped.

"Oh my word. Beautiful. Thoughtful."

"How?" I asked, shaking my head.

"He asked if I had a card or letter from your mother a couple weeks ago. Said it was for a gift. He must have used that."

Tears fell from my eyes as I sank to the chair.

"He's a good one," Herb said as we all sat in silence, taking it in.

And he was, I thought, touching the delicate necklace and thinking about how special it was. He was a good one in so many ways. Could that be enough to save us?

———

AFTER ATTENDING A CHURCH SERVICE, we headed into the bakery to set up for the holiday party. The bells rang, and I looked up to see Serena walking through the door. I was so happy to see her. I needed someone to spill all my feelings to.

"I've never seen you this tired, even when you pulled that all-nighter to finish your first book," Serena said as I handed her a coffee. Noah was back at the hotel dealing with some work calls. He wanted to give us time to ourselves, which I was grateful for.

"I'm so tired. It was a lot."

"It was wonderful, though. Everyone was talking about how it was the best festival ever. And all the dogs that came got adopted at the Mistletoe Kissing Booth. You should be so proud. I know I'm proud of you, all of you," Serena said.

"I'm thankful you were there to help out, but also because I've missed you."

I stirred creamer into my coffee, sitting at a table in the bakery thinking about what I'd accomplished in just one month. I *was* proud. I'd not only pulled off the manuscript deadline but also managed to help the bake-off happen. It was a good feeling to know I'd been a big part of both of those crucial elements. Now, though, with the whirl of the festival over and my book with the publisher for edits, I was able to process everything completely.

"So, what's next?" Serena asked, cradling her coffee in her hands.

I exhaled. "Well, Anna called. The publisher loves my book. I have a meeting at their office coming up on January second."

"That's wonderful, Lucy. But *that soon?*" she asked, looking alarmed.

I nodded.

"What about Will?" she asked quietly.

I sighed. "I don't know. Things have... changed. For one, his ex was at the festival. She entered her bakery, which used to belong to her and Will."

"What?" Serena asked. I promptly explained the scenario. When I was done, she shook her head. "That's crazy. First New York—and now here? Poor guy. What are the chances?"

"I know. It had to be hard. But still. The way he looked at her, Serena... And afterward, she told me to be careful, that he didn't let go easily. I feel like maybe what we had wasn't that special. Maybe he's still hung up on her. Maybe I was just a rebound." It felt good to get those very real fears out in the open.

"Oh, stop it. No way. I saw the way he looked at you. That man adores you. And I've known from the first time you mentioned him that you adore him too. So yes, he was thrown off by seeing his ex. Who wouldn't be? But that doesn't mean he's wrapped up in the past or doesn't want a future with you."

I wanted to believe her, and my fingers instinctively went to the necklace I was wearing. The nagging doubts stayed put.

"But what about New York? I'm going back on Friday."

"You can just go for the meeting and then come back here," Serena said.

I sighed. "I feel like it's a sign, this whole book thing. Being back in the city when I took Will reminded me how much I fit there, how energized it makes me. And I love Star Creek, I do. But can I really just give up on my dreams of New York so fast?"

"Couples do long distance all the time," she answered. And she was right. It all made sense.

But in reality, I was terrified. I was scared of getting hurt again. I feared losing out on love. I was afraid Will and I wouldn't be the magical recipe for love everyone seemed to think we could be.

"I just don't know where things stand. It was awkward yesterday, and plus, I told him about going to New York. I don't know if he's ready for something serious. Seeing Marissa rocked him, which rocked me. Maybe we just got caught up in the thrill of the festival. After seeing him with her, I wonder if it's too soon for him and, in truth, maybe for me too."

It decimated me to admit it. I'd been playing the thought over and over in my head since Saturday. It just felt like everything was coming to a close—including Will and me. That stung worse than I ever could have expected.

"I just don't want to see you give up because you're scared," Serena said. "I know you've been hurt, but I saw how you and Will were together. You're so happy together. Sure, seeing Marissa probably threw him for a loop. But I think you can recover. If that's what you want."

"I don't know, because the other part of me is afraid saying yes to a future with Will means saying goodbye to my dreams. His dream is here in Star Creek right now. And mine is—well, I don't know where mine is. How do you reconcile that?"

Grandma was wiping off the counter. Hearing my words, she put the rag down and walked over, helping herself to a chair. She exhaled as Serena and I looked at her.

"I don't know if you ever reconcile your dreams and love, darling. It's a constant push and pull, a constant taking from one area to make another work. But if you find the right person, the one who makes you want to pursue your dreams in the first place, then you do make it work. He helps make it work. You sort it out together, constantly reassessing where you're going and how to make sure each of you is living the life you were meant to.

"In a sense, love doesn't take away dreams. It just shifts them, and sometimes, it shifts them to something sweeter and richer. It's like baking. You might start out with one recipe and think that's exactly how it's going to turn out. But along the way, you might have to change it up a little bit depending on the temperature of your ingredients, the altitude, and your customers' preferences. I might think I want to make chocolate chip walnut cookies but by the middle of the recipe recall that some customers are allergic. I might end up swapping out the nuts for white chocolate chips or caramel. It's a different cookie in the end, but it's still delicious."

I smiled at Grandma's baking analogy. Still, it did make perfect sense. I just didn't know yet if Will really was the missing piece of my dreams—or the piece that would make me abandon everything I thought I wanted.

"Grandma, do you ever regret staying in Star Creek? Staying in one place? Do you ever regret that you didn't get out and experience more of the world?" I asked her because perhaps that was at the heart of my fears. I didn't want to live a life that felt too small.

"No. Not at all. Sure, I could've traveled around or started my bakery in a huge city or in Europe or something like that. But Star Creek was my home from the beginning. It's what made my dream the special thing it is. I don't think a bakery anywhere else would have fulfilled me—mostly because your grandfather wouldn't have been there. It wasn't the bakery by itself that made me happy. It was sharing the bakery with your grandfather, with this community. That was what made it beautiful."

I thought about her words. It wasn't just the dream. It was about who you had to share the dream with and where you wanted to do that. It didn't make it any easier, though, because Will and I weren't my grandma and grandfather. We were our own complex unit of pasts, hardship, and uncertainty.

Was I willing to risk it all to make it work?

Was he?

There were so many questions, very few answers, and a whole lot of work to do, any way I looked at it.

THIRTY-NINE

The next morning, I glanced around the bakery, inhaling the familiar scents and committing them to memory. Grandma was at the front counter after I insisted she didn't need to put off her plans to help Will today. It was the day after Christmas, and there would be a rush of customers throughout the day to try the new Holiday-Bake-Off-winning cupcake from the festival.

It felt bittersweet that I was heading back home already. I had spent the past month focused on everything to celebrate the holiday—and now, I was leaving. Alone. I tried not to let that thought sting. I tried to focus on New York, on Serena, and on the amazing news about my book.

Christmas dinner had been beautiful with several couples, a few singles, and a few families joining us for dinner. Laughter, holiday carols, and baked goods were passed around as we all joined in the festivities. Still, I couldn't help but glance at the door and hope that maybe, despite everything, Will would come.

He didn't. Things had changed. I was leaving. I had to face the facts.

Grandma and I had breakfast with Herb early that morning, and my car was packed. I wanted to get back to the city a few days early to settle back in. Mostly, I wanted to yank off the proverbial bandage since I'd made my decision. Still, as I stood there in the front door of the bakery, tears filled my eyes. It felt impossible that I was leaving, especially after all that had happened.

I thought about that first time I'd walked in. Could it only have been a month ago? Will was singing the song that, at the time, stabbed my heart. Now, I could hear that song and it didn't mean a thing about the past. It just meant Will.

He'd done that for me, but he'd done so much more. He'd made me see who I was again and see that love didn't have to be the enemy. Love wasn't the enemy, but maybe differing dreams were.

He was staying here, where he now belonged. I was glad for it. Grandma needed him, and he needed to be in the bakery. It was where his heart was.

And, as much as my heart felt like it belonged to Star Creek, I had responsibilities to return to in the city as well as dreams.

I switched my weight to my left foot as I stared at Grandma, who had come to the bakery with me that morning, beaming at the customer at the register. She'd had it all—dreams, love, and even a second and third chance at love. I had my writing dream, of course. But why didn't that feel so spectacular anymore?

After the customer walked away, Grandma came out from behind the counter and hugged me.

"I'm going to miss you," she said. "As much as I didn't want you putting your dreams on hold for me, I'm selfishly glad you came. It's been so nice having you here, honey."

The tears flowed, and Grandma just held me. I

breathed in her cinnamon and floral perfume and felt the love from her. It seemed impossible to leave. My heart jolted with a twinge of guilt, especially with all the health issues she'd had. But the doctor said she was improving, and with Herb by her side, she would have eyes on her at all times. Still, it was hard to be so far away. I made her swear to call if she felt tired, dizzy, or anything less than excellent. She nodded in agreement for the tenth time—we'd had the same conversation repeatedly for the past day.

After a long moment, I wiped at the tears in my eyes and tried to pull myself together. I sighed. "Anna called to talk about the meeting. She said the editor at the publishing house can't stop raving about my book. They love my story. Well, your story," I said, and Grandma's face lit up.

"That's wonderful, darling." I'd told her about the book news at Christmas dinner, and she'd squealed, cried, and toasted to my success at least three times. She'd been happy for me, and her excitement made me feel better about everything. Almost.

"I'm sorry I didn't tell you the day after the festival. I just didn't want to overshadow your news with Herb. I should have told you as soon as I found out." I felt guilty that I hadn't let her in on the news immediately, since it was her story.

"It's okay. But you're not overshadowing anything. I'm so proud of you."

It was good news, I'd decided. The dreams I'd had as a girl of living in the city, of strolling to the publisher's office in my stilettos, of the exciting energy, had come true. But why, then, did it feel like I was leaving home all over again? Why did I feel so sad going back to the city if it was really where I was meant to be?

Will emerged from the kitchen, towel draped over his

shoulder. I hadn't seen him since our food truck dinner when I told him I was going back. It was like I'd ripped out the final bit of his heart that Marissa had left in his chest. Looking at him now, a despondent version of the man I'd come to know, my own heart broke. It was painful to think I'd shattered him like she had, even if perhaps it wasn't as severe.

"You're leaving today?" he asked, his voice a solemn whisper.

I nodded. Grandma stepped away, busying herself with Mrs. Stella in the corner of the bakery to give us privacy. I slid my hands in the back pockets of my jeans and rocked onto my toes.

"My agent has that meeting for us with the publisher to talk about marketing. I need to get back a few days early so I can settle in before it."

"That's great, Lucy," he said, and his tone was genuinely happy. That broke my heart even more—the fact that in his sadness, he could still be rooting for me, sincerely excited for what it meant for me.

"So, what's the plan after the meeting?" he asked.

I sighed, staring at the floor. "I haven't told my grandma this, but remember how I told you I wanted to go to Paris? Well, my flight departs January 13. I bought the ticket before coming here. I think I should go. The trip is for a month, so I'll probably tackle that before settling back into New York life for good."

He raised an eyebrow. "That's huge."

"Yeah," I admitted, shrugging. There didn't seem to be anything else to say that fit.

He exhaled, and I thought he might try to stop me. Deep down, I wanted him to tell me not to go. In truth, it wouldn't have taken much to change my mind.

Instead, he just smiled. "I'm happy for you, Lucy. And I'm glad I got to meet you. I hope you have an amazing life."

He reached out then and hugged me. I tried to memorize the scent of his cologne, the feel of his arms around me. He pulled back, and it felt like my sense of safety went with him. I stood there, alone, in the center of the bakery. He turned and walked back to the kitchen, door closed, case closed. That was the end of it.

Grandma came back over, hugging me again. "You have to follow your heart, Lucy. Always. Dreams change. Dreams stay the same. Love comes. Love goes. But your heart and what it wants—that's all that matters."

She touched my cheek and looked into my eyes. And then, before I headed for New York, she leaned in, kissed my cheek, and said, "Your mother would be so proud of you."

I wiped at the tears and told myself to stand strong. I accepted the box of cupcakes Grandma pulled for me for the road and waved goodbye to her from my car as I backed out of Star Creek Bakery for the final time.

As I watched Grandma waving from the rearview mirror, I let the tears flow freely. I don't think I stopped crying the entire drive to New York.

FORTY

One Week Later

I sat at the table in our favorite coffee shop with an espresso, staring out the window as the snowflakes flung themselves about the city skyline. Tourists and regulars shared the sidewalks, bundled up and rushing to their assorted destinations. The bells of the café jingled and Serena blew in. I waved to her and she rushed over.

"Sorry I'm late," she said, huffing as she unwrapped her scarf and coat and claimed her seat. I shook my head. Serena was still working on a major case, so it was hard to carve out time to spend with her. I, on the other hand, had nothing but time. I'd met with the publisher earlier and had our marketing meeting, which went well. Now, I was waiting on edits, and with no writing inspiration striking, I'd been filling my days aimlessly wandering about the city that once felt like home.

"How are you?" Serena asked. "Or do I even need to ask?"

I sighed. "I'm sorry. I know I've been a downer since I got home."

"Hey, no need to apologize. You have a lot going on."

I did. And I didn't. I sipped my espresso, thinking about how so much had changed. I was home, back in the apartment with Serena. Gary, my plant, was still thriving. My writing career was in a better place than it had been in a long time. Still, I felt... stagnant. Lonely.

"Are you ready for your trip?" Serena asked. "I feel like it will be a good thing for you to get back to that trip you were so excited about."

"I've finished my research and have all my spots mapped out," I said practically.

"Are you sure you still want to go? You don't seem excited about it."

"The ticket is non-refundable. It might be good to have a change of scenery."

That had been the original intent of the trip—to get away from all the things that reminded me of Jed. I'd booked it at a time when life felt impossibly complicated and I was lost. But now that I'd returned to the city, there was another problem.

It wasn't Jed I was thinking about. I'd pass the bakeries we used to visit, and it wasn't Jed's face that came to mind. It was Will's. I'd see a Christmas tree and remember that night we decorated the tree at Grandma's. I'd hear someone singing karaoke, and his face would come to mind. The haunting memory of Jed had been replaced. I saw Will everywhere now, and the realization was gutting.

"Have you talked to him since you left?" Serena ventured as if she could read my thoughts.

I shook my head. "No. He texted to see if I made it to the city okay, and I just replied yes. But we haven't talked since then. There's nothing left to say, really."

Grandma, of course, had kept me up to date on everything happening in Star Creek during our daily conversations—and that meant keeping me apprised of Will's situation too. Which, although she meant well, only made it harder.

Paris. That would be the answer, I told myself. It would be the answer to getting me back on track, to resetting my life.

"It's not too late," Serena said.

I eyed her suspiciously. "For what?"

"To change your mind. Look, I love you. I love having you in the city. But you haven't been happy since you came back."

"It's just—complicated."

"It always is, Lucy. But that doesn't mean it isn't worth it."

We finished our espressos, changing the subject and talking about our favorite show and the band we were going to see the next day. Still, as I walked to our apartment alone when Serena had to return to the office, I couldn't help but think about what she'd said.

It wasn't too late.

I sat on a bench outside our apartment complex, the snow still whirling about, wondering what Will was doing— and if he was thinking about me too.

After a long while, I went back inside the apartment to plan for my adventure, my chance to go out on my own and explore part of the world.

I spent the rest of the week wandering the city, watching too much TV, and thinking about Will. Finally, after the days slowly passed by, it was time for my trip. I boarded a plane to Paris, leaving everything behind. At least that was what I told myself.

FORTY-ONE

Two Weeks Later

I slipped my key into the bakery door lock and walked through the doors, the morning fresh and bright. I thought about how it still looked the same—yet it also didn't. So much had changed since I'd last stepped foot inside. As the familiar bells jingled, the knot in the pit of my stomach grew. Nerves kicked in. What if this was a terrible idea? I hadn't even told Grandma I was coming.

My plan had been a little crazy, driving all night to get to Star Creek after I just returned to the city from Paris. I felt like I hadn't slept in weeks—because I hadn't. Serena begged me to wait another day, reeling from my return home from Paris weeks earlier than planned. But when I got an idea, I had to follow through.

The bakery was empty because they weren't open yet, but a song rang out from the kitchen. It wasn't the first song

I'd heard him sing the day we met. I smiled at it being a different song, one that maybe would become our song.

But maybe not. I had no idea how things would go. The knot in my stomach morphed into butterflies. It would be okay either way, I told myself—even though I knew that was a lie.

He walked out from the kitchen, perhaps ready to greet Grandma, who didn't seem to be there. I hadn't seen Herb's car outside. The towel was draped over his shoulder, just like I remembered. When he saw me standing in the doorway, he paused. He blinked. He froze and seemed to process. Finally, standing behind the counter with his head tilted, he spoke.

"Your grandma said you were in Paris."

"I was." I shrugged. "But I didn't end up staying."

He waited for an explanation. It was an explanation I had considered for the past two weeks as I thought through my options, as I anguished over making the right decision while staring at tourist attractions in Paris. It was a decision I'd replayed over and over as I sat in cafés and ate scones that weren't as good as the ones in Star Creek. It was the choice I'd thought about as I saw couples in love in a city that was far from the picturesque ideal I'd had in my mind.

In truth, Paris wasn't all it was cracked up to be. Sure, it was pretty and stunning, full of vibrancy just like the movies. But as I took the tours and visited the museums, I realized there was one major problem. My heart wasn't there. And it wasn't back in New York City either.

It was in Star Creek with Will.

So I'd done what seemed crazy. I left Paris early, spending way too much money on an early flight home. And as soon as I walked into our apartment, exhausted from travel, I packed up my things, told a confused but happy

Serena goodbye, and piled into my car to return to Star Creek. To return home.

For good.

Grandma was right. It wasn't about dreams or love or what Will wanted. It was about my heart and what felt right.

So I began.

"When Jed cheated on me, I thought I needed to escape in order to be happy again. I thought I needed to do something crazy like go to Paris for a month to find who I was and what would bring me to life again. So I made the plans. When I went back to the city after Christmas, I even kept the plans. I got on the plane, and I went to Paris. But there was a problem. It didn't fit anymore. Not Paris. Not even New York. Nothing felt the same."

I stepped around the counter, staring up into his eyes. My heart was beating wildly. It was a risk. Maybe it was too late. Maybe I'd hurt him too much.

"What changed?" he asked, his voice uncharacteristically soft and shaky.

"You. You did. Being here in Star Creek with you, I've never felt more alive, more creative, more passionate. My writing flourished here. And it wasn't just the change of scenery or hearing Grandma's story that did it. It was you. I came here with a shattered heart and a broken sense of direction, but you fixed that. From the first moment I looked into your eyes, Will, I saw safety, protection... and love. I saw love. And if I've learned anything from Grandma's story, it's that when you find that, you hang on to it because beautiful things emerge from that sort of connection."

He stood staring at me with tender eyes. We were wordless for a long moment, and my stomach clenched. Still, I went on. I was in this now, no matter what. I would put all the cookies out on the table.

"I know our lives aren't all figured out. I know we're both still haunted by the past. I know we have some healing to do. And we've both got crazy dreams, and we don't know where those will take us. But no matter what dreams we're chasing or what pasts we're overcoming, I want to do it together. I want to see what we could be together. And if that means putting New York on hold, that's fine with me. I'm moving back to Star Creek for good. I don't have it all sorted out yet, but that's okay. I want to spend time here with you so we can figure out where we're headed. Together. If that's what you want."

"But I don't want to keep you from your dreams. What about New York? What about the publisher?" he asked.

"You're not stopping me from anything," I said, smiling. "You're helping me find new dreams, which, as I've learned, is an absolutely beautiful thing. We've both been hurt. I know that. And I know we still have pain. But I think together, we can build something sweet."

At that, I saw his walls come down. It was as if I could see his heart patching back together, just like mine. He stepped forward and put his flour-covered hands on my waist. I didn't care.

"Something as sweet as love?" His face was so close to mine, I could feel his breath on my lips, could taste the cupcakes on his breath.

"Maybe even sweeter," I murmured. And then his lips were on mine. The kiss was soft and sensuous. It sealed the deal. I was exactly where I was supposed to be, and so was he. There were no more questions or conversations. Our hearts were on the same page, and we were ready to build a life we knew could be worthy of its own book. It wouldn't be perfect, and there was certainly still pain to overcome and conversations to have. But right then, I wasn't worried.

In that moment, I knew Grandma was right. It wasn't about where in the world you were. It wasn't about the excitement of New York or the romance of Paris. It wasn't about a coast in Maine or anywhere else in the big, wild world.

In life, it was really only about who you were with and how you walked through life together, exactly as you were but also better somehow. As Will Westerly kissed me beside the counter of the Star Creek Bakery, I knew that with him dreams I didn't even know I had yet could come true.

EPILOGUE

One Year Later

I stood at the counter waiting for my espresso while Serena talked to Grandma and Herb at a table in the corner. The wind howled outside, and every guest who walked through the doors of the Star Creek Bakery was shivering. Snow reminiscent of the snowball cookies we served sprinkled the front entrance. Still, the line was wrapped around the building, and my heart warmed. In truth, my heart had defrosted a year ago when I'd moved back to Star Creek for good.

"Is there a famous author named Lucy here for an espresso?" a deep voice called out, and I smiled at his silly but adorable sense of humor. The espresso machine had been my idea and one of the many changes we'd made at Star Creek Bakery. I'd been spending a lot of time there for obvious reasons. I claimed my drink from Will, but as he handed it to me, he pulled me in for a kiss. When he leaned back and handed me Serena's coffee as well, he had a huge grin on his face. "The line's getting even longer. You better get back over to your spot."

I kissed Will one more time before he sauntered back to the kitchen to put in another batch of cupcakes as I strolled anxiously over to my place behind the stacks of books Carissa Beesworth had graciously ordered for me. I handed Serena her coffee before claiming my seat at the front window. I ran my hand over the smooth cover of the book, Grandma and Grandpa's wedding picture staring up at me.

I'd asked to use them as the cover because they really were the inspiration for the book. It was their love story—dramatized, of course, but still their tale. I'd had to fight with the publisher, but eventually they agreed that *The Second's Even Better* could at least have a trial run with the cover I wanted. My grandma had burst into tears when she saw the book—and of course told everyone all about it. I was pretty sure she'd purchased at least one hundred copies already.

I wasn't sure how many people would come out for my Star Creek Bakery and Books event. It was the weekend after the Star Creek Holiday Bake-Off, and we were all exhausted. But apparently the town wasn't over cupcakes yet. Will had even made up a special cupcake flavor called "Leave Room for Seconds." It was a cupcake infused with beer as a tribute to how my grandparents met. I had a book talk scheduled at the Star Creek Bookstore next week, at Carissa's insistence, and Will was working on a different recipe for that event. It was all coming together in a beautiful display of dreams.

I spent the afternoon signing books, watching people enjoy their cupcakes, and eating the snowball cookies Will kept delivering to me for sustenance.

"Your mom and dad are smiling down," Grandma whispered to me when there was a lull in the line. She leaned in to hug me.

"Grandpa too," I replied. She embraced me even tighter, and we stayed like that for a long moment.

Grandma was doing better. The doctor said her heart sounded great, and as long as she took it easy and didn't overdo it, she would be just fine. It had been a long road to recovery, but Herb had been there to watch her every step of the way. She'd slowed down because of him in some ways —but they certainly weren't living a boring life.

Their Las Vegas wedding ceremony, for example, had been one crazy affair. Will and I had gone together and had a blast. I was glad for it because now that Herb and Grandma had tied the knot, he'd moved in with her. Since then, she was showing up at the bakery less and less. The two of them were enjoying their free time, something that used to be a curse word to Grandma. They were taking trips to the casino, to the beach, and everywhere in between. Even Edmund and Sylvester had become fast friends.

I'd also found a new living situation. Herb had let me take over his house, so I was still close enough to keep an eye on Grandma and go over for dinner often, but they had their space. After a day of writing, I would spend the evenings on the front porch, watching the few cars straggle by. A few days a week, I joined Will at the bakery to help out but mostly just to be with him. Even though he rarely let me touch the cupcake batter, he was proud to announce I was a good muse for cupcake flavors, so that was something. And he had been a great muse for my work, as well.

I looked over at him now, that kitchen towel draped over his shoulder like it was the first day we met. He smiled at me, a smile that said he wasn't afraid to love. We'd grown over the past year, had learned to trust again. We'd both let go of our demons from New York and found our way to whole hearts once more.

Together. It was always together.

We'd found that love really could be sweet if you found the right recipe.

I missed the city sometimes. I missed my favorite pizza shop and meeting Serena for drinks after work. I missed karaoke nights on Wednesdays at the dive bar we sometimes went to. I missed the dream I had in my heart when I was younger. But dreams changed, whether by circumstance or choice. Sometimes, the dreams we thought we had morphed into new ones. When they did, they often turned out even better than we could've first imagined.

I'd thought Paris was the answer to my writer's block and my lack of passion. I'd thought I needed to jet around the world to find myself again. But it turned out that I found myself in a tiny town surrounded by genuine people who loved me, really loved me.

I visited Serena often, and she actually retreated to Star Creek quite frequently with Noah in tow. They were still going strong. She'd gotten her promotion, too, so life was changing for her. Still, our friendship was solid, and I was glad Star Creek could be a quiet space for her to escape where the cinnamon rolls were delicious—and free for good friends like her.

The townsfolk started trickling home, the bakery emptying as my event ended. I couldn't imagine how many books and cupcakes we'd sold, and I beamed with pride at the thought.

"Why don't you all head home? Will and I can clean up," I said to Grandma, Herb, Noah, and Serena as the final customer left. I'd already started gathering up the few left-over books. None of them made a move, though.

I eyed them suspiciously. "What's going on?"

At that, they all scrambled to their feet, busying their hands with plates and imaginary tasks. I turned to the kitchen to see where Will was. Something was definitely going on. And then, as if on cue, he strutted out from the kitchen wearing a suit. He was carrying a plate with a cupcake on it.

"Will?" I asked, my heart racing as I heard Serena let out a squeal from her table. The four of them had reclaimed their seats. I suddenly felt like I was in a theater performance that I didn't have a script for.

"Lucy," Will said, now standing in front of me. A chocolate heart was on top of some fluffy icing on the cupcake. I could see the powdered sugar and smell the almondy scent. He'd spelled out *I love you* on the edge of the plate in strawberry sauce. It was a masterpiece, and I smiled at him.

"When you walked through that bakery door for the first time, I was a broken man. I'd come home to Star Creek, but it didn't feel like it. My heart was still smashed in New York, my belief in love destroyed by a woman who seemed to think I wasn't good enough. I came here with broken dreams, a broken sense of my worth, and a broken heart. But then, from that first moment I saw you, I felt healed somehow. Brighter. You inspired me to chase my own passions. You reminded me what it was like to laugh again, to work hard, and to be invested in something worthwhile. If I'm honest, I loved you from that first day when you messed up that batch of cupcakes, even though I didn't want to admit it."

He flashed me a toothy grin, and I heard Grandma chuckle behind us.

My heart was racing, but I interrupted him. "It wasn't my fault."

"It kind of was. But anyway, I knew then what you would mean to me. I just couldn't tell you because I didn't want to admit it. Because it was scary after what I'd been through. It was terrifying to let someone in again. Plus, I didn't want you to think I was crazy."

"I definitely did when you were singing to yourself."

He laughed. "Will you stop interrupting? I had this all planned."

I pretended to zip my lips, and he continued.

"I know things weren't easy for you. Moving here, taking over the Holiday Bake-Off. You'd lost in love, and you'd lost your parents. Your heart was broken too. But I think, Lucy, somehow, us finding each other here in this bakery was exactly what was supposed to happen. Because this past year, I think we've both found that our new dreams here in Star Creek were even better than the old ones. Here, we're together. Here, we're hand in hand, taking on life. Here, our love was able to flourish. I love you. So much. Forever."

Tears were flooding down my cheeks now because it was true. We'd grown so much over the past year as individuals—but also as a couple. In Will, I'd found a refuge. In Star Creek, I'd found the life I actually wanted. I'd found the inspiration to believe in love again and everything that went with it.

"This is a new but also old flavor of cupcake. It's an almond cake with a light, airy frosting. There's a drizzle of caramel sauce and a sprinkle of powdered sugar. And there is, of course, a heart on top for good measure. But I need you to do the taste test and make sure I got the recipe just right."

I teared up as I realized he'd remembered the recipe for the cupcake from my childhood, the one inspired by my mother's snowball cookies. It felt like a piece of her was here, and my heart leaped. He handed me a fork, and I turned to look at Grandma, Herb, Noah, and Serena, who were watching as if we were putting on a play. I smiled at them and looked back at Will before digging into the frosting of the cupcake and taking a small taste. It was the best cupcake I'd ever had, a perfect concoction from Will's brain and mine.

"I love it."

"You didn't get any of the middle. There's a special ingredient there," he whispered. I noticed the plate was shaking a little bit. I'd never seen Will so nervous.

I eyed him suspiciously, and then I dug straight down into the middle. My fork clanged against something metal, and my heart fluttered. I fished out a ring, gold with a ruby stone in the middle.

Will pulled the towel off his shoulder and wiped away the cake so I could get a better look. As I gasped, he dropped to one knee in the middle of Star Creek Bakery, and I heard Grandma's sniffles. I couldn't pull my gaze off the man in front of me.

"Lucy Carter, I love you forever. We came together over the Holiday Bake-Off, but our love has really grown all year long. I want to keep growing our love. I want us to keep inspiring each other. Will you do me the honor of marrying me?"

I smiled, unable to hold back or keep him in suspense.

"You bet!" I shouted with a smirk, our signature catch-phrase the perfect response. He leaped up, wrapping me in his strong arms. I kissed him, the taste of the almond cupcake still on my lips. Grandma, Herb, Noah, and Serena cheered and clapped in the corner. Tears rushed down my cheeks. The bakery was a cacophony of happy noises, sniffling, and clapping. When Will pulled back, I looked down at my hand to see the ring he had placed on my finger. It was a little sticky and still sort of chocolate-covered, but the ruby stone shimmered.

"I thought you should have a unique ring. Also, someone may have told me you had mentioned wanting a ruby instead of a diamond," he said, looking over at Serena.

I turned my attention to her then.

"You knew?" I asked, heading over to apprehend my supposed best friend. I couldn't wipe the smile off my face.

"Honey, I knew from the first time you called me and told me about Will Westerly," she said, hugging me. "I'm so happy for you."

"Even if you'll have to do your chick flick marathons without me sometimes back in the city?" I asked.

"I've kind of started liking the drive. You'll just have to save me a sofa to sit on here."

"Deal," I said.

Next, Grandma came over and hugged me. "I'm so happy for you, darling. I felt so sad when you came to town, gave up on your city life for me. But now, I'm pretty glad."

"Me too. Although next time, you don't have to scare me with heart issues to get me here to meet your new baker," I teased.

"Speaking of that," Grandma said, moving to the center of the floor. "Now it's my turn to make a speech."

Will came over to me, standing with his arm around me.

"You all know what Star Creek Bakery means to me. It's been my lifeblood, my legacy. Your grandfather and I spent our marriage here. We built our love, our lives, in this kitchen. I thought I'd spend my final days here, alone with the memories. But as a little romance book I read recently says, sometimes another love is exactly what you need."

She turned to look at Herb, who was also standing

beside us. He wore a blue button-up shirt with a sunshine-yellow sweater vest that really made his eyes pop. But as Grandma looked at him, all I could see was the deep red color of his cheeks. He grinned.

"Herb, I thought I was done with love after Paul died. I thought I would never even consider it at my age. But you've changed that. This past year with you has shown me I still have so much life to live, so many memories to make. And I want to make the most of that time, sweetheart."

"I love you," he murmured.

"I love you too."

All of our hearts melted at the sound of the words.

"And that's why it's time for me to move on from Star Creek Bakery. It's served me well, and I will always love this place for what it's meant. But it's time for a new couple to take it into the next generation."

She reached into her pocket and pulled out a key with a red ribbon tied on it. She walked forward, extending her hand to Will and me.

"It's yours, darlings. I know you'll help the legacy live on."

Now tears were gushing down my face.

"Grandma, are you sure?" I asked, hesitantly.

"I'm positive. As long as you both want it."

"Of course," Will replied, hugging Grandma. He, too, had watery eyes. I joined in the hug, wrapping my arms around both of them. "I can't believe this. I can't believe it. Thank you."

"I love you, Grandma. Thank you," I whispered.

"You're welcome. I hope this place will bring you as much happiness as it did us. I'm sure it will, by the sounds of it. And don't worry. I'll still be in now and then to check up on the place."

"We're counting on it," Will replied. He wiped his eyes. I knew what this meant to him, and what it meant to me. We were both shaken, standing there staring at the key in Will's hand and thinking about all the possibilities. A long moment passed as I processed it all. And then Serena stepped forward.

"So now it's my turn?" she asked, and we all turned to her.

"Does everyone have a secret surprise but me?" I asked.

Herb shrugged. "I don't, kid."

I laughed and nodded. Serena stepped into the center of the floor, Noah by her side, as always.

"A little over a year ago, I watched my best friend fall apart because of some guy who didn't appreciate her. And as happy as I selfishly was to have her back on my couch to eat ice cream with me and watch sappy movies, I was also so sad to see her lose her passion. Lucy, I watched your writing voice shrivel up. I watched your confidence and excitement die off, too, long before you left Jed. I was heartbroken for you. But then you made the decision to go to Paris, to see some of the world and try to find what you were missing. I was happy for you because I hoped you'd get back in your groove. I wanted that for you. I guess there were other plans at play, though, weren't there?"

I nodded through my smile, squeezing Will's hand.

"At first, I was worried you were trading in your dreams for some guy who might break your heart. I was worried you'd passed up your life in the city for a small town that might not give you what you needed. But that first time you called from here, I knew, Lucy. I knew you'd found your place, your person, and your dream. I just knew. And I couldn't be happier."

"Thank you," I said through my shaky voice.

"Now, I know you made it to Paris, but not really because your heart was somewhere else. I think if you've learned anything this past year, it's that you can have your cake and eat it, too, when it comes to love and dreams."

"Oh, great analogy," Grandma said, winking, and we laughed.

Serena stepped forward and handed me an envelope.

I opened it and gasped.

"This is too much. Way too much," I argued, shaking my head as I handed it to Will.

"It's not. I've got money to waste—and this is the furthest thing from a waste. Make those memories."

"What is it?" Herb asked.

Will looked up, stunned. "It's a honeymoon in Paris for a week. Next spring."

I ran over to Serena and grasped her in a hug.

"I love you," I whispered.

"I love you. I thought you could use a redo on Paris. Maybe the City of Love will treat you differently this time. And I'm so glad your dreams are working out."

After a long moment I pulled back, still beaming.

"Well, that was a lot of excitement for one evening," I said, and everyone laughed.

"So when do you think the wedding's going to be? I can't wait. We have to start thinking about cake flavors," Grandma asked.

I looked at Will, and his deep brown eyes confirmed what I already knew. He nodded, and I turned back to the group.

"Well, I'm thinking the Star Creek Holiday Bake-Off might require a little extra planning next year. And maybe the cupcake will be called something like The Westerly? Or I Do? What do you think, Grandma?"

She smiled at me. "I think that it will be the best Holiday Bake-Off this town will ever see. It's perfect."

As the six of us cleaned up the bakery, laughing and talking about all that had transpired, I knew she was right. No matter what happened, it would be perfect and sweet. It would be everything we could've asked for—as long as I was with Will.

A NOTE FROM LINDSAY

Dear Reader,

Thank you so much for picking up and reading my book *The Holiday Bake-off*. I hope Lucy and Will's story put you in the holiday spirit and reminded you that anything is possible when it comes to love.

If you'd like to know when my next book is out, you can sign up for new Harpeth Road release alerts for my novels here:

https://www.harpethroad.com/lindsay-detwiler-newsletter-signup

I won't share your information with anyone else, and I'll only send you a quick email when new books are released or books go on sale.

If you enjoyed *The Holiday Bake-off*, I would really appreciate if you'd take the time to write a review online. Getting feedback from readers helps me grow as a writer and encourages others to pick up my book for the first time.

I'd love to hear what you thought of Lucy and Will's love story, so be sure to drop a line or two on your favorite retailer's site.

Thank you for reading,
Lindsay Detwiler

ACKNOWLEDGMENTS

As always, I want to thank my husband, Chad, for supporting my writing dreams and for being my best friend. I'm so glad we get to do life together. I love you forever.

Thank you to my friends and family who have been here for my writing journey since the beginning. Thank you to my parents, Lori and Ken, for instilling a love of books and writing in me from the time I could talk. Thank you to Grandma Bonnie for always coming to my book events and to my close friends who always support me, especially Christie James.

I also want to give a shoutout to some of my dedicated readers over the years. I appreciate you giving my books and characters shelf space—and spaces in your imagination. I want to especially thank Kay, Alicia, Lynette, Ronice, my local Barnes & Noble, and everyone else who has tirelessly supported my dreams.

Thank you to my amazing agent, Erica, for always rooting for me and helping me see my dreams come true. I don't know where I'd be without you!

Finally, last but not least, thank you to my best four-legged friend, Edmund, who inspired the Great Dane in this book and who reminds me every day what matters most. I love you forever. And to my mastiff, Henry, who was there for the beginning of my journey—thank you for always being by my side.